She studied ~~as~~ our free library ~~app~~
career as a hotel receptionist ~~following on from her~~ library
glamorous two years working in a bank. The moment that
one of her colleagues received the much coveted carriage
clock for fifteen years' service was the moment when she knew
she had to escape. She quit her job and returned to university
to train to be a teacher. Three years later, she emerged wide
eyed and terrified that she now had responsibility for the
development of thirty young minds. She taught for four
years and then escaped the classroom to teach history
workshops, dressing up as a Viking one day and an
Egyptian High Priestess the next. But the long journeys
around the UK and many hours sat on the M25 gave her a lot
of time to plan out her stories and she now writes full time,
doing what she loves.

Holly has been writing for 9 years. She was shortlisted for
the New Talent Award at the Festival of Romance. Her
short story won the Sunlounger competition and was
published in the Sunlounger anthology. She won the Carina
Valentine's competi-tion at the Festival of Romance
2013 with her novel The Guestbook. She was
shortlisted for Best Romantic Read, Best eBook and
Innovation in Romantic Fiction at the Festival of Romance
2014. She is the bestselling author of 20 books.

Also by Holly Martin

The Guestbook at Willow Cottage
One Hundred Proposals
One Hundred Christmas Proposals
Tied Up With Love

A Home on Bramble Hill

HOLLY MARTIN

ONE PLACE. MANY STORIES

HQ
An imprint of HarperCollins*Publishers* Ltd
1 London Bridge Street
London SE1 9GF

This paperback edition 2018

First published in Great Britain by
HQ, an imprint of HarperCollins*Publishers* Ltd 2018

ISBN: 9781848457720

MIX
Paper from
responsible sources
FSC® C007454

This book is produced from independently certified FSC™ paper
to ensure responsible forest management.

For more information visit: www.harpercollins.co.uk/green

Printed and bound in Great Britain by
CPI Group (UK) Ltd, Croydon, CR0 4YY

To all the wonderful book bloggers and authors out there who have tweeted, retweeted, blogged, reviewed or shouted about this book, you are incredible and your support touches me every day.

One day we will all meet in a big room with lots of cake and I'll get to go round and hug you all – for now, this book is for you.

Prologue

Joy crouched down behind the bush, her heart hammering against her chest. Someone had called the police and now, after two years, she was finally going to get caught.

Her car was hidden in the dark trees behind her and she glanced towards it, trying to decide whether to make a run for it. It was quite far, maybe a hundred metres or more. She peered through the leaves at her would-be captor. He was a lot older than she was and held a bit of weight on his stomach. She was certain she could outrun him. But running would draw his attention, as would the noise of the engine.

She couldn't get caught, her life would be over.

The policeman walked slowly towards where she was and she tried to make herself as small as possible. He was only a few metres away now. If she was going to run, now was the time to do it.

Suddenly, another policeman came round the edge of the house with a dog; a great, snarling Alsatian.

'Come on Phil, there's nothing there,' the dog handler called. 'There's no sign of a break in, no damage, it was probably just kids messing about. They'll be long gone by now. Or shall I release Tiger; he's dying for a run around?'

Tiger? Joy swallowed as she felt cold sweat prickle her neck.

'Keep that savage beast on the lead, you know we don't see eye to eye,' Phil called back, rubbing his bum as he obviously remembered his last run in with the evil hound.

Tiger and his owner disappeared back round the house and with a last look in her direction Phil turned away too.

Just then her stomach gurgled loudly and Phil whipped back to face her, grabbing his baton like it was a loaded gun.

'Colin!' called Phil.

Her heart in her mouth, she leapt up and ran.

'Oi! Police!' yelled Phil. 'Stay where you are.'

Joy leapt over a log and tore through the trees. Behind her she heard Tiger bark and she pushed herself faster. The branches caught her clothes and hair, like fingers dragging her back.

Black metal gleamed in the moonlight and she ran for it. She threw her rucksack into the passenger seat as torchlight danced through the trees towards her.

She quickly started the car, threw it into reverse and seconds later she hit the road. Thanking her brother for teaching her the darker side of how to drive, she slammed her foot on the brake and spun the wheel, executing a perfect J-turn manoeuvre, before tearing off up the road.

The road stayed empty behind her.

She took the first turn off and her wheels screeched as she took several other corners in quick succession. She turned the engine off as she parked outside a quiet, unassuming row of cottages and threw herself across the passenger seat.

A minute later she heard the sound of the police car tearing along the main road. The siren faded into the distance and she knew she was safe.

With a shaky hand, she pushed her hair from her face and waited for her heart to stop pounding. That was close, too close.

Chapter One

'Please let me lick it,' Joy said.

'Uh uh, no way, not in my car,' Alex said. 'I'm driving as fast as I can. Bloody stupid country lanes, could you have picked anywhere more remote than this to live?'

She smiled as they passed the village sign: 'Bramble Hill; Voted Britain's Friendliest Village for the Last Nine Years.'

'I love that it's in the middle of nowhere. It's so cute and quiet. Fifty-six people live in this village Al, can you imagine. Pretty soon I'll know them all by name. There'll be Mrs Twinkly Eyes who will invite me in for a slice of homemade lemon drizzle cake whilst she regales me with stories from her youth. Mr Silver Hair who will come round to offer advice on my garden, and lovely mummies who will invite me round for coffee and we'll chat in the garden whilst the angelic little cherubs play quietly nearby. And there's a local pub, a proper local. Do you know how long I've wanted a proper local? Somewhere the landlord knows your name, knows your usual tipple and has it waiting for you on the bar as soon as you walk in. There'll be cake sales and village fairs and people will give me eggs and fresh vegetables in return for my delicious apple pies. I can't wait.'

She surreptitiously licked a tiny droplet of chocolate ice cream

3

off her hand and looked up at Alex who was smiling at her.

'What?'

'What's it like in your head Joy, is everything slightly rose-tinted? Your glass is permanently overflowing isn't, it? When it rains you smile because it's good for the garden. Joy by name, Joy by nature.'

She smiled at the turn of phrase he had used for years as he pulled up outside the house.

He leaned over her looking out on the tiny whitewashed cottage. 'Are you sure about this place? It's quite close to Blueberry Farm.'

She frowned slightly. 'I know. That wasn't my intention. When I agreed to move here, I had no idea it was so close. Maybe it's fate though; maybe it's time I came home.'

His face darkened at this. It was the same disagreement they'd had for the last few years. He put his fingers to his heart. 'Home is in here, you know that, it's not a much-revered bunch of bricks. And you shouldn't allow fate, tradition or sentiment to dictate where you live. You just need to open your heart to new possibilities.' He brushed a stray hair from her face. 'This is a fresh start for you; I hope you get everything you want from this.'

'I've had a lot of fresh starts and none of them worked. But I have a good feeling about this place.' She ignored the protest that Alex was quickly forming and pressed on. 'It's not just its proximity to Blueberry Farm. There's something about here that feels like coming home.' She negotiated the door handle with her little finger and carefully clambered out, holding the two ice creams precariously in her hands. 'You'll see. Moving here will be the best thing that has ever happened to me.'

She ignored the look from Alex. Admittedly, she'd said that for the previous eight places she had lived in over the last few years, but this time she hoped it would be different. She turned back towards the house and walked straight into someone.

'Oh sorry.' Joy leapt back and to her horror realised that the man now had two large round chocolate stains on his gleaming, white shirt – almost as if two fake breasts had been painted on. An expensive shirt too, she recognised the little logo on the breast pocket.

'Oh god, I'm so sorry, I…'

He glared down at her and then down at his shirt in shock. She balanced the ice creams in one hand and fished a tissue from her pocket. But as she started to wipe away the ice cream, all she succeeded in doing was mushing the chocolate stain into a larger area across his shirt. He stood watching her as she desperately tried to get some off but made the stain bigger every time she touched him. Now tissue bits were sticking themselves to the shirt too. She abandoned the tissue, which was now hanging off him, and used her hand instead. As she felt his heart thud against her fingers, he abruptly caught her hand and moved it off him.

Joy's mouth went dry. The man was huge, the largest man she had ever seen in her life. He was almost like a bear in terms of size and build, the hand that had pushed her own hand away was like a giant paw. His hair was a shaggy, dirty blond mess that fell across his eyes. Slate grey eyes, like thunderclouds.

In stark contrast to the angry bear before her, a shaggy grey mongrel stood at his side, wagging his tail, his tongue falling out of his mouth in what looked like an amused grin.

Emboldened by the dog's smile, she tried one of her own. 'I really am very sorry. I'll pay to have your shirt cleaned of course and…'

Suddenly, Alex was by her side, obviously sensing there was trouble brewing.

'Hey, there's no harm done here – we'll pay to have your shirt cleaned or for a new shirt, and as it was obviously an accident it would be a shame to start off on the wrong foot. This is Joy, your new neighbour, and I'm Alex, her brother.'

Joy watched as the big man tore his glare away from her and his eyes slid to Alex.

'Brother?' he asked, deliberately ignoring Alex's outstretched hand.

Alex nodded.

'For Christ's sake,' he muttered as he stormed away.

'Well, you certainly know how to make a good first impression,' Alex said.

'I'm sure I can win him round.'

'I'm sure you can. You're my favourite person in the world and if he can't see how fantastic you are, then he's blind.'

Joy passed Alex his rather squished ice cream and followed him into the house. She glanced back at the large man disappearing down the road and tried to ignore the butterflies that were fluttering with unease around her stomach.

*

The sun was setting over Bramble Hill as Joy drove down towards the tiny village with the last load of her stuff. She had picked it up from Alex's house, nearly an hour's drive from her new home, and waved away offers for him to spend the first night with her.

Next to the village sign she'd just passed was another that she hadn't noticed before. It was weather-beaten, decorated in tiny delicate flowers and said; "Bramble Hill, Home of Finn Mackenzie." She wondered who that might be; the village founder perhaps, or some old scout leader who had taken boys camping and taught them how to make fires since before she was born. She was sure she would find out over the next few days.

The village looked beautiful basked in the rosy glow of the sun as she drove down the hill towards the cluster of whitewashed cottages. It was peaceful and quiet. There was a tiny duck pond, glinting pink and gold as the little white ducks bobbed on the water, an old beamed pub, called charmingly The Peacock's Pride, a tiny shop, and that was it. Life here would be as idyllic and quiet as the village itself.

She drew up outside her house and sighed. Home, sweet home.

Opening her boot, she hefted her large chainsaw over her shoulder, picked up a smaller one and grabbed a bag of some of her other power tools.

'Hey, would you like some help?' came a voice from behind her.

She turned to see a man hurrying towards her. It was the smile she saw first – an honest, genuine smile that spread to his denim blue eyes. He was quite broad in the shoulder, and wearing very tight jeans. His dark hair was floppy over his eyes, in a sexy, unruly, unkempt kind of way.

Although she had carried the large chainsaw many times over the years and she was used to the weight, she wasn't about to turn down an offer of help from someone – it might appear rude. Besides, he was the first person who had actually spoken to her since she had arrived.

'Sure, that would be great.' She carefully passed the chainsaw into his waiting hands.

'This isn't the twelve tonnes of makeup and hair products I was expecting,' he said, following her into the house.

She smiled at the dig. 'I've already unpacked that.'

'Now if my detective skills haven't let me down, you must be Jo Carter.'

'I'm afraid they have. Joy Cartier, my landlord is Joe Carter.'

He was clearly thrown by this.

'I know, weird isn't it? Similar sounding names, but no relation.'

'This could be a problem,' he mumbled, clearly more to himself than to her. She looked at him waiting for clarification but his lovely smile quickly returned and he changed the subject. 'I'm Casey Fallowfield, my brother Zach lives next door. This place looks great.'

They walked through the house and towards the shed. 'Thanks, though I can't take any of the credit. Joe did all the decorating.

I'm just renting from him. Just put that on the shelf up there.'

The shed was very small and Casey leaned up over her to put the chainsaw on the shelf, revealing a flash of brown, toned belly. She swallowed. He was standing so close and his fresh citrus smell made something clench in her stomach.

He flashed her a grin as he let go of the chainsaw and she blushed. He knew she had just been staring at his stomach.

'So the chainsaws, what are they for?'

'Cutting wood,' she said.

'This is a very expensive chainsaw though, and are those your initials engraved onto the side?'

She brushed past him as she headed out the shed.

'You're not… The Dark Shadow are you?' He grinned, clearly not believing she was.

She laughed. 'Isn't he supposed to be some eight-foot-tall alien, or a time traveller, or a demon from the underworld?' Some of the conspiracy theories surrounding The Dark Shadow were ridiculous.

'I heard it was animals, trying to send us a message. Or fairies, definitely fairies.'

'I heard—' she looked around to make sure no one was listening '—that it was a Scotsman.'

Casey gasped theatrically. 'Nooooo.'

'A nine-foot Scotsman with a twelve-foot-long red beard, eyes of coal, arms of steel, teeth made from razor blades.'

'Those Scotsmen are savage.'

'Well I'm sure the Scottish are perfectly wonderful people, it's just this one that's savage. Some say he's actually a vampire and he's hundreds of years old. Can I offer you a beer?'

'Sure, then you can tell me about the chainsaws.'

She smiled at him over her shoulder. 'You're nosy, aren't you?'

'People interest me – you interest me, Joy. Where have you come from? Why did you come here? Was it to run away from something or towards something? What do you do for a job?

Though it must be something good to afford the rent in this place… and what's with the hulking great autographed chainsaw in your shed?'

'Wow, those are a lot of questions.' She passed him a beer and came back to stand on the decking, watching the sun sink behind the hills. 'Maybe one day I'll tell you the answers.'

'Ah, a woman of mystery. I suddenly like you a whole heap more.'

She chinked her beer against his. 'To friendship then, and to sucking out all the gory details of each other's personal lives.'

'I like it, that's what true friendship is all about; being beholden to each other over our deepest darkest secrets.'

She smiled. 'So what are yours?'

'I'll need more than just a sip of beer inside me to tell you that.'

She turned back to the view.

Just then, the large man she had literally bumped into earlier walked out into his garden. Her heart leapt. He wasn't wearing a top and his whole body seemed to shout muscles. He was so tall, nearly two feet taller than her tiny five feet. He was filthy and sweaty and Joy had never been so turned on in her entire life.

She watched him pick up a large tree, as easily as if he was picking up a daffodil, and place it carefully into a large hole. He patted the soil gently around it, as if the tree was made from china. More soil was added until the tree was secure. He stood up and drank long and deep from a bottle of water. As he moved, the sunlight caught a piercing in his nipple. Joy tried to swallow but realised her throat was now parched. She took a long swig of beer before she remembered Casey standing next to her.

She quickly turned to him, blushing furiously at the thought that he would have caught her gawping so avidly. To her surprise his attention was well and truly caught by the beautiful man next door as well. His eyes, as she imagined hers were right now, were dark with lust and desire.

Joy took another sip of beer, whilst she pondered this, watching the man next door pick up his tools and take them to his shed. As he turned back, he caught them watching, scowled first at her and then broke into a huge grin when he saw Casey and waved at him before going back into his own house.

Casey took a long sip of beer, which he had clearly forgotten about whilst he had enjoyed the show, and then looked at Joy in what he clearly hoped was a nonchalant way.

She arched an eyebrow at him and he sighed.

'That… was Finn Mackenzie, my best friend and the man I've been secretly in love with for the last fifteen years.'

Joy smiled at him in sympathy. Unrequited love was the worst.

He chinked his beer against the side of hers, dryly. 'Come inside and we can start on at least one of my dark and gruesome secrets.'

She followed him in, and sensing this unburdening was going to need a bit more than cheap beer, she grabbed a bottle of wine from the fridge and a huge slab of chocolate. She went through to the lounge where Casey was already sitting on the sofa with his head in his hands.

'You saw it didn't you, the way I looked at him,' he said.

'What, the same look of desire that I had on my face? Yes, I saw it.'

Casey looked up with a sheepish smile. 'He is beautiful, isn't he?'

Joy shook her head with admiration and sat down next to him. 'He's magnificent. If we're sharing secrets, I might as well share mine with you. When I saw that pierced nipple, I wanted nothing more than to run over and lick it.'

Casey laughed, loudly. 'Oh, I know. I went with him when he got that done. It gave me a good excuse to touch it, you know, purely out of curiosity.'

She grinned. 'Of course.'

Darcy, her great, beloved Newfoundland, hauled herself up

from the cool tiled fireplace to finally greet the new visitor. Casey stroked her absently, but his smile faltered as he thought. 'Do you think he saw how I was looking at him?'

'I doubt it. Men are blind to these things. Besides, he waved at you. All I got was a scowl.'

'Yeah, I clocked that. It's your hair, he has a thing about redheads, can't stand them.'

Joy felt her mouth pop open. 'That's a bit… hairist.'

Casey smiled again. 'To be fair, he's anti-all-women at the moment.'

'Oh… so he's gay as well?'

Casey laughed even louder at this. 'Oh god, I wish. That would be all my Christmases, birthdays, dreams and wishes come true in one fell swoop. No, Finn is straight. He just hates women after his ex-wife cheated on him. He hasn't been with anyone since. Though not from lack of offers from the entire female population of Bramble Hill and the other local villages. They were queuing up once Pippa left, but he hasn't shown a flicker of interest. He has been sullen to the point of rude and still they fancy their chances.'

'Maybe his marriage broke up because he was gay.'

'You're just saying that to cheer me up. No, he's definitely straight. But it's not just women he has a problem with. He's rude to everyone; well, he has been for the last eighteen months. So don't take it personally. He says very little, keeps himself to himself, never gets involved with village life. Never gets involved with anyone. You'll be no different. Well, except that you have red hair. He'll hate you for that.'

Joy frowned.

'Pippa was a redhead so now he has tarred all redheads with the same brush,' Casey explained as he finished his beer and opened the wine.

'And how do the villagers take to his rudeness?'

'They love him.' Casey obviously saw the look of confusion on her face. 'You know who he is, right?'

She shook her head.

'Finn Mackenzie, the actor?'

She shrugged, still none the wiser.

'He was in that vampire trilogy years ago – *In the Darkness*, *The Taste of Blood* and, my personal favourite, *The Spoils of War*. God, that bit when he bathes naked in the moonlit lake… I think I ruined my video by pausing it so often in the same place. I should have realised back then that I was gay, when all my friends were drooling over the beautiful Scarlet Rome and all I could see was Finn.'

He must have seen the blank look on her face.

'You haven't seen them, really? You must be the only living woman not to. What exactly were you doing twenty years ago?'

'I was nine, so…' She trailed off as she realised exactly what she was doing twenty years before.

'You might have been a bit young to appreciate the first film, but the second and the third? How could it have passed you by?'

She shrugged. 'I guess it did.'

'He was fourteen when he filmed the first one and nineteen by the time the last one came out. Overnight he became this Hollywood sensation, the press followed him around everywhere. He hated it. I don't think he had any idea what it would be like for him to be famous overnight. After *Spoils* was finished he withdrew from public life. He had so many offers to do so many different projects, but he wasn't interested at all. He hasn't done anything for the last fifteen years.'

She smiled at Casey's enthusiasm for Finn. 'I guess it's safe to say, you're his biggest fan.'

'I am, yes, but we've been friends since we were both knee high to a grasshopper. It wasn't the fame thing that attracted me. Hell, you've seen him – the man's a god.'

'I take it you haven't told him how you feel?'

'Good lord, no, definitely not. No one knows I'm gay. You're the first person I've told, and I wouldn't have told you if you

12

hadn't caught me drooling. I'm normally better at disguising it than that. Well, I hope I am.'

Joy frowned slightly. 'You've been gay for fifteen years and never told anyone?'

'No. Not really. I mean yes, my inappropriate crush on my best friend has lasted fifteen years but I guess I never really accepted I was gay until recently. A year, maybe two.'

'But why haven't you told your parents? Would they be awful about it?'

Casey poured two large glasses of wine, broke off a huge chunk of chocolate and shoved it in his mouth. It took him a few moments to answer whilst he chewed on it.

'Honestly, I think they would have been OK with it. I come from a very loving family and all they've ever wanted was for me and Zach to be happy. But I think their friends would give them hell over it. They're... Mum's incredibly wealthy and there's always social gatherings – balls, seven-course dinners, big charity events that they used to attend with Lord and Lady Chalsworth, the Earl of Menton Hall, and Sir Ronald Chase-Matthews.' He affected a posh voice as he reeled off his fellow socialites. 'I've always shied away from it myself, which I think disappointed them slightly. Zach is more into the social networking, keeping up with the Joneses malarkey than I am. As the oldest son, they would have loved nothing more than if I attended these functions with some beautiful lady on my arm. If I were to turn up with a beautiful man on my arm instead... well, I don't think their friends would be as understanding.'

Joy broke off a chunk of chocolate and chewed on it, thoughtfully. 'So you're never going to tell them?'

'I suppose, if I found someone I loved, truly loved and who loved me too, then perhaps I would be brave enough to say, "this is the man that I'm going to spend the rest of my life with". But it's hard to find that man when no one knows I'm actually gay.'

'My brother's gay,' Joy said and then laughed at the look on his face. 'No, don't worry. I wasn't trying to set you up with him. I hate that when people do that to me, "oh you're single, he's single, why don't the two of you get together?" No, you're not his type at all. Alex prefers big men, just as you do it seems. No, I just meant maybe he could take you out to some gay bars, give you a chance to meet some men that are in the same boat.'

'He's… openly gay?'

She nodded.

'And how did your parents take to that?'

'They didn't. They were both killed in a car accident when he was seventeen. I'm not sure if he had even figured it out by that point. He came out to me a few years later.'

'Oh god Joy, I'm so sorry, that's terrible. Your parents being killed obviously, not your brother being gay.'

She swallowed the lump in her throat that was always there when she spoke about her parents. 'It's fine. It's been twenty years.'

'You were nine?'

She nodded again.

'That's what you were doing twenty years ago. I was fawning over my best friend dressed in leather and you were mourning the loss of your parents. I'm sorry. Who raised you after they'd died?'

'Al did. He was three weeks away from being eighteen. He lied about his age, told the authorities he was eighteen and as such was my legal guardian. By the time they checked, he was eighteen.'

'He raised you on his own?'

She smiled. 'I know, looking back, I just took it for granted that he was there. He had always been there, always would be there for me. I didn't think until I was eighteen myself what he should have been doing – that going clubbing, getting drunk, going to parties should have been a way of life for him. He wanted to go to university, train to be in the film industry. He put it all on hold to look after me. He did a superb job too. He wasn't just my brother, he was my dad, my mum and my friend. Can you imagine, when all his friends were graduating university, or coming back from travelling the world, he was sitting down with me explaining to me about periods. He was amazing.'

'Sounds like someone I'd like to meet.'

'You should, just so you have at least one gay friend to talk to about all this stuff. Maybe he can help you to come out to your family. Or at least help you find someone other than Finn to set your sights on.'

Just then there was a loud knock on the door.

Casey stretched back into the sofa. 'Well, I don't think we've done too badly in the sharing of our deepest, darkest secrets for one night. Maybe we'll stop there before I discover that the chainsaw is for hacking up bodies.'

'Damn it, now I'm going to have to kill you too.' She moved to answer the door and Darcy followed.

Joy opened it and the man standing on the doorstep was so obviously Casey's brother, Zach. He had the same washed denim eyes, the same black floppy hair, but where Casey's unkempt style had probably taken seconds to achieve, Zach's unruly 'I don't care about my hair' look had probably taken hours of styling. He had the sexy designer stubble in comparison to Casey's clean-shaven face. But feeling horribly disloyal to her new friend, she had to admit that Zach had the edge when it came to sex appeal.

'What have you done with my brother?' asked Zach, his mouth twitching into a smirk. 'I know he's in there with you. I saw him carry that chainsaw into your house, and he hasn't come out since. If you've chopped him up into tiny pieces you'll have me to answer to.'

She fixed him with a dark look. 'Why don't you come down to the cellar and I'll show you what I've done with him.'

'Ha, I've seen that film. I go down to the cellar with you and the next thing I'm manacled to a table as you cut out my innards. Not a chance. Unless it's bondage you're into, then I wouldn't mind a bit of manacling.'

She laughed. 'I'm Joy, you must be Zach?'

'Ah, he mentioned me, did he – just before you brutally murdered him?'

Just then Casey appeared behind her. 'Fret not little brother, she tried to kill me, but I fought her off. Are you ready to go down the pub?'

'Yep, is the murderer coming with us?'

'She sure is. We'll introduce her to the *friendly* folk down The Pride.'

Joy couldn't fail to miss the sarcastic way Casey had said friendly.

'Hey, they're OK… just not keen on newcomers,' Zach said. 'They'll take a while to warm to you but I'm sure you'll win them round.' He moved closer to her, his eyes casting over her. She stroked Darcy, a useful prop to focus on as she found herself embarrassed by the sheer hunger in his eyes.

Casey moved to stand by her side, forcing Zach to move back a bit. 'Go and grab my wallet would you, I left it on the coffee table.'

Zach nodded and with a last dark look in her direction, he scooted back to his house. Joy tried to calm her heart down before she turned back to Casey. What was wrong with her? Three times her pulse had quickened in the last half hour, each time with someone different. It had clearly been too long since she'd been with a man.

Casey closed the door behind Zach and turned to her.

'I like you Joy, so let me give you one piece of advice. Don't get involved with my brother. Women are like a game to him. He'll lavish you with attention and charm but once he's had you, he'll move onto the next. If he had notches on his bedpost, he would've gone through several bedposts by now. I shudder to think how many women he's actually slept with. Don't be one of them. Now—' he opened the door and offered her his arm '—let me escort you down The Pride.'

Zach was already waiting with his dark looks of appreciation. Joy sighed inwardly; she really didn't need to get involved with a serial womaniser. And with her definitely not being Casey's type, and Finn hating the ground she walked on, it didn't seem her dry patch would be ending any time soon.

Chapter Two

The Pride was a rustic, country pub, with low, beamed ceilings and a great fireplace which Joy could imagine sitting by in the winter months, chatting with her new friends. Zach and Casey were funny and friendly and the fact that she wouldn't be getting involved with either of them made things very easy and comfortable between them. She would just have to ignore the way her heart raced every time Zach brushed against her or looked at her.

The unfriendliness of the locals didn't seem to be a problem either. Chloe, standing behind the bar and serving them, was as overenthusiastic as a puppy. She was sweet and had a huge smile that lit up her entire face.

'So you're friends with Zach?' Chloe said, finally diverting her attention from the man himself, as he chatted with her.

'She's my friend actually,' Casey said and Joy was thrown by the slight protective tone to his voice.

Zach obviously picked up on the tone as well and he slid an arm round Joy's waist, clearly trying to piss his brother off or make him jealous. Little did he know. 'He's always been the same, Joy, never wanted to share his toys.' He turned back to Chloe. 'Joy's just moved in next door, so I'm just showing her the sights, making her feel welcome.'

Chloe let out a girly, high-pitched giggle, twisting her hair round her finger.

Joy looked around at the scattering of customers. Was it her imagination or did the pub suddenly go quieter when Zach announced that she had moved in next door? They were bound to be curious about any newcomers to their tiny village, but the room seemed colder all of a sudden. Although a nearby pair of older men were seemingly focused on a game of chess, and three old ladies – all supping pints of dark coloured bitter and wearing thick woolly cardigans, despite the heat of the night – were chatting quietly in a small booth. None of them seemed to be interested in her. She must have imagined it.

Sitting in the corner, reading a paper, was Finn Mackenzie. And there it was, the huge tidal wave of desire crashing over her again. She could see why Casey was head over heels in love with him. The permanent scowl did nothing to detract from his appearance.

She hadn't made the best first impression on him. But even if she wasn't his type, they should at least be civil to each other for the sake of neighbourly relations. She turned back to Chloe.

'Can I get a pint of whatever Finn is drinking?'

Casey and Zach sucked in their breath.

'Seriously, you really want to go there?' Zach said.

'This is not going to be pretty.' Casey shook his head in warning.

'Look, I'm not chatting the man up. I just think we started off on the wrong foot after I got ice cream all down him earlier. If we're going to live next to each other, it makes sense that we can at least be on talking terms.'

Chloe put a pint of bitter on the bar. 'Good luck.'

'When he shoots you down, we'll be over in the corner.' Zach gestured to the part of the pub that was the furthest away from Finn.

A smile and a free pint went a long way with most men, so she picked up the bitter and walked over to him.

'Finn, hi,' she said, gaining his attention. His eyes cast over her for a second, before he returned his gaze to the paper again. She was undeterred – determined to get one civil word from him, she pressed on. 'Look, I know we started badly, but I'm sure we can at least be polite when we see each other. I'm Joy Cartier and...'

'I don't care,' he said, without even looking up.

Annoyed, she stepped closer. 'I'm not hitting on you and I know I'm not your type but...'

He looked up, appraising her with what appeared to be a look of disgust. 'You've got that right; you are most definitely not my type. Now I suggest you run along back to your friends.'

He turned back to the paper again and Joy felt her jaw clenching at the dismissal. She slammed the bitter down on top of his newspaper, so it splashed over the glass, soaking the article he was reading. 'You're welcome.'

With that, she turned and stormed back to the warmer side of the pub.

*

Finn watched her go. The girl could certainly flounce. The black dress she was wearing seemed to flounce as well; it shook dramatically around her bum and legs as she moved. Damn it. He didn't like short women. He was so big that kissing someone small was always a problem. And redheads? No way, not again. He would just ignore the flash of heat that surged through him when she had walked over.

Joy Cartier though, not Jo Carter as everyone thought. Joy Cartier from Ascot. So she was rich. She probably had a pony called Princess and a butler called James. Even the way she said Cartier screamed of wealth, not Car-te-er but Car-te-yay. She drove a Range Rover too, big flashy thing that had probably never seen a fleck of mud in its life. He didn't like snobs.

As she walked, the eyes of every single person in the pub

followed her. They weren't friendly either; some glared at her with mistrust, but most eyes were filled with pure venomous hatred.

He pushed away the sudden need to protect her. He forced his eyes away from her and back to his paper. The ale stain was spreading slowly across the article about The Dark Shadow that he had been avidly reading. He tried to pick out the words through the watery mess. He would not get involved.

*

Joy knew she had a big, stupid grin on her face. Apart from the cretin in the corner, life in the tiny village had started just as she had imagined it would. She already had two friends and was sitting in her local, putting the world to rights. Zach was very funny and, as Casey said, very charming and attentive. Finn was a git, but she wouldn't let that spoil her mood.

Casey got up to get another round in, coincidentally at the same time that Finn went to the bar. As the appreciative gaze from Zach returned, Joy excused herself to go to the toilet.

It was as she was washing her hands that Chloe came into the toilet behind her. Joy turned around to speak to her, but she was thrown by the look on her face. Gone was the giddy over-exuberance and huge smile – Chloe's eyes were dark, filled with hate.

She grabbed Joy by the scruff of the neck and threw her against the wall. Pain seared through her as something stabbed into the back of her shoulder. Joy reacted instinctively, without thought. Her self-defence teacher had taught her well and in that moment when her mind was still processing the attack, her body seemingly reacted by itself. She kneed Chloe hard in the stomach and as she staggered back, Joy kicked her legs out from under her and slammed her into the floor, pinning her down with her foot to her chest.

Shit.

She hadn't meant to do that. But as Chloe struggled against her, she didn't think it was safe to let her up any time soon.

'What's your problem?' Joy said, concerned by the amount of blood that was pouring down her arm. She looked round to see some kind of nail or picture hook hanging out of the wall, which Chloe had inadvertently thrown her against.

'Zach's mine,' Chloe growled.

'Seriously! You've just attacked me over Zach? Honey, I have absolutely no interest in Zach whatsoever. Casey has already warned me off him, says he's with a different woman every week. I have no desire to be another notch on his bedpost. I've just moved next door to him, that's all.'

'He loves me. Those other women mean nothing to him. He's just sowing his seed. When he's finished, he'll come back to me. You'll see. He's mine, so keep your filthy hands off him.'

Joy shook her head at the lack of comprehending on Chloe's part. 'And you're welcome to him.'

'And Casey is with one of my friends, so you can't have him.'

'He…? Erm… I'm not interested in Casey either.' That was a turn up for the books.

'Or Finn…'

'The man's an arse, I'm definitely not interested in him.'

All the fight seemed to go out of Chloe. 'Zach does love me.'

Still not sure whether to let her up, Joy kept her foot on Chloe's chest a moment longer. 'I'm sure he does.'

The toilet door opened and another lady that worked behind the bar came in. Joy presumed she was the pub landlady. She was a large, short woman who would look right at home on a rugby field.

'What the hell is going on here?'

Joy thought this might be an opportune moment to let Chloe off the floor. 'Just a difference of opinion, right Chloe? I think we've sorted things out now.'

Chloe scrabbled up, clearly still winded by the knee to the stomach, and shot Joy a filthy look. 'She attacked me Pam, said I was to stay away from Zach, she just threw me to the ground for no reason.'

Joy opened her mouth to protest, but stopped. The landlady's face was like an open book. Joy could tell that Pam knew Chloe was lying, Pam clearly knew of Chloe's inappropriate infatuation for a man who didn't return her feelings, and she had already seen the blood trickling down Joy's arm. But apparently Pam had decided whose side she was on, and it wasn't the side where the customer was always right.

'How dare you come into my pub and attack my staff like this. Get out now.'

'But…'

Pam took a threatening step towards her and, recognising that this was one fight she certainly didn't want to have, Joy held up her hands in a symbol of defeat and surrender. 'I'm going.'

'And don't you dare show your face in this pub again.'

Joy scooted out, past Pam and into the pub. She hurried over to Zach's table and grabbed her jacket.

'Hey, where you going? I've just bought you a drink.' Casey said, as he sat back down.

'I've got to go. Sorry, you boys stay here, enjoy your evening. Don't worry about me.'

'Are you OK?' Zach stood up, filled with concern. 'You're bleeding. Here, let me walk you back.'

She edged to the door. 'No, I'm fine. My house is only a minute away. I'll be fine. Stay here, please and finish your drinks.'

With concerned looks from both of them, she hurried out the pub.

*

Finn glared at Joy as she ran out the pub. He felt annoyed by the protective feelings she provoked in him.

23

Chloe was about as unhinged as Kathy Bates's character in *Misery* so when he had seen her stalking into the bathroom after Joy, he'd known it was going to lead to some confrontation. He had to physically stop himself from going into the bathroom after them. He was shocked to see Joy hurrying out of the bathroom a few minutes later, bleeding and shaken, but stunned that Pam had to physically help Chloe out of the bathroom seconds after Joy had left. Little Joy Cartier had obviously given as good as she'd got. But he still had this need to go after her to make sure she was OK.

He would not get involved. That would only lead down one path and he wasn't going to let that happen again.

His eyes flitted to Mrs Brannigan who was hurriedly finishing her pint and heading out the door after Joy. Albert Cole, with a dark look of venom in his eyes, met her at the door and with a mutual nod of understanding between them they quickly left.

Finn was already on his feet as he slammed down the pint that he knew would now go to waste. He cursed Joy for making him care and stormed out of the pub after them.

*

Outside, Joy slipped off her shoes and leaving her jacket on top of them, she walked down to the edge of the small pond. Moonlight bathed the waters with silvery ribbons. The village was so quiet. There was not a single sound to be heard. It was a beautiful place and she was so desperate to finally find a place that she could call home. But now it seemed that Bramble Hill would go the same way as the other places she had tried, though she had never left because she had been involved in a fight before. She had thought the tiny little village would be the answer. London and the other big cities, where her neighbours had barely said two words to her for the entire time she had lived there, certainly hadn't been.

She hadn't even been here a day and she had alienated her

neighbour by spilling ice cream down him, had a fight with a barmaid and been banned from her local. It wasn't the rose-tinted start to village life she had hoped for. Suddenly, she was pushed hard from behind and as she tumbled head first into the inky cold water she heard a man speak.

'Piss off back to Ascot, you little bitch.'

But then she also heard a far-off shout that sounded like, 'Oi, leave her alone.'

The coldness of the water was shocking against her hot skin, reeds closed around her like fingers, dragging her down as she fought against them to reach the surface. She gasped out as her head burst through the water and she struggled against the reeds to get to the side. She grabbed a log and pushed her hair out of her eyes, shivering against the cold.

Finn was standing on the edge of the pond, his expression thunderous and she wondered if he was capable of any other expression.

'Oh, very good, payback for me covering you with ice cream was it? A bit childish, but yes revenge is certainly a dish best served cold.' She was trying to laugh it off, keep some dignity even though she looked like a drowned rat, but she had been shocked by the maliciousness of the push. She heaved herself out of the cold water and clambered up onto her knees, aware of pain in her ankle and shin. The heat of the night did nothing to stop the chill of the cold water on her skin.

'It wasn't me,' he said.

She looked around; the village was quiet and deserted. 'Well, who then? The ghost of the pond perhaps. Oh, was it Chloe?'

'No, she was still clutching her stomach when I left. People here are not going to take kindly to you after what you did.'

'To Chloe? She attacked me, I just defended myself—'

'I'm not talking about that nut job, everyone round here knows what's she's like – though beating her up certainly isn't going to curry favour with the locals. I'm talking about Mrs Kemblewick.'

She looked up at him in confusion. He was a lot bigger than her, but from her position kneeling on the floor, the feeling of intimidation that seemed to seep from him was certainly more prevalent. She moved to get up, but quickly realised that the pain in her ankle was from a bad twist or sprain. She was determined that he wouldn't know he had hurt her as well as soaking and embarrassing her, so she stayed where she was. She would wait till he had gone before she hobbled home. She shivered again.

'Who's Mrs Kemblewick?'

'The lady you kicked out so you could move in. Classy, you don't even know who was living there. Did Daddy's solicitor handle everything for you?'

Her head was swimming with cold, confusion and pain and he clearly wasn't going any time soon. She stood carefully, deliberately trying not to put any weight on her ankle. Her dress clung to her and she realised her bra had come undone at the back. She stood in absolute horror as one of her breasts fell out the top of her dress.

To her surprise, as she quickly scooped her breast back in, Finn's coat was suddenly around her. It was huge, swamping her from neck to toe, making her feel like a child in her dad's clothes. It was warm and smelt earthy.

She glared at him. 'What the hell is wrong with you? You push me in the pond, then hang around so you can see how humiliated I am, give me some cryptic warning about some Mrs Kemblewick and then give me your coat because you feel guilty?'

'As I said, it wasn't me and if you don't want my coat I'll take it back.'

'Fine.' Joy shrugged out of it and passed it back to him, then wobbled a bit when she inadvertently put weight on her twisted ankle. Finn grabbed her arm to stop her falling back in.

'You're bleeding.'

Joy looked down at her shoulder. 'I know, where Chloe attacked me, silly cow threw me against a picture hook.'

26

'I meant your shin.'

Joy glanced down and sure enough her shin was pouring with blood from a large gash just underneath her knee. Though the water was probably making it look worse than it was.

'Just… go away Finn. You don't like me; you've made that perfectly clear…'

Just then Casey came running down the banks towards them, closely followed by Zach.

'What happened?! Joy, are you OK?' Casey shrugged out of his jacket and wrapped it round her.

'Someone pushed her in,' Finn said.

'Over Mrs Kemblewick?' Casey said, rubbing her arms trying to get her warm.

Finn nodded then turned to walk away but stopped when he came face to face with Zach. If she thought the look of anger and hate that he had given her was bad enough, it was nothing in comparison to the look he gave Zach. It was pure venomous loathing. Zach stepped back under the weight of it, and with another filthy look in his direction, Finn stormed off.

Zach watched him go, then quickly moved to her side.

'Are you hurt?' he said, his arm round her shoulders.

'No, not really – my ankle is twisted, I've cut my shin, but my pride is hurt more than anything.'

'Here, lean on me, I'll help you get back.'

Casey grabbed Joy's shoes and jacket and with Zach supporting her she hobbled the short distance back to her house. On the way, she explained what had happened between her and Chloe and then with Finn and the pond.

'It wasn't Finn,' Casey said, as he opened her front door for her. 'I know he can be a moody sod, but there's no way he would do that.'

Zach nodded. 'Me and Finn don't get on, as you no doubt saw, but I'd have to agree with Casey, Finn would never do something like that.'

Joy sighed as Zach helped her onto the sofa.

'Then who, and more importantly why?'

Zach moved into the kitchen, probably to get some ice and Casey sat next to her.

'My guess would be Albert Cole and Mrs Brannigan, they left the pub straight after you. I only thought it odd when Finn got up and went after them. He must have known something was wrong.'

Zach came back with a bowl of water and a towel. He knelt at her feet and started to clean up her cut. There was something about the way he ran the damp cloth up her leg that was incredibly intimate. His eyes were on hers as he moved the cloth over her and swallowing the desire to lean forward and kiss him, she tore her eyes from him and focused on Casey instead.

'Who's Mrs Kemblewick?'

'A very sweet old lady that lived here for twenty years or more – so say the gossips.' Casey said. 'It seems she was the lover of the man that owned the house…'

'Joe?' That was a surprise. Her landlord was young, very good looking and had struck her as a bit of a ladies' man. Who knew those ladies were of the elderly variety?

'His father apparently, Eric Carter from Ascot. He would turn up two or three times a week, keep her entertained, so to speak. He died a few months ago, leaving the house to his child. Joe then gave Mrs Kemblewick notice that if she wanted to stay there she would have to start paying rent; seemingly paying rent in sexual favours for the last twenty years wasn't going to cut it with the recently bereaved offspring. Mrs Kemblewick, having no income of her own, was forced into a retirement home. Something that the residents of Bramble Hill were less than impressed with. She died last week and I think the locals are baying for blood.'

Zach moved to sit on her other side, so he could clean up her shoulder.

'We all thought that it was Joe Carter that was moving in. Or

Jo as in Joanne. When you introduced yourself to me as Joy Cartier and told me you were renting, I knew we were going to have some problems. Though I didn't expect this,' Casey said.

'Are you saying that my landlord Joe kicked out some old lady from her home and I'm now being punished for it?'

'Sums it up, yes.' Casey eyed his brother suspiciously over her shoulder.

Joy turned around to see what Zach was doing and regretted it immediately when she nearly clashed mouths with him. She shuffled away from him and he moved back as well.

'Er… your cut to your shoulder is pretty deep and as it was a nail, I'd recommend getting a tetanus jab.'

She narrowed her eyes at him. 'And what the hell is this thing with Chloe about?'

'She is an absolute fruit loop. I slept with her, three, four years ago, just one drunken night. She's been like my stalker ever since. I've made it clear that it was a one night only thing, that I'm not interested, but she won't listen. Sorry about that. I'll talk to her.'

'So… that's your thing is it, sleeping with a different woman each week, not worrying about the broken hearts you leave behind?'

'No.'

'Yes,' Casey said. 'She summed you up pretty quickly.'

'With a little help from you, no doubt.' Zach glared at his brother. 'I'm looking for love, Joy. It's just very hard to find. And when you know that the person you're with is not the one you're going to spend the rest of your life with, there's no point in continuing with it, is there?'

His eyes were so honest and she suddenly felt like she'd found a kindred spirit. That's what she had felt about all the places she had lived in over the last few years. She knew almost instantly that a place wasn't going to be her home, so there seemed little point in sticking it out.

She felt her frown soften slightly. 'I suppose not.'

She smirked when she heard Casey let out a sigh of exasperation behind her.

'Listen both of you, get out. I need to think about how I'm going to persuade the village I'm really very lovely.'

Zach stood and with the sexy smile fixed back on his face, he moved towards the door. 'I'm already persuaded.'

Casey rolled his eyes as he watched him go, then turned back to her. 'You OK?'

She nodded.

He leaned forward and kissed her on the forehead. 'I'll probably see you tomorrow.'

She smiled as she watched him go. Damn his sexual preference.

*

Finn was lying in bed when he heard Joy come upstairs and start to move about in her room. He switched the TV off and listened.

The four houses in Blackberry Row used to be two larger houses and had been converted into four smaller cottages many years before. He shared floorboards with Joy. Zach shared them with Mr and Mrs Butterworth. The split had been done very successfully downstairs, so that you would never know that it once had been one large house. But up in the smaller back bedroom, they had either run out of time, money or patience and the dividing wall between his and Joy's houses was so thin that he could hear everything. This hadn't been a problem when Mrs Kemblewick lived there. Her bedroom, the one she shared with the previous owner of the house, was the front one, so Finn didn't get to hear their sexual antics two or three times a week. But Joy, it seemed, preferred the amazing view that the back bedroom gave, which was the very reason he had chosen it to sleep in too.

The wall was so thin, or built so badly, that he could even see a thin sliver of light underneath the skirting boards. He rolled over to his side to watch the shadows move around the room as she did, finding it oddly comforting to have her there.

He heard her on the phone, putting the person she was calling on loud speaker as she no doubt got undressed.

'Hello, my lovely,' said a man's voice, which gave Finn an unexpected surge of jealousy.

'Hey Al,'

Alex. That was her brother.

'How's your first night going?'

Finn heard the hesitation in her voice. She clearly wanted to tell Alex all about Chloe and the pond incident and the nasty man next door, but she didn't.

'Fine.'

'Joy, I know that tone, what's happened? Is it that moody sod that you spilt ice cream over, is he giving you grief?'

Little did Alex know that the moody sod next door was the least of Joy's worries.

'No, well I don't think I'm going to win him round with my famous apple pie, but… everything's fine. I've met some other people, there's Casey, he's lovely. I may give him your number actually; you might be able to advise him on a few things.'

'Oh yes?'

'Well, I'll let him tell you all about it, it wouldn't be fair for me to tell you. And I've met his brother Zach who lives the other side of me.'

There was a pause from Alex and Finn could hear the laughter in his voice when he spoke.

'And Zach, is he lovely too?'

Joy laughed. 'Yes he is, but by all accounts he's a complete tart. Casey warned me off him, so I'm staying well clear. We can just be friends.'

'Men and women can't be friends.'

Finn nodded in agreement. He certainly didn't want to be friends with Joy, because then it would be friends who would

hang out together, friends that would kiss, friends that would…
no, it would be better all round if he stayed as the moody sod
next door.

'Sure they can. You've got lots of women friends,' Joy said.

'That's because I'm gay. That's like being an honorary female.
Besides they know they're never going to get anywhere with me,
so they don't have to worry about impressing me or making me
jealous, they can just be themselves. That's the only time male-
female friendships works. You can sort of be friends with the
husband of a female friend, that's OK as long as the female friend
is laidback enough or comfortable enough in their relationship
not to get all jealous and psycho every time the two of you speak.
Other than that, being friends with a man doesn't work, especially
not when you're both single and both attracted to each other.'

'Well, I'm going to prove you wrong. Absolutely nothing is
going to happen between me and Zach.'

'How much do you want to bet?'

'A million pounds.'

'Done.'

Finn sat up. Bloody hell. Was she that rich that she could so
easily bandy about that kind of money?

'Anyway, I'm going to sleep now, that's if I can shift Darcy off
the bed, she's slept all afternoon, lazy sod.'

'Joy, are you sure you're OK?'

'I'm fine, everything's OK. Goodnight. I love you.'

'Love you too, kid.'

There was a beep to indicate the call had finished and then
there was a heavy sigh.

'Yeah, everything's fine Al, the moody sod next door hates me,
the locals are going to run me out of the town with pitchforks
and burning torches, I was pushed in a pond, had a fight with a
barmaid and I'm now covered in so many cuts and bruises I look
like I've had a run in with Mike Tyson. Yeah everything is absolutely fine.' She sighed again. 'Shift your arse Darcy, you big fatty.'

There was the sound of the bed creaking, the light went out and then silence.

Finn lay back on his pillow. She'd not had the best start to village life and he was part of the reason for that. He couldn't help feeling guilty. The villagers were going to make her life hell; he didn't need to add to it. In fact, he was probably the only one that could stop it. His position in the village as local celebrity should be able to afford him some weight in these matters. But then again, her moving out wouldn't be such a bad thing either. Then he could just go back to his uncomplicated life.

Just then, there was the sound of a really loud fart.

He sat up in surprise. Surely not.

'Darcy, I swear, if that stinks, I'm shoving a cork up your bum.'

He smiled to himself. Maybe having her next door wouldn't be so bad after all. Just as long as they weren't friends.

Chapter Three

Finn was standing at the bottom of his garden, staring at the heather-covered hills that swept up from his back fence. It was early morning and the sun, if it had bothered to come out at all, was currently hiding behind heavy rain clouds. He had never minded the rain. In fact, he loved it, it was always so peaceful. The only noise he could hear was the soft thud of raindrops hitting his hood. That was until he heard a wailing behind him.

He turned quickly, wondering if someone had been hurt, and immediately saw Joy dancing around in her bedroom window, seemingly singing or rather shrieking her version of 'It's Raining Men'. She was wrapped only in a towel, a tangle of red wet hair hanging down her back. She spun around and as she did the towel fell away. His eyes drank her in. In a flash, his hands were caressing her pale, milky skin, feeling the fire of her hair between his fingers, pulling her warm body against his.

Unashamed, she carried on dancing. If it could be called that. Every part of her seemed to be wiggling as if she was attached to strings and controlled by a very drunk puppeteer. Her arms were punching up and down, her hips going side to side and her knees knocking together. But none of this detracted from the incredibly beautiful body. The innocent enthusiasm was incredibly endearing. After the night before, he expected her to be moping around, but it seemed nothing could keep Joy in a bad mood. He couldn't help but smile at her.

The music obviously changed, because the next thing she was screaming along to 'Lady Marmalade' by All Saints. He didn't need to be fluent in French to know the lyrics meant 'Do you want to sleep with me tonight.' Every teenage boy on his university trip to France made sure they knew those words if nothing else. The terrible dancing had changed too. It was still terrible but was now what could only be classed as provocative, as she ground her hips round in slow circles.

He couldn't take his eyes off her. What an absolute creep he was. But no matter how much he despised himself, he could do nothing to stop it.

Suddenly, anger flooded through him. She knew he was out here, that's why she was dancing like this. How could she not see him? He was wearing a bright yellow hoodie; it'd be pretty hard to miss. She was either trying to turn him on, or she was just teasing him to wind him up.

Either option was not pleasing in his book.

He stormed back into the house, out onto the street and hammered on her front door.

It took a few moments for her to answer, and when she did she was thankfully wrapped in a white robe. Her face was flushed with happiness, which immediately vanished as soon as she saw him.

'Let's get one thing straight, I don't like you, and I certainly don't fancy you. That little show you've just put on for my benefit only made you look ridiculous.'

Her mouth fell open, her face going a bright shade of red. She'd clearly had no idea he was out there. But he'd started now, so he was damned sure he was going to finish.

'I suggest if you want to dance, badly may I just point out, that you put some bloody clothes on or draw the curtains. That way I won't see something I really don't want to see.'

With that he marched back to his house.

But she was hot on his heels.

'You arrogant, conceited, jumped up little shit. I was not dancing for you. I didn't even know you were there. And you know what, if I want to dance naked in the privacy of my own home, I will. I suggest if you are offended by my nudity, you look away, instead of perving on me like the disgusting creep that you are.'

She flounced away.

He caught her arm and span her round.

'Hey!' came Zach's voice, protectively, though he was wise enough not to come any closer.

Finn stared down at Joy, his jaw clenched. Her eyes, currently filled with hatred, were an intense olive green, tiny freckles covered her nose and shoulders. Her lips…

He let her go, taking a step back before he closed the gap between them and kissed her. What was wrong with him? She infuriated him; he certainly didn't like her in that way.

He flashed Zach an obligatory filthy look, looked back to Joy, at her wet hair dripping down her neck, at the swell of her breast that was peeping out the top of her robe, and then stormed back into his own house.

*

Joy watched him go, her heart pounding.

'You OK?' Zach stepped up to her a fraction too late.

She nodded, aware that her hands were shaking.

'What was that about?'

'Er…' She tore her eyes away from Finn's front door and looked at Zach instead. 'Just Finn making it very clear he doesn't like me.'

'Oh that. Don't take it personally, he doesn't like anyone.'

She noticed Zach's eyes travelling down her body, his pupils widening with lust. She looked down to see that her wet hair was making the robe damp and see-through. Folding her arms across her chest she moved back towards the house.

'I'll see you later.'

His face fell slightly as she closed the door.

How strange to be so desired and so hated within a matter of seconds. Her heart was still pounding furiously. In part, it was because of her anger at Finn's arrogance and comments, but she knew mainly it was down to a wave of desire and need that had crashed over her when he had grabbed her and spun her around. If he had thrown her over his shoulder and carried her back to his cave right then, she would have only protested out of principle.

At that moment, a disgusting smell hit her nose. She looked around to find the source and saw a piece of paper on the floor, with what could only be dog poo on it. Scrawled across the paper in large angry capital letters was the word BITCH. It had clearly been posted through her letterbox that morning, but because she had opened the door, she had dislodged half the poo and it had mushed into the carpet and underneath the door.

Retribution for Mrs Kemblewick was swift indeed. She stomped into the kitchen to get a bowl of hot soapy water to clean up the mess and knew she would have to come up with a plan and quick.

*

Casey let himself in through Finn's back door and helped himself to a bottle of beer from the fridge before moving through to the front room. Finn was sprawled out on his sofa, reading a book and he looked at Casey over the top of it when he walked in.

'Could have got one for me while you're raiding my fridge,' Finn said, marking his place in his book and throwing it onto the coffee table. He stood up and stretched, showing the toned muscles in his stomach for a brief second. If Casey didn't know better, he'd think Finn was deliberately torturing him.

Casey sat down, picking up the book as Finn went to get a beer for himself.

'Any good?' He waved the book in the air as Finn returned.

'I have no idea,' Finn sighed.

Casey smiled. 'Yeah, I thought you might say that. Are you doing OK?'

'Not really.'

'Joy's incredibly beautiful.'

'She's not my type.'

'Oh come on, are you saying that to convince me or yourself?'

Finn sat down. 'Me, obviously. If I say it enough, I might start to believe it.'

Casey stroked the head of Billy, Finn's straggly dog. His heart went out to Finn. For him to have his heart broken twice by the same woman must have been horrendous. Finn's child would have been a year old now and Casey wondered how often Finn must think about that.

'Admittedly Joy has red hair like Pippa but that's where the similarities end. She's lovely. You'd really like her if you gave her a chance.'

Finn stared at Casey as if he'd just suggested he should chop off his own head.

'I can't do a relationship again, I just can't. Pippa hurt me spectacularly and I never want to be hurt like that again.'

'Mate, I'm not suggesting you marry her or even jump into bed with her, I'm just saying be nice. Don't treat her like scum just because she has the same hair colour as your ex-wife. She's had a bit of a rough life...' He hesitated in telling Finn about Joy's parents, but there was a vulnerability in Joy that he wanted to protect. 'Her parents were killed when she was a kid. I feel like she's come here for a fresh start and now the villagers are all giving her grief over this stupid Mrs Kemblewick fiasco – which has nothing to do with her, by the way. Her landlord is Joe Carter, the man that kicked Mrs Kemblewick out, she just has a similar name.'

'You're kidding?'

'No, she has no idea who Mrs Kemblewick is. Look, she needs a friend and if you can't manage that, then at least be civil to her.'

Casey put the empty bottle of beer on the table. 'I'm going next door to see if she's OK after last night. Anything you want me to say to her?'

Finn shook his head as he stared at the floor. Casey smiled sympathetically at him. Finn had gone through a rough time too, but Casey was damned sure he wasn't going to let Finn take his anger out on Joy just because he was still messed up over his own heartbreak.

*

Finn watched Casey go and groaned. Joy's parents were dead. That made things so much worse. He had this innate need to protect, to comfort. That was how he had met Pippa. She had driven her car into a ditch at the side of the road and although she was unhurt, she was very shaken and tearful when he had pulled over to see if he could help. Her tears, her clinging to him as he held her, was what had done it. He had been lost, beyond redemption from that point on.

Now he wanted nothing more than to wrap his arms round Joy and hold her.

An orphan. She could only be about thirty and she had lost both parents. He would be distraught if he lost his, he couldn't even begin to think what that would feel like. And she had moved here and the welcome party was well and truly out.

He would have to try to be civil to her from now on. He wouldn't be friends with her, that would lead to trouble, but at least he could be polite.

*

There was a knock on her door as Joy was knee deep in tissue paper and pretty lilac notelets. The kitchen smelt delicious and Darcy had moved downstairs in the hope of scrounging some morsels. She should have taken poor Darcy for a walk ages ago, though she seemed happy to sleep on the cool tiles of the kitchen floor at the moment.

She hurried to the door; Casey was standing there, looking lovely and dishevelled.

'Hi, how you feeling today?'

'I'm good, come in, you can help me.' She turned back down towards the kitchen and Casey followed her.

She watched him look at the chaos and mess across the breakfast table and then at her with amusement. She tried to look at it through his eyes; the desperation of a mad woman.

'What are you doing?'

'These are my friendship cakes. I've made one for each house in the village. I'm wrapping them in tissue paper and putting a note in with each one explaining who I am and inviting them all to a housewarming barbeque this Sunday. Here, read the note and tell me what you think.'

He picked up one of the lilac notelets and read it. It explained that she was Joy Cartier and was renting from Joe Carter, that though their names were similar she was not related to him or the previous owner. It said she was very sorry for what had happened to Mrs Kemblewick, but it really had nothing to do with her. It was brief, and friendly but to the point – had taken her hours to construct those few little lines.

'It's fine,' Casey said. 'But I don't know if it will work. They seemed to be quite irate when I was in the village shop this morning. I tried to explain to them who you were, but they practically shooed me out of the shop, telling me it was village business and as such was none of mine.'

She stopped in the middle of wrapping up another cake in red tissue paper. 'You don't live here?'

'No, I live in Ashton Woods, the next village.'

'Oh.' This bothered her more than it should have. She thought that she had at least two friends in the village, now it was down to only one – and Zach was only friends with her because he wanted to sleep with her. 'Well, it's clear they're never going to be my best friends but maybe I can persuade them not to push me in the pond again or post dog poo through my letterbox.'

'What?' Casey's eyes widened as he picked up one of the cakes and artfully arranged the tissue paper around it in a way that she could never achieve.

'Found it this morning, with a note telling me I'm a bitch.'

He shook his head. 'Well then, you certainly can't make it any worse. I'll give you a hand.'

They worked diligently between them for a while until all the cakes were wrapped.

She sat down, her back aching a bit, and looked out the window at the rain that hadn't stopped all morning. The hills looked dramatic, silhouetted against the grey sky.

'It needs to stop raining by tonight, I really need to go out to work,' she said, then wished she hadn't as that was bound to lead to questions.

'A lady of the night, are you?' Casey's eyes gleamed with excitement. 'A prostitute? A spy?'

'Yes to both. Spying doesn't pay well, so I supplement it with a bit of prostitution.'

'Noble.'

'I thought so. Oh, that's what I meant to ask you.' She quickly changed the subject. 'When Chloe was threatening me to keep away from Zach, she also said that I couldn't have you because you were with one of her friends.'

Casey picked up a crumb of cake from the baking tray. 'Umm… yes, Arielle.'

She waited for more details but clearly none were forthcoming. 'You're dating a girl?'

'Yeah, well not really dating, sort of…'

There was another knock on the door, interrupting what Casey was clearly finding embarrassing to tell her. She presumed it was Finn or Zach and found herself straightening her hair as she moved to answer it, then cursed herself for doing it.

Opening the door, Joy came face to face with a spaghetti thin blonde, her hair scraped back in a very severe looking French roll. She was dressed in a very expensive, very short dress with matching jacket and her face had the look of someone who had sucked a lemon. She was pretty, Joy supposed, and would be even prettier without the excessive makeup and angry pursed lips. She was holding an umbrella over her that matched the colour of her dress suit exactly.

'Is my fiancé in there with you?'

Joy felt like she'd just received a smack to the face with that news, but quickly collected herself. Clearly this woman had come to the wrong house.

'Arielle, hi,' came Casey's voice behind her.

There was a silence as Joy processed this information and Arielle cast her beady eye over her.

'This is Joy, she's just moved in next to Zach,' Casey said.

'Evidently,' said Arielle, icily.

'Er…' Casey fumbled for something to say. Gone was the happy, relaxed Casey – he had rapidly been replaced by someone who was clumsy, awkward and clearly petrified of his fiancée. 'Joy is my cousin. Remember me telling you about Uncle Raymond, well, this is his daughter.'

Arielle stared at Joy vacantly for a moment as well she might. Joy was feeling equally confused. Finally, Arielle nodded and stretched out her hand for a delicate and formal handshake. 'Of course. Cousin Joy, it's a pleasure to finally meet you. You'll be coming to the wedding next week?'

'Yes, we invited her ages ago, she RSVP'd straightaway. We were quite close growing up.' Casey squeezed past Joy who seemed to be frozen in the hallway.

Arielle cast her eyes over her again. 'Of course, well if I don't see you before, we'll see you then. Casey, do come along, we must meet with Jules to discuss the flowers. Apparently I can't change the roses to daffodils as they aren't in season. You need to talk to her.'

Without waiting for an answer, Arielle marched down the path to a little red convertible that was gleaming on the street. Casey glanced at Joy as he followed.

'I can explain, I promise,' he said and hurried after Arielle.

'I can't wait,' Joy shouted after him.

But whether he heard or not, she didn't know because her voice was lost in the noise of the engine as the car roared up the road.

*

Joy delivered the cakes to each doorstep in the village, though she hadn't quite been brave enough to knock on the doors. Then it was time to take Darcy for a walk.

She intended to trek along the hill range past Menton Hall. She had a job to do there that night, if the rain stopped, and she wanted to get an idea of the lay of the land.

That's what she was telling herself, it wasn't at all because the hills held sentimental attachment to her.

When one of Alex's friends had mentioned that his cousin was doing up a place in the country with a view to renting, Joy had taken it as a sign that it was time to move on from the busy town of Milton Keynes. She had been a face in the crowd there and had no more than a nodding acquaintance with her neighbours of three months.

It was only as she had driven round to see the house that the village names started to sound familiar. She had rounded a corner and was met with the striking hills that bordered the cluster of villages, the same hills that she had trekked over every weekend with her dad, right up until the weekend before he died.

Even before she saw the house, she knew she was going to say yes. Maybe she could never go back home, but maybe walking these hills with Darcy, as she had done many years before with her dad, would be all she needed to feel at home.

Joy sighed as Darcy left her side and went galloping up to greet Finn's straggly dog. Seemingly, in the dog world, you just had to shove your nose up the other dog's bum and you were best friends for life. She wondered what Finn's reaction to that would be if she tried it. She hung back a little, hoping Finn would try to avoid her, but he was obviously on his way home now, so their paths had to cross if she intended taking Darcy on the walk she had planned. Finn called his dog away from Darcy, but Billy, tongue hanging out, stupid grin in place, was very interested in her. He had that demented look about him when a dog smells a bitch in heat. Damn it. Darcy had been a bit listless the day before, but Joy had put it down to the move. Still they wouldn't be here long enough for Billy to get lucky. Hopefully Finn would pass without a single word.

He drew closer. He always looked so cool. Even today tramping over the rain sodden fields with his dog, he looked like he'd just stepped out of a clothes commercial. He was wearing a simple baseball cap and a waterproof hoodie, but he still looked sexy. And also, as he drew closer, she saw he was wearing a sneer just for her. Her heart sank. Well, attack was sometimes the best form of defence.

She marched up to him. 'Why is it you hate me so much? It can't possibly be about the ice cream, that would be unbelievably petty. And as you don't get involved with village matters it can't be about Mrs Kemblewick either, which by the way had nothing to do with me. So it's either like Casey said, you hate me because I have red hair, which would be very shallow and small-minded or it's just that you're a bastard for no other reason than you like to make people's lives a misery. So tell me, which is it?'

He glared at her but when there was clearly no answer forthcoming, she turned away from him. 'I'll take that as the latter then. Darcy, heel!'

She walked away from him, her hands clenched into fists in her pockets, and refused to look back.

*

Damn it. Finn watched her go, his hand on Billy's collar, who seemed very keen to follow them. Just like his owner. She was right, he was a bastard. He felt beyond guilty for shouting at her that morning just for singing and dancing – and then as she walked towards him, he had been appalled by how turned on he was after seeing Joy dressed in her waxed jacket and cap. It was a waxed jacket and cap, how could it be sexy? The black dress she had worn the day before was sexy. Not a waxed jacket and a pair of battered walking boots. He was determined to be polite, regardless of these insane feelings for her slamming through him. He was going to say hello, that was as good a start as any, but as his emotions clawed away inside him his face must have been a picture as he battled with a sudden fear of redheads, a fear of intimacy and a fear of what might happen if they got too close. And whatever she had seen in his face had not been good, and she'd gone on the defence before he attacked her again.

So now not only did he have to be polite to a woman, a redhead none the less, but he was going to have to work on his facial expressions too. He practised a smile; the feeling of his mouth turning upwards felt alien to him. He looked down at Billy with the rictus grin stuck on his face, Billy glanced up at him and whined with something akin to fear. Finn sighed and headed for home.

*

The sun finally decided to make an appearance late afternoon as Joy came back home from her walk.

Though would it ever be the place she could finally call home? She would give Bramble Hill a chance, just like all the other places she had tried over the years. Joe, her landlord, had said if she wanted to stay, permanently, he would sell the place to her, but he was quite happy to rent in the meantime. She could easily afford the asking price if she decided to buy it; her job paid her ridiculously well. But as with the other places, she rented first, in a "try before you buy" type of way. So far, she'd not found anywhere that she had wanted to buy.

As she drew close to her house, she noticed a collection of flies and wasps around her front door. More dog poo? But then the wasps wouldn't be interested in that.

She moved closer and realised, with a crashing wave of disappointment, that many, if not all, of her lovingly made friendship cakes had been deposited on her doorstep. Some had seemingly been stamped on and some had even been forcibly shoved through her letterbox. They either hadn't bothered to read the notes once they spotted it was from her, or hadn't believed the declaration that she'd had nothing to do with the ousting of Mrs Kemblewick. It did seem slightly implausible that she was Joy Cartier and her landlord was Joe Carter; she and Joe had laughed about it when they'd first met. It was much more believable that she was lying about who she was.

She couldn't even get through the front door, there were so many wasps. She had legal access to her back garden through Finn's garden. There was a side gate that allowed her to walk through his garden and into hers. She hadn't used it yet, though she had every right to do so. She thought that it would be the polite thing to do to check with Finn before she strolled across his land. But since the man was an arse, she certainly wasn't going to extend that courtesy to him.

She opened his back gate, which legally had to be kept

unlocked, and walked purposefully towards her own gate, biting her lip as she hoped she could get past unnoticed. She would just walk across his garden as if she had every right to do so, which of course she did. Five metres away, four, three… and if he had noticed her he hadn't come out and yelled at her yet. Suddenly, something in Finn's downstairs window caught her eye, and despite her best intentions to be in and out in mere seconds, she couldn't help but look.

There was Finn, stark naked, drying his wet hair with a towel.

Chapter Four

He had evidently come downstairs to answer the phone, as he was chatting away on it, and wasn't expecting anyone to stroll across his back garden.

His body was glorious, he was so tall and big. His great broad chest, with that tantalizing pierced nipple. Muscles screamed from every part of him. Every single part. She couldn't help but let her eyes wander, following the thin smattering of hair down from his navel to his groin. She swallowed. He really was big in every single sense. She wondered if he had to have some special licence for it, an operator of heavy machinery. His thighs were huge too, there would be a lot of strength and stamina in those hips and thighs. She imagined what it would feel like to be wrapped around those hips, to feel that much strength under her hands, against her own body.

Suddenly aware of what she was doing, that she had been frozen to the spot for at least a minute, if not more, she looked back up at Finn's face. How long he had known she was there was unclear, but he was staring at her – his mouth partly open in shock. Not only had she looked through his window and caught him naked, but she might as well have opened a bag of popcorn and pulled up a chair for the amount of time she had spent enjoying the show.

She turned away and hurried through the back gate. Out the

corner of her eye she saw Finn quickly wrap a towel around himself and move to the door to confront her.

'Oi!' came Finn's voice through the gate. 'Get a good enough look, did you?'

Stifling the smirk from her mouth, she whirled to face him. He was so tall that even though the gate was closed, she could still see his head and chest above it. That chest with the pierced nipple.

'Let's call us even shall we, since you stood perving at me in my bedroom this morning.'

'I was not...' He paused, clearly fighting with the decision to shout at her or accept she was right. 'Fine, let's call it even.'

This surprised her. She fumbled with her keys, trying to get inside as quickly as possible, but the damned key wouldn't turn and he was still standing there watching her. Finally, she undid the lock and tumbled through the door, knowing her face was burning bright red yet again.

*

Dusk fell on Bramble Hill, leaving trails of plum and tangerine across the sky. The village, as always, was peaceful and quiet. Though next door to Finn was a sudden hive of activity.

For the last few minutes he had watched Joy load up the back of her car with boxes and bags. She was dressed entirely in black.

But the weirdest thing was what she was doing now, obscuring her number plates with a purpose made black cover. He wasn't an expert on the law, but he was pretty sure that was illegal.

She hopped in the car and to his great surprise, she tied a black bandana round her head, like a pirate. With a great wheel spin, she disappeared up the road.

One thing was for sure, she was up to no good.

*

Joy stood in the darkened trees, gently touching what she had achieved. It was beautiful. The dragon almost glinted in the moonlight. A huge sense of pride filled her and she wanted to stand and stare at it all night. But now she needed to be gone before anyone discovered her.

She quickly loaded her gear into the back of the Range Rover and manoeuvred out through the trees with the skill of someone with years of experience in off-roading at night. It wasn't long before she hit the road, and minutes later she arrived back at her house.

This was the first job she had done so close to home. She had always worked far away in case she got caught, but this particular job was going to pay very well.

She moved silently into her garden, diligently unloading all her gear into the shed. Her tools would need cleaning the next day, so she quickly disassembled them ready to be cleaned and left their parts spread out on the work bench.

She moved out into the garden, stretching her arms above her head as she looked up at the stars that glittered like diamonds above her. Thousands of them peppered the inky blue sky, some were in great white clusters but others were separate, proudly standing alone. Without the lights of the city here, the night sky seemed endless above her. She lay down on the chair swing to look at them properly. She and her mum used to lie and look at the stars sometimes. She tried to remember some of the constellations that her mum had pointed out to her all those years before. Orion was easy, as was The Plough and Cassiopeia. And there was Draco – the dragon constellation. Joy smiled fondly as she remembered what she had achieved that night. The Seven Sisters was harder, the constellation you could only really see when you didn't look directly at it.

She smiled as she put her hands behind her head. She would just stay there a while longer and find a few more.

*

Finn stood annoyed at the window. For someone who never got involved, he was doing a pretty poor job of it.

He had watched Joy take all her boxes back to the shed and then lay down on the chair swing and she hadn't moved since. That had been over an hour before. She had evidently fallen asleep on the chair and all Finn could think about was how cold she would be.

He was determined not to care so he'd forced himself to go back to bed. Sleep evaded him and periodically he kept sitting up to look out the window to see if she was still there.

Knowing he wouldn't be able to sleep until he resolved this, he grabbed a thick blanket off his bed and stormed down the stairs. It was like having a child next door. She was old enough to look after herself, she certainly shouldn't be falling asleep outside.

He opened the connecting gate and walked straight over to her. One arm was behind her head, her eyes were closed, casting shadows over her pale cheeks with her long dark lashes. Her red hair, glinting in the moonlight, looked like curls of fire as it hung over her shoulders.

Cursing himself, he placed the blanket gently over her, and tucked it in around the edges. She stirred slightly and he prayed she wouldn't wake up and see him.

'Dad?' she mumbled.

God, his heart ached for her. He had to physically stop himself from carrying her into the house and putting her to bed.

He went back to his own house, happy that she was now at least warm, though it was still several hours before he actually fell asleep.

*

Joy woke the next morning and smiled when she realised she had spent the night outside. Her grin broadened even more when she realised she was tucked warmly underneath a blanket.

51

It had to be Zach. He really was lovely. It was such a shame that he had this reputation. She would be silly if she thought she could be the person to change him.

She stood up, wrapping the blanket tightly round herself to protect her against the cool chill of the morning.

The man himself was standing in his garden, smoking a cigarette. Startled to see her there, he quickly stamped it out, grinning at her sheepishly.

'Morning.' Zach stepped closer to the fence. He smelt of smoke, and though it was not a particularly attractive habit, the smell of it always reminded her of her dad. He leaned across the fence to touch her face and to her horror he gently pulled a snail from her forehead. She blushed as he placed the snail on the fence between them.

'I erm… fell asleep on the chair,' she explained lamely.

'So I see.'

His eyes were so gentle, filled with amusement.

She gestured to the blanket. 'Thanks for this, that's very sweet.'

He paused for a moment then smiled. 'You're very welcome. I didn't want you to get cold.'

She buried her face in it, relishing the earthy smell.

'Joy, would you like to go out for a drink with me, maybe a meal somewhere? Somewhere that's not The Pride obviously.'

She wanted to, of course she did. But unless she entered into it knowing it would only ever be a one night stand, she would be very disappointed. And she had never been the type for casual flings. She was an old romantic at heart and ultimately was looking for The One. Her mum and dad had been together for years, and every memory she had of them together was of them giggling, kissing and holding hands, just like they were in the first throes of love. They would sit under the old oak tree in the garden and kiss and cuddle every night. She wanted that, to grow old and grey with the man she loved. And although she had dated a few men over the years, never really knowing whether they were going to be The One until she had been with them for a few weeks or months, it was quite clear that with Zach, it was only going to last a few days.

Zach smiled at the length of time it was taking her to answer. 'Well, at least it wasn't a straight out no.'

'It's still a no, I'm afraid. I like you Zach, I really do, but I'm not the sort that has one night stands.'

'Neither am I.'

She arched an eyebrow at him.

'I know my track record isn't great, but I genuinely am looking for love. So many times I think I've found it and so many times I've been disappointed.' He took her hand, stroking his thumb over the back of it. 'But this time I really do think I may have found the one I'm looking for.'

She smiled but shook her head. 'And how many women have you said that to?'

'You're the first, I swear. Look, what can I do to prove to you that you're the only one for me?'

'No sex for a month.' She didn't know where she plucked that one from but it seemed to put him off her all of a sudden. He dropped her hand like he had been burnt, his face fell and she almost thought he might start to cry.

'A month?!'

'If I'm the only one for you, then you should have no need to pursue other women.'

He clearly toyed with the idea for a moment. 'OK, no other women for a month, I promise, and then will you sleep with me?'

'I'll go out with you.'

He scowled slightly, but then nodded. 'OK, you have a deal. I will prove to you that you are the only woman for me, that we can be happy together. Look, I have to go, I'll see you later.' He sent her one last dark appreciative look before he went back into the house.

She watched him go with a smile.

'He'll break your heart,' came Finn's voice behind her.

She turned and quickly looked away when she realised he was standing in the garden with no top on.

'He won't because I'm not going to give it to him. You know him better than I do, but I'm pretty sure he won't make the month.'

'He's a determined sort. When he wants something he'll keep going after it until he gets it.'

'You make that sound like a bad thing.'

'It is if it belongs to someone else.'

'Well, he isn't going to get me.'

He looked at her with disbelief and she rolled her eyes as she moved back towards the house.

*

Finn watched her go back in and went back into his own house. He had two gardens to sort out today, one on the far side of Bramble Hill and one in the nearby village of Strawberry Green. He was good at gardening and he loved the satisfaction it gave him of seeing plants grow and flourish under his care.

He had started off doing odd gardening jobs at the weekends when he was fourteen, helping his dad. It was when he was working in one of the large houses on the outskirts of Ashton Woods where he grew up, that he was spotted by a casting director for *The Darkness* trilogy. He was freakishly tall even back then and was apparently perfect for the role of the dark and brooding Seth. After the films were finished and Finn wanted to retire from movies, he thought perhaps he would start his own landscaping and gardening business. He didn't need the money, *The Darkness* had set him up for the rest of his life, but he certainly wanted something to keep him occupied.

When he had posted leaflets through the doors of the surrounding villages, hoping to get a few jobs, he had been inundated with responses. It seemed having your garden tended to by a world-famous movie star was very popular indeed. He had been kept busy for over three years, doing a different house every day. He loved it, working outdoors and with his hands. As his popularity slowly faded so did the demand, but he still had a large handful of clients who he saw on a regular basis. That was enough for him, just as long as he wasn't stuck in the house every day. Well, Billy made sure he went out at least once a day for long walks over the hills; the gardening gave him something to do when he got back. Too much time doing nothing allowed too much time for thinking and brooding. Since Pippa had left eighteen months before, he had brooded far too much.

He grabbed a bottle of water, shoved his baseball cap on his head and was just about to turn the radio off and head out when he heard the words 'The Dark Shadow' on a news bulletin. He had followed the career of The Dark Shadow avidly since he first appeared on the scene two years before. This man was clever, very clever. He didn't seem to do it for the money but for the adulation and reputation he gained. Finn had to admire him for it – for his obvious skill but also for the continued secrecy, for never getting caught. He smiled as he listened to the story, but his smile quickly fell off as the newscaster continued. Menton Hall, in the next village of Chalk Rise, had been robbed. Diamonds had been taken from a safe and from a jewellery box, most notably a diamond necklace shaped like a dragon. It seemed the thief had entered through the loft window of all places, as all other doors and windows were alarmed. No one had seen him come and go and there was no other evidence at all, other than the loft door being left open. There was no damage and nothing else had been taken. Police were appealing to anyone who might have seen anything suspicious in the immediate area.

Finn stroked Billy absently. His neighbour dressed in black, wearing a scarf round her head and covering her number plates was very suspicious indeed. Was Joy the diamond thief?

He had strict rules about not getting involved in people's affairs, and phoning the police to turn in his neighbour was definitely getting involved. Maybe her going out dressed in black was merely a coincidence. Maybe he should talk to her to see what she knew. Maybe he should keep his head down and get on with his gardening.

He grabbed his keys and headed out.

*

Casey was listening to the news as well as he drove round to Bramble Hill. The Dark Shadow appearing in Chalk Rise, now that was very interesting. He had been down to Menton Hall that morning as soon as he'd heard. The grounds were filled with local and national journalists, much to the annoyance of the police. Surely it was merely a coincidence, he thought, that Joy and that chainsaw had moved into the neighbouring village just a few days before. And, by her own admission, she worked at night and she was repeatedly vague about what she did. He smiled; he was damned sure he was going to find out just how much of a coincidence it was. Though if he was right, it did seem that Bramble Hill had another celebrity in its midst – a celebrity who was just as reluctant as Finn was to bask in the limelight.

*

After putting fresh food down for Darcy and making a fuss of her, Joy stepped out into the hall meaning to have a shower and tackle some of the unpacking she had been putting off.

Sitting on her door mat was another pile of dog poo, but she'd had the foresight to put newspaper down the night before just in case of another attack. She scooped the newspaper up around the poo and opened the front door to throw it in the bin outside. She wasn't looking where she was going and as she stepped outside she toppled straight over something large on her doorstep. With a shriek she landed headfirst in the nearest bush, the parcel of poo flying out of her hands.

She wiggled around trying to gain enough leverage with her hands to right herself, but the branches were in the way and there was too much of her in the bush to flip herself up.

Suddenly, strong hands were around her calves, and with the ease of great strength she was pulled free of the bush and righted back on her feet. She pushed her hair out of her eyes and came face to face with Finn again. Well, sort of face to face since he was almost two foot taller than she was. He seemed determined to always be present in her most ungraceful moments.

'Thanks.' She was annoyed that she had to thank him.

'You should look where you're going.'

She looked back to the doorstep to see what had tripped her up – there was a bucket of soapy water but that hadn't been it, it had been something much bigger than that. She glanced back at Finn, who had a scrubbing brush tucked into his pocket and was covered in soapy water.

'You tripped me up, it was you, wasn't it? What were you doing on my doorstep?'

He flushed. 'I was… there was dog shit on your doorstep, I was trying to clear it up.'

She stared at him. 'Why?'

He shrugged, snatched the bucket up and headed back into his own house. She stared after him. Was that Finn's attempt at being nice?

Just then Casey pulled up outside in a purple Ford Focus, not the neat little convertible he had taken off in the day before with Arielle.

He saw Joy, and shielding his face, he quickly made for Zach's front door.

She smirked as he peered through his fingers at her. 'Casey Fallowfield, you have some explaining to do.'

He sighed theatrically. 'Damn it, how did you know it was me?'

She indicated that he should go into her house. 'I think you and I need to have a little chat.'

He slunk past her like a naughty schoolboy. 'If this is stage two in the unburdening of our gruesome secrets, you can start off by telling me what you were doing last night?'

She followed him through to the lounge; so news of it had hit the headlines already. 'I watched Romeo and Juliet on the TV and was tucked up in bed with a hot chocolate and a fat dog for company by ten.'

Casey pulled out a very official looking notepad. 'And do you have an alibi, a witness that will testify to this?'

She sighed, pulling affectionately on Darcy's ears as the dog sat down on Casey's feet to be stroked. 'If only Darcy could speak, she would confirm my story.' She watched him make a hasty note in his notebook. She leaned round him to see what he had written and he snapped it shut before she'd seen it, though she was pretty sure Casey had just drawn a quick doodle of a flower. 'What are you, the local constabulary?'

'Actually, yes.'

She stared at him; his eyes were so honest. 'Really?'

He fished his wallet out of his pocket and showed her his ID. 'Detective Inspector Fallowfield, CID.'

'You're kidding?'

He smiled and shook his head. 'As I said before, people interest me, but taking an interest is actually part of my job.'

'That's so cool, bet you've seen some interesting cases.'

'Yes, they've been some weird ones. There was a squirrel killer.'

The smile fell off her face. 'An actual squirrel killer?'

'Yes.'

'I wouldn't think CID would get involved in that.'

'Normally we wouldn't. The bodies of mutilated squirrels kept turning up on people's doorsteps. But the first person to receive a squirrel was found dead a week after the squirrel was reported. Then, when more dead squirrels started appearing we thought it might be the calling card of a serial killer, we thought that those that received a dead squirrel would be killed too. Turned out it was just some sicko who liked killing squirrels who used the opportunity to get his own back on a bunch of people he didn't like. The first death was merely a coincidence.'

'That's horrible, did he go to prison?'

'For six weeks, and a hefty fine for animal cruelty.'

'Six weeks?'

'Legally you can kill squirrels, grey ones, it's just the method that has to be humane.'

She shook her head over the lack of justice.

'Oh, there was Bonnie and Clyde, a husband and wife crime duo. Jewellery shops, petrol stations, car jackings, they left behind quite the trail of guilt wherever they went.'

'They weren't really called Bonnie and Clyde, were they?'

'She was, Bronwyn was her real name but everyone called her Bonnie.'

'What was his name?'

'Derek.'

She laughed. 'Did you catch them, did they go down in a hail of bullets?'

'Not quite as dramatic. We thought it was mainly the wife, that she was the brains and he was the brawn. We finally caught up with him when their car ran of petrol just round the corner from a petrol station he'd robbed. But all the evidence pointed to him – we couldn't pin anything to her, even though we knew she was as involved as he was. He went down for three years, she walked away scot-free.'

The legal system really did have a lot to answer for.

'It does sound like an interesting job.'

'It is, I love it, no day is ever the same.'

'But… why aren't you at work? In fact, you've not been at work since I've met you.'

'I have a few weeks off, for the erm…' He trailed off.

'The wedding?'

Casey flushed obligingly. 'Yes, this Saturday, a week today. You will come, won't you?'

'I'm your cousin, Uncle Raymond would be very disappointed if I didn't show my support.'

He grinned at her, but then the smile fell off his face.

She squeezed his arm. 'Casey, what are you doing, marrying someone you clearly don't love?'

'It just sort of got out of hand. I've dated a few women in the past, years ago, before I really accepted I was gay. Of course, they never worked out. I'd been single for years and Mum came to me and said one of her friends wanted to set me up with one of their children. When she told me it was one of the Carmichael kids I was delighted. I only knew of the Carmichael boys, big strapping lads, really fit. It turns out they had a little sister too.'

Casey sighed. He grabbed a flower from a vase and started slowly demolishing it, ripping the petals off one by one.

'Mum was so excited about the date and when I came downstairs to find Arielle waiting for me, I could hardly say, "Urgh, a girl!" So I went on the date and when I next saw Mum, she was as giddy as a school girl about how well Arielle had said it went. In truth, there was no chemistry at all, not even as friends. I found myself telling Mum that of course I'd be seeing Arielle again. I didn't want to upset her. It just spiralled out of control.'

With the flower ruined and confetti-like petals scattered about his feet, Casey reached for another one. Joy didn't really mind. She'd only picked them from the garden.

'I'm not quite sure how I ended up engaged. Of course, that had never been my intention, and to Arielle of all people! She's an absolute cow. We'd only been dating a few weeks and I was desperately trying to find a way out. But there I was walking through the woods one day with Arielle and her parents and my mum. I spotted a ring on the floor, knelt to pick it up and the next thing, she's squealing, her parents are squealing, my mum was crying, proper tears of joy and everything. I don't even know how the ring got there, but it fitted Arielle like a glove, so I wouldn't be surprised if she threw it on the floor in front of me. Well, it quickly snowballed from there. Before I knew it there was an engagement party, marquees were ordered, a band, a harpist, flowers, the best champagne from France. I couldn't stop it. I have never seen my Mum as happy as she has been over the last few months organising this wedding and I just couldn't break her heart, I couldn't do it.'

'So you're just going to get married? Live happily ever after with a woman you can't stand?'

Casey sighed. 'My dad died, three years ago.'

'Oh Casey, I'm so sorry.'

'Mum was a wreck, but after the initial grieving was over, the constant crying, she just became this empty shell, devoid of any life. She'd get up, get dressed, meet friends, she was involved with the village council, but... she wasn't really there if you know what I mean. She was always this sparkling woman who laughed a lot, who had this zest for life, and when Dad died he took all that with him. Her eyes were flat, her skin was grey. She never laughed anymore. She moved through life, she engaged with people, but she was lifeless, a living corpse. It devastated me to see her like that and year after year, it never got any better. It was almost as if she was just biding her time until she could die herself and be reunited with him. This engagement has brought her out of that shell – she laughs now, she's excited, she has plans, she has a purpose. My old mum is back and so yes, I'm going to marry Arielle if that's what it takes to keep my mum happy and to keep the smile on her face, because I never want to see her go back to how she was before.'

'Your mum would be devastated if she knew you were doing this for her,' Joy said quietly.

'I know, but I'm just enjoying her being happy again. I'll deal with the fallout when it happens. It won't last Joy, Arielle doesn't like me either. I'm pretty sure she's shagging our pool boy, or the gardener or maybe both.'

This was madness. 'So why is she marrying you if she doesn't like you?'

'The Fallowfields are pretty high up in the social scheme of things. If there was a food chain made up of Lords, Ladies, Earls and Countesses, the Fallowfields would be at the very top. We're richer than most of the nobles in this country.'

He wasn't saying it to show off, in fact he seemed quite embarrassed by the whole thing.

'So it's safe to say you don't actually need to work?'

'No, I just enjoy it. But Arielle, despite her flashy clothes and car, would be down at the bottom of the food chain.'

Joy bit her lip. 'Have you slept with her?'

'No, lord no. I made the excuse that I wanted to wait until after we were married.'

'Honeymoon?'

He let his head fall into his hands and nodded. 'Two weeks in St Lucia. I think she'd like to try for a baby.'

'Oh Casey. What are you going to do?'

'Hope that I catch her with that pool boy before she walks down the aisle.'

*

Finn was busy tweaking things in his front garden, tying up the trailing clematis when the police car pulled up outside.

He had spent a good few hours tidying the two gardens of his clients earlier and had come back to work on his own. Joy had just left about ten minutes before to walk Darcy, dressed in that sexy jacket and cap again. She had flashed him a small smile as she walked past. He didn't give one back; in fact, he was pretty sure he glared. He cursed himself for getting involved, for feeling sorry enough for her to try to do something about the dog shit on her doorstep before she found out.

He straightened from pulling a stray weed out from near the roots of the clematis as he watched the policeman and policewoman walk up Joy's garden path.

'She's out,' he said, wondering why he couldn't stop himself from getting involved. 'She's just left.'

They turned to face him and gave him that look that most people gave him when they met him for the first time. A look that said, 'My God, he's huge.' He was used to it now. At six foot ten he always got that look. He was broad as well, and he understood that some people found him intimidating.

The policeman found his voice first. 'Do you know which way she went? We really need to talk to her.'

Instinctively and not really knowing why, except for having this intrinsic need to protect her, he found himself pointing in the opposite direction to the one she had just taken. 'She normally walks through the village to The Pride and follows the little path up to the old beacon.' God, now he was lying to the police as well.

The policeman nodded. 'We would appreciate it if you didn't tell her you saw us. We'd like to speak to her first. We wouldn't want her to worry.'

'No, of course not.' Finn nodded, feeling his stomach clench with that exact same worry.

The police got back in their car and drove off in the direction that Finn had pointed. Finn threw down his tools, whistled for Billy and quickly followed in Joy's footsteps.

Chapter Five

Joy had made for the tallest peak in the range of hills. The one that looked like a face. Old Woman White, her dad used to call it or White Lady Hill to everyone else. It was a good long walk, but Darcy had enjoyed it. Joy knew, as she approached the side that held the hooked nose, she would have excellent views of the valley below. There would be the River Quail, which was nothing more than a tiny stream in this part of the country. It would curl lazily through Hollyhock Woods, down Blueberry Hill and most importantly straight past Blueberry Farm. It was the farm she was more interested in seeing than anything else. She hadn't been brave enough to go and visit it yet. But when she did she would give the man that owned it a piece of her mind. For now, she would settle for looking at it. Maybe she would sit for a while and remember.

Her dad had said that she should never look back, that dwelling on the past was a mistake. He said that time was well spent planning for the future, but more importantly it should be spent living for now, enjoying the moment, because you could never go back and change things, so there was no point wishing you could. She wondered if he would be disappointed that she had come to the farm that day, if he would be shaking his head over her plans.

As the farm came into view, she realised she had been holding her breath. She stood looking at it for a moment, then sat down to indulge in the past.

*

Finn had easily spotted her about a thousand yards ahead, her red hair flying like a scarlet banner behind her. He had followed her, slowly closing the gap between them, as she had walked with purpose across the range. As he drew closer she finally stopped and sat down, staring out on the view below. He approached, but now he was here he didn't know whether to talk to her about the police or not. Surely it was best for both of them if he just kept walking. He really didn't need to be there for her, or to know the reason for that sad, faraway look on her face. He would just keep on walking.

'You see that farm down there Darcy, that's my farm.' Joy pointed down towards Blueberry Farm. Intrigued at the lie more than anything else, he moved to stand near her side.

She looked up, clearly embarrassed at being caught talking to her dog, and annoyed to see Finn was the one to disturb her, she moved to get up.

'No, don't go on my account, I was just enjoying the view. Surely we can be civil enough to enjoy the same view at the same time.'

She nodded reluctantly and he sat next to her. They sat in awkward silence for a while, probably while she wondered if he had some sort of split personality disorder. He'd been scrubbing her doorstep this morning, then he refused to smile at her when she had smiled at him, and now he was sitting down next to her as if they were best friends. He was confused by it himself.

'I… couldn't help overhearing you telling Darcy that Blueberry Farm was yours. I know the person that actually owns it and you look nothing like him.'

He watched her jaw clench but she didn't say anything.

'It's an odd thing to lie to your dog.'

Her eyes flashed. 'It *was* my farm. I was born there, lived there till I was eighteen. I still consider it my home, even though it belongs to some arsehole now.'

'Oh.' Oh crap, thought the arsehole. The woman that had been trying to buy him out – the woman that had made repeated calls, sent many letters and emails asking him to sell his farm to her, the woman he had largely ignored for the last few months – was sitting next to him. 'Why did you leave if you still consider it to be home?'

'I...' She stared back down at the farm, pulling her knees up to her chest. 'I didn't have much choice.' She bit her lip, clearly considering whether to tell him or not, and every part of his brain was screaming at him to get away before she unburdened herself with her story. By the look on her face it wasn't going to be a happy one. He was trying to ignore the need to put his arm round her and comfort her and he hadn't even heard the story yet. If she started crying, that would be it, he'd be lost for good.

'My parents died, they were killed in a car accident when I was nine.'

And there it was, he was lost, beyond the point of no return.

'My brother raised me after they died, but there was seemingly very little money. Alex didn't know a lot about farming, I was always the one that followed Mum and Dad around, asking loads of questions about the dairy cows. Alex was always building stuff, robots, animatronics. He did a course on it at college and was set to go to university to study special effects in film.

When they died, he had no clue how to carry on what they had started and though he had a part-time job it wasn't enough to pay the bills. I know, in the first few months after they died, he started working more hours, though he was always there to take me to school and pick me up at the end of the day. I know that he was worried about money, I heard him on the phone talking about how he was going to keep a roof over our heads. Slowly, over the years, he sold off pieces of land to neighbouring farms, sold the cattle, the crops, the machinery. The only thing we had left in the end was the farmhouse.

I found out that he had sold everything when I was about fifteen, after I had spent the last six years tramping over ground that wasn't mine, stroking the cows that were no longer mine. I was so angry that he had practically sold everything without telling me. The other farmers never said anything, even when I'd see them working in the field I assumed they were doing it to help Alex. I was so stupid.'

'You were a child.'

'A child that had no idea how much things cost. I just took it for granted that there would always be electricity in our farm, that there would always be food on the table. And there was. Only looking back now, I realise how hard Alex must have worked to ensure that.

When I was eighteen I applied to go to university and Alex sat me down and told me there was no money to do it. Tuition fees, rent in halls of residence, food – all that would cost money that he simply didn't have. He told me of his dreams to go to university too, that these dreams were put on hold when our parents died. He told me that if we sold the farm, there would be enough money left over to pay for us both to go to university, to pay our fees and rent and maybe even a small deposit on a house for us once we came back out the other side. As much as I wanted to go to university I wanted my home more, I wanted to live there for the rest of my life, raise my children there. But I knew that Alex's life had been put on hold for the last nine years, that he should have travelled the world, gone to university, got the job of his dreams... and he couldn't because of me. As I was eighteen, I knew he should start living his life again. We sold the farm, but I vowed one day I would come back and buy it.

I've lived in many places since then, a few months here, a year

67

there, but nowhere has been my home. I don't know what I'm looking for if I'm honest. It's just a feeling I suppose, a silly sentimental feeling.'

'You spend eighteen years in the same place, nothing else is going to compare to it. It's not silly at all.'

'I was going to buy it back last year when it came up for sale but I dithered. I didn't want to take a step back. It felt somehow that I wasn't moving forward but still living in the past. But I decided that even if I wasn't going to live in it, I wanted to own it. It's belonged to the family for over seven generations and it feels wrong that it now belongs to someone else. Unfortunately I was too late, and despite very generous offers to the idiot that's now living there, he won't budge. Sorry if the idiot is your friend.'

Finn shrugged. 'I don't like him much.'

'I think that's part of the problem, it being owned by an arse. If it was owned by a husband and wife who loved it, who had three little kids and a donkey out the back, I think I could let it go.'

How on earth was he going to tell her that he owned the farm? It would be weird between them, and he still wasn't sure what he was going to do with it. In the last year since he had bought the farm he had become very attached to it. It had been in a bad way when he first bought it as an investment, a project for him to undertake, but he had spent months lovingly restoring it and now he'd fallen a little bit in love with the place. Clearly not as much as Joy loved the place. He still hadn't decided whether to sell it on when it was finished or to move in himself and until he had decided he needed to keep the fact that he owned it quiet.

She let out a deep breath. 'Wow, I don't know why I told you all of that, I've never told anyone that before. It seems so silly to be clinging onto my childhood home like this, but I can't seem to let it go.'

He was silent for a while and looked down to see her hand held in his, but he had no recollection of how it got there. Damn it. He needed to get back to the original reason why he came up here.

'The police were looking for you.'

She paled significantly and he wished he'd just kept his big mouth shut.

'Did they say what for?'

He shook his head. 'Did you know there was a diamond robbery at Menton Hall last night?'

'At Menton Hall? Oh my god.' She paled even more, which was not the reaction he was hoping for. 'Do you think they want to talk to me about that?'

'Why would they?'

'I… don't know.' She stood quickly. 'I… I'd better go.' She hesitated for a moment. 'I'm having a housewarming barbeque tomorrow night. I invited all the villagers. I doubt anyone will come but… will you?'

He shook his head. 'I have Casey's wedding rehearsal dinner thing tomorrow night. I'm not entirely sure what the whole bloody thing entails, only that I have to be there as Casey's best man. Sorry, I would come otherwise.' Would he? Would he have gone as her friend?

'I take it Casey and Zach won't be there either.'

He smiled. 'I don't think they can rehearse without Casey. Maybe we can come by after.'

She nodded and then hurried off down the hill. He watched her go. She'd been spooked by the police coming, that was for sure.

*

The police looking for her had bothered Joy. She had spent most of the night worrying about it and whether they had any connection that might link her with the robbery. But as it was now nearly lunchtime the next day and they hadn't come back, she had to assume it was for an entirely innocent reason that they wanted to talk to her.

She had spent the morning busily preparing for the house-warming barbeque that night. She had marinated chicken, made salad and punch and decorated her garden.

But now, with the sun warming the day outside, it was a perfect time to enjoy a pint of cider in the beer garden of her nearby local. Though being banned from her nearby local might put a dampener on those plans. Could she perhaps go in disguise? Would a fake nose, a pair of googly specs and walking with a limp be enough to get past the astute eyes of the landlady Pam? Unlikely.

Though she wasn't just limited to Bramble Hill. There was a cluster of villages in the surrounding area, almost all of which had a local pub. Ashton Woods was about a thirty-minute walk from Bramble Hill. A good walk would be just what she needed to work up a thirst for a pint of cider. Calling for Darcy she headed out, scooping up the daily offering of dog poo that had been posted through her letterbox on the way.

*

She stopped outside the small thatched pub in Ashton Woods. It had a low white picket fence around the outside and small tables and chairs in a pretty little garden, complete with multi-coloured parasols. The pub sign swung gently in the breeze, its slight squeak drawing her attention. Instead of the arrogantly named Peacock's Pride, in large friendly writing was the cosy-sounding Ale and Custard. It made her smile and she crossed over the road to get a closer look.

As she drew nearer there was a sign outside that declared that the Ale and Custard welcomed dogs. She just hoped that the customers and landlord were as welcoming to their human owners – and that her reputation of throwing old ladies from their homes hadn't preceded her this far.

She pushed the door open. The pub was empty save for three elderly men playing dominoes and two middle aged ladies, one of which, the larger of the two, was serving behind the bar. She was chatting to a lady with long blonde hair. The blonde lady looked up and smiled at Joy and then the smile slid from her face, as she went an almost deathly shade of pale.

Oh god. She just wanted a pint of cider and to sit for a few hours and read her book. Surely Bramble Hill's small-mindedness couldn't have stretched this far.

Joy hesitated on the threshold, then decided to brazen it out. Striding to the bar purposefully, she knew she looked braver than she felt.

'Joy Cartier?' said the blonde lady, her voice barely a whisper.

Joy Cartier, not Jo Carter?

'Yes?'

The lady stared at her for a moment then came towards her.

'I'm Rose, I'm Casey's mum. He's spoken so much about you, it's a pleasure to actually meet you.'

'Oh.'

This was so not what she was expecting and didn't explain the look of fear that had crossed the lady's face when Joy had walked in.

Rose smiled at Joy's uncertainty. 'You look so much like your mum, I thought for a second… when you came in… I used to be friends with her.'

And though that did explain it, it did nothing to quell the confusion.

'Let me buy you a drink and we can have a chat.' Rose indicated a booth at the side of the room and Joy nodded numbly. Rose was soon sitting opposite her nursing a glass of whisky whilst Joy took a much-needed sip of her cider. Her throat was dry all of a sudden.

'We were best friends, me and your mum. We grew up together, she was maid of honour at my wedding and I reciprocated for her. I'm Alex's godmother, though you'd never know it, I wasn't around at all whilst he was growing up. Your mum was godmother to Zach and Casey too.' Rose sighed. 'We had a row, not long before you were born, over Zach. Right little tearaway he was, he must have been about four years old at the time. He used to play up at Blueberry Farm regularly, he loved your parents' cows. Well, he found a tin of spray paint, bright orange stuff it was, and Zach decided to use it to graffiti all over the side of one of your barns. Your mum was heavily pregnant with you, very emotional because they'd just had to put down one of their dogs and they'd just finished painting the barn too. I think the graffiti just pushed her over the edge. She was furious – took Zach over her knee and smacked him. Of course I would have smacked him myself had I got there first but I was so angry that she had hit my son. We had a blazing row about it and we never spoke to each other again. It was such a stupid thing to row over, especially after we had been friends for so long. So many times I wanted to pick up the phone and apologise but I didn't, too bloody stubborn. As time went on it became harder and harder to do it, until eventually it was too late. When your mum died I was gutted that nine years of stubborn pride had stood between me and my best friend, that I had never righted things between us before she died.'

A distant memory flooded Joy's mind. 'You're Rosie?'

Rose's face lit up. 'Yes, that's what your mum used to call me.'

'Mum spoke of you fondly,' Joy said, honestly.

'She did?'

'We used to look through the wedding album regularly and she'd tell me who the people were in the pictures. She told me all about you two sliding down the bannister in the hotel where she got married, and skinny-dipping in Brighton where she had her hen night.'

Rose smiled. 'Good lord, I'd forgotten that. I thought we would die of hypothermia. Becky thought it was hilarious.'

'When I asked where you were now and why she didn't see you anymore, she just said that sometimes friends drift apart. That pride was a silly sentiment and that she missed you a lot.'

'Oh.' Rose took a big swig of whisky.

'I presume Zach didn't have lasting scars from my mum's beating.'

'No, and he certainly didn't do anything like that again. I think he turned out OK.'

'I don't know him that well, but he seems like a nice lad.' Of course she couldn't tell Rose that she'd imagined doing all manner of inappropriate things with him, that he was desperate to get her into bed. She quickly changed the subject as she was aware she was blushing. 'Casey is lovely.'

Rose seemed to glow with pride. 'He is, isn't he? So kind and sweet. I presume you've met Arielle.'

Something about the way Rose said Arielle's name made Joy sit up straighter. 'You don't like her?'

'No love, I don't. Nasty little cow. I can't believe Casey proposed to her, I wouldn't believe it if I hadn't seen it with my own eyes. But if Casey's happy then I'm happy.'

'What if he's not?' Joy immediately regretted saying that. If Casey didn't want to tell his mum, it certainly wasn't her place to say something.

Rose frowned. 'Has he said something?'

'No, just… I think he feels it's all moving very quickly.'

'That's Arielle, she can't wait to get her hands on our money. Oh, I must admit, I've been helping a bit with all the arrangements. I love a good wedding and I never thought I'd see the day when either of my boys got married. Zach has been with more women than I could possibly count and for a long time I thought Casey might be gay.'

Joy nearly choked on her drink. 'You did? How funny. Would that have been a problem?'

'No of course not, I want him to be happy, to spend the rest of his life with the person he loves, man or woman, but he never said anything, or showed any inclination towards men. He does seem genuinely happy now with Arielle so I must have got it wrong.'

Joy bit her lip as she stared at the bubbles in her cider. How could Rose have got it so wrong now? How could she not see how unhappy Casey was? She had to tell Rose the truth and that would let Casey off the hook in marrying Arielle. Casey would hate her for spilling his secret. But that was a small price to pay for his happiness.

'I thought he was gay too,' said the large brown-haired lady from behind the bar as she collected Rose's empty glass. 'I thought he was in love with my son.'

'They would have made a cute couple,' Rose smiled wistfully. 'I think Casey would have been good for him too, better than that horrid ex-wife of his.'

Oh dear lord, Joy had to tell her.

'Oh, where are my manners, this is Sally, this is Joy, a friend of Casey's,' Rose said.

Sally shook Joy's hand hard, she was surprisingly strong. She struck Joy as a no-nonsense sort of woman. Whilst Rose was clearly fantasising about Casey and Sally's son living happily ever after, Sally seemed to have something important to get off her very ample chest. She took the seat opposite Joy.

'I couldn't help overhearing, you used to own Blueberry Farm?'

Joy didn't want to get distracted from Casey's problem. She just had to form the right words to out her friend. She nodded vaguely.

'My son owns it now. I presume you're the one who has been trying to buy him out for the last year.'

Sally immediately had Joy's fullest attention.

'When the house came up for sale, I wanted to buy it, but your son got there first. I've been very generous trying to buy him out but he won't budge.'

'I'm telling you now, Mac won't sell it, so you might as well stop trying.'

Joy opened her mouth to protest but Sally wasn't finished.

'When he bought it, it was a bit of a project for him, something to keep him occupied after his wife left him. You probably know that the previous owner left it in a right state.'

'Yes, I'd heard that, part of the reason I was so keen to get my hands on it.'

Joy had heard rumours of broken guttering which left mould growing up the entire front of the house, that the garden had been left to grow wild, that the window frames were broken and chipped, roof tiles had come off and not been replaced. Inside was apparently worse.

'Mac said he wanted to complete the project before he sold it on. But what started off as neutral, impersonal decorating and renovating, slowly started to get personal. There's so much of him in that house now, you can see his personality in every room. Every time he's there he's so happy and animated. It makes me smile just to see it. He's done all the work himself and he's become really proud of it. He's even started to find pieces of art or blown up photos to decorate it. The bedrooms look wonderful, he's created a gorgeous nursery right next to the master bedroom, a little boy's room decorated with spaceships and rockets and the little girl's room is hand painted with unicorns and fairies. He built a treehouse in the garden. He said he'd never had a treehouse growing up and he wanted his kids to have one. That was when I realised this wasn't an investment any longer, he was building a home, somewhere to raise his kids. If he's refusing to sell it, it's because he's fallen in love with it.'

Joy stared down at her glass, watching the condensation trickle onto the table. She didn't know what to do with this information. That was her home; she didn't want anyone else to be in love with it. Though if it was being looked after that was slightly easier to deal with.

Sally took her hand. 'I don't mean to speak out of turn, you clearly have a lot of happy memories of the place, but I think it's time you let go of the past and let someone else have a chance to make their own memories there. Mac will take care of it, I promise you that, and when he has children of his own, they will love it too.'

Rose nodded. 'I think your parents would want you to move on too.'

Sally perhaps realised that she had overstepped some mark. 'Come on Rose, let's leave the girl to her drink. I want to talk to you about what I should wear to the wedding this weekend.'

Rose's face lit up with talk of the wedding. 'Maybe, if you're interested, some other time I could show you some photos of your mum, when she was younger.'

'I'd really like that.'

Rose smiled and then followed Sally back to the bar, chatting excitedly about the wedding.

What Sally had said was at odds with what Finn had told her about the man that owned it. Finn had said the man was an arse. Maybe she would go round and see the farm for herself.

She dug out her book, sat back in the booth and started to read with Darcy slumbering peacefully at her feet. The book was good and as the pub stayed relatively empty apart from the old men that continued to play dominoes in silence, she devoured three chapters before she was disturbed by the pub door creaking open.

Finn came in, temporarily blocking out the light with his enormous frame, before he walked up to the bar. He didn't notice Joy sitting in the corner, something she was thankful for. That delicious feeling of lust shot through her. How could he affect her so much? She couldn't take her eyes off him.

Sally finished on the phone and came round to him, embracing him in a big hug. She obviously knew him. He bent his head down to kiss her fondly on the cheek, pulling her into a great bear hug.

'Hi Mum,' Finn said.

Joy smiled. Sally was Finn's mum and he obviously adored her. Then the smile slid from her face. Finn Mackenzie. Mac.

Chapter Six

Sally obviously said something to him about her because he looked over, his smile falling from his face.

Furious at his deception, Joy threw her book back in her bag, and stalked over to him. Darcy, sensing she was going, scrabbled to her feet behind her.

She jabbed a finger into his chest. 'You treacherous, lowlife scum. You lied to me.'

'No, I didn't.' He held up his hands in defence.

'You let me sit there bawling my heart out about my farm and never once mentioned that you owned it. I bet you were sitting there thinking, "She's desperate to live there, I can fleece her for so much more than the farm is worth."'

She was vaguely aware that the old men had dragged their attention from their riveting game of dominoes and were staring at her with their mouths open.

'Do you two know each other?' asked Sally, clearly hoping to calm down the situation.

'Well enough to know that your son is an absolute wan—'

'Now just a minute, I will not have bad language in my pub.'

'Well, that's fine because I was just leaving.'

Joy grabbed Darcy's lead and stormed out, though by the heavy footsteps behind her she knew that Finn was following her. She managed to make it to the picket fence before he grabbed her arm and pulled her back.

'Wait. I'm sorry I didn't tell you, I really am. You didn't exactly make it easy for me. You were sitting there saying the bloke that owned it was an arsehole and an idiot. I didn't feel like I could say, "Hi, I'm the arsehole, pleased to meet you."'

She yanked her arm out of his grip, but didn't walk away. He had a point.

'And no, fleecing you was not part of my agenda either. I made a fortune on my films, do you think a couple hundred thousand is going to make any difference to that? If I choose to sell it, it will be at a fair price but at the moment I'm not sure if I want to sell it. I know you're attached to it, but I am too and I didn't want to be pressured in to selling it just because…' He trailed off.

She felt her temper slowly ebb away at his words. 'Because?'

He sighed. 'Because a beautiful woman with sad eyes and a very sad story wants to buy it.'

'I don't need your pity,' she said. A beautiful woman?

'Exactly. That wasn't the right reason to sell it, not when I've spent so much time and effort restoring it. Not when for me it represents a fresh start, a new home and future. For you, by your own admittance, it was a step back. If I was going to sell it, it had to be the right thing for me and until I made that decision I thought it best to keep my ownership to myself. I'm sorry if that seemed selfish, I never meant to hurt you.'

She stroked Darcy's great head, embarrassed by her earlier outburst.

'I'm sorry for… poking you in the chest,' she said. She still felt angry that he hadn't told her, but she could at least apologise for the poking.

He smiled, rubbing his chest. 'You have quite the strong finger there. Would you like to see it?'

His chest? Mm, yes please. Damn it what was wrong with her, she really did have a one-track mind.

'The farm?' he prompted.

'Oh.'

After all this time, and with the sentimental attachment she still had for the place, she had to see it.

'We can go in my truck, if you like?'

They were going to see the farm now?

Finn was already striding across the road towards the beaten up old pick-up truck. He opened the back door for Darcy and then held the passenger door open for Joy. Darcy leapt in without any preamble, though Joy was slightly more hesitant, her nerves getting the better of her. What would it be like, how would she feel after all this time?

She got in and he drove off.

Feeling hot with nerves, she wound down the window, letting the cool breeze pull at her hair.

'I do have air con, if you'd prefer.' Finn indicated the dashboard.

'No, I prefer fresh air, the breeze on my face, it's such a nice feeling.' Small talk was good, anything to distract her from the sudden butterflies in her stomach. After all this time she was going home.

'Pippa always preferred the air conditioning,' Finn said, more to himself than to her.

'Oh, I don't mind, it's your car.' She started doing the window up.

'No, leave it. I like it.'

She watched him as he put his hand out the window, letting the wind race across his fingers. The beginnings of a smile touched his mouth. She liked it, he didn't smile often enough. It was kind of him to take her, especially after she had called him scum. Her gaze wandered from his huge strong hand, playing in the breeze to his slightly stubbly jaw, his large, strong shoulders, his full lips… she wanted to kiss those lips. He suddenly turned to look at her and, embarrassed that she had been caught staring, she quickly found something to say. 'Your mum says you've fallen in love with the place?'

His whole face lit up and she felt a sudden pang of jealousy.

'It's a beautiful place. I love going there. Bramble Hill has bad memories now.'

Finn pulled into the driveway that led down to the farm and she knew she had to keep talking.

'Why haven't you moved in then?'

'It was only ever supposed to be a project for me; I had no intention of living there, but now...'

Joy got the feeling that he had wanted to move in, but now with her stamping her feet over some sentimental attachment to her home he was feeling guilty about staying there. She didn't want him to feel guilty enough to sell it to her.

'I've spent a lot of time doing the garden, that being my forte. The downstairs and the bedrooms are done but the bathroom still needs some work, the shower doesn't work at all at the moment. Maybe when that's done... I want it to be finished before I move in... if I move in.'

And suddenly there it was – the farmhouse. Her home came into view and the longing, the sentimentality for it all came rushing back. Finn stopped the truck. The fields either side of the farm no longer belonged to it, as Alex had sold them off years before – it was just the farm, two nearby barns and the back garden that belonged to Finn now.

Finn came round to open her door for her, though she was reticent to get out. He opened the back door for Darcy, who scrabbled out, excited about being somewhere new. Joy reluctantly followed.

'Look what I found the other day.' He took her hand and gently pulled her over to the larger of the two barns. She knew he was trying to make it easier for her. He pointed at the side wall that was still painted white, as she remembered it, but Finn traced his fingers over letters that had been scratched into the side. JC and DS carved inside a tiny heart.

Joy laughed. 'My first boyfriend, Dave Sampson. I was five. We held hands for a week and I thought we were going to get married. Then he stuck his tongue in my mouth and left his chewing gum in there. I dumped him after that.'

'French kissing at the age of five, I'm shocked.'

'Hardly. It wasn't a kiss. He told me to open my mouth like I was at the dentist and then he just poked his tongue inside. He didn't even move it around. He said he'd seen his brother do it. I'm hoping his brother had more skill than that.'

If they were going to rehash old memories, she could do that, she had a tonne.

'You know this barn was where I'd always go when I was in a bad mood. There were lots of big machines in here and I could hide behind them and no one would know I was there. I ran away from home once when I was seven, and I came here. Alex brought me food so I wouldn't starve.'

'How long did you stay here?'

'I left after breakfast and was back in time for dinner. My parents knew where I was as well, so as runaway attempts go it wasn't that successful. But it was my refuge, when things got rough I'd always come here. There was something about the smell, I'm not sure what it was but it was… comforting. It was my secret place, I'd spend hours drawing in here, and later Alex made it into a bit of a studio for me.'

She moved round the front to the door and lifted one of the big plant pots. Underneath there was a key and she laughed. 'The spare key is still there, after all this time.' She took it out and slotted it into the lock; it turned easily. Finn stared at her with his mouth open. She pushed the door open and looked inside. This was easy, she could do this. The barn hadn't changed at all. The big machines were gone and there were now tins of paint, a step ladder and a lawn mower, but other than that it was exactly how she remembered it. The comforting, musty smell was still present. Smiling at the memories, she closed the door again, locked it and handed him the key.

'You might want to put that somewhere safe.'

He stared at the key for a moment and then slid it back under the pot. 'It's been safe there for eleven years, so I imagine it's still safe there now.'

He hesitated then turned towards the house. 'Shall we?'

She nodded and followed him.

'So… you're an artist?' She knew he was trying to distract her. Although she was willing to grasp any subject now that wasn't about the farm, what she did for a living was a tricky subject.

'Sort of,' she answered, deliberately being vague.

They were heading towards the front door. She had always used the back door, so it felt weird to be entering the house this way. The front door was now painted red, which was different to the green door she remembered. Red did look smart though. The wooden windows had recently been replaced with PVC ones but in a similar style to the windows that had been there before. Other than that, the outside looked the same.

He opened the front door and let her walk in ahead of him. But if she was waiting for all those childhood memories to come flooding back, she would have been disappointed. Standing in the hall, there was no semblance at all of the home she remembered. Her heart started pounding. The staircase was the first thing she noticed, that had changed completely. Instead of straight up at the side of the hall, it now curved outwards from the top floor so the bottom stairs were much wider than the top. It had been made into a feature of the room and the curvy black wrought iron rail was much more interesting than the plain wooden one. The stone floor, where she had fallen and broken her arm at the age of six had been replaced by soft, cream carpets. There was a large window halfway up the stairs that had not been there before, and it made the whole room lighter.

'Would you like to do downstairs first?' he asked quietly, his eyes filled with concern. He knew how hard this was for her and she felt touched by his compassion.

She nodded, unable to speak, a slow feeling of panic starting to clutch at her gut.

'There's just two rooms now.' He opened the nearest door to his left.

Two rooms? There had been a lounge, dining room, study, kitchen and conservatory downstairs, how could there only be two rooms now? She followed him into what used to be the lounge and felt her mouth fall open.

'This is the family room.'

It was the lounge, dining room and study all knocked into one great big room. The chimney was the first thing she noticed. In her time, it had been in the middle of the joining wall between the lounge and dining room, but as that wall was now gone it stood alone in the middle of the room, so you could walk all the way round it. It was a beautiful stone column tapering to a smaller circumference near the ceiling.

There was a large brown leather sofa that took up the entire end of the room, stretching out in a horseshoe shape round the three sides and facing a huge widescreen TV, fixed to one side of the chimney.

In the middle, across one wall there was a huge bookcase and several brown leather armchairs, perfect for curling up in and reading one of the hundreds of books that were on offer, everything from the classics – *Treasure Island*, *Robinson Crusoe*, the works of Shakespeare – to *James Bond* books, a huge Tolkien collection and the entire *Harry Potter* series.

Next to where she stood in stunned silence was a huge pool table and a large black piano. Gone were the white walls of her childhood, it was replaced with the warm autumn colours of red, gold and rich creams. The doorway between the dining room and study had also been removed – it was here that her dad had marked her and Alex's height every year on their birthdays.

Finn moved towards a door at the end and waited for her there. On shaky legs she followed him.

'This is the kitchen.' He pushed the door open.

But it wasn't her kitchen that met her, in fact there was nothing recognisable about it at all. It had been incorporated into the conservatory. The wicker chairs and flowered walls she remembered were also gone. The whole of the back wall of the house was now glass, there was also three large skylights making the room bright. The wooden kitchen units had been replaced with sleek cream ones, with black granite surfaces. There was a breakfast bar with bar stools in the middle and a vast dining table with eight black leather chairs up one end.

She wandered over to the window that had views of the back garden, and in the distance the river that curled through the surrounding fields and woods like a silver ribbon. The back garden had just been a patch of grass with the large oak tree on one side – now it had shape, flowers and plants spilt over from borders that had never been there before. There were huge pots that held more plants on the wooden decking. There was stepping stones, leading to several benches that were dotted round the sides. And up in the oak tree was a great treehouse, complete with curtained windows and a little front door.

Finn opened the back door, letting the heat spill onto the warm terracotta tiles.

'Are you OK? Do you want to sit down for a minute?'

Had he asked that because she'd gone pale, because her breathing was erratic, because her eyes were wide with panic? Her heart was racing, her brain was buzzing, she felt numb.

'I just need a few minutes,' she said as she walked out into the garden, hoping that he wouldn't follow her. She walked up to one of the furthest benches and sat down staring back at the house.

It was no longer her home, that was the problem. In her rose-tinted view of the world, the farmhouse would still be there waiting for her, exactly as she had left it eleven years before. She had mentally prepared herself that the décor would be different but nothing had prepared her for the completely different house that she had just walked round. There had been nothing of her childhood home left, that home now only existed in her memories. She felt an enormous sense of loss all of a sudden.

Finn approached with a glass of water. He slowed warily as he drew nearer; eyeing her like she was a wild animal. He passed her the glass and sat down next to her. He didn't speak though, probably thinking she was a right nut job.

'All this time I've been searching for a place that I could call home, but I never found it. I realise now that I wasn't waiting for that special something, that secret missing ingredient that I just couldn't put my finger on. Nowhere matched up because I didn't want anywhere else, the only home I wanted was this place. I knew that one day I would come home and subconsciously anything in between was just a stopgap so I never allowed myself to fall in love with it. Beautiful houses, perfect towns and villages and I turned my back on all of them because it wasn't here. And now I find that the home I was longing to return to has gone. There's nothing for me here either.'

She looked down to see her hand in his again.

'I'm sorry.'

'Don't be. It's a beautiful house; you've done an amazing job with it. It's a proper home now and one day you will fill it with a wife and children. That's how it should be.'

She passed him back the glass and stood up but he caught her hand.

'You still have your memories Joy, no matter where you live you will always have them. Being physically closer to them won't make those memories more real. You keep them alive by remembering them, by talking about them.'

'You're right.' It had been silly to hold out for this place. As

Alex had said, the memories were in her heart not the four walls of her childhood home. 'I guess I was just scared that the memories were fading and I was trying to cling onto them in any way I could.'

'Well, if you want to come up here, any time, if you want to make mud pies in the garden or play in the barn, you're more than welcome.'

She smiled, her heart swelling a little bit more for him.

'I'm glad you bought it. It's good to know it's in safe hands. And Mum would have loved what you've done to the place.'

He stood up. 'Shall I take you home?'

'No, I'm fine, I'd like to walk.' She reached up and Finn obliged by bending his head down. She kissed him on the cheek. 'Thanks for taking care of it.'

With that she walked back round the side of the house, whistling for Darcy as she went. Though the loss hurt, it was now tinged with a sense of relief. She could never go back home now, so she could stop waiting. She could finally draw a line under that part of her life and make a real effort to settle in one place. It was time to stop running.

She had the housewarming barbeque that night. Maybe she could make some real friends here in Bramble Hill, maybe her house could finally be the home she had been searching for.

*

When she got home she phoned Alex. He had been worried by her plans to buy the farm. It was a cathartic release to be able to honestly tell him she no longer wanted to live there, that for the first time in her life she was looking to the future. Alex couldn't disguise the relief from his voice; he had been concerned that she couldn't let go of the past.

They chatted for a while and then she remembered Rose.

'Alex, do you remember a lady called Rose, a friend of Mum's?'

There was silence for a moment. 'Rosie, yes I do. I haven't seen her since I was about eight, she just stopped coming round. She had two boys – I remember Caz but I can't remember the little one's name.'

'Zach, he vandalised the side of our barn with a can of spray paint. Mum smacked his bum. She and Rose had a big row over it and never spoke since.'

'Oh, that explains a lot. Wow, Mum never hit us, she must have been really mad. I was gutted, when they stopped coming. Caz was brilliant, so funny and cute.'

She smiled, hugely. 'Caz as in Casey, Casey Fallowfield?'

'Caz Fallowfield, that's it.' Alex gasped. 'Oh my god, is that the Casey that texted me the other day?'

'Yes, small world or what?'

'I guess it was bound to happen, you living so close to where we grew up.'

'Look, I need to go, my barbeque is supposed to start shortly.'

'Have fun kid, I'd better go to sleep. We're kidnapping the prime minister at midnight.'

'Well that sounds like much more fun than my little barbeque.'

'I don't know, I'd rather be there with you.'

She smiled, her heart aching a little bit. 'Love you Al.'

'Love you too, always.'

*

It was late by the time Finn got back from the wedding rehearsal. Zach and Casey had stayed up at their mum's house chatting and socialising with the elite. He had no part in that world and didn't want to. He loved Casey's mum dearly, as much as he loved his own parents, but the dinner parties and balls that she continually invited him to held no interest for him.

He went up to his room, determined to be out of his suit and tie as quick as he could. As he slid the tie off his neck, he noticed fairy lights strung across the trees next door. He stepped closer to the window and saw twinkling decorations adorning every fence, tree and bush and around the roof of the summer house. Candles were in jam jars and dotted periodically throughout the garden. It looked beautiful. The embers on the barbeque seemed to be dying out, and a table covered in plates and bowls of food seemed to have been demolished. It looked like the end of a good party. Just then a whoosh of light exploded from the garden, shattering glittering gold stars into the night sky. Fireworks. So the party must still be in full swing.

He turned to go down and join her, then stopped himself. Just because he had taken her to the farm earlier, it didn't make them friends. He didn't want to be friends with her, because as her brother so wisely said, men and women couldn't be friends. It would soon develop into something more and he didn't want something more. He never wanted to be hurt again the way Pippa had hurt him. He turned back to the window then, cursing himself, he stormed down the stairs. He did say he would go when he came back after all.

He let himself through the connecting gate and watched what was obviously a slightly tipsy Joy light another firework and then run quickly away from it before it exploded. She was wearing a long black floaty dress that clung at the breast and floated down to her ankles – she was barefoot, her long hair trailing down her back. The firework lit up the garden for a moment, sending silvery shadows across the lawn, long enough for Finn to see Joy was completely alone. There was music playing on a nearby stereo – The Killers' 'Mr Brightside' – which Joy was cheerily singing along to, as she poured herself a glass of dubious looking brown liquid from a punch bowl.

'Joy?'

She whirled around spilling most of the brown liquid on the floor.

'Finn! You came!' A huge smile split her face from ear to ear.

'Would you like a drink? I have alcoholic punch, which tastes like shit, and non-alcoholic punch which also tastes like shit, or I've got a beer which might be a bit warm as it's been outside for a while.'

'Warm beer is fine.'

'Good cos I'm not really sure which is the alcoholic punch anymore.'

She passed him a beer and skipped across the lawn to light another firework. It boomed blue lightning across the sky.

He sipped his beer and watched her.

'Good party?'

'I had a great time. The burgers tasted great, I made them myself, the salad didn't get eaten, but then it never does at barbeques. I have danced for most of the night and I might be a tiny bit tipsy. So yep a bloody great party.' She took another swig from her dubious punch, and he smiled for her. Maybe the villagers had been persuaded by her note, or at least some of her friends had obviously been and gone. 'No one came,' she said, as she lit another firework. 'But it was still a great party.'

'What do you mean no one came, you mean none of the villagers?'

She ran as fast as she could away from the firework, covering her ears, grinning, hugely. 'This one's a big one. The Finale.'

He waited. She waited. But there was nothing.

'Stupid thing,' she muttered, moving to go back to it. He caught her arm and pulled her back.

'Have you never heard of the old adage, never go back to a firework once it's been lit?'

'That's just an old wives' tale, like don't go swimming after you've eaten or don't eat yellow snow.'

He laughed and was surprised by the sound of it. It had been a long time since he had laughed. 'I'm not sure about the swimming after you've eaten one, but not eating yellow snow sounds like good advice.'

'It probably just needs to be re-lit, or I could give it a kick or something.'

'And lose your foot or your face in the process, I don't think so.'

'Spoilsport, that was The Finale.'

'So you said, but not this time my love.' He froze. Did he just call her 'my love'? Luckily, she hadn't noticed. 'What did you mean, no one came?'

'Just that. It was just me and Darcy all night. Until you arrived.'

His heart bled for her. 'No one. What about your friends?'

'I don't have any.' She laughed. 'No, that's not true. I have brilliant friends. When I went to university I spent four years in the pockets of Libby, Annie, Suzie and Eve. We all studied Fine Art and Sculpture. We were inseparable. We went everywhere, did everything together. But when we graduated Libby went back to the furthest northern shores of Scotland, Suzie went back to Jersey, Annie went back to Iceland and the last I heard Eve now lives on a ranch in Texas, married to a huge cowboy called Red, with five equally huge children. God, I miss them. We all stay in touch with Skype or email but obviously we don't see each other that often.'

'So everyone went back home and you didn't have a home to return to? What did you do?'

She smiled darkly. 'When university finished I was in the middle of a passionate whirlwind affair with Jake Aldbury, a guest speaker that had talked to us about carving wood. He was such a marvellous man – he had travelled the world, he'd seen so much and he could do things with wood I couldn't even begin to do. Jake taught me so much about wood carving and the sex was amazing. When he travelled to Italy, I went with him. Then he travelled to Australia and I went too. We parted ways soon after that, but I had the travelling bug and as you said, I had no home to return to, so I didn't see any point in coming back. I spent the next four years travelling the world. I worked in bars, I danced on tables…'

She laughed when she saw his angry face.

'No, not like topless dancing. I worked in one of those Fifties-style restaurants in San Francisco, where the waiters are costumed. Mainly I was Rizzo from *Grease*, but sometimes I was Marilyn Monroe in a blonde wig, apparently I had the tits for it.'

He refused to let his eyes wander to them to check them out.

'So I was dancing on tables, cleaning hotels, I washed cars, delivered pizzas and in between I'm carving, whittling, sculpting wood and selling my pieces to tourists. The Aboriginals and the Native Americans taught me a lot about carving wood too. Then I met a chainsaw artist, and that was inspiring. I went to every single little pocket of the world – Alaska, Easter Island, Christmas Island, Greenland, Thailand, New Zealand – and I met the most amazing people who I still keep in touch with, but unfortunately they're all a bit far away to be coming to my little barbeque. I came back to England three years ago and for a while I was involved with Ed, he had loads of friends and suddenly I did too, but after what happened...' She trailed off, frowning.

'What happened?'

'Nothing, it doesn't matter.' Leading Finn to believe it did.

'Did he cheat on you?'

'No.'

'Did you cheat on him?'

Anger exploded in her eyes. 'No, I would never do that, never.'

'Then what?'

'It doesn't matter, we broke up and all my friends, his friends that had been so nice to me in the year that me and Ed had been together, well, as soon as Ed dropped me, they went back to being just *his* friends again. In the last two years, I haven't been anywhere longer than three months. You don't tend to make lasting friend-ships when you've only known someone for a month or two. So although I have friends, none of them live close. Oh, listen to me warble on. My mouth does seem to disengage itself from my brain when I'm drunk. You should just tell me to shut up. Oh, I love this song.' She started dancing, swirling round in circles, her arms above her head as she sang along to Cyndi Lauper's 'Time after Time'.

He watched her, his heart physically aching for her. Every single one of the villagers had snubbed her. She'd been thrown in a pond, been in a fight, had dog shit posted through her letterbox and she was still dancing. Nothing seemed to keep her down. It seemed she had gotten very good at being on her own, creating her own fun, but it shouldn't be like that. She needed a friend. He could be her friend.

'Dance with me, Finn.' She held out a hand for him and he instinctively took it, with the other hand at her waist, pulling her close against him. She tried to loop her arm round his neck, but she couldn't reach so she settled for her hand on his shoulder instead, leaning her head against his chest. With her warmth, her smell, her body against his, a wave of desire crashed through him like he had never felt before. He'd had girlfriends in the past, women he had found attractive, but right then he wanted Joy like a drug addict wanted heroin. He nearly pushed her away – the need for her, to have her, was so strong.

Just then the redundant firework blew up with a deafening boom, Joy jolted a bit and he automatically pulled her closer. Ribbons of gold, silver and red shot across the sky and they both looked up, admiring the view.

As the light faded from her eyes and she stared into his, he knew they could never be friends, not when he was now seemingly falling in love with her.

Chapter Seven

Joy woke the next day to find her head was pounding and her mouth was dry. She was in bed, in her pyjamas with no recollection of how she got there. Her head was sticking out the bottom of the bed, but then she always did wriggle around a lot in her dreams when she was drunk. She sat up carefully, holding her head in her hands when it pounded even harder with the excessive movement.

Images of the night before flooded through her mind. The barbeque, the fireworks, Finn, dancing with Finn. She had felt so safe there in his arms, so protected. She groaned as her cheeks burned red. She remembered trying to kiss him. She remembered him stepping back from her, pushing her gently but firmly away, before he disappeared back through the gate without another word. The shame of rejection washed through her.

Darcy rolled over, resting her great head in Joy's lap, her beautiful doleful eyes staring up at her.

Joy stroked her ears. 'Oh Darcy, maybe I really should just stick my nose up Finn's butt, it seems to work for you.'

Suddenly, Joy heard a spluttering, a coughing from next door – it was so loud, so clear it was almost as if Finn was in the room with her. It sounded like he had just drank some water and spat it out again. Had he choked on it in shock over what she'd just said? If she could hear him coughing so clearly, he would definitely be able to hear her speaking. She was sure her cheeks were glowing crimson right now.

She scrabbled out of bed and went to stand near the adjoining wall.

'You heard that, didn't you?' she asked the wall.

There was silence for a moment then she heard a shifting of weight as someone moved closer to the wall.

'Yes,' came Finn's voice.

She closed her eyes. Silence stretched between them. There were no words she could find to lessen her embarrassment. She wondered, if she prayed and wished really hard, if the gods, fairy godmothers, guardian angels or whoever else might be listening might be persuaded to turn the clock back five minutes. In fact, whilst the gods of time were messing about with the timeline, they might as well turn the clocks back forty-eight hours. That way she wouldn't, rather embarrassingly, bare her soul to Finn about her parents and her home, she wouldn't have gone to all that trouble for the barbeque if she'd known no one was going to turn up, then she wouldn't have got drunk, told Finn she hadn't got any friends and then tried to kiss him.

She kept her eyes scrunched for a moment, hoping that when she opened them she would be lying on the chair swing, wrapped in the blanket that Zach had covered her with and everything would be right with the world.

She opened her eyes and to her disappointment she found she was still standing next to the wall.

Joy sighed. She knew she would have to speak to Finn at some point and at least talking to him through the wall was easier than doing so face to face.

'I'm… sorry about last night.'

She heard a shifting of weight again as he moved closer. She couldn't say why, but she felt sure he was pressing his hand against the wall, almost like he wanted to touch her. It was a silly thought, if he wanted to touch her, he would have done so the night before.

'It's fine.' His voice was cool, clipped. She sighed. They had been making headway in their friendship. The day before, when he'd been so nice about the farm, had been lovely. Now it seemed that they were going to revert back to how they were when she first moved in.

'Darcy, let's go for a walk,' she said, indicating to Finn that their conversation was over. She stormed out, but then hesitated near the door as Darcy ran past her and thundered down the stairs. She frowned in confusion at the lack of movement from Finn's side, almost as if he was still standing there, next to her wall. Turning away, she went into the bathroom to brush her teeth.

*

As Joy walked back from the fields with Darcy, she thought back again to the night before. The way Finn had held her when they had danced, the way he had looked at her right before she tried to kiss him, had indicated to her that perhaps he had feelings for her too. The rejection confused her.

She sighed. She'd revealed some of her deepest, darkest memories. He now knew more about her than most of her friends. Why she felt so compelled to share her innermost secrets with him, she didn't know. All she had to do now was tell him of the time she was attacked in London and that would be it, all her secrets would be laid out before him.

Almost all of her secrets. There was still one that she held very close to her chest.

She had given away too much information about her wood carving and chainsaw experience to Finn the night before. If he saw her with the chainsaw or Casey told him about it, Finn might put two and two together. They both could, especially if they compared notes. The unfortunate timing of the Menton Hall robbery was too close for comfort as well. She had spent the best part of two years keeping the identity of her alter ego hidden, she couldn't afford to be found out now just because her tongue got a bit loose when she was drunk.

She let herself back in, filled Darcy's water bowl and opened the back door so Darcy could lie outside.

Blanking out the number plates outside her home just before her last job had been a mistake. Normally she did it just round the corner from where she would go off road, but as Menton Hall had been so close, she'd done it at home and that had been careless. If anyone saw, if Finn saw that, then suspicions would certainly arise.

She had another job to do tonight, another local one. Maybe she would start to load a few bits now so it didn't look quite as suspicious as it would if she did it all in one go later.

'Hey!' called Zach from his garden, disturbing her from her reverie. 'Sorry I couldn't make your barbeque thing last night. I wish I could have come, I bet it would have been much more fun than the stupid rehearsal dinner thing.'

'A rehearsal dinner does sound a bit strange. What do you need to rehearse? She says I do, he says I do, job done.'

Zach laughed. 'You're right, it is silly. Casey's just doing anything for a quiet life at the moment. That's why he keeps hanging round here all the time, trying to keep out of Arielle's way whilst she goes mad with all the wedding preparations.'

She stepped closer to the fence. 'What do you make of Casey marrying Arielle?' She had to be careful what she said here.

'I think it's the stupidest thing I've ever heard. I've never known two people less suited to each other. I'm pretty sure she's shagging Robert Franks, the local plumber, so I doubt it will last. She makes Casey miserable and if Mum stopped getting so excited about this big wedding of the year for just a second, she would see how unhappy he is. I do worry about him.'

Joy was surprised by this. Although Zach seemed like a nice bloke, she had always thought that he was quite self-involved. To hear him so concerned about his brother was incredibly endearing.

'Listen I have something to ask you,' he went on. 'And just hear me out before you say no. I know you're coming to the wedding on Saturday but I was wondering if you would come as my date. No funny business,' he added quickly. 'It's just that there will be a lot of single women at this wedding and a lot of them are interested in me...'

'Poor you, that must be so hard.' She smirked at him.

'Well, normally I wouldn't mind, but since I fell in love with the girl next door, I've sworn off women for the next month. It would make it a lot easier if I had a date to the wedding – that way no possible suitors will come after me. I'm not asking you to pretend to be my girlfriend or anything, just to accompany me. Maybe dance with me once or twice.'

She barely heard what he said; her mind was still processing the fact that he'd just said he was in love with her. No one had ever said they loved her. There'd been boyfriends in the past, but no real long-term relationships. Ed had been the longest and he'd never uttered those words. But then it was clear he'd never loved her – if he had, he wouldn't've dumped her over what had happened that fateful night.

But Zach had just said it so casually, so simply, the words didn't seem to matter at all. She had always envisaged hearing those words for the first time in much more romantic circumstances. Did he really love her? The 'can't breathe, can't sleep, can't eat, can't think,' kind of love?

She found herself nodding, inwardly cursing herself for being so flattered that he loved her, or at least had said it. 'OK then, just as long as you know that it's not a proper date, there'll be no kissing or anything else that your dirty little mind can imagine.'

He pretended to look offended. 'I'll have you know that my mind is squeaky clean.'

'Well, that's OK then. We'll just be two friends going to the wedding together.'

Zach crossed his heart and held his fingers up in a boy scout's salute. 'I promise, I won't even squeeze your butt when we dance.'

'I should hope not too.'

He grinned. She heard the phone ring in his house and he waved goodbye to her as he ran to answer it.

'Jesus, you women are a sucker for the love word, aren't you?' came Finn's voice behind her. She turned to face him, determined she wouldn't be embarrassed after what had happened the night before. 'It didn't even come with flowers, chocolates, a ring, or a violinist to serenade you and I could still see your heart fall out of your chest and the little birds singing gaily as they flew around your head.'

'What's it got to do with you?' So they had gone full circle then. Finn's niceness the day before was very short-lived. The sneer on his face was back. Though she couldn't understand why he was so angry about it.

'Nothing at all. I couldn't care less. I'm just amazed at how easily you were swayed. One moment you're standing your ground, refusing to be another notch on his bedpost, and the very next second, he tells you he loves you and now you're going out on a date.'

'It's not a date, we're just friends.'

'Men and women can't be friends, Joy.'

There was something about the way he said that, that made her think he was talking about them not being friends. She moved closer to his fence. 'We seemed to do OK yesterday, at the farm.'

'Don't mistake kindness for friendship. Besides, you crashed straight across those boundaries when you tried to kiss me.'

She hated that she gave him the satisfaction of blushing. It was mortifying. Of course he didn't want her. He was magnificent, the great Finn Mackenzie, he could have any woman he wanted. He'd shown a little bit of tenderness to her and she'd fallen for him because of it. Idiot.

'That's why men and women can't be friends, someone always wants more.' Finn's eyes were cold. Arrogant sod.

He was so inconsistent, she couldn't keep up. He had been rude, but then he had been so kind, so considerate the day before at the farm, and the way he had held her when they had danced the night before was so… loving, but now this anger over a kiss. It was exhausting. Maybe it was better if they weren't friends. Though being friends with him was far easier than this continual angst.

He must have thought so too. 'Look, if you understand that I don't want more, with you or anyone else, if you realise that nothing is ever going to happen between us, that I don't find you in the least bit attractive, then maybe we can be friends.'

Egotistical, conceited little… 'I tell you what Finn, you can stick your friendship up your arse.'

With that, she stormed back into the house.

*

Finn scowled as he pulled up outside Joy's house a few hours later, glaring at her front door. He had hurt Joy but he wasn't going to feel guilty just because he didn't want a relationship. He was perfectly happy with his life as it was, he didn't need her crashing into it with her beautiful red hair, her intense green eyes, her sad stories and her stroppy moods.

He glanced at himself in the rear-view mirror. Two angry grey eyes glared back at him, the frown between his eyes was an almost permanent feature now, as it had been for the last eighteen months. Oh yes, he was perfectly happy!

He got out and slammed the door, grumpy that the blasted woman had such an effect on him, and was just unloading his car when the police car pulled up outside again.

He deliberately dawdled with his stuff as he surreptitiously watched the policewoman from the other day get out and walk up the path towards Joy's front door.

A few seconds later the door opened and Joy gasped. 'Oh god.'

'Hello Joy, can I come in?'

And that was it. The policewoman went inside and the door closed firmly behind them. Not a lot to go on.

He was perturbed slightly at the lack of information. He went through to the back garden to put his stuff in the shed and attempt to fix the lawn mower that had died the day before.

It wasn't long before he heard Joy's front door open and close and presumably what sounded like the police car driving away.

Had she been arrested?

Though that theory was quickly dismissed as she came outside and stood on the decking. She looked very pale.

He looked determinedly down at the lawn mower.

Out of the corner of his eye he saw her walk on shaky legs down to the summer house. The lawn mower; that's what he was out here for. He was not going to get involved.

He glanced over again and saw she was now sitting with her head in her hands.

Shit.

No, it had nothing to do with him. His eyes slid back towards her again. Was she crying?

He stared back at the screwdriver in his hand, threw it down in annoyance and pushed his way through the connecting gate.

She was crying. No doubt about it. He could hear the stifled sobs as he walked closer. She hadn't seen him yet, he could still back out.

'Are you OK?'

She jolted in shock, looking up and quickly wiping the tears from her face. Damn it. A woman's tears were the most powerful tool in the world. He would have done anything for her right then; he would have lain down and died for her if she'd asked, or thrown her into the back of his pick-up truck and spent the rest of their lives on the run, hiding from the law.

'I'm fine,' she snapped, clearly embarrassed.

'Well, you're obviously not.'

'Like you care.'

He felt his jaw clench. 'You're right, I don't.'

He turned and stormed away, angry that his offer of help had been refused.

*

She wouldn't let it affect her, Joy thought as she loaded her boot with her chainsaw and a collection of other power tools. She'd had a little cry and that was only natural, but she wouldn't think of it again. If she dwelled on it, allowed herself to be scared, then the bastard had won – and he wouldn't win, she was damned sure of that.

She jumped in the car and drove off up the road, deliberately ignoring Finn as he watched her from his window.

But she was angry and she was entitled to that. The justice system had let her down. If she hadn't fought back, if she had let the bastard have his way, he would still be rotting in prison, probably for another four years. Instead he had got out in just under two. The fact that he'd confessed and that his solicitor had said there was mitigating circumstances had made the sentence much less. Mitigating circumstances. Bullshit.

She stopped the car in a layby and when the road was quiet, she quickly got out and covered her number plates. She drove round the corner and as the road was still empty she turned off and drove through the trees, allowing the greenery to swallow her, hiding her from the view of the road. She drove on as far as she could before she had to stop; the trees were getting too close together to go any further.

It was a good five-minute walk from where she'd stopped to get to her target, so she'd kept the luggage to a minimum, one large rucksack on her back and she carried the larger chainsaw in her hands.

It was quiet in the woods, trees stretching as far as the eye could see in every direction. This was the perfect place to work. Working in the public grounds of Menton Hall the other night was not ideal, it was more likely she would get caught in such open places like that. But not getting caught was part of the thrill and it was also integral to being The Dark Shadow. Without the mystery, there would be no demand, well, very little.

She had fallen in love with chainsaw carving when she stayed with a chainsaw artist for a week in Alaska four years before. She had become hooked on the excitement of using such dangerous equipment and relished in the skill needed to use chainsaws to carve such intricate pieces.

On her return to the UK, she had gained her chainsaw qual-ifications at a local agricultural college and spent months refining her skill. She had contacted a local chainsaw artist, Dan Cordell, with the hope that she could get some pointers from him. His work was stunning. She expected to get little or nothing back. Based on her limited experience of those in the art world, people didn't really have the time or inclination to help their peers. Chainsaw carvers were a different breed. What she had got from Dan had been amazing. He taught her so much about the use of different power tools and their effects. He introduced her to loads of other chainsaw carvers who were also more than willing to pass on their tips and expertise. She had met Matt George, another carver, who had lived just down the road from her at the time with his lovely wife Emily and three beautiful daughters. Matt had firmly taken her under his wing. He had been more than happy to let her follow him around for weeks as he did commissions and attended events. The carvers were a family of great people who looked after one another and were genuinely happy for each other's successes. She was quickly accepted as one of them and not just Matt's weird little stalker. She attended events, small school fetes, craft fairs, demonstrating her skills and slowly, very slowly, building a name for herself.

Although she got a few commissions, work was still very thin on the ground.

She had been keen to show Jake Aldbury, her former lover and mentor, how much she had learned in wood carving since they had parted in Australia all those years before. One night, she had snuck into the grounds of his farm and using the chainsaw had carved a huge flying unicorn into the trunk of a dead oak tree. It was fantastic and to this day was one of the pieces she was most proud of.

She presumed she would get a text or a phone call from him the next day but instead Jake went to the press. Hamming it up for the TV cameras, he stood in a pork pie hat, chewing on a blade of grass, looking confused and a bit simple. He explained to the journalists that he had gone to bed the night before and when he woke in the morning the unicorn was there as if it had quite simply grown out of the wood. He spoke of aliens and of time travellers, but kept saying 'why me, why did they choose me?' Joy's favourite part of the news clip, which she had played hundreds of times since, was Jake looking round at the unicorn in bewilderment, shaking his head, but as he turned back to the camera, for a split second there was a fierce pride in his eyes. When the journalists asked if he had seen anything, he told them of what had appeared on the CCTV, a shape, a dark shadow that moved so quickly it was impossible to tell who or what it was. The news programme then played the clip of the CCTV in slow motion, and as Jake said it was nothing more than a shadow and subsequently The Dark Shadow had inadvertently been born.

Joy had quickly followed up with two more strikes, one in Western Scotland and one in Dartmoor the day after, using old dead trees as her canvas. Suddenly, there was a media frenzy, with everyone wanting to know who and what The Dark Shadow was.

Alex had quickly helped her to set up a website with photos of her "strikes" and hundreds of people had started contacting The Dark Shadow offering to pay her to come and do something in their grounds. Mainly she had only accepted offers from public places, attracting more visitors to come and see them. And it was only ever dead trees that she carved, bringing life where there was none anymore.

In a matter of months, she had gone from living on baked beans on toast and wondering how she was going to pay the rent to having more money than she'd ever had in her life. She'd paid cash for her second-hand Range Rover and had enough money in the bank now to buy her little house outright and still have some left over. But she wasn't stupid. She knew the popularity of The Dark Shadow would be short-lived, people would tire of it, or her identity would eventually be revealed. Although she would still get commissions on the back of The Dark Shadow's success, she would never be as popular as she was now once her identity was out there. She had to be careful with her money, make sure she had enough to live on after the frenzy died down. But for now, she could enjoy the glory.

In the months that followed, the demand for The Dark Shadow grew and grew until she was doing strikes three or four times a week. The Dark Shadow had gained so much in popularity there were now treasure maps showing where the strikes were across the UK. There was a special geocache website set up exclusively for her pieces, people would follow co-ordinates to find them and have their photos taken with some of the pieces and post them online. There were even T-shirts printed by a company that sold the rather provocative phrase 'The Dark Shadow did me last night', printed across a range of different coloured styles.

The great thing about the secrecy was that although the clients had paid for her services, they never knew when she was going to strike and sometimes it would be weeks after she had carved the pieces that it would be discovered and news of it would hit the headlines. Sometimes two strikes would appear in the news on the same day hundreds of miles apart, leading to more conspiracies about the identity of The Dark Shadow.

As time went on, these conspiracy theories as to the true identity of The Dark Shadow became more and more ridiculous, which just added weight to the intrigue. But none of them suggested it was a five-foot girl from some little village in the middle of nowhere. In fact, as some of her sculptures were quite high up, many people believed it must be a very tall man. Though a few tree surgeons had said how easy it would be to get up a tree to carve, using ropes, harnesses and spikes strapped to the feet. She had been slightly annoyed at that – hanging from a harness to cut off a few branches was one thing, but doing so while carving a detailed, intricate piece was a whole other ball game. Other chainsaw carvers she knew erected scaffolding to do high pieces, but she didn't have that luxury, she had to be in and out in a matter of hours.

The Dark Shadow had even made international strikes, two in Alaska where it had all begun for her, and ones in Washington, France, Madeira and Spain. That was harder. Strict airport security meant she could never take her own chainsaws on a plane, she had to hire them or ask for her clients to provide the tools in a secret drop off. The Americans loved the secret drop offs, going to a park and placing a chainsaw in a secret location for her to collect, it added to the thrill for them too. For her second anniversary the month before, she had been invited to do a piece in Central Park in New York. For the city that never sleeps, keeping her strike a secret was very tricky, but fun.

Joy looked up at the tree she was about to carve. Her strikes always had to be recced before she carved and she would take photos from different angles so she could plan what she wanted to do. Mostly people gave her a free reign as there were certain things that were beyond her repertoire, but now and again, like tonight, people had specific requests. Tonight, it had to be themed around Lord of the Rings. It would be very easy to do an Ent, like Treebeard the talking tree – carve some eyes, mouth, nose, hands and feet and she could be out of there in half an hour.

But in her sketches over the last few days, as she roughly drew some ideas, and with the maquettes she had made from plasticine, she had settled on a Ringwraith, a hooded faceless creature, with clawed hands, the evil ones in search of The One Ring. The folds of the cloak would be particularly tricky to carve, and the hands would require some intricate detail. But she needed the distraction of the challenge tonight.

Chainsaw carving allowed her to escape – it gave her control which she so desperately strived for after her attacker tried to take it away from her. The skill needed to control such a powerful piece of equipment with such precision gave her shattered confidence an incredible boost. She felt strong here, amongst the trees. No one could ever take that away from her.

It wouldn't be long before she had to light her lanterns so she could see what she was doing, but for now she would make use of the fading daylight. She tied her hair back with a bandana and pulled on her safety goggles. She switched on her iPod, and flicked through her extensive collection to find something to drown out the white noise of the chainsaw. Her most recent playlist showed an eclectic mix of Snow Patrol, Westlife, Green Day, Bach, Ed Sheeran, Debussy, Kings of Leon, Guns N' Roses and Jessie J. But tonight's mood needed something big – not just to drown out the noise, but her bad mood too. She selected Two Steps from Hell's epic album *Invincible* and hit play. She pulled on her ear defenders, picked up her chainsaw and started to carve.

*

Finn woke to a noise from Joy's side of the wall. A muffled noise, like a scream smothered by a pillow or duvet. He sat up, concerned slightly. It was after two in the morning. Joy had returned from her night job just after midnight, unloaded her boxes and gone straight to bed. He had heard her mumble goodnight to Darcy and then there'd been silence. But now there was a noise, some sort of commotion, a struggle?

Then her voice rang out, the urgency of which sliced through the silence of the night like a knife.

'Get off, don't touch me, someone help, HELP!'

Chapter Eight

He was out of bed and down the stairs in a blur. He broke through her front door, vaguely aware that he had smashed it to smithereens and charged up her stairs. He ran into her bedroom, which was in pitch darkness and pain seared through his nose as he was punched hard in the face. As he was still reeling from the attack and trying to see anything through the gloom, his attacker stamped painfully on his foot and then punched him in the gut.

There was silence from Joy and Finn was concerned by what this bastard had done to her. He slammed his attacker into the wall, pinning him with his weight. To his horror, with his body pressed against hers, he realised it was Joy. He felt sickened by the force he had thrown her against the wall and quickly stepped back, but not before she kneed him hard in the nuts. Stars popped in his eyes, as he doubled over in excruciating agony.

*

Her heart was racing in her ears. Joy quickly turned on the light so she could see her attacker more clearly. There was Finn, crouched over in agony, finding it very difficult to breathe.

'Finn? What the hell are you doing here?'

He moved slowly to the bed, gingerly sitting down.

She was suddenly overwhelmed with a huge sense of relief and she sat down next to him. She felt tears pricking her eyes and she let her head fall into her hands. Her body was shaking with the fear and adrenaline that had just pumped through her veins.

She knew now that it had been a nightmare. The police visit earlier that day had reignited all those fears and bad dreams that she'd had years before. Finn must have heard her through the ridiculously thin wall and thought the worst.

He would hate her. There'd be swearing and shouting. Maybe if she let the tears come like they were clearly threatening to do, she could persuade him to save the shouting till tomorrow.

To her utmost surprise, when he finally spoke, his voice was gentle. 'Are you OK?'

She looked at him in shock and was thrown by the tenderness and concern in his eyes. She quickly wiped away the tears that spilt over her cheeks.

In a move that was so quick she didn't have a chance to stop it, he scooped her up and pulled her onto his lap, holding her tightly in his arms. She sat frozen, numb with shock at the sudden show of affection. He started stroking her back and arms in small soothing motions, presumably to try to calm her down. This did nothing of the sort. His hands were warm and strong and at his touch, her breath caught in her throat. Where her heart had just been slowing down after the attack, it was now roaring in her ears for an entirely different reason. It took every ounce of restraint not to look up and kiss him.

'Please don't do that,' she said, deliberately staring at a small bruise on her knee and not at him.

He stopped stroking but didn't let her go. She looked at him. God, his mouth was so close to hers and she couldn't even move back as he was holding her so tight.

'Do you have any idea what it makes me feel with your arms around me like this?'

He quickly let her go. 'Scared? Jesus Joy, I'm not going to hurt you.'

'I'm not scared of you, Finn. But you're not doing anything to stop my heart from racing. In fact, it's pounding even harder now than it was a few minutes ago when I thought you were trying to attack me.'

His face flickered with confusion for a moment, then he blushed. He deliberately changed the subject and moved on from the fact that he had just unknowingly been pressing all of her buttons.

'I think you owe me an explanation.'

'I don't owe you anything.'

'You just kneed me in the bollocks after I rushed in here to save you; you damn well owe me something.'

Anger ripped through her. 'It was just a nightmare. No big deal.'

'Since the nightmare coincided with the police visiting you earlier, the police visit that made you cry, and since you're still shaking now, I'd say there's a hell of a lot more to it than that. Besides, talking it through might help.'

'What are you, my therapist? You've been mean, you've repeatedly told me you don't like me and now you want to be my best friend all of a sudden? I don't think so. I'm grateful that you would come to my rescue like that, but I'm not about to spill my innermost thoughts and feelings to you.' She'd already done enough of that about her parents and the farm.

His arms slid round her again, but this time not protective but restraining. 'Then we're going to stay here until you do.'

She moved to stand up but his arms tightened around her. She fought against him, but he was a lot stronger and in the end she gave up. He would give up and go home before she gave in, she was damned sure of that. She folded her arms across her chest and leaned back into him.

*

111

Finn was good at waiting. When he had been filming *The Darkness* trilogy, there had sometimes been hours in between takes that he'd had to wait. He was quite prepared to sit there and wait all night if need be, but he was damned sure he was going to get some answers.

He felt her shift to get more comfortable. With his arms so tight around her he could feel her heart beating furiously. What the hell had scared her so much? It made him feel sick to think of her having nightmares and what had caused them.

He eyed Darcy lying on the floor. She hadn't moved during the fracas, some guard dog she would turn out to be. Unless, recognising Finn's scent, she knew she wouldn't have to defend her mistress against him. Long minutes stretched on but he could wait hours if necessary.

He forced his mind away from the warmth of her body next to his, the sweet smell of her and started to think about the garden at the farmhouse and what he would do to it instead. It had just been a patch of grass with a few shrubs when he had bought it, but he wanted it to be a proper garden, one that children could grow up in. He would grow cherry trees along the left-hand fence and a forsythia bush at the back that would spread big and out of control across the corner and... she was wearing purple nail varnish on her toes, tiny, sexy little toes... and... and a summer house, painted pale blue with great big comfy chairs and large windows to look out on the garden. She had fantastic legs, shown off spectacularly in the tiny shorts she was currently wearing. Benches, he could have benches on the patio or some other stylish garden furniture. Her legs and hands were covered in tiny little scars and bruises, similar to the sort he got from gardening, nothing severe, they seemed to be scratches from plants, though he hadn't seen her do any work in the garden since she arrived. Some kind of large barbeque area, maybe a brick one or one of those ones with the large chimneys. Her breathing on his neck was one of the most erotic things ever. The treehouse, maybe he'd paint it or should he leave it natural so it was more in keeping with the oak tree. Her breathing was very heavy now, almost as if…

He looked down at her and realised she had gone to sleep, or at least was pretending to be.

He watched her suspiciously, waiting for a flicker of consciousness, but there was nothing. She was limp in his arms, her mouth parted slightly in sleep. It was safe to say he wasn't going to get any answers out of her tonight. Not unless he woke her up. But he wasn't an idiot, as a man he knew it was potentially fatal to disturb a woman whilst she was sleeping. He'd already had one knee to the nuts that night – if he wanted children someday, to play in this fantasy garden with them, he'd better avoid being kneed in the nuts again.

With Joy still in his arms, he shuffled back a bit. She jolted a bit at the movement and he felt her heart leap as perhaps her dreams fell back into the one she was having before. He stroked her hair, hoping that in sleep he could offer her some comfort.

'Finn?' she mumbled, barely awake.

'Yeah I'm here, go back to sleep, we'll talk in the morning.'

He lay down with her. The little voice at the back of his head was screaming at him. What was he doing, was he really going to spend the night with her? She shifted slightly, stretching her legs out at his side.

'You don't have to stay.' She snaked her arms round his neck, nuzzling into the side of his throat.

He swallowed and pulled her tighter against him. 'I'm here,' he repeated.

'You're so kind.'

'This doesn't change anything, you know.'

'I know.'

'I still don't care.'

He felt her smiling against his neck. 'I know.'

'You're not my type.'

'That's fine.'

He kissed her on the head and hours after she had fallen back to sleep, he finally managed to snatch a few hours' himself.

*

Joy woke the next day and was a bit shocked to find she was wrapped tightly in Finn's arms, lying on his chest. That was certainly a turn up for the books. She lay there for a while, enjoying the cosiness, the feel of his chest rising and falling as he breathed. But the intimacy of him absently stroking her hair made her heart swell for him. He liked her, she was sure of it.

She propped herself up on her elbow to look at him; he looked back, his hand still in her hair. 'Well, this is new.'

'You scared the crap out of me last night.'

She sighed. 'You're not going to let this go, are you? What about the fact that we just spent the night together, we could talk about that instead.'

He scowled, though it was less threatening when he was holding her so protectively. 'It's been a while since I've spent the night with a woman. I'd have to say, this one wouldn't feature in my top five.'

'No? What about your top ten?'

She saw him smirk.

She stretched and felt him tense as she realised exactly where her leg was. She carefully removed it from in between his legs. 'How is everything down there? Nothing permanently damaged I hope.'

'It seems to be OK. Are you going to tell me what I risked never having children for?'

She narrowed her eyes. 'You know practically everything there is to know about me, I know next to nothing about you. How about you tell me something?'

He nodded. 'That's fair. You go first.'

'I'm serious Finn, you have to share something about you too.'

'I promise.'

She bit her lip, letting her gaze fall from Finn's face. 'I was attacked in London, a little over two years ago. I was walking back from a bar late one night to the flat I was staying in with Ed, it was a hundred yards away, so I didn't get a taxi. I was grabbed and forced into some nearby parkland. Craig Peters, I don't think I'll ever forget that name. My god, did I fight back, I punched and stamped and kicked and bit, but he fought back too and he was strong, broke one of my ribs just from one punch. Then he pulled a knife on me and I just froze. He forced me to the ground and I just lay there numb as he fumbled with his jeans. He stank of alcohol, I remember that much. He was clearly very drunk as he could barely undo his jeans. But as I lay there, frozen on the damp floor, I knew that there was no way I was going to let it happen.' She swallowed a wave of revulsion as she remembered what happened next. 'As he continued to fumble around inside his jeans, pinning me down with one hand, I reached for him. I offered to help him. He was drunk and horny and was keen to have any sort of help as he clearly couldn't do anything himself. I slid my hand into his jeans and found what he had been desperately searching for. I grabbed it tightly and twisted until I felt something snap inside. As he howled and screamed in blind agony, I scrabbled up and ran.'

'You fought back, that was brave.'

'Or stupid. He had a knife. But I didn't think about what could have happened, I just thought about what I didn't want to happen. I didn't want him to win. Though I suppose he has if I'm still having nightmares after all this time.'

'It's only natural that your mind will play it back, it's your subconscious trying to see if there was anything you could have done differently. It's how you deal with the nightmares that's important. Do you hide under the bed crying or do you get up fighting?'

She looked at him in surprise. She had fought back. That night in the park with Craig, when she heard Finn break into her house, there hadn't been a choice. To fight back had been the only answer. 'When you broke down my door it woke me up. I heard you thunder up the stairs and the only thing I thought of was there was no way I was going to let it happen again. Hiding didn't even enter my head.'

'You see, you're brave. You fought well.'

'Ha, you didn't fight back. If you'd fought back it would have been over very quickly. You're ten times bigger than I am.'

'And you still had me doubled over in agony.'

'Lucky shot.'

'Clever shot. You know a man's weakness. So I could take you very easily, I'm bigger, stronger, uglier—' she smiled '—and if it happens again, he might not be drunk, he might be stronger, you might not be lucky enough to take that clever shot, but you damned well give him something to think about. You bite, you kick, you scratch, you make sure he goes away with war wounds of his own.'

She nodded. It was intrinsic now, like when Chloe attacked her in the toilets, she reacted without thinking.

'And what happens if I fight back and he kills me?'

'Then you make sure you have some of his DNA under your fingernails so they can find the bastard. And then come back and haunt me for encouraging you to fight. Most importantly, you learn from your mistakes. Don't put yourself in harm's way again. There are many nut jobs out there, psychos that will stab people for no reason, terrorists that will blow up buildings, gunmen that will walk down the street killing anyone that moves. There's nothing you can do about that, if you're there when that kind of shit goes down, you've just got to put your head between your knees and pray or run as fast as you can in the opposite direction. But don't tempt fate. Don't walk home alone through deserted park land late at night. That was a pretty stupid thing to do.'

She rolled her eyes. She'd had the same lecture from Alex. 'Yes, Dad.'

He ignored her insolence. 'I presume they caught the bastard.'

'There were luckily police nearby and when I told them what had happened, he was still there, lying on the floor, crying when they went to investigate. It went to court but despite the bruises and broken bones he left me with, attempted rape is not the same as rape. He got thirty months but nowadays thirty months means twenty-four apparently. He will be released on Friday. That's what the police were here to tell me. I'm fine about it, really. I've barely given it a thought over the last year. I think it was just a shock to see the policewoman again, the one that dealt with my case, it all came flooding back.'

Finn brushed a stray hair from her face and she looked at him. 'He wants to see me.'

'What?'

'On Friday, the day he comes out, he wants to meet with me.'

'No fucking way.'

'That's what I thought at first. That I never wanted to set eyes on him again. But now I'm thinking about it. The police will be there with me and if I agree, we'll meet somewhere public like a coffee shop. It might be good for closure.'

'I'll come with you.'

Joy's heart filled with sudden love for him. 'No, I can't ask you to do that.'

'I'll come and then I can kick the bastard into a bloody pulp.'

'No, I don't want you to do that. If you come, you have to promise you won't say or do anything. I need to handle this myself. Having you fight my battles for me is not going to help me feel in control about this.'

Finn clearly fought an internal battle with himself but he eventually nodded. 'OK I promise, not a word.'

'I haven't decided whether to go or not, but if I do it'd be great to have you along for moral support.'

He frowned slightly as he clearly thought of something else. 'You were with Ed when this attack happened?'

'Yes, we were dating, he obviously wasn't physically with me at the time. He stayed in the bar, I was tired and wanted to go home.'

The frown deepened. 'He didn't walk you home?'

'Well, no. The bar was literally a few hundred yards from the flat. You could see the lounge window from the bar. He probably thought nothing would happen. *I* didn't even think about walking home alone, not such a short distance.'

'I would have walked you home,' he muttered. 'He dumped you after, didn't he? That's what you were talking about the other night, you said after what happened, he dumped you. You meant this.'

She nodded. 'Obviously he felt bad for not walking me home and he was very sympathetic and concerned for me, but after... he didn't want to touch me, like I was dirty in some way. To him it was almost like I'd been unfaithful to him, the fact that my hand had been around another man's dick... he couldn't get past that.'

'That's ridiculous.'

She shrugged. 'In hindsight, the man was an arse, I'm better off without him.'

There was a silence from Finn as he clearly struggled with the next question. 'Have you... had sex since?'

'Yes, but... I've only ever gone on top.'

'So you can stay in control.'

'Yes, it's hard to hand over control like that. I guess it will come with trust.'

There was another awkward silence and Joy wished she'd never had to tell him.

'Change of subject?' he asked.

She nodded with relief.

'OK...' He paused as he clearly searched around for a suitable topic. 'What are you doing going out dressed in black for the last few nights?'

'I'm a ninja.'

He laughed. 'What is it that ninjas do?'

'Covert stuff.'

'Like?'

'I could tell you but then I'd have to kill you.'

'You're not going to tell me, are you?'

'I can't,' she said honestly and she sensed that for now at least he was going to leave it. She fixed him with a look. 'Your turn now.'

'Very well, what do you want to know?'

'Easy one first, why did you hate being famous?'

'Oh, so you know who I am?'

'I have no idea. Finn Mackenzie, actor in some vampire thing says Casey. I was a bit young for it myself, though I was never into TV and films, they sort of passed me by, still do, mainly.'

'Well, I never wanted to be an actor. I was spotted, my abnormal size brought me to their attention and they asked me to audition. I thought it might be fun, a bit of money, and it was. I spent five years sword fighting, riding horses, going to exotic locations around the world. I loved it.

But nothing prepared me for the fame thing. When the first movie hit I was a star overnight. I was sixteen and the paparazzi were following me around, shoving cameras in my face. Girls are coming up to me in the street and throwing their arms round me, screaming and following me wherever I went. And as many people as there were who loved me and wanted to be a part of my life, so many more people hated me. I got so much bad press, because I apparently never smiled, because I smoked at the time and they said I wasn't a good role model for children. I had no idea at all about being a role model; I was still a child myself. Every day there'd be some story in the paper slagging me off. One paper followed me around the supermarket taking photos of everything that I put in my trolley, and featured it on a double page spread. I had condoms in the trolley, Mum was mortified.

Then when I was a bit older and I started dating women, they only wanted to be with me because I was Finn Mackenzie, because of my money, the glitzy parties they hoped I would take them to. And every single one I slept with sold their story to the papers. It was humiliating. So after I'd finished with *The Darkness* trilogy, I decided that was enough. The press still followed me around for a while, made out I was a has been, that no one wanted to work with me, when the reality was I was getting offers from all over the place. I didn't want it anymore and eventually the interest died down and I was left in peace.'

'OK, next question.' He scowled but she ploughed on regardless. 'Why do you hate Zach so much?'

'That one's easy, he was my best friend and he slept with my wife.'

'Pippa?' She was shocked at this. That was so not the answer she had been expecting.

'I've only had one wife, so yes.'

'I'm so sorry.' The betrayal of that must have hurt so much, not only had his wife cheated on him but with his best friend of all people. 'What happened?'

He arched an eyebrow.

'I mean, was it a one night stand or an affair?'

'Does it matter?'

'No, it doesn't. But I guess the betrayal would be worse if it had been going on for months.'

'I suppose. I think it was only once. Things happened very quickly between me and Pippa. It was one of those stupid, fall head over heels type of loves. We were married just six months after we met and almost four months to the day that we got married, I caught them together.'

'What was she like?'

'She was highly strung, attention seeking. She was a singer.

She was good too. But she wanted the world to sit up and pay attention. She struggled for years to make a name for herself and never made it, she used to get so angry over it. She got bored so easily, she always wanted to be doing something, she could never just sit. She took shooting lessons, learned how to rock climb and abseil, learned circus skills, acrobatics, trapeze. She did art classes, yoga, archery. But she'd get bored of them quickly and move onto some other hobby. Sex was the same, she was always rushing me, and as soon as she took what she needed, she was off doing something else. And we never did it in bed either. It had to be on a table, on the floor, in the shower, outside.

I was so in love, I would have done anything for her. I spent almost every day with her coming up with new and exciting ways to keep her interested. I took her to Paris, to Rome, we'd end up in Brighton or Edinburgh on the spur of the moment. We'd go to theme parks, to wine tasting nights, to the theatre – it was a new thing every day. But deep down I knew I was doing it all so she wouldn't grow bored of me, and I could see she was. She told me I was boring too. If I was reading or doing the garden, she would moan at me until I did something she wanted to do. I thought by marrying her it would settle her down, but it didn't. She laughed at the prospect of having children, said she was too busy having fun. And I wanted kids, I really wanted them.'

He sighed heavily, his eyes filled with agony. 'She got pregnant and for three days I was the happiest man alive. I was going to be a dad. And then she came home one day and told me she'd had an abortion. My child – and she killed it like it was nothing more than an annoying wasp. She didn't tell me until she'd had it done either. Didn't even think to talk about it with me first.'

'Oh, Finn.' Her heart bled for him.

He fingered her hair absently. 'I knew then that we didn't have a future together, but I was in shock. It wasn't even two weeks later that I caught her with Zach. Zach interested her, I knew that. From the very first moment she laid eyes on him, she was keen. To his credit, he declined her advances for months. Me, Zach and Casey had been best friends since before I can even remember, we grew up together. Me and Zach moved to this village at the same time, we thought it would be brilliant, being neighbours. I never thought he would betray me. I could see her flirting with him, and he would just politely decline. Though as time passed, I could see he was interested too.

On her birthday, we'd planned a big party barbeque thing round my house, although after the abortion I was in no mood to celebrate, but as it had already been planned we went ahead with it anyway. Zach got really drunk and about halfway through the night he and Pippa disappeared. I went into his house and there they were on his sofa.'

'I'm sorry,' she said again. There really were no other words she could say. She'd lost all respect for Zach in that moment. Yes, he'd been drunk but still there should have been some loyalty there. You didn't just throw away thirty years of friendship for a quick drunken grope on the sofa with your best friend's wife. Especially when it seemed Zach wasn't short of offers from other women.

'Of course I kicked her out and I thought they might get together. I might have been OK with that, eventually, if it had been real love and not just a drunken shag, but Zach didn't want to know her.'

'Maybe Zach felt guilty for what he had done.'

He shrugged. 'Maybe he did. It makes no difference. I want nothing more to do with him now.'

'And Pippa?'

'She left Bramble Hill and I haven't seen her since. I didn't realise till after she'd gone what a relief it was that we were no longer together. She made me so tense. I spent ten months trying to be someone that I wasn't. Her betrayal hurt a lot but in the end I suppose it was for the best.'

'What did you see in her?'

'Her vulnerability. A woman's tears are the most powerful tool at her disposal. I wanted to protect her. Love at first sight, I was trapped and was unwilling or unable to escape.'

'So…' Joy bit her lip, but didn't take her eyes off Finn's. 'Are you learning from your mistakes too? You've already fallen for one redhead so you don't want to fall for another?'

He gaped like a fish for a moment and she knew she'd hit the nail on the head. She ploughed on. 'You like me, but you're trying really hard not to, trying to hate me even, because you're scared of falling in love and of being hurt again? The wall you've built around your heart since Pippa cheated on you, you're scared I'm going to break it down. That's why you keep pushing me away, being horrible to me, because you don't want to let me in.'

'I don't like…' he started but stopped. He could clearly see it was useless to deny he liked her, not when he'd spent the night holding her in his arms, not when he had been absently stroking her back for the last ten minutes. 'Fine, I like you, but I don't *like* you. Maybe I've been a bit mean…'

'A bit?'

'OK, a lot mean, but I've had so many women in the last eighteen months think, "Oh poor Finn, his wife's cheated on him, I'll look after him, I'll fix him". I don't need fixing Joy, I just want to be left alone. It was easier to push you away by being mean than have you try to fix me. But I'm just not interested in a relationship right now.'

'So you have no feelings for me at all?'

His jaw clenched as he clearly fought the automatic denial that was forming on his lips.

'You just spent the night in bed with me. If there were no feelings there at all, wouldn't you have just gone back to your own bed when I fell asleep?'

'I stayed with you as a friend, nothing more.'

'Are you always this intimate with your friends?' Casey would be delighted.

'You were upset, I was trying to comfort you.'

'Which I'm very grateful for.' Too grateful, as she had fallen a little bit in love with him because of it.

Seemingly reading her mind, he took her chin in his large hand. 'Don't fall for me, Joy. You'll get hurt and I really don't want to hurt you.'

'But you can't just shut the chance of love out of your life forever. You deserve to be happy again.'

'I'm happy alone.'

She tried another tack. 'So you're never getting married again?'

He shook his head.

'No one to have children with, no one to grow old and grey with? You've built this beautiful home to raise a family in, you can't let it go to waste.'

She saw him hesitate at this and the pain in his eyes he must still feel about the abortion. She decided she wasn't going to push it anymore.

'So… how about we're friends instead?' she said.

He offered her his hand to shake, which seemed a bit too polite for the fact that she was lying on his bare chest, but she took it anyway and shook it. 'Friends.'

She rested her head on his chest for a moment, before she got up, and his hand almost instinctively fingered one of her curls. It was such an affectionate gesture.

If this was friendship, then she could certainly get used to it.

*

Finn headed out into his garden and passed a bottle of beer to Casey. He had left Joy on good terms earlier and he was relieved that he was no longer going to have to push her away. But her comments had bothered him, she bothered him. He had taken Billy for a very long walk to think about her and when he came back Casey had been sitting on his doorstep. But even though he'd had hours to think through his emotions, his thoughts, and even though Casey was talking to him, he couldn't clear his head of her.

He had set the boundaries quite clearly. Friends, simple as that. He knew she liked him, but there wasn't going to be anything between them, he would see to that.

But that comment about never having children, not growing old with the person you love, that had settled into his brain and refused to go away. He still wanted that, he had wanted that so much with Pippa. That's what Blueberry Farm had been about, creating a home for his wife and kids. Should he really throw away his chance of happiness just because of what happened between him and Pippa? She had hurt him spectacularly and he never wanted to live through that kind of hurt again. Though was it time to put the hurt behind him and move on? Could Joy really be the person he moved on with?

'Hey, are you listening to me?' Casey waved a hand in front of Finn's face.

'Mm? Sorry mate, what were you saying?'

'There's been another one.'

Finn focused on Casey, his best friend, and pushed away thoughts of Joy altogether. Well temporarily at least. 'Another what?'

'Diamond robbery, last night. Strawberry Green this time. They took a load of diamond rings and a diamond brooch shaped like an owl. It seems the thief is working their way through the local area.'

Finn frowned. Joy was out again the night before, dressed in black. He really hoped she wasn't the diamond thief. She didn't seem to have a job and as she didn't appear to have come from wealth, having to sell her home when she was eighteen, she had to be getting her money from somewhere.

Hoping Casey hadn't noticed his eyes sliding to Joy's house when he spoke of the diamond thief, he changed the subject slightly. 'I thought you were supposed to be on holiday, you're not involved in this case, are you?'

Casey frowned. 'It's my case. It's the same thief that hit five houses in my patch in spring. We're trying to play down that we have a serial thief on our hands, the press don't know, but he wants us to know that's it the same man. He always leaves behind a plasticine animal.'

'Plasticine? What is he, a child?'

'A very talented child, the animals are so intricate, obviously a lot of work has gone into them. It could be a child, though. The size of some of the openings he's got through are tiny.' Casey swigged his beer thoughtfully. 'Could be a woman.'

Finn cleared his throat uncomfortably, just as Joy walked out into her garden.

'Hey.' Casey waved at her. 'Were you out by any chance last night?'

She stopped and Finn saw her eyes slide momentarily to him. She knew he had seen her go out dressed in black.

'Yes, for a drive. I... couldn't sleep so drove around for a bit, getting to know the local area.'

'And did you perhaps go near say... The Orchards or... Strawberry Green?'

She paled, she definitely paled. Though Casey seemed to think the whole thing was hilarious.

'I don't really know where I drove, Ashton Woods, your neck of the woods, I was definitely there, Chalk Rise. I don't think I was near The Orchards.'

She seemingly had deliberately not mentioned Strawberry Green, though the small village of The Orchards backed onto it. She stroked Darcy as she ambled past her. 'Casey, pop by later when you've got a moment. I need a word.'

Casey nodded and Joy disappeared into her shed, closing the door firmly behind her. Finn eyed Casey, who was watching Joy suspiciously, and fought back the sudden urge to give her an alibi.

When Joy had finished cleaning and sharpening her chainsaws later, and replacing a new disc on her angle grinder, she emerged from the shed and was relieved to see Casey and Finn were gone. Just because Casey had seen her with the chainsaws, he had now decided that she must be The Dark Shadow. There was no more proof than that, but still he knew and she had always been a bad liar. It was the local jobs as well, she should never have taken them. She had one more to do in Ashton Woods but after that she wouldn't work so close to home again.

Zach was in his garden, smoking again, but after what she had heard about him that morning she wasn't in the mood to talk to him. He smiled and waved at her as she walked past, but she ignored him.

'Hey, wait up, what's wrong?' Zach came through the connecting gate, his eyes filled with concern. 'You OK?'

'You're not the person I thought you were.'

'Wait, wait.' He quickly followed her into her kitchen. 'What has Casey been telling you now?'

She whirled to face him. 'It wasn't Casey, it was Finn, he told me about you sleeping with Pippa.'

His face fell and a real sadness filled his eyes. 'Oh. Worst thing I've ever done. I can never go back and change that; I can never undo the hurt that I inflicted on Finn. He was my best friend...'

'And you betrayed him.'

'Do I not even get a chance for my side of the story, or is that it, you've already made up your mind about me?' She could see he was hurt but he didn't deserve the chance to explain.

'What are you going to say, that it was an accident, that you tripped over and your dick accidentally fell into her?' She turned away from him.

'No, listen.' He caught her arm and pulled her back. 'She had been after me for months, touching me, trying to kiss me, but I didn't want anything to do with her. She was Finn's and he was so in love with her. She was beautiful though, any idiot could tell that. I was attracted to her, I can't deny it, but I would never have done anything with her.

At her party I got so drunk, Pippa had mixed some weird punch and kept plying me with it all night. I have never been so drunk in my entire life. I went back to my house and passed out on the sofa. God I had weird dreams, I still remember them, so vivid – Angelina Jolie was in them, always had a bit of a thing for her. So I'm with her, kissing her, and ahem… other things… and the next thing she changes and it's Pippa I'm making love to, Pippa who is sitting on top of me, stark naked, Pippa whose breasts I'm…'

'OK, OK, I get the picture.'

'Well, suddenly Finn's there and there was a lot of shouting and well… you know the rest. Finn has barely spoken to me since. I swear Joy, I would never have intentionally slept with Pippa, I could never do that to Finn.'

She watched him, his shoulders slumped, his hands thrust in his pockets, his face crumpled and she couldn't help but feel a bit sorry for him.

There was a knock on the back door and Casey was standing there, looking between her and Zach with narrowed eyes.

'Clear off little bro, me and Joy have some serious talking to do.'

Zach took a step back away from her, watching her carefully. 'We're OK, aren't we?'

'I… don't know.'

'Just think about it before you cast the first stone,' he said as he walked out looking very dejected.

As soon as he was gone she turned to Casey, who was scowling at her.

'Him and Pippa, do you believe his side of the story?'

'Yeah, I sort of do. Zach is many things, most of them are not good but I doubt he would ever have deliberately slept with Pippa behind Finn's back. Alcohol can make you do some stupid things.'

She sighed, not sure what to think.

'What's the deal between you two anyway? Finn says you're going to the wedding with him.'

'As friends.' She turned to put the kettle on. Although why had she agreed to that when she'd much rather go with her new best friend she had made the night before?

'Just make sure it stays that way. He'll hurt you, Joy – and I'd hate to see that happen.'

She didn't say anything, just busied herself with the mugs. She had to prepare herself for what she wanted to say next.

'Have you seen the new sign on the road into the village,' he said behind her. 'You know at the top of the hill, where there's a sign saying, "Home of Finn Mackenzie", there's a new one now, it says, "Home of The Dark Shadow."'

She dropped the mug she was holding and it smashed on the floor.

Chapter Nine

She quickly bent to pick up the pieces, deliberately not looking at him.

There was silence from Casey for a moment, then he spoke. 'Shit, Joy – you are, aren't you? I was joking the other day, I was just teasing you because of the chainsaw, I didn't think you actually were. Oh my god.'

'Of course I'm not, what a silly thing to suggest.' She grabbed the dustpan and brush and started to sweep up the fragments. 'What on earth makes the villagers think that he lives here?'

He paused, obviously watching her carefully. 'One of the villagers, Mr Brackley I gather from the gossip, was in The Orchards last night visiting his sister when he saw a black 4x4 emerge from the woods. Well, The Orchards is directly above Bramble Hill, you can see your village from the road. He watched the headlights of the car follow the road down towards Bramble Hill and past The Pride and they went out shortly after that. It was impossible to tell which house it stopped outside, but as there's only one road into Bramble Hill it stands to reason that the driver of the vehicle lives or at least was staying in Bramble Hill, otherwise they'd have no reason to drive down here quite so late at night.'

'That's silly, it could just have been a farmer, or someone looking for firewood.' She concentrated on sweeping up all the fragments so she wouldn't have to look at him.

'In August? And the news is filled with another Dark Shadow strike in The Orchards this morning; a Ringwraith apparently. The villagers are very excited. They all think it's Mark Dempsey who moved into the village about three months ago, he owns a dark blue BMW 4x4, which might have looked black in the night. Though to be honest, as this is quite an affluent area, most of the villagers own dark 4x4s, it could have been anyone.'

'And now they've put up a sign?' She looked up at him and he nodded. Crap. Wait till the press got hold of that, they'd be swarming all over the place trying to find out exactly who it was. Ashton Woods would have to wait a few days, maybe even weeks until the furore calmed down.

She had worked so hard for this; she couldn't let it all go now. She realised her hands were shaking as Casey knelt down by her side.

His eyes were serious, concerned. 'Joy, there's CCTV footage of the grounds of Menton Hall, from the night of the robbery. There's a black 4x4 in the background of one of the shots, driving through the woods. It's very far away. It's the only sign of anything suspicious from that night. The only clue we have. We were going to have it analysed, get specialists to zoom in to see if we can make out the driver. Is this something I need to get hold of and accidentally lose or delete?'

She swallowed. Asking him to do that would be admitting she was The Dark Shadow. How much could she trust Casey? There were probably only two people that knew who she was – Jake Aldbury and Alex. To get hold of this footage she had to trust Casey more than she'd trusted anyone in her life.

But then even if she did ask him, that was a dreadful imposition on him. He could get in serious trouble for tampering with evidence like that, even if her presence in the video had nothing to do with the diamond robbery. He could lose his job over it, she couldn't ask him to do that. She would just have to hope the specialists couldn't identify her through the footage. But what if they could? She would be called in for questioning, they might think she had something to do with the diamond robbery, she would have to tell them who she was and what she was doing. She could easily prove who she was but there was no way a whole team of police would keep her identity a secret.

She finally found her voice. 'I erm... I know someone who might be able to help you with that evidence. Alex actually, he works in the film industry, he has access to that sort of equipment that allows you to enhance footage. If you get me the footage, I could pass it to him and he could look at it for you.'

She knew she had just handed herself to Casey on a plate. It was down to him now whether he would serve her up to the police and the waiting press.

He stood up. 'We normally have our own people for such things, but... we have limited budgets, we don't have access to the really cool stuff that MI6 have, and I expect Warner Brothers and their associates have an even bigger budget than they do. It would be good to pass on this evidence to someone skilled enough to handle it. I imagine I can trust Alex to pass on any details that he finds?'

'Absolutely.'

He nodded and fished his phone out of his pocket, then walked into the lounge. 'Hello it's DI Fallowfield. You know the CCTV footage of the Plasticine Diamond case, from Menton Hall. I need you...' His voice faded as he moved to the front of the house and Joy realised her heart was thundering against her chest. She quickly made the tea, having to do something with her hands. Alex to the rescue once again.

He had done so much for her, not only putting his life on hold to raise her, but financially supporting her for the first few months when she had returned to the UK and was trying to make a name for herself as a chainsaw artist. Where other parents might have encouraged their child to get a job somewhere, anywhere just to get some money, Alex had been fierce that she had a rare talent and that her career would take off just as long as she kept working at it. Eventually she'd gotten a few commissions, in her life previous to The Dark Shadow, and it was enough that she could move out of Alex's home and rent a place with bad plumbing and several dubious damp patches. It was here that she had lived on a diet of porridge and baked beans on toast, and where she was determined that after everything Alex had done for her, she would not be reliant on him again. He had his own life and it was time enough that he started to live it.

She couldn't go back to wondering where her next meal was coming from, or rely on Alex to put her up again.

But here she was, relying on him to get her out of this bind, pulling him into the lies and the deceit, now she'd be asking him to lie to the police for her.

Casey came back in and he smiled at her when he saw her worried face.

'I've just spoken to Alex, he'll be more than happy to have a look at the footage for me.'

She frowned slightly, confused. 'You spoke to Alex?'

'Yes, you gave me his number, remember, so we could chat about being gay and my inappropriate crush on my best friend.'

'Of course, but I didn't know you had spoken.'

'We actually met for coffee yesterday; he really is a lovely bloke.'

She beamed. 'He is… did you…'

He must have seen her innuendo. 'No, no, no. Definitely not my type. I mean funny, kind, fiercely loyal to you, but I'm not remotely attracted to him. He's way too thin for my liking. In comparison to Finn, Alex is like a blade of grass. Alex pretty much said the same about me, that if this was your attempt at setting the two of us up, then it hadn't worked, he likes them big too – men that is.'

133

She smirked. 'I didn't think the two of you would leap into bed with each other just because you're both single and gay, I was just hoping that you could become friends.'

'Well, we've certainly done that. We're definitely going to meet up again, probably after the wedding or the honeymoon. Anyway...' he fixed her with a serious look. 'He says he'll take care of the CCTV for you, I mean, for me.'

'Thank you.'

'And perhaps, if you know this Dark Shadow man, you'll tell him to keep his head down for a while.'

She nodded.

'And that's the last time I'll speak of it, I promise.'

She knew it would be too. She knew she could trust him completely. She stepped forward and hugged him. He jolted in surprise as she rested her head on his chest and then he hugged her back, holding her tight in his arms. She felt a tightening in her throat as she held him and she smiled as she pulled away.

'Damn it Casey, why do you have to be gay?'

He laughed as he kissed her fondly on the head, picked up his mug of tea and walked into the lounge. 'What did you want to talk to me about anyway?'

She cast her mind back to her previous problems, grabbed her mug and followed him.

'Finn.'

'Oh yes?' He threw himself down next to Darcy who was sprawled out upside down on the sofa, with her tongue hanging out of her face. He rubbed her belly absently which earned him a half-hearted wag of the tail. Joy sat down on the big comfy chair opposite him.

'It's just that... there's a code, between friends.' How could she put this? 'When me and my friends would go out, if one of us called dibs on a guy the rest of us would stay well clear. Normally we all went for very different types anyway but occasionally we would overlap. I remember once I fancied this guy Steve for months, though he was blatantly not interested in me. Anyway as the months went on, Libby started to notice him too and when he asked her out, she came to ask me if it was OK.'

'And was it?' Casey asked with a smirk, clearly knowing where this conversation was going.

'Yes,' she said, honestly.

Casey took a big breath. 'You're asking me if it's OK if you go after Finn?'

'Yes. I won't do anything with him if you're not happy with it. You've been in love with the man for fifteen years, it would be a bit mean of me to…' She sighed. 'I think I'm falling for him.'

He took a big swig of his tea and swallowed it thoughtfully. 'Does he feel the same way?'

'I don't know. He likes me, I know that much. I think it could be something more. He's still hurting over Pippa and I don't think he's ready for a relationship yet.'

He shifted uncomfortably. 'I'm going to tell him.'

'What? That I'm falling for him, that's hardly fair.'

'No, that I love him.'

She had no words, though she was aware that her mouth was flapping open like a fish.

'I have to know Joy. I know deep down that he doesn't see me that way, that he's not gay, but I have to know for sure. I have to hear it from him. Maybe then I can finally move on.'

'You're going to tell him you're gay, that you love him and have been in love with him for fifteen years?'

Casey nodded. 'I know it's stupid, but I have to.'

'But what if… what if he's homophobic?'

'Finn? No way, he may be a moody sod, but he's not that.'

Her heart ached for him. He was not going to get out of this what he wanted and he knew that. But maybe this would be the first stage in him coming out, in finally being brave enough to accept who he was.

'When are you going to do it?'

'Friday. I'm having a sort of mini stag do, just me and him. I don't want a big fuss and if Zach had his way there'd be strippers and lap dancers. Me and Finn are just going to have a few drinks, maybe play on the Wii. I'm going to tell him then.'

She moved to sit next to him, taking his hand, but she couldn't find any words to offer hope when she knew it was hopeless. She could only hope that Finn was kind about it.

'After that Joy, after I've told him and been spectacularly rejected, you can have him. I want him to be happy and I know he won't find that with me so if he can find it with you then I'll be happy with that. Just give me till then.'

She nodded, almost hoping that Finn would turn out to be gay, and Casey at least would get his 'happy ever after'.

*

Joy was busy making a maquette, a mini model from plasticine as she planned out her next carving. Many ideas and plans were formed in her head, but it wasn't until she made a model of it could she see the limbs and detail in scale. She liked to make a scale model of the tree first based on photos from her recces. Then she experimented with what she could achieve from the canvas she had been given. Sometimes branches would become part of the design, sometimes she would chop them all off and work with a plain round canvas. She often wished that trees would grow square instead of round, it would make her job an awful lot easier.

The backdoor was open and the late afternoon sun was spilling across the kitchen floor. She heard Darcy bark and looked out to see what she was doing. Her heart dropped when she realised Darcy wasn't in the garden. She ran out and saw her with a girl of about seven years old in Finn's back garden. Her hair was a white blonde curtain over her face and she was busy painting Darcy's claws with pink sparkly nail varnish. Joy smiled and let herself through the connecting gate which Casey must have left open earlier.

'You know, you should probably practise your skills on someone who isn't likely to lick it off.'

The girl jumped and Joy saw the smile that had been on her face quickly fall off.

'Is this your dog?'

For someone so young, Joy was surprised to see such an angry expression on her face.

'Yes, her name is Darcy.'

'Do you have Billy then as Uncle Finn has your dog?'

'No, Billy's not next door, I think Darcy just wandered through the open gate.'

The girl looked back at Darcy. 'She's a Newfoundland, isn't she? My granddad had one, Boris he was called.'

'Your granddad or the dog?'

The girl smiled again. 'The dog, Granddad was Frank.'

Joy noted the 'was' and the sudden sadness that had entered the girl's eyes.

'I'm Joy by the way.'

The girl shook her hand so hard that Joy's whole arm was almost yanked out the socket.

'I'm Lily.'

'So, Lily, why don't you practise your makeover skills on me instead, and then you can tell me all about your granddad and Boris.'

'I don't like to talk about it.'

'OK, I'd like purple nail varnish please.' Joy sat down and laid her hands on the table, knowing there'd be more to come.

Lily dived into her bag and pulled out a bottle of bright purple nail varnish. 'Well, that's what Mummy says when people talk about him, she tells them "I don't like to talk about it" and then they stop.'

Joy nodded as Lily stuck her tongue out and carefully applied the nail varnish to her thumb nail. 'And would you like to talk about it?'

'I miss him.'

'I bet you do.'

'He died two weeks ago and the funeral is today. I'm not allowed to go.'

Children and death were such tricky subjects. There was a fine line between trying to shield your child from death and allowing them to grieve properly. When her parents had died, no one had spoken to her about it, apart from Alex. Everyone thought she was too young, or that mentioning it would upset her even more. Talking about it helped but no one was prepared to take that risk.

'Tell me about Frank, what was he like?'

*

Finn put the phone down and went out towards the garden. Lily loved pizza; maybe that would cheer her up. She'd been so sad for the last two weeks and nothing seemed to make her smile for very long, if at all. He didn't agree with his sister's decision to not let Lily come to the funeral, but it meant he got to spend time with Lily and that was always a good thing in his book.

He stepped outside and froze.

Joy was holding Lily on her lap, her arms around her to stop Lily toppling off as Joy struggled against her. Joy's lips had already been painted red, she had pink glittery eye shadow, deep red blusher in little cute round circles on her cheeks and Lily was desperately attempting to put ribbons in Joy's hair. Joy was moving her head out of Lily's reach, but Lily had her pinned down, giggling uncontrollably, she quickly attached the ribbon before Joy could move away. Then she added a pair of huge plastic orange clip-on earrings and the outfit was complete. Joy slumped in defeat.

'Now would you like purple nail varnish or red on your toes?' Lily asked, rummaging in her makeup bag.

'Red, I suppose,' Joy grumbled, looking at the ribbon in her hair. 'It will go with my ribbon.'

Finn snorted with amusement and Joy turned to look at him. Suddenly, he felt a huge lump in his throat. Every time he thought he had successfully pushed her away, she did something to pull herself closer. She looked adorable.

'I caught this reprobate putting nail varnish on Darcy and the next thing I know I'm being made over like some kind of Barbie princess.'

'What's a rebro-bate?' Lily had found some glitter gel and was applying it to Joy's cheeks.

'It means troublemaker,' Finn said. He finally tore his eyes from Joy and glanced around the garden. The back gate leading to the road was open and his heart leapt.

'Where's Billy?'

Joy and Lily looked blank and he quickly ducked back inside and called him. Billy didn't appear. He raced upstairs. Billy normally came when he was called, but it wasn't completely unheard of for him to be in a very deep sleep. There was no sign of him upstairs either. He ran back downstairs and back out into the garden. He couldn't have gone far.

'Lily get your shoes on, we need to look for Billy.'

Joy stood up, her eyes underneath all the makeup were alert and concerned. 'He's missing?'

Finn gestured helplessly to the open gate as Lily ran past him into the house.

'Look,' said Joy, 'she can stay with me, you'll probably cover more ground without her.'

He shook his head. He couldn't leave his niece with a complete stranger. Besides, he was supposed to be cheering her up.

'I can't, she's had a rough few weeks, she's barely spoken—'

'I know, her granddad died, she told me all about it. And him,

139

he sounds like quite the character. I'm presuming as you've not said anything that he wasn't your dad?'

'My brother in-law's. She told you? She hasn't wanted to talk about it at all.' His sister had been quite adamant not to mention it in front of Lily.

'It turns out she did.'

Finn felt angry at this. Lily had known Joy for all of five seconds.

Joy must have seen his face. 'Sorry, I didn't mean to tread on any toes. Maybe she felt more comfortable because she didn't know me. Regardless, you can shout at me when you get back, you need to look for Billy. Give me your number and I'll call you if he comes home. They normally do once they're hungry.'

Joy was right, he would be quicker looking for Billy without Lily.

Lily came running out with her pink spotted wellies on. 'I'm ready, do you think Billy's OK?'

He knelt down. 'Would you rather stay here with Joy? The pizza has been ordered, and I'll be back really soon.'

Lily wavered. 'What kind of pizza did you get?'

'Your favourite, ham and pineapple, and there's chocolate ice cream in the fridge.'

'I'll stay and we'll save you some pizza.'

He smiled as he stood back up. He scribbled his number in lipstick on a piece of paper and gave it to Joy. 'Thanks, there's money on the table for the pizza.'

He quickly kissed her on the cheek and ran out the gate, wondering why he'd felt the need to kiss her. Maybe Joy wouldn't notice.

He heard Lily giggle as the gate closed behind him. 'Uncle Finn just kissed you.'

He winced.

'Yes, he did.'

'Does he love you?'

140

'We're just friends.'

'He doesn't kiss Casey like that.'

Finn nearly stopped to hear what Joy would reply to that, but he imagined it would be quite a lengthy reply.

Chapter Ten

Finn stomped back towards his house almost two hours later with Billy at his side. He was in a foul mood. Some people were so rude and Mrs Browne was by far the rudest, stupidest person he'd ever had the misfortune to come across. Why would she walk all the way home with Billy following and not turn around and bring him back? How could she not ring to say Billy had followed her and her bitch home? Billy had his collar on, with Finn's number on the tag. How hard would it have been to phone him? Why would she leave Billy sitting outside her house for two hours and not do anything about it? It was only sheer luck that Finn had been passing and saw Billy scratching at the back gate. Obviously the bitch had been in heat. Mrs Browne had come out and laughed about how Billy had followed her little Princess home. Finn, who had been frantic with worry, had wanted to throttle her.

The pizza would be cold, he was starving, he had a headache, he'd barely slept whilst he held Joy in his arms the night before and was now really tired and the lovely night he'd had planned with his niece had been ruined.

He walked back through the gate and heard giggling coming

from Joy's. He went into her garden and the temper that he had carefully reined in when speaking to Mrs Browne snapped when he saw Lily, covered head to toe in a thick layer of mud. She looked like she had been at a festival – her hair, her face, every inch of her clothes was splattered in it. Joy, also covered in mud, was chasing her up the garden, obviously pretending she was a monster. Lily was shrieking, laughing loudly, the biggest smile splitting her face.

Lily saw Finn and launched herself towards him.

'Lily, no...' Joy started but Lily had already splatted against his trousers.

He wouldn't explode at Lily, this wasn't her fault.

'Uncle Finn, did you find Billy, oh there he is. We've had the best time ever, we had a water fight and then Joy fell over in the mud and I slipped on top of her and then we were laughing and doing mud angels and the mud was so cold and Joy was shrieking. Oh, and Joy said that we could do a proper goodbye thing for Granddad with balloons and we can send notes to heaven for Granddad to read, we can do that can't we?'

He kept his voice calm when he spoke. 'Lily, it's nearly time for bed, get undressed and I'll be up to give you a bath in a minute.'

'But you promised we would watch *Shrek*.'

'We will, in bed, but only once you've had a bath.'

'Yay! Can we have popcorn?'

'Yes.'

'Can Joy join us?'

'No.'

Lily obviously sensed the anger coming off him because she backed off. She waved at Joy uncertainly and walked into the house.

Joy approached. 'Sorry about the mud, I was just about to give her a bath myself and... oh, you're really angry.'

His head was pounding and he could feel his heart racing.

143

'You're supposed to be the responsible adult, I do not expect to come back and find her looking like that. I trusted you to look after her.'

'I did, she had a great time. It's just mud, it will wash off.'

'And what's this stupid goodbye thing you've planted in her head. It's down to her parents to help her with her grief, you shouldn't interfere. You think because your parents are dead it makes you some kind of expert. Well, butt out, it's got nothing to do with you.'

Instantly he regretted saying that. He wanted to take it all back. It was just mud, and Joy had made Lily laugh like she hadn't laughed in ages. He wasn't even angry at Joy, he should have shouted at Mrs Browne rather than coming home and taking it out on Joy. And he'd hurt her with that comment about her parents, he could tell that.

For once, Joy didn't have some smart comeback. After staring at him in shock she just turned away and walked back into her house.

Damn it. He really was scum.

*

Joy was waiting for a call from Alex. She knew he was out rigging explosives and some big car stunt for the latest James Bond film, but he had promised to call her as soon as he got in.

She had been in Bramble Hill nearly a week now, and though she had promised herself that she would make a go of it, the long-term prospects weren't good. There had been more poo posted through her letterbox that morning. She had popped down to the local shop earlier and had been pelted with eggs before she so much as put a carton of milk in the basket, and the volatile 'friendship' she had with Finn wasn't really a selling point.

But where to go next? What was it exactly that she was looking for? How would she find it if she didn't know what 'it' was?

Maybe she could move to Casey's village. She had a good friend there and that at least was a start. Though if he or Arielle decided to make a go of this marriage, she guessed she wouldn't really be seeing him a lot.

And what of Finn? With Casey still in her life, seeing Finn would be quite likely too, and after tonight's little episode she didn't think she could cope with that anymore.

Idly, she sat on the bed, picked up her notepad and started sketching ideas for her next strike. A stag soon stood proud on the page, its liquid eyes staring out from the stark white background.

The phone rang and as she added the detail of his fur, she flicked it onto loud speaker.

'Hello.'

'Hi, you OK?' asked Alex.

She stopped drawing for a moment. 'Yeah, a bit worried, but I'm OK.'

'Does Casey know? The conversation I had with him earlier about the CCTV was very vague, but reading between the lines, he knows.'

'Yeah he does. I've not confirmed it but he knows. Al, I don't want you to lie for me. Especially not to Casey, he's your friend and CID, you could get into trouble. Just… if I'm on the CCTV, just give me some warning before you tell him so I can prepare myself.'

'Of course I'll lie for you; I'll do anything in my power to protect you. Casey's my friend but you come first.'

She smiled with love for him. 'No, just tell me if you find anything and I'll tell Casey. Then he can choose what he wants to do with it.'

There was a cough from the other side of the wall and she went cold, realising that Finn had heard every word they had been saying. Had she mentioned The Dark Shadow? No, she hadn't, but still she had to be careful in case Finn put two and two together.

She quickly snatched up the phone and took it off loud speaker. 'Hang on Al, let me take this call downstairs.'

She really didn't need to give Finn any more ammunition.

*

Joy stared sleepily at the saucepan and its contents that smelt and looked like vomit. She had carved intricate pieces that were twenty feet long on fallen trees, she had scaled trees with very limited equipment to carve into the tallest limbs, but something as simple as cooking, was clearly beyond her. Maybe if she chopped her vegetables with a chainsaw she might have more luck.

Her puddings were legendary; crumbles, pies, cakes, trifles, tarts – she could do them all with her eyes closed. But something like soup just seemed to be beyond her capabilities. She had tried many times over the years to teach herself to cook, but whatever she made tasted disgusting. She had thought soup would be easy. But even she wasn't tempted to try the vomit smelling soup de jour before her.

The back door was open and the black acrid smoke was drifting out, probably creating another hole in the ozone layer. The smoke alarm had finally stopped, though it was still echoing in her ears. It seemed she would have another microwave meal for lunch again.

Just then there was a knock on the back door. 'Is everyone still alive?'

She turned around to face Finn, not sure whether she should still be angry with him. She really couldn't hold a grudge for long but she was certainly still hurting over the whole Lily incident. He was holding a huge bunch of flowers and she felt herself soften almost immediately.

He stepped in, blocking out all the light temporarily with his enormous frame.

'I'm really sorry about last night. I wasn't even angry with you,

146

it was the whole Billy situation that had riled me. I said some really hurtful things and I'm so sorry.'

He offered her the flowers, which she took. They weren't even shop bought ones, these were handpicked from his garden – which just made them so much more personal. They smelt divine and were arranged beautifully.

'Was Billy OK?'

'Yes, he'd followed some bitch home and the owner didn't think to call me and tell me Billy was sitting outside her house for two hours. I was so annoyed.'

'I could tell.'

He winced at the dig. 'I am sorry. Lily didn't stop talking about you all night, how wonderful you are. You really made her happy.'

Joy smiled into the blooms and Finn obviously took this as a good sign as he came further into the kitchen.

'Still friends?'

She hesitated but found herself nodding anyway.

He moved to the saucepan and pulled a face as he poked the contents. 'What is that?'

'Soup,' Joy said, defiantly. 'A… Moroccan recipe.' She took a big spoonful and swallowed it. As suspected, it tasted like vomit as well. She kept the smile on her face. 'It's delicious, probably not to your taste though.'

He looked around at the chaos in the kitchen, the remains of chopped up vegetables sitting in pools of water or gravy and every single bowl, plate, pan, jug, knife, fork and spoon littering the surfaces. It was quite obvious to even the untrained eye that she had no clue what she was doing. She had looked in recipe books but they spoke of techniques and ingredients that she had never even heard of before, so in the end she had made it up, which was now obvious to Finn.

He started picking up the mess and loading the dishwasher. She supposed she should feel embarrassed but she couldn't find it in her.

'Do you want me to show you how I cook my soup sometime?

I'm sure your Moroccan masterpiece is delicious, but… well, it's always good to have alternatives.'

She sniffed. 'Well, it would be nice to add to my wide repertoire of delicious recipes.'

'Of course.' He moved round her kitchen, tidying and wiping the sides and she realised that he still felt guilty. 'How about tomorrow night, we'll cook together and then we can eat it.'

Joy blinked at the sudden offer. They had gone from a vague 'sometime' to an actual date. The thought of working companionably alongside him tugged at her heart.

'As friends,' he quickly said.

'Of course, as friends, I'm not your type.' She tried to suppress the smirk.

'Definitely not.' His mouth twitched as he turned away busying himself with some imaginary stain. 'I prefer blondes.'

She felt the smile growing at the stupidity of it all. 'Good, I don't really like big men.'

He turned back. 'You don't?'

'No, not at all, I prefer my men quite short.'

'That's er great, I'm glad we've set the parameters. So tomorrow night we'll just be two friends who aren't remotely attracted to each other, cooking together.'

She nodded and he bit his lip to stop himself from laughing.

He suddenly took her chin in his huge, strong hand which sent another wave of desire crashing through her.

'You look exhausted, didn't you sleep last night?'

She wrestled with whether to tell him but didn't have the energy or the incentive to lie.

'Someone threw a brick through my window last night, when I came running downstairs I found this.'

She passed him the note she'd found wrapped around the brick telling her to 'fuk off'. She didn't know which was worse – the idea that it was a kid, influenced by his parents to hate her or that the residents of Bramble Hill were illiterate morons.

'What the hell is this?'

'The villagers hate me.'

'Right, this is going to stop. I thought the dog shit was a childish prank, I didn't realise it had escalated to this. I should have done something before.'

'I don't need you to fight my battles for me.'

'Well that's good, what are you going to do about it?'

She had nothing. A fair few practical jokes and tricks had entered her mind – from writing rude messages in bleach on their perfect lawns to stealing all their garden gnomes or posting an ant nest through their letterboxes – but although it might make her feel better, it wasn't going to solve anything.

'Right, do you have a copy of your lease or the contract for the house, naming Joe as your landlord and you as the client?'

She went to a drawer and sifted through a pile of envelopes. 'I thought about doing this myself, but they won't give me a chance to talk.' She passed him the contract.

'Let me take care of this.'

'Finn…'

'You don't have to be so fiercely independent all the time. It's OK to ask for help now and again. You're my friend, let me help you.'

At this stage she was willing to try anything. She nodded and he strode out, a man with a purpose.

*

Joy was on her way back from walking Darcy when she saw Casey up ahead, obviously on his way round to Zach's again. She called him and then caught him up as he waited for her. She smiled to herself when he greeted her with what seemed a habitual hug and kiss.

'How goes the wedding plans?'

Casey rolled his eyes. 'That woman changes her mind faster than I change my underwear.'

'Once a week?'

Casey nudged her. 'Currently it seems like five times a day.'

'That's a lot of underwear.'

Ignoring the jibe, Casey pressed on. 'Last week we were having a cellist to welcome the guests, then it was a violinist, then I think it was a twelve-piece choir. Why do the guests need to be welcomed at all? I'm going to be there with Finn to shake hands and ensure they all have drinks, isn't that enough of a welcome? Why don't we have a brass band or a dancing clown or a trapeze artist or how about a great banner saying "Welcome" in fifty-foot-high letters. I've been to loads of weddings in my time, some good, some bad, some indifferent, but I've never gone away thinking that I wasn't made to feel welcome enough.'

She squeezed his hand as they walked. 'Casey, do you really have to go through with all this? I never told you the other day, what with all the erm... Dark Shadow stuff, but I spoke with your mum. She just wants you to be happy, she even said that if you were gay she would be happy for you.'

'I know, she'd be fine about it. But it's gone too far now. If I tell her now she'll know that I was only going through all this to keep her happy, she'll be heartbroken that I couldn't tell her the truth. And she's so deliriously happy organising this wedding, I just can't seem to find the courage to break her heart.'

'Are you seriously going to commit to a long and unhappy marriage, bring children into a loveless relationship, deny who you are for the rest of your life... just to keep her happy?'

'It won't last, maybe a few months before Arielle leaves me or slips up enough for me to catch her in one of her many affairs. Then at least, once the divorce is over, I might be able to finally tell her the truth. But Mum needs this right now, the project, the excitement. I can't take it all away from her, for all her efforts to turn to nothing.'

She sighed sadly for him. It must have been agonizing to see his mum reduced to a lifeless shell with no passion for anything anymore. If she had been in Casey's shoes, she probably would have done the same thing just to make her mum happy again.

They heard a door slam and they watched Finn, from a distance, stride away from a house angrily and walk up the drive of the house next door. Was he visiting every house in the village to tell them who she really was? From the looks of it, he wasn't getting a positive response.

As she and Casey neared the pond, they stopped to watch a small group of villagers hanging bunting from the trees

'What are they doing?' Joy said.

'I'm no expert, but it seems like they're hanging bunting from the trees.'

'Excellent deductions, Holmes. CID must be so proud to have you on their team. I meant why?'

'Oh, for the Friendliest Village Competition. Last day of the month I think, there'll be a fete type thing; cake sales, face painting, bouncy castle, free jam tasting.'

She shook her head in disbelief. 'Kind of ironic that they win Friendliest Village award nine years in a row, when they seem hellbent on making my life a misery.'

'Still no progress on that?'

She told him about the cakes that had been shoved through her letterbox, the daily offerings of dog poo shoved through her door or left on the doorstep, the eggs and what had happened the night before with the brick through her window.

'Jeez, this is getting serious. Have you told the police?'

'Yes, I phoned the local station this morning, the one halfway between here and Ashton Woods. The policeman there told me, in no uncertain terms, that it would be better for everyone if I did leave.'

Casey rolled his eyes. 'Mr Burton.' He almost spat the name out. 'He and Mrs Kemblewick were very good friends. I can take this higher if you want?'

She turned away from the pond and headed towards her house. 'It's a bit beyond CID's remit isn't it?'

'Yes, but I have contacts.'

'No, it's fine, I'm not sure what they could do anyway. We don't know who is doing it, whether it's two or three people or a whole village of haters.'

Casey whistled for Darcy who was seemingly transfixed by the bunting. 'How about some revenge of your own?'

'Post Darcy's poo through all the letterboxes, with a note saying "Screw you and Mrs Kemblewick"?'

'Not quite what I had in mind. My mum is on the committee for this Friendliest Village award, she despairs that Bramble Hill wins it year after year.'

'Yes, how is it that they've won so often? Friendliest village in Hertfordshire I could understand. Well, not really considering their attitude to me, but OK, it's believable – but Friendliest Village in Britain?'

Casey dug in his pocket and offered her a Starburst; she chose a strawberry before he chose a lime green one for himself with relish.

'Really?' She gestured to the lime green sweet in shock.

'They're my favourites,' he said, defensively. 'It's a nonsense award Joy, a self-proclaimed title. No one contests it, because no one in Britain even knows Bramble Hill exists, let alone their much-exulted status. It started ten years ago when somebody in Bramble Hill decided there should be a competition between the local villages to see who could be classed as the friendliest village. A committee was raised, existing of the well-to-do ladies, one from each village, and some of the owners of the big manor houses in the area. No one really had a clue how they could prove their village was the friendliest, though it was deemed that the committee would visit each village in turn on a certain day to see what it had to offer. On the day that they visited here, Bramble Hill held their now annual fete. The committee were most impressed with the auction where the villagers auction off their time as prizes – mowing lawns, cutting hair, cleaning, all that sort of thing – with all the money going to charity. The committee said the auction showed real camaraderie and community spirit and as the other villages had done nothing, they declared Bramble Hill the winner. I think the second year a few of the other villages held fetes, but as Bramble Hill were offering free car washes to all who attended their fete they won again. After that, the other villages didn't bother to try to win and Bramble Hill has won year after year.'

'So bribery goes a long way?' Joy gestured for Casey to follow her into her house, though he was already walking up her path as if he belonged there.

'The point being, the committee are getting a bit fed up of Bramble Hill winning every year, they know it's all a load of nonsense. But some of them, my mum included, would love to see Bramble Hill get its comeuppance. They know that their attitude to newcomers is less than desirable, that they're rude to tourists. There was talk the other day of setting up a Most Miserable Village award. Something like this would be like adding fuel to the fire. They would love to hear about how they are treating you, that would end Bramble Hill's gloried reign once and for all.'

Joy smiled as she boiled the kettle. It was tempting, very tempting for a bit of swift retribution of her own. But she shook her head. 'I'd really like to make a go of living here. I've moved around so much over the last few years and I think it's time to stop running and finally settle down. If I go to the committee with this, if I took away their treasured crown, there's no way I could stay here then. My life would be made a living hell.'

'More so than it is already?'

'I'm sure a few bits of dog poo would be the least of my worries.'

*

Joy was staring out of her window at the village, when Finn came running from his house, leapt in his truck and tore off up the road. Something was clearly up.

She finished her cup of tea and was just about to wash it up when there was a knock on the door.

When she opened it, she was surprised to see Lily standing on her doorstep, with three helium balloons in her hand.

'Hello ragamuffin, have you come round to see Finn? He's just gone out,' Joy looked around for Lily's parents but she seemed to be completely alone.

'What's a ragamuffin?'

'It means you're a dirty little mud monster. Where's your mum or dad?'

She saw the wobble of Lily's lip. 'I've run away from home.'

Crap.

'Well, I'm glad you came to me, in you come.'

Lily shuffled in, her shoulders slumped. 'You won't tell them I'm here? I'll run away again if they find me.'

'No of course not, it'll be our secret. Do you want some ice cream, it's coconut flavoured?'

Lily nodded, her whole face lighting up.

Her parents would be worried sick by now, that was probably why Finn had sped out of the village so quickly to join the search for her. She'd have to text Finn somehow without Lily knowing.

Joy grabbed the ice cream from the fridge and started dishing up two portions while Lily watched her astutely.

'So what's this about?'

'I told Mum and Dad about the balloon thing we talked about, about sending notes to Granddad in heaven and Dad said there was no such thing as heaven.'

Good lord, why didn't he tell her there was no Santa, Easter Bunny and Tooth Fairy whilst he was at it?

'He said the balloons would float in the air and eventually come down and get stuck in a tree and it was a silly idea.'

Joy and Lily had chatted a lot about her granddad the day before and Joy had mentioned what she had done when her parents had died with little messages tied to balloons. She hadn't realised that Lily would grab onto this with both hands.

'Is that true?' Lily asked, the wobble back on her lip.

This was tricky ground. 'What do you believe?'

'I think that Granddad is still here sometimes, watching over us.'

'So, it doesn't matter whether he reads the note in heaven, or whether he is here when you write it.'

'No…' Lily seemed doubtful.

'I guess what really matters is that you have a chance to say goodbye to him, to tell him how you feel, and I bet somehow, he'll know.'

This wasn't just chatting now, this was full on interfering, exactly what Finn had told her not to do the day before. But clearly Lily needed to say goodbye to her granddad and as she had been denied that chance at the funeral the day before, that was what was at the root of her running away. Joy sucked on her spoon. Really, she should phone Finn, tell him where Lily was, that she was still upset over her granddad and they needed to do something to help her to come to terms with it. It wasn't her place to do this.

'I've bought three balloons from the shop, one for Granddad, one for Boris and one for you to write to your parents too.'

'Oh.' So there was no choice. If it wasn't resolved today, if Joy let her down, then Lily might run away again and this time she might not come back to Joy, she might go off on her own and that was terrifying. Lily just needed some closure and if her parents and Finn were angry with Joy for doing this then so be it. But she still had to tell Finn where Lily was.

'Where do you live?'

'Chalk Rise,' Lily said, playing with the string of one of the balloons that were bobbing around on the ceiling, desperate for their freedom.

That was a ten-minute drive away, five minutes at the speed Finn was driving earlier. They would have to be quick before her parents came round and shouted at Lily for running away and at Joy for interfering.

'I have some purple notepaper upstairs by my bed, go and grab it for me and we'll write some messages together. Do you know what you want to say?'

Lily nodded and ran out the room.

Joy grabbed her phone and fired off a quick text to Finn. *'Lily is here, she doesn't want you to know, give us some time.'*

Her phone burst into life immediately, with Finn's name flashing on the screen. There really was nothing subtle about him. She heard Lily thundering down the stairs and she quickly dismissed the call and turned the phone off. Finn would be furious.

Lily sat down at the table and started writing. Joy sat next to her.

'Will you read mine to see if it's OK?' Lily asked as she wrote.

'I'm sure it will be, but yes if you want me to.'

'And I'll read yours too.'

'Oh, OK.'

Joy stared at the piece of paper, wondering what she could say to her parents – something that would sum up twenty years of missing them in just a few lines. She couldn't even remember what she had written on the balloon twenty years before. Now, when she knew Lily's dad was right about the message landing in a tree somewhere, she was finding it even harder. But Lily needed to know that this was something serious for Joy too. If she could see them again, one more time, just for a few seconds, what would she tell them?

She swallowed the sudden lump in her throat and started writing.

Out of the corner of her eye, she could see Lily had finished her note to her granddad and had now, presumably, started on Boris's note.

156

'Finished,' Lily declared, proudly.

'Me too.'

Lily slid hers across the table for Joy to read.

'To Granddad. I will miss you and think of you every day. You gave the best piggy backs and you made me laugh a lot. I love you. Don't eat too many toffees in heaven, they will rot your teeth.'

Joy smiled and then she read the note to Boris and she nearly burst into tears.

'Dear Boris. Please look after Granddad and go on lots of long walks with him. He missed you so much when you died so I'm happy that you are together again. He might miss us now too so if you play with him often and wag your tail and roll on your back and make him laugh then he might not miss us too much. I love you Boris.'

Lily was trying to read what Joy had written. 'What does it say?'

Joy cleared her throat. 'It says, "To Mum and Dad, there hasn't been a single day that I haven't thought of you or missed you. You should know that Alex has turned out to be someone you would have been very proud of. You did a brilliant job in raising him and because of you he did a brilliant job in raising me. I have so many happy memories of my life with you, but now for the first time, I'm looking to the future and not living in the past. I love you and I always will"'.

Lily stared at her, clearly not understanding half of what she had written, but she nodded her approval.

Joy helped her to tie the notes to the balloons and they went outside, just as she heard Finn's truck pull up out the front.

'You ready?' Joy said, bracing herself for the assault that was bound to come. Lily took her hand and nodded. 'After three?'

'Wait.' Lily scrunched up her eyes. 'Goodbye Granddad. I love you loads and loads and if you can hear me, give Boris a big hug from me.'

Joy smiled and Lily opened her eyes. 'Now I'm ready.'

'OK. One, two, three.'

Lily released the two balloons. They floated upwards and Joy let hers go too. Lily started waving at the balloons and as they drifted further away, Joy found herself waving too. She smiled at the thought of her parents somehow reading the note, knowing what a brilliant legacy they had left behind in Alex. For the first time, the lump in her throat that was always there when she thought of them was a little bit smaller. Lily had helped her too.

Lily leaned into Joy's side and Joy knelt down and hugged her. She spotted Finn and presumably Lily's dad over her shoulder, watching them from Finn's back garden. Finn was obviously angry but thankfully Lily's dad just seemed to be relieved that Lily was OK.

Joy pulled away and indicated to Lily that her dad was there. Lily hung back, clearly worried that her dad would be angry.

Her dad came through the gate and ran across the grass towards them and Lily, obviously realising she wasn't going to get shouted out, ran straight into his arms.

'Oh Lilyloodles, I'm so sorry,' he said as he held her tight. 'I was so caught up in my own grief that I didn't think about yours.'

'That's OK, Daddy, losing your parents is very sad,' Lily said, clearly now the expert on grief. 'Joy lost both her parents twenty years ago and she still misses them every day.'

Joy blushed and chanced a glance at Finn who had also come through the gate into her garden. Yes, he was definitely pissed.

'We can go and visit his grave tomorrow if you like,' Lily's dad was saying.

'I know it makes you sad, Daddy, but I'd just like to talk about him sometimes.'

'We can talk about him any time you want.'

Still holding her in his arms he stood up and smiled at Joy. 'Thank you.'

She smiled and he carried Lily back into Finn's house. And then she was alone with Finn.

In one giant stride he was in front of her. She started to defend herself but was silenced with his mouth as he kissed her.

Her heart leapt, and she felt herself go hot and cold simultaneously. Something inside her melted like an ice cube sizzling on hot skin. Her mouth was still open – half in shock, half with the unsaid words she'd been about to say. And then she started kissing him back, her hands in his hair as he pulled her against him.

His tongue touched hers and something zapped through her, all senses and synapses firing up, so his every touch washed over her in great waves of desire. He was really good too, but so not what she expected. Despite his size, she imagined his kisses to be gentle and soft, and though there was an element of that, there was also passion, an undeniable hunger from him. This was a kiss that was about to lead to something more – in about five seconds, clothes were going to get torn off and Joy didn't care that they were in broad daylight and people might see them.

But as abruptly as it had started, it was suddenly over as Finn snatched himself away, obviously aware of where the kiss had been heading.

He didn't say anything as he stared at her but he didn't look pleased, as if she had just grabbed him and kissed him.

His hand was still on her arm and he let it fall to her hand, linking fingers with her. 'Thanks for looking after Lily.'

'That was some thank you kiss.'

He let go of her hand and after a few seconds of avoiding her eyes, he walked back towards his house without looking back.

*

Finn took a swig of his beer and stared up at the stars. The sky was clear, thousands of stars peppered the darkness like glitter. What was he going to do about Joy? He'd now got a date with her tomorrow to cook together, and he'd kissed her. His strict rule of not letting anything happen between them was quickly crumbling. He'd seen her briefly that afternoon, a few hours after the kiss. He'd been in the front garden when she had popped outside to put her rubbish in the bin. She hadn't noticed him at first, as there was what appeared to be a pie dish left on her doorstep, which caught her attention. He'd watched as she'd lifted the foil and smiled at the contents underneath. Something from Casey no doubt, the man was a devil in the kitchen and he had left numerous things for Finn over the years.

Then, just as she'd been about to go back in the house, she saw him and the smile she flashed him was like a punch to the heart. How could he love her? It didn't make sense. He had known her for about a week, he couldn't possibly love her. But with Pippa it had taken mere seconds and he wasn't going to make that mistake again. It was lust, pure and simple. Especially if that kiss had been anything to go by. It had almost developed beyond the point of no return right there on her back lawn. He just had to back off a bit. He wouldn't hurt her by reverting to his foul moods, but he could still cool things down between them.

He heard Joy's back door slam open, and despite his best intentions, he found himself looking over the low wall at her.

She came rushing out, her breathing fast, accelerated, as she seemingly tried to get something off herself. She was patting down her arms, legs and clothes, desperate to be rid of it. But whatever 'it' was, he couldn't see anything.

Suddenly, she ripped off her vest top, quickly followed by her bra. Seconds later, her shorts and pants joined the pile of clothes on the floor. She was completely naked as she rubbed her arms and legs down, shaking her hair out too, making small little whimpers of panic as she picked things off her skin.

Chapter Eleven

He found himself taking a step towards her, concerned by her panic, but then a movement caught his eye behind her. Zach was standing in his garden, staring at her too. But where Finn was looking at her with worry, Zach was looking at her only with desire.

Zach let himself through the connecting gate and moved quickly to her side. His hands on her made Finn furious.

'Joy, are you OK?' Zach said.

She looked up, noticing his arrival for the first time, even though he was standing right in front of her, with his hands on her waist.

'Zach, they're everywhere.'

'What are?'

'The ants, they're all over me, look they're on my arms, they won't get off.'

'There's nothing on you.'

'God, your eyes are amazing.'

'Erm… thanks.'

'So blue. Like turquoise. No purple, they're bright purple, like Cadbury's purple. They're so vivid. Oh look the ants are on you too, quick get your shirt off.'

To Finn's disgust Zach was very quick to respond; yanking his shirt over his head and letting it fall on top of Joy's discarded clothes. As his hands moved back to her waist he moved in closer. His eyes scanned down her body as she tried to pick the ants off him too.

'You're so beautiful, Joy. Why don't we go inside and we can pick the ants off each other?'

Finn felt his hands clench into fists at his side.

She must have caught the look of desire too because she suddenly giggled.

'You're trying to get me into bed.'

'I've been trying to get you into bed since I first laid eyes on you. Tonight's no different, except you're already naked.'

'Except tonight, I might just let you. I do feel very horny.'

Zach couldn't help the stupid grin from spreading on his stupid face. 'You do?'

'Oh yes, I think it's the ants, they make me horny, them and Finn.'

His face fell at that, and now Finn found himself smiling with a smug satisfaction.

'Finn makes you horny?'

'Oh yes, god yes. I keep having sex dreams about him. Can't help it. At first it was bloody annoying, but now I really like them.'

'Have you had any dreams about me?'

'No, but it doesn't matter, I'll still shag you anyway.'

Zach clearly thought about this for a moment. Joy was obviously settling for Zach rather than him being first choice. But it didn't damage his ego that much that he was going to pass up on the chance of sex when it was offered so willingly.

He shrugged and took her hand and started pulling her back towards the house. Joy, giggling like a school girl, followed.

Finn found himself striding through the gate and blocking their way back into her house.

'As much as I'd hate to interrupt this little party, you're not sleeping with her tonight,' Finn growled.

Zach laughed. 'Jealous?'

'No, she's clearly off her face on something and I don't think she's in the right frame of mind.'

'Finn!' Joy finally realised he was there and grinned up at him. He looked down at her, her pupils were huge.

'Shit, what the hell did you take?' He took his shirt off and wrapped it round her.

'Nothing.' She grinned again, then her eyes travelled over his body in the same way Zach had looked at her a few moments before. 'I had some quiche, mushroom quiche, then I started feeling funny, but my god did that quiche taste good. I nearly ate the whole thing.'

'Shit,' Finn muttered. 'Magic mushrooms?'

'Is that bad?' Zach said.

'It causes severe hallucinations, hence all the talk about the ants and your eyes being purple.'

Her eyes were wide with excitement. 'Magic? Do I have magical powers now?'

'Where did you get these mushrooms from? Don't tell me you just picked them from the woods?'

She frowned slightly. 'They were in the quiche. Someone gave me the quiche. Did fairies bring it, magical mystical fairies with magical mystical quiche?'

'Someone gave you the quiche?'

Joy nodded absently as she moved to stroke a hand across Finn's chest.

'Are we going to have a threesome?' she asked, her eyes lighting up with delight. 'I've never had one before, it might be fun.'

Finn tried to stop her from unbuttoning his jeans.

She tutted with annoyance and turned back to Zach. 'Are we going to have sex or not?'

'Yes.'

'No, you're not. If she wants to have sex with you when she's not high on something that's her problem, but I'm not letting you

163

sleep with her when she's in this state.' Finn glared at Zach, daring him to argue, daring him to take one step closer to the house with Joy. But he clearly could tell this was not an argument he was going to win. Holding his hands up in defeat, he backed off.

'Maybe another time, eh Joy?'

With a look of amusement at Finn, Zach disappeared back through the connecting gate again.

Finn looked back down at Joy who was busy trying to get ants off his chest, seemingly not even aware that Zach had gone. She was clearly wearing some pink glittery lipstick that Lily often wore, making her look childlike and vulnerable.

'What are you wearing on your lips?'

'It's Lily's, I just found it, I thought it made me look pretty.' She tried to pout in a sexy way, but failed.

He sighed, cursing himself for getting involved. He'd promised himself he was going to have nothing to do with her and yet she had forced herself into his life whether he liked it or not. He didn't want to have this need to protect her, yet it was inherent in him, like the need to breathe.

He took her hand and, leading her back through the connecting gate, he went back into his own house.

'Are we going to have sex, Finn?'

'No.'

'Because I'm not your type?'

'That's right.' He pushed her gently down onto the sofa.

'And because you hate me?'

The hurt and pain in her voice threw him. He pulled the shirt around her, helping her to put her arms through the sleeves and then buttoning it up. He sat down next to her.

'I don't hate you Joy, that's the problem.'

She turned towards him, curling her knees up and resting them on his lap. She started picking ants off his body again.

'They won't come off,' she mumbled.

'They won't hurt you, just try to ignore them.'

She brushed her hand over his chest, trying to sweep the 'ants' away, until her hand came to rest on his nipple, the pierced nipple. He shifted uneasily. If she thought the piecing was an ant and tried to rip it out, that would hurt a lot. She was staring at it, her eyes wide. For safety's sake, he gently removed her hand from it.

'You know what I want to do Finn, more than anything?'

'What's that?'

Suddenly and unexpectedly, she bent her head and ran her tongue over his nipple, straight over where the metal bar went through the skin.

A wave of desire crashed through him and he had to swallow back the moan that nearly erupted from his throat.

She sat back up again, her eyes were still so dark, but lust filled now. 'I've wanted to do that for so long.'

Finn didn't trust himself to speak at all.

She looked at him and blushed furiously. 'I'm so sorry. I don't know why I did that.'

She moved to get up, but he stopped her, his arm round her as he pulled her against him.

'It doesn't matter. Stay here till your head is a bit clearer, why don't we watch some TV for a bit?'

She looked into his eyes in confusion. 'You're not angry?'

He shook his head, and grabbed the remote, switching on the TV in the hope that he could distract her from doing it again.

She leaned into him, which did nothing to stop the inappropriate feelings from flooding through him. She laid her head on his shoulder and a few minutes later she was fast asleep.

He pulled a blanket over her and kissed her head.

How could she possibly think he hated her? He was head over heels in love with this crazy, beautiful redhead and there didn't seem to be a single thing he could do about it. But enough was enough, he wasn't going to hurt her anymore.

*

Joy stirred and opened her eyes. For a second, she had no idea where she was, then she saw Finn watching her from the chair on the other side of the room.

She sat up in confusion, realising she was in his lounge. Her head was pounding and her stomach rolled. She quickly realised she was only wearing Finn's shirt, that she was naked underneath. She pulled the shirt down to her knees in embarrassment.

His bare chest was covered in a thin sheen of pink glitter, though around his nipple, the pink glitter was concentrated in what was clearly the shape of a mouth. Suddenly, memories of the night before flooded through her. Memories of stripping naked in her garden, of Zach's offer of sex, and with horror she recalled licking Finn's nipple.

She let her head fall into her hands. 'Oh god, oh no.' She couldn't look at him. 'I'm sorry, I'm so sorry.'

'Don't be.'

She peered at him through her fingers. He didn't look angry. He stood up and knelt in front of her, offering her a glass of water. 'Are you feeling OK?'

She took the glass and stared at him. 'Why are you being so nice?'

'I can be nice.'

She rubbed her hand across her face. 'Oh god it's like Jekyll and Hyde. One second you're been all sweet and lovely and wonderful, and the next you're yelling at me over something stupid. Two days ago you shouted at me because I'd managed to get Lily covered in mud when I was looking after her, yesterday you apologised, brought me flowers, practically asked me on a date—'

'It wasn't a date.'

Joy ignored the interruption. '—and kissed me. You kissed me. Jesus, that kiss was like nothing else. You can't tell me that you didn't feel anything from that kiss. Then you ignored me for the rest of the day. You couldn't even smile at me when I saw you last night. Now, you're being all sweet and looking after me. I

166

molested you. Oh god, I'm no better than Craig Peters, forcing myself on you when I was...' She tried to recall what had happened, had she been drunk?

'Hallucinating,' Finn supplied helpfully. 'Probably from a dodgy mushroom quiche.'

There had been the quiche that someone had left on her doorstep, she had presumed it was a peace offering from someone in the village. She had eaten the quiche, made some more maquettes for her next few strikes, eaten some more quiche and then... the ants. They had been all over her, in her hair, her clothes, even under her skin. She shuddered as she thought about it, but now her mind was a bit clearer she knew she had been hallucinating. Finn had said as much the night before, that she was off her face on something.

'The big difference between you and Craig Peters is that you molested someone that actually wanted to be molested.'

Joy felt her eyebrows shoot up into her hair.

'I really fucking like you, shit – it's driving me insane how much I want you. I've been trying to deny it and punishing you for my feelings. It's not fair on you and I'm sorry. That kiss, you... licking my nipple, it's just making it so much worse. But it's not just lust or sex. I want to take care of you, not because I think you need taking care of, because you clearly don't, but because I want to look after you and protect you.'

Joy put her hand on his face, stroking the stubble on his cheeks.

'But this is exactly how I fell for Pippa and I can see it's happening all over again.'

She let her hand fall from his cheek. 'I'm not Pippa.'

He shook his head. 'I can't do a relationship. I just can't. And I don't just want sex either because I'd get hurt or I'd end up hurting you and I really don't want to do that. I promise, no more angry looks or stupid mood swings. But I'm hoping we can be friends. And as your friend I'd like to take care of you. So are you hungry?'

167

She nodded, unable to find any words.

'Eggs on toast? Eggs are supposed to be good for settling the stomach.'

She nodded again and Finn stood and quickly made for the kitchen.

*

'I need to have a shower and walk Darcy,' Joy said, sleepily, trying not to stare at the strange nice version of Finn that had manifested itself overnight. Over breakfast there had been secret smiles and little looks and it was confusing as hell for her. At least she knew where she stood when he was angry and grumpy.

'I can walk her. I have to walk Billy anyway so it's no hassle.'

She peered at him through heavy eyes. Why did he have to be so nice? Every time he was kind she felt herself falling for him a little bit more and it hurt even more the next time he was angry with her. She just didn't have the energy to argue against his offer of help.

She stood up and Finn offered her his hand and she took it, glad of the support – her legs were wobbly and she had the worst hangover of her life.

Finn led her out into his garden and then through the gate to hers. Zach was in his own garden and he glanced over as they came out of Finn's house, hand in hand.

'Oh, I see,' Zach said, letting himself through the connecting gate. 'So you had a problem with me sleeping with her but it was OK for you to fool around with her?'

'Nothing happened,' Finn said.

'So what's with all the glitter all over your chest then?'

Finn tried to wipe it off but it stayed resolute. 'It's not what it looks like.'

Joy's head was pounding and she had no time for Zach today. 'Before you start getting all judgemental, you should look at your own morals. Last night I was high on magic mushrooms or something. I was clearly having hallucinations yet you were more than willing to take advantage of my vulnerability and sleep with me. I have no time for men like that.'

Zach looked mortified.

Joy made to walk into her house but Zach stopped her with his hand on her arm. Finn moved closer, glaring down at Zach, and he quickly released her.

'Joy, I'm not… I didn't… I'm attracted to you. Look, I'm sorry if you thought I was a bit of a creep. You know how I feel about you. It was hard to ignore those feelings when you were naked and so horny.'

She brushed past him, pulled Finn in after her and closed the door on Zach's horrified and guilty face.

'I'm going for a shower.'

'Do you need some help?'

'Ha!' She gestured to their hands that were still linked. 'We've already crossed over the boundaries of friendship in so many different ways. Showering together is going to destroy any last hold of the friendship that you're clinging to so tightly. I really like you, you know that, but if you honestly think that we can shower together with all these sparks flying between us and nothing happen, then sure by all means, you can come and wash my back.'

She walked upstairs, not even sure anymore whether she actually wanted him to follow her or not.

*

Finn watched her go upstairs, her red hair looking like fire against his white shirt. It took every ounce of strength he had not to follow her.

He turned away before he got a glimpse of her bum under his shirt as she reached the top of the stairs.

Friends. How long was that going to last exactly? He put some fresh food and water down for Darcy, let her out into the garden and went back to his own house to get changed.

When he came back into Joy's house a few minutes later with Billy, he could hear the sound of the shower upstairs and he closed his eyes and counted to ten.

Who was he kidding? He stood more chance of sprouting wings and learning how to fly than of succeeding in being just friends with Joy.

He opened his eyes and spotted the quiche on the kitchen unit. He broke it apart with his hands, keen to see the mushrooms himself to put his mind at ease. He wasn't an expert on mushrooms but his dad was a gardener, just like him, and had taught Finn what different mushrooms looked like. He knew that some mushrooms had different effects; some caused hallucinations, some caused sickness and stomach pains and some caused organ failure and death. Death in many cases was prolonged, sometimes two or three weeks after eating them. Thankfully, these weren't deadly ones but they were highly hallucinogenic and nothing like any variation of edible mushroom. Someone had deliberately used these to poison her.

The reaction to him sharing Joy's lease with the villagers the day before had been met with various degrees of disbelief. As much as they all adored him, they wanted to believe that Joy was a monster even more. This was going to have to stop. He gave Casey a quick call and he agreed to come round in an hour.

He put Darcy on her lead and was about to go and that's when he saw them. Sitting on the breakfast bar were three intricate plasticine animals, a stag, a scorpion and a bear. They were fantastic, so detailed, so lifelike... and so going to get Joy into trouble if Casey saw them. He looked around for somewhere to stash them. He opened a drawer, threw them in, grabbed Darcy and Billy and left.

Chapter Twelve

Finn sat down on the hilltop. Billy was sniffing around behind him, but he had Darcy still on the lead next to him. She wasn't his dog and he had no idea whether she would come back when he called.

God, that woman. He couldn't stay away from her, couldn't stop thinking about her. It was lust, pure and simple. If he slept with her, things would be better between them, the air would be clearer. At the moment there was so much sexual tension flying around that it was impossible to ignore. He had tried to push her away, but she had clawed her way into his life and his heart whether he liked it or not.

And now it seemed she could be the diamond thief. He didn't want to believe that of her but the evidence was mounting up.

Suddenly aware that Darcy was no longer sitting at his side, he whirled round to find her. There was Billy, getting the quick, hard shag he so desperately needed. His tongue was hanging out of his mouth with a demented grin on his face. Darcy, though quite willing to stand there and let Billy have his wicked way with her, seemed quite bored by the whole affair. Women, they were all the same, they bored easily and were soon onto the next willing man. Pippa had been bored very easily, and Joy would be the same. She would move on soon, once she tired of this village, this home – and he would never see her again. He wasn't going to allow himself to get hurt again.

He stood up and clapped his hands at the two dogs, but Billy was already finished. Dismounting the huge dog, Billy looked at her hopefully as if waiting for some compliment on his prowess. Darcy didn't even give him a backward glance as she ambled over to a pile of poo and sniffed at it half-heartedly. He grabbed her lead and headed towards home. Billy had a skip in his step as he trotted along, and grinned up at Finn as if to say, 'See, that's how you do it, a quick, harmless shag and everyone is happy.'

*

When Joy came downstairs later, Finn and Casey were waiting for her. She smiled at her friend, though she wasn't sure what look to give Finn. They certainly couldn't be friends, that much was clear and she didn't really know where that left them.

It took a second to realise that Casey was very serious.

'Finn told me about the magic mushrooms.'

Joy's face fell. 'I don't take drugs if that's what you're thinking. Jeez, Joy lives in a nice house, drives a nice car, she must be a drug dealer. Well, thanks very much, both of you.'

'Calm down, little firecracker,' Casey laughed. 'Come and sit down. I'm under no illusions that you're making meth in your cellar and selling cocaine to the kids at the school. Finn said someone made you the quiche with hallucinogenic mushrooms in it. This is very serious.'

Joy sighed. 'I can't believe someone would try to kill me over this Mrs Kemblewick fiasco. Maybe it was a gift from someone really naïve about mushrooms.'

'Did the quiche come with a card?' Casey said.

Joy shook her head.

'You seem very blasé about all this, someone tried to poison you,' Finn said.

'I'm not blasé. I want this to stop, I do. But we don't know who's doing it. I'm not sure if it's one person or every idiot in the village. I've tried to tell them who I am, you've tried, how did that work out for you?'

'Not good.'

'Exactly. What am I going to do, sue the whole village for harassment? I'd like to see that stand up in a court of law.'

'You can't let them win,' Finn said.

'If I'd let them win, I would have moved out by now.'

'I'm going to take the quiche tray in for fingerprinting, see if we can start from there,' Casey said. 'I'm also going to arrange for CCTV to be installed round the front and back of the house, see if we can catch these little bastards. In the meantime, I'd like you to keep a diary of all the events and as gross as it sounds, the next time that dog crap gets shoved through the door, I want you to keep some of it.'

'Are you kidding me?'

'That dog crap is coming from somewhere. That can be analysed too. If we can link it to a specific dog, then we can link it to the owner. We're going to stop this.'

Joy nodded wearily.

Casey stood up to go. 'Come on firecracker, show these bastards some of that fire.'

She smiled and he kissed her on the head and left, leaving her on her own with Finn. Immediately the atmosphere crackled with sparks and tension.

She stood, not really knowing what to do with herself, Finn stood too.

'Thank you for taking Darcy for a walk.'

'My pleasure.'

Wow this was all very polite, she could go and shake his hand in a minute.

'You look better.'

'I feel better.'

Silence. Man, this was awkward. She felt at a loss for something to say. She wanted to kiss him. She wanted him to grab her and kiss her like he'd done in the garden the other day. Surely he wanted that too. She had to say something now. The silence was dragging on too long.

'So I guess your carer duties are officially over.'

Finn reached out with one finger and briefly stroked the back of her hand. His touch sent a jolt of electricity zinging through her. 'Pity. I was kind of enjoying it.' He stepped back, a smile playing on his lips. 'Well, you know where I am if you need me. Big spider in the bath or scary movie you don't want to watch alone, I'm your man.'

'I'll remember that.'

He smiled and ducked out the back door.

Joy had to stop herself doing a little giddy dance. She was sure she could find something he could help her with. Then the phone rang and as she answered it the smile fell off her face.

*

Finn was attempting to read again when Joy knocked on the back door with a bottle of wine. She looked stunning in a simple green summer dress that swished and sparkled as she moved.

'I've come for my date,' she smiled shyly.

He stared at her and then remembered the arrangements they'd made the day before. It seemed like a lifetime ago.

He stood up and moved over to her. 'It wasn't a date. I was just going to teach you how to cook. If it was a date, there would have been candles, romantic music, great food, maybe a bit of dancing. And probably some amazing sex to finish off the perfect night.'

Joy laughed at his candour. 'Wow, that's some date. Could we maybe skip all of the food and music and go straight for the hot sex?'

He stared at her, all the words he wanted to say stuck in his throat.

'I'm joking Finn, though I could really do with a distraction tonight and someone to talk to.'

'OK.'

'We can do that, can't we? We are friends after all.'

He thought for a moment. She needed a distraction, but it had to be something that wasn't remotely romantic. They didn't need any further temptation. They were friends, what did friends do?

'Board games.'

'What?'

He took the wine off her and pulled her into the dining room. 'I'm a demon at Jenga.' He opened a cupboard and pulled out a box. 'And I'm pretty good at Cluedo too. Anything you fancy, I've got Monopoly, Pictionary, Trivial Pursuit?'

Joy leaned round the cupboard door and looked in, clearly confused with how the evening was turning out. 'Ooh Hungry Hippos, I used to love that as a child.'

'You do realise you're speaking to the regional Hungry Hippo champion?'

Joy laughed. 'That sounds like a challenge.'

*

Finn laughed as Joy tried to bounce the ball into the cup for the thirty-eighth time.

'Stop laughing, this is really hard.' The ball hit the rim and bounced off onto the floor. Again.

'I've never seen someone play The Cube before with so much ineptitude and so much lack of skill.'

Joy disappeared under the table to retrieve the ball, grinning

175

to herself. She hadn't stopped laughing all night. They had played one board game after another after another. Finn had pretty much ruthlessly thrashed her at every game they'd played. The sexual tension had completely disappeared and she was just really enjoying being in his company.

'I can't find the ball.'

'Oh well, I think it's best we called it a night anyway. You can go home and lick your wounds about how truly terrible you are at playing games.'

She pulled herself up from the floor and went and sat on the sofa.

'Thank you for my date tonight, I had a lot of fun.'

'It wasn't a date.'

'That's a shame because there's one part of your list for an amazing date that I'd be very interested in.'

'Oh yes?' He was teasing her now – his face was straight but his eyes were filled with mischief.

'I'd like to see you dance, I think that would be very amusing.'

He laughed. 'I'm a very proficient dancer I'll have you know.'

'Well, if you ever ask me out on a date, I'll be the judge of that.'

He frowned slightly and she thought perhaps she might have pushed the conversation too far.

'Well, Casey told me it was your birthday next week, Wednesday was it? I thought maybe we could go out, do something for the day, that's if you don't have plans?'

She stared at him.

'It's not a date, so you don't need to bring your dancing shoes. Just two friends out together.'

She smiled. 'I'd like that.'

'Good. And as for the slur on my dancing ability…' He got up and loaded a CD into the stereo. He hit play and the dramatic sound of the traditional waltz music filled the room. Finn came towards her and took her hand.

'No, Finn. I trust you, you can dance, I get it.' He pulled her to her feet. 'Please, no, I don't need proof.'

But he wasn't taking no for an answer. With one hand in hers and the other at her waist, he was suddenly sweeping across the room in a seemingly faultless waltz. And although she had always thought of herself as clumsy and ungainly, she was now waltzing seamlessly too. Finn looked down at her with a huge smile on his face. It filled her heart to see it. The song went on for a good five minutes and Finn didn't miss a step but eventually the song came to an end and as Finn released her she flopped back onto the sofa, exhausted.

'You really can dance.'

Finn turned the stereo off. 'I had to learn for *The Darkness* trilogy.'

'I must watch these films one day. I expect your partner was some beautiful movie star.'

'Hardly, they paired me with some six-foot-five woman who kept stamping on my feet through every take. I got my own back though when I ripped her throat out.'

'What?'

He laughed. 'I was a vampire. I danced with her and then killed her. She hated the fake blood all over her so I kept screwing up the take so we'd have to reshoot it again and again. Pissed her right off.'

'You really have a way with women, don't you?'

'I have my moments. Now do you want to tell me what tonight was about before you go home?'

Joy's face fell and she sighed, her little bubble of happiness popping as she remembered what she wanted a distraction from. 'PC Annabel French rang me earlier, asking if I wanted to meet up with her and Craig Peters tomorrow? I said I'd go but now I'm wishing I hadn't.'

Finn took her hand. 'You don't have to meet him.'

'I think I do.'

'Then I'll come with you.'

This time she wasn't going to argue.

*

Joy was lying on the chair swing early the next day, watching the pink morning clouds roll lazily across the pale blue sky. Determined not to spend the night worrying about Craig Peters, she had allowed herself to think about Finn instead. How lovely he was. Although those thoughts had quickly been replaced with thoughts of that amazing passionate kiss in the garden. Regardless of the wonderful 'friend' night they'd had the night before, she wanted to finish that kiss and her dreams had been filled with finishing that kiss in the shower, sometimes up against a wall – and her favourite was on Finn's huge dining table. Desire and need bubbled through her. She felt like a coke can, all shook up and waiting to explode.

'Knock, knock?' called Zach, as he let himself through the connecting gate.

She sat up, annoyed at the distraction. He was carrying a big bunch of flowers. Casey was right; Zach was good with the charm. He offered them to her, a collection of white roses and tiny little purple flowers interspersed between them, an artfully arranged shop bought bouquet but she didn't take them.

His face fell when he saw she was still angry with him and that made her feel guilty. She hadn't seen him since she accused him of being a letch and she wanted to clear the air between them. Nothing was going to happen between them, the desire she'd first had for him had well and truly passed but Casey seemed to think Zach wasn't a bad person so maybe they could at least be friends.

'I'm so sorry for what I did the other night, it was completely inappropriate and I'm really sorry. I just… I really like sex and you were so keen for it and… I just thought at first you were drunk and I know that's no excuse either. God, I'm sorry. I'm glad Finn was there.'

'So am I.'

He looked distraught.

'Look, you should know more than anyone that it's a horrible thing to take advantage of someone when they're drunk, like Pippa did to you.'

He nodded, sadly. 'I'm not a bad person. I know I like to fool around with women and have a good time but I'm not bad.'

He looked so low, she couldn't help but feel sorry for him.

'You're not bad and I don't want this to come between us anymore. We all make mistakes.'

'We can be friends?' Zach looked at her hopefully.

She nodded in defeat.

His face split into a grin.

'Just friends though, Zach. Nothing is ever going to happen between us, you need to know that.'

'Just friends, I promise.' He grinned mischievously as he stuck out a hand to shake and she reluctantly shook it. 'Does that mean you're still going to come with me to the wedding tomorrow?'

'No, it's not appropriate. I'm sorry, but I think it would mean something different to you than it would to me.'

His mischievous grin faded slightly. He stood to leave and passed her the flowers which she duly took this time. He shoulders were slumped slightly as he walked out, but she knew he wouldn't stay down for long. He was like a jack-in-the-box, he always seemed to bounce back.

But as Finn stepped out from the back of his house, she knew she had bigger problems facing her.

'You ready to go?' he asked.

'Not really.' She stood anyway. 'But let's get it over with.'

*

179

She sat outside the restaurant on a bench, with Finn sitting quietly next to her. Why was she here? She had asked herself that question several times on the train journey into London. She had asked herself that question several more times in the taxi on the way here from the station. What did she want to gain from meeting him today? She never wanted to see his face ever again. Why was she putting herself through this? She took a calming breath and Finn took her hand.

She needed to prove to herself and maybe to Craig that she wasn't scared of him. It had been two years and she was a stronger person because of it. She had learned to fight and to defend herself well and she wouldn't be scared of him. She refused to let him have any control over her and that included any subconscious fears too.

She stood up with renewed determination and walked straight into the restaurant with Finn still holding her hand.

She spotted the policewoman, Annabel, sitting quietly at the table nursing a cup of coffee, and next to her was Craig Peters. He was a lot thinner than she remembered and he'd acquired a bald patch in the last two years too. He sat biting the nails on his hand, looking sad and pathetic.

He stood up when he saw them approach.

'Joy, thank you for meeting with me today.' He stuck his hand out and she ignored it.

His eyes cast to Finn and he paled slightly.

'This is Finn.'

'Her fiancé,' Finn said, staring down at Craig with sheer hate and loathing.

She was surprised by the sudden upgrade in their relationship but she was glad she had Finn there for support.

Craig sat down and Joy and Finn sat opposite him. Annabel smiled warmly at Joy but she didn't say anything, that was down to Craig.

'I wanted to say how sorry I am. What I did that night was

unforgiveable and I'm going to have to live with that for the rest of my life. I have never done anything like that before and nor will I again. I was drunk, I was emotional, my wife had just told me she was cheating on me.' He shook his head. 'There is no excuse, no reason that I can give you that will justify my actions, but I wasn't in the right frame of mind that night. It was never my intention to hurt anyone.'

'You had a knife, what exactly was your intention when you left home with a knife?' Joy spat.

'When your world falls apart, you don't think logically or calmly.'

Joy looked over at Finn who had lost everything the night his wife had aborted his baby and then had it confirmed just over a week later when his wife was caught sleeping with Zach. He'd been angry and moody and determined not to let himself get hurt again, but she knew without having to ask that Finn at no point during his grieving process had ever thought about going out and raping a woman to exact some kind of sick revenge on the gender that had hurt him so spectacularly.

Craig placed his cigarette stained hands on the table. 'I went out that night to scare the shit out of the man that had been screwing my wife. Then after a few drinks I thought I would hurt her by screwing around with someone else, only I couldn't find anyone who was interested. This made me even angrier. I spent my whole school life being rejected by women. I went out the bar and I saw you. This beautiful woman, the type that rejected me at school and in the bar that night. I was furious.' He looked down. 'Everything happened so quickly.' He closed his eyes as if it pained him to remember what he did. Joy felt anger boil through her. How dare he feel pain over what he had done? He had made that decision to rape her, to take away control from her. He deserved to feel all the pain and guilt that he was feeling. She wanted it to chew him up from the inside. If he wanted forgiveness he would have a long wait.

She was done here, she didn't need to hear his feeble excuses anymore. She had proved to herself that she wasn't scared of him – but also, now that she had seen him, she had also seen that he wasn't as tall or foreboding as she had remembered. He was a small, pathetic little excuse for a man and she was so much stronger than him in many, many ways.

She stood up to leave and Finn stood too. 'Is everything working OK down there, since I…' She motioned squeezing with her fist and Craig swallowed.

'It… erm, seems to be'

Joy leaned over the table and got right in his face. 'If I ever find out that you've hurt another woman, I will find you and rip it off, do you understand?'

Craig stared at her in shock and then at Annabel who was busy staring at the inside of her coffee cup as if the world's problems might be solved in there.

Joy slammed her hand on the table and Craig leapt back in shock. 'Do you understand?'

Craig nodded and Joy walked out, followed quickly by Finn.

*

Finn watched Joy step out from the restaurant and look up, smiling at the sun on her face. She laughed to herself and then rounded on Finn with a big grin on her face.

'Are you OK?'

'Better than OK?'

The restaurant door opened and Annabel came out.

'Joy, are you doing OK?'

Joy nodded, still smiling.

Anger swirled in his gut where it had been ever since they had boarded the train. It had now manifested itself into a white-hot ball of rage. This not doing anything was killing him, but he had promised. But there was no way he could leave today without doing the one thing he had promised himself he'd do.

Now was his chance.

'I might just pop to the loo, while I'm here,' Finn said. Joy was too euphoric to notice, though Annabel gave him a look.

'If you see Craig tell him, I'll be back with him in...' She looked at her watch. 'One minute.'

He smiled. That was clear code for, 'don't do anything stupid but you have one minute to say what you need to say.'

He strode in as Annabel distracted Joy outside and as soon as Craig saw him he scrabbled to get out of his seat, but Finn towered over him before he could even stand up. Craig cowered back into his chair.

'I just want to make it very clear, if I ever see you anywhere near my fiancée again I will break every single bone in your fucking body. I would rather go to prison for the rest of my life for murder than have you touch her or any other woman again.'

'Are you guys done here?' Annabel asked sweetly.

'Yes. I just wanted to explain something to Craig, but he understands, don't you?'

Craig nodded again.

Finn nodded his thanks to Annabel and walked out, snagging Joy's hand and walking with her back to the train station.

'I feel great, like this weight has been lifted off me. Did you see him? He was nothing. You on the other hand, with your stupid grumpy face and your split personality, you are simply marvellous.' Laughing, she swung her arms round his neck and kissed him. There wasn't a single bone in his body that was going to stop it. He wrapped his arms round her tight and right there in the middle of the street, as shoppers and parents with children and businessmen and women hurried round them, he kissed her back. She tasted sublime. He knew he could kiss her forever and never tire of it. As someone bumped into them, he shuffled her back into a side alley, not taking his lips from hers. Pinning her against the wall, he felt her pulse skitter with desire along her throat as his hands caressed against her skin. Her hands were in his hair and as he kissed her hard, a moan rumbled in her mouth.

He lifted her and she immediately wrapped her legs round his hips. He pressed into her and she tore her mouth from his, groaning as she arched against him. He moved his mouth to her throat and eyed the hustle and bustle that was going on mere metres away from them on the pavement. It was broad daylight but no one could see or care about what was happening in this darkened part of the alleyway.

Suddenly, she stopped him. 'Let's go home.'

He nodded, keenly, not caring what boundaries had been crossed. He needed her right now and he could deal with his demons later.

Then a thought struck him. 'No, we can't, I have Casey's stag do tonight.'

She paled, her face stricken with guilt. 'Oh god, I'm a terrible friend.' She disentangled herself from his grasp and straightened her dress.

'What's wrong?'

'Oh Finn, I'm no good for you. I'm such a horrible person.'

She walked out the alley and out into the bright sunshine. She waited for him and then they walked back to the train station in complete silence. What the hell had just happened?

*

Joy sat on the train next to Finn without saying a word. Tonight, Casey was going to tell Finn that he loved him. She winced with guilt. Casey had asked her not to do anything with Finn until he'd told him how he felt. They had kissed in the garden, had a sort of date, danced and nearly had hot amazing sex in an alleyway in London. It wasn't the romantic affair of the century but there still should have been some loyalty there. Damn it. She had done exactly what Zach had done with Pippa, she had taken what was rightfully Casey's. He had asked her to wait a few days and she couldn't even do that.

And poor Casey could not only be spectacularly rejected that night, but he could also lose his best friend at the same time. Finn might be really cruel about it. There was nothing she could do to take back what had happened between her and Finn but she had to do something to make sure that Finn treated Casey kindly. Though quite how she was going to do that without revealing Casey's big secret was beyond her.

The train rattled to a stop at their station and they walked back to Finn's truck. He started the engine and drove home. He looked so forlorn.

They pulled up outside his house and he got out, looking thoroughly confused.

'Finn, we need to talk.'

Chapter Thirteen

His face fell a bit. 'I'm not sure I'm ready to have that conversation yet.'

She gestured to go into his house and she followed him into his front room. 'Not about us.'

'Oh. Well, I'm not being funny, but you sort of need to be quick. Casey's coming round in a few minutes, we're having a few drinks to commiserate his last night of freedom.'

'It's Casey I need to talk to you about…' How could she say this without giving away what Casey wanted to say for himself? She took a deep breath. 'Casey's really special.'

Finn arched an eyebrow. 'Yes, he is. Don't tell me you've fallen in love with him, it's a bit bloody late for that.'

'Just listen. He's your best friend?'

'Yes.'

'You've been friends forever?'

'Yes, you know all this, why are you…'

'Friends like him don't come around very often. He's sweet and lovely and generous and fiercely loyal to you. Just don't throw that away.'

'What are you—'

'I'm just saying, don't throw away thirty years of friendship over male pride. He needs you now, god knows this marriage to Arielle is going to be a disaster and he'll need a friend when it's all over.'

'And he'll have one. Two by the looks of things.'

She opened her mouth to continue but he held up a hand to interrupt her. 'Look I'm not sure what this is about, but Casey's my best friend, I love him,' he said simply.

This threw her. Maybe Casey would get his happy ending after all.

His eyes were soft and she was angry that she had doubted him.

'You'd die for your friends, wouldn't you?'

'I'd prefer not to, but yes.'

'Then a kiss isn't too much to ask for, is it?'

He frowned, slightly, still clearly confused. He moved his hands to her waist. 'Is that what you want?'

She touched his cheek. 'Yes, more than anything. But I wasn't actually talking about me.'

This obviously confused him even more, but she was saved from any more awkward questions then by a knock on the door.

Finn continued to stare at her for a moment, then took her hand and started leading her back to the door. 'Maybe we can chat more about this kiss another time, but you need to go, boys only tonight.'

'Hey.' Finn acknowledged Casey as he opened the door.

Joy saw Casey look down at her hand in Finn's and with a huge pang of guilt she watched as he gave a small sigh of defeat.

'Don't worry, Joy was just going.'

Finn gave her hand a little squeeze and then walked back inside. Casey cocked his head at her as he followed him in.

'Good luck,' she whispered.

He gave a small smile and closed the door behind him.

She stood staring at the door for a moment, desperate to know what was going on inside. She hovered, biting her lip. Hoping that Finn or Casey weren't near the front window, she got onto her hands and knees and crawled underneath it to the safety of the side of the house. Her heart was pounding as she edged along the wall towards the kitchen window, which was open a crack. She could hear voices as she approached, inching closer she strained her ears to hear.

'Beer please,' Casey said, from somewhere above her. 'How's things going with you and Joy?'

'I… don't even know how to answer that question. Good, bad, terrible and wonderful all at the same time. You know she's not at all my type.'

Casey and Finn laughed, and Joy had to smile at the absurdity of it all. He'd said it so often he almost believed it himself. Almost.

Joy heard the noise of a beer bottle being opened.

'What is your type?' Casey asked

Ooh, good lead onto the gay topic.

'No one. I'm not interested in any women at the moment, they're a minefield. I prefer to keep my legs and my heart intact.'

Finn couldn't have set up the topic of conversation for Casey more perfectly. And sure enough Casey took the bait.

'What about men?'

His voice was faint though and there was no answer from Finn. In fact, there was no noise at all. Chancing a look, she realised that the kitchen was now empty and they had evidently moved into the lounge. She hurried round the back of the house and then edged round the window, peering through the branches of a climbing rose to see what was going on in the lounge. They were sitting opposite each other Casey on the chair, Finn on the sofa. The windows were closed and she could only surmise what was being said.

Casey was talking – he looked nervous, embarrassed, but he didn't take his eyes off Finn as he spoke. Finn's eyebrows shot up, his mouth falling open slightly as Casey continued to speak.

Finn started shaking his head, he looked really apologetic, though Casey looked sad – his shoulders slumped as he looked down at the floor. He stood up and moved to sit next to Finn and she found herself holding her breath hoping that Finn wouldn't move away, or hurt him. He didn't. Whatever Casey said next though must have been very shocking as Finn's eyes nearly fell out of his head, but then he was nodding and Casey laughed.

She watched as Casey wiped his hands on his jeans and took Finn's face in his hands. Finn watched him carefully and Joy moved closer to the window, her own mouth falling open in shock as Casey leaned forward and kissed Finn on the lips. Resting her face almost on the window she tried to get a better look. She wasn't sure whether Finn was kissing Casey back, but he certainly wasn't pulling away. The kiss continued, long seconds dragged on with her heart hammering in her mouth.

So that was it. Finn was confused about his feelings for her because he was gay or at least bisexual. Maybe he hadn't known himself until now. Maybe he had been trying to deny it, but now Casey had come out to him, he clearly thought it was a good time to come out too.

She was jealous, insanely so, but at the same time she was so pleased for Casey, that he would get his happy ever after. Finn would be happy too, finally finding someone to love that he could trust. His best friend, it didn't get any better than that.

With the kiss still continuing and with tears smarting her eyes, it was time to leave.

She turned away and walked into a clay pillar, the type that plant pots would sit on top of. It toppled and seemingly in slow motion, fell to the floor and smashed. The noise hung heavy in the air and she stared at the broken pieces for a few seconds before she turned and ran. She stepped straight into a plastic flower pot, her foot getting wedged between the sides and the bottom. She was still hobbling about trying to get it off seconds later when Finn opened the French doors and stared at her.

'Enjoy the show, did you?'

She couldn't tell if he was angry or embarrassed.

'I didn't… I…'

There were no words to make the situation better and to her utmost annoyance, the tears that had threatened to come moments before now spilled over.

He stepped towards her. Finally freeing herself from the flowerpot, she turned to run, now more embarrassed than guilty for watching. He caught her arm before she managed to get one step away from him.

Just then Casey appeared in the doorway.

'Ah leave the poor girl alone, she can come in and join us for a few beers.'

'No, god no, I wouldn't want to intrude.'

'Finn, go and get her a beer. I insist you stay, it is my stag do, and you can't say no to the groom the night before the wedding.'

Finn continued to stare at her for a moment, before he let go of her arm and moved off towards the kitchen.

Casey immediately stepped towards her and wiped the tears away from her eyes. He smiled at her. 'He's all yours Joy. I told him everything and as we both knew, he doesn't see me like that.'

'But… you kissed?'

'I asked him if he would let me kiss him, to see if there was anything there, any spark at all.'

'And he agreed?' Joy couldn't help but notice how high-pitched her voice had got.

'He said it was only fair, if I'd been in love with him for fifteen years, then a kiss wasn't too much to ask for.'

Joy smiled at the use of her own words. 'And after? There was nothing?'

Casey shook his head. 'No, not for him. Strangely, not for me either. For a few moments it was like "Yes! I'm finally kissing him," but after that I was surprised by the complete lack of zing in the kiss.'

'Zing?' She smirked.

'You know, the va-va-voom, the pizzazz, the… magic. It just wasn't there. He did say I was a very good kisser though.'

She laughed, wiping away the last of her own tears.

'So, you can have him, with my complete and utter blessing.'

'I kissed him.' She had to tell him. 'He kissed me first, but I kissed him back. And today we kissed again. I'm so sorry.'

But Casey was smiling. 'Was there zing?'

She blushed. 'There was definitely zing.'

'Good. Now come inside and get drunk, I insist.'

He took her hand, and ignoring her protests, dragged her inside.

*

Joy lay on the floor, gripping onto the carpet for dear life – she knew that if she let go, she would slide straight out the lounge door and end up out on the street. The house had tilted and was lying on its side. The room had taken on a very steep incline. The windows were up somewhere where the ceiling had been and the door was down on the floor.

Urgh. She made a mental note never to try to keep up with Finn in a drinking competition. The man had nearly polished off a whole bottle of whisky and still seemed sober.

There had been shots, vodka, tequila, some other foul-tasting stuff. They had drunk a lot of beer. There were drinking games, which she had lost at spectacularly, and they had played on the Wii. After a particularly savage go at horse racing, Joy had fallen against the chair as she tried to sit down and slumped to the floor where she had been ever since.

Casey was now sprawled out, seemingly unconscious on the sofa, and Finn was sitting on the chair above her head, his long legs stretched out over her back, his bare feet crossed at the ankles. He had very large feet.

Finn suddenly got up, carefully ensuring he didn't tread on her as he did so. 'I'm going to bed, I have to be up early tomorrow to look after the groom and deliver my best man speech.'

She wasn't sure who he was speaking to. Casey didn't even respond and she was too busy clinging onto the floor. He disappeared from the room, but came back moments later holding a blanket, identical to the one that she had been wrapped in that day she had woken up in the garden. She lifted her head a little in confusion. So Zach and Finn either shopped in the same place, or Finn had covered her and Zach had lied about it.

Finn covered Casey carefully, tucking him in, and Casey stirred.

'Thanks mate. I still love you.'

She saw Finn smile. 'I love you too.'

Casey giggled, as he drifted back off. 'And do something with that over there.' He waved in her general direction. 'Don't leave her there all night, she'll get cold.'

'Don't worry about her, I'll sort it.'

He ruffled Casey's hair affectionately and turned and picked her up in one easy, fluid movement.

She closed her eyes as the room span around her, then clung to him as she felt him take the stairs.

'What are you doing?'

'Taking you to bed.'

She heard the gasp of shock escape her lips before she could stop it. 'You are not. You can't expect me to sleep with you just because I'm drunk and you're horny, I mean because you're drunk and I'm horny.'

'You're horny?'

'Yes, but I'm not going to jump into bed with you because of it.'

'Love, I don't expect you to jump anywhere tonight, you're a drunken disgrace.'

'I am not.' She surprised herself then by nuzzling into the side of his neck. Her brain didn't seem to be in control of her own body anymore, her limbs responding without any prior consent from her. She watched as her arms wrapped round his neck.

Seemingly unperturbed by this sudden show of affection, Finn continued to the top of the stairs. 'So when you're drunk, you have high moral standards. I must remember that when I want to get into your pants.'

'I do not have high moral standards.' She really didn't. If Finn started to make love to her now, there wasn't a single bone in her body that didn't want it or would stop it. But she had obviously turned argumentative and stubborn all of a sudden.

Finn manoeuvred into the bedroom and lay her down on the bed. 'You don't? So I can get into your pants?'

Joy felt her toes curl with delicious anticipation. 'Yes please.'

He smirked as he pulled off his T-shirt and she was embarrassed by another gasp that fell from her mouth. He was magnificent.

'Here, let me help you get undressed.'

Finn pulled her T-shirt over her head and, feeling like a kid at Christmas who was about to unwrap the best present of all, she quickly reached for the belt on his jeans. He stopped her.

'Joy, I'm not sleeping with you.'

'We don't have to sleep.' She waggled her eyebrows in what she hoped was a saucy way. In the back of her mind, her dignity was slapping herself on her forehead and groaning with disbelief.

'I'm not going to make love to you because you're drunk and I would have to be a complete arsehole to take advantage of you like this.'

'You're drunk too, I could take advantage of you.'

'That's a really tempting offer.' He was teasing her now but she didn't care. 'How about we take a rain check.'

'My dad used to say, "Don't put off till tomorrow what you can do today."'

'That's a good point.'

She watched as he took his jeans off, enjoying his thighs and hips and the obvious bulge behind his pants.

193

He came back to the bed, eyeing her. She swallowed.

'Are you getting undressed or are you sleeping in your jeans?'

Embarrassed, she wriggled out of them. He didn't take his eyes off her for a second. He knelt next to her on the bed. God, she wanted him so much.

'Now... budge over, I can't fit in to the bed unless you do'

Stunned, she did as she was asked. She watched as Finn got into bed next to her, her heart hammering, her palms sweaty. He turned the light off and rolled over to face away from her.

'Goodnight Joy.'

She stared at his back for a moment, then huffily rearranged the duvet over her.

'Comfy?' asked Finn dryly.

'Yes.'

'Good.'

A few minutes later, to her utmost annoyance, Finn was snoring softly.

*

Joy woke with a start and stared straight into Finn's eyes. Just a single look from him melted her insides. She couldn't tear her eyes away and the desire to have him crashed over her in waves. She was falling for this great beast of a man and she knew he was falling for her too.

'You're in my bed,' Finn said, quietly.

'Yes. How are we doing with this whole friends thing?'

'Not good.' He ran a finger down her arm.

She swallowed. 'No, me neither.'

'You know if we just shagged each other, we'd get over each other very quickly and we could just get back to hating each other again.' He laughed, clearly trying to disperse some of the tension in the room.

'That sounds so tempting – but if we hated each other, I'd

194

miss playing Jenga and The Cube with you, I'd miss the dancing and you holding my hand when times get tough.'

Shit, where did that come from?

Finn's eyes softened. 'I will always be here for you.'

Her heart swelled and without a moment's warning she found herself kissing him. Taking her face gently in his large hand, he leaned forward and kissed her too. Her heart exploded in her chest as his lips moved gently against hers. But as her breath shuddered through her lips, the kiss suddenly changed. It was urgent, filled with need. He moved to roll on top of her then paused.

'Sorry,' he mumbled, leaving her confused as he kissed her again, rolling her on top of him, instead.

His hands trailed down her ribs and then back up, running his fingers through her hair. She felt her body quiver under his touch as his hands moved towards the top of her pants.

But as quickly as it started he frustratingly pulled away.

'Damn it, I have a wedding to organise, for my gay best friend apparently. I haven't got time to get into this with you now – and believe me, I really want to get into this with you – but my duties as best man are unfortunately going to have to come first.'

Joy sighed with frustration and rolled off him.

'Look, this isn't me being an ass and changing my mind again – this is me genuinely not having enough time.'

'I know, it's OK.' She hesitated for a second. "Why did you apologise when you were kissing me? You rolled on top of me and rolled straight back off again.'

'I… didn't want you to feel trapped or scared by me being on top.'

She stared at him with a huge lump in her throat. And then rolled on her back groaning with frustration. 'You are making it impossible for me to hate you, you do realise that.'

She climbed out of bed and got dressed as Finn watched her.

'I guess I'll see you later.' She fastened her jeans and pulled her T-shirt over her head.

He climbed out of bed and caught her hand. 'Come to the wedding with me today.'

'I was supposed to be going with Zach.'

'Seriously? Still?'

'Well, I'm not now after his little stunt the other night but I don't think it's fair that I go with you instead. That's kind of rubbing his nose in it. That kind of feels a bit nasty and I'm not that person, especially if he has fallen for me, which I doubt. But just because he's a bit of an ass, doesn't mean I want to hurt him.'

'OK, OK.' He held up his hands in defeat. 'Will you at least dance with me?'

She smiled. 'That I can do.'

He kissed her again, just briefly this time.

'Go take care of your friend.'

He nodded and quickly left the room.

*

Casey sat on the chair with his head in his hands. It was ten past one and he was supposed to be marrying Arielle at one. Finn was outside now, placating the crowds in the beautifully flowered marquee. Everything was perfect out there, his mum had ensured that. The big, expensive country hotel with the salmon and duck canapés awaiting the guests as soon as the ceremony had finished. The welcome drinks of Pimms and lemonade, Buck's Fizz and the finest champagne. The gold chairs positioned either side of the aisle, the flowered archway, the violinist and harpist ready to play the fateful 'Here comes the bride' or whatever else that Arielle had chosen for her big day. The dress, the photographer, the videographer, the waiters and waitresses, the chocolate fountain, the five-tiered cake, the fairy lights that adorned the trees. He felt sick, physically sick.

There was a knock on the summer house door, where he had sought refuge, and Zach walked in.

'How you doing, mate?'

Casey stood. 'I can't do this, I can't.'

Zach moved to straighten Casey's bow tie, watching him carefully. 'Any reason you want to tell me?'

Casey sighed. 'Zach, I'm gay.'

'I know. That's why I've been trying to persuade you for the last few months to call off the wedding, why I've been all but pleading with Mum to lay off you.'

'You know?' Casey was incredulous. 'Why didn't you say anything?'

'I figured you'd tell me when you were ready, preferably before you walked up the aisle and married the bitch from hell.'

'Zach, what am I going to do?'

'Well, you can slip out that window there and run as fast as your scrawny legs can carry you. I'll give you a ten-minute head start then go out and tell everybody the wedding is off.'

Casey laughed, sorely tempted. 'No, if I'm going to cancel the wedding, I need to do that myself. Mum will be heartbroken.'

'Yes she will, but you can't marry Arielle just to keep her happy.'

'I can't break her heart either, she's so excited, so happy for me. It's been so long since I've seen her smile.'

'I know but if she knew the truth, that you're considering marrying someone just for her, she would be even more hurt.'

'I know, but...'

Just then there was another knock on the door and his mum came in. She was flushed with excitement and worry. She was beautiful, dressed in a pale blue suit, which matched her eyes exactly. The only woman he had ever loved. He couldn't do it to her.

'Caz, you OK?'

'No, he's not Mum, he doesn't want to marry Arielle,' Zach spoke quickly and Casey glared at him.

Real hurt flickered in his mum's eyes and her hands shook as she smoothed out his wayward hair. 'Then we'll cancel it,' she said simply.

He gathered her close, resting his head on her shoulder a minute. 'It's fine Mum, it's just nerves. Come on, let's go face the hordes.'

He took her hand and stepped out into the sunshine, ignoring his brother swearing under his breath as he followed them.

*

The wedding was one of the strangest that Joy had ever attended. During the ceremony Casey looked genuinely terrified, Arielle looked bored.

At the point where the registrar asked if anyone here present knew of any reason why they shouldn't get married, almost every single one of Casey's friends shuffled awkwardly. They all knew, despite his best intentions, they knew. To her consternation, several men on the bride's side also shuffled awkwardly as well. It seemed, even to her untrained eye, that Arielle had been spreading herself a bit thin, or spreading her legs a bit too wide.

The ceremony was over quite quickly. There were photos taken, with Casey and Arielle barely cracking a smile and then it was onto the reception inside the hotel.

Her brain was a whirl of emotion. She felt for Casey and what he must be going through, standing up in front of hundreds and declaring his love for someone he couldn't stand. And with the rejection from Finn the day before, he must be miserable.

She kept seeing Rose wandering around and she honestly didn't look happy either, maybe because her husband wasn't there to see the happy day, maybe because she didn't want Arielle as a daughter-in-law or maybe because she could obviously see that Casey was so unhappy.

Zach kept passing her glances that ranged between the guilty hound dog look, to big friendly smiles and even the odd look of lust and desire too. The man just didn't give up, and with a few drinks inside him he was as randy as a dog.

But the final cherry on the top of her trifle of emotions was Finn. The kiss in his bed that morning, the way he had touched her, held her. How much she wanted him. The glances they shared throughout the day were hot – it sizzled and sparked between them. But he was keeping a respectful distance, at least for now.

The band started playing some slow number and those guests on the dancefloor that weren't in a relationship awkwardly moved off it and those that were, clung together, obviously very much in love. Her parents loved to dance, she remembered that. And how they would look at each other as if no one else existed.

A strong hand was suddenly on her back. She looked up into the warm grey eyes of Finn.

'Dance with me?'

She allowed herself to be led onto the dance floor, feeling that delicious surge of lust slice through her at his touch.

He placed his hands on her waist and pulled her gently against him, as she leaned her head on his chest.

'We're rubbish at being friends,' she said, feeling his heartbeat thunder against her ear.

'I know. Are you staying here tonight? Many of the guests are.' Was that an invite?

'I have to be back for Darcy.' She leaned her head against him again, listening to his heart, feeling his warmth.

'I have to get back for Billy, so we can share a cab back if you like.'

'OK.' It was a small thing but she liked the companionship of it. He wanted her and maybe he wasn't ready for a relationship yet, but with time he might be persuaded to risk his heart on her. And she had time. She had decided for the time being at least that Bramble Hill was worth sticking at. The residents were less than welcoming, but she was determined to win over at least one of them.

The song ended way too soon for her liking and Finn kissed her fondly on the head.

'I'm going to get a drink, do you want one?'

She nodded. 'Just a water.'

He disappeared off to the bar and she found herself on the side of the dancefloor, next to the chocolate fountain. Arielle was standing on the other side of the fountain, feeding a chocolate-covered strawberry to a tall man in a grey suit. She didn't seem to care who saw them, Joy noted sourly – she was already married to Casey now, a done deal in her book.

Zach walked past, handing her a flower and a very flirty, drunk smile. He walked away without saying a word, but the hungry look on his face was unmistakable.

'You little bitch,' said a voice Joy recognised immediately as Chloe. Her body's shift into defence mode was a bit slow, either because of the wine and champagne, or because she was still feeling cosily happy after dancing with Finn. But before she had a chance to turn round, Chloe grabbed her hair and forced her headfirst into the chocolate fountain. Joy tried to fight her off, her arms and legs flailing everywhere but not making contact with her attacker. For someone so small, Chloe was freakishly strong. Joy was struggling to breathe, chocolate was everywhere – up her nose, in her mouth, her ears, eyes, pouring down her back. Death by chocolate had taken on a new and terrifying meaning. She fought against Chloe and with her hand on the edges of the fountain she forced her way back up, gasping for breath. The fountain suddenly seemed to tilt and it disappeared from her grip altogether.

There was a collective gasp and the room went deathly quiet as Joy struggled to get the chocolate out of her nose and mouth so she could breathe.

'You cow, you absolute cow,' came Arielle's voice very nearby.

There was chaos then, and Joy had no idea what was happening. There were shouts, screams and the sounds of a fight breaking out. Seconds later, a hand was in hers and she was pulled to one side.

'Stay here.' Finn's voice was quiet and authoritative in her ear. 'I'll be back in a second.'

She still couldn't see and she tried to wipe the chocolate from her eyes, but there was so much on her that as soon as she wiped it away, more flooded back into them.

Finn's hand was back in hers and he pulled her along quite quickly. It felt like they went outside and still he pulled her away from the shouts and crowds. She stumbled in his wake and Joy figured they were heading towards the pool, where there were pool side showers.

Water rained down on her head, it was cold at first but quickly heated up. The chocolate was so thick and the water didn't seem to be doing anything to rid it from her eyes. Hands were on her shoulders, in her hair trying to wipe away the chocolate and then they trailed to her face. Suddenly, Finn was kissing her. She didn't hesitate, after the huge disappointment of not having him that morning, her body responded quickly now before he could change his mind. She kissed him back, matching his hungriness, finding it hugely erotic to kiss him when she couldn't see him.

It took her brain about five seconds to work out that something was wrong with the kiss, something was different from how he had kissed her that morning. She pulled away and wiped the chocolate from her eyes. Blinking blearily through the water, she realised with horror that she had been kissing Zach. And worse, much worse, was Finn standing about ten metres away, his face like thunder.

Chapter Fourteen

He turned and stormed away and Joy immediately chased after him, leaving chocolate puddles across the lawn.

'Finn, wait, please.' She caught up with him and without thinking grabbed his arm with a very chocolatey hand.

He flinched away from her. 'Don't touch me, don't ever come near me again.'

'Wait.' Joy ran round in front of him, blocking his way. 'I thought I was kissing you – you told me to wait for you and the next thing I'm being dragged away, I thought it was you, I couldn't see, you know that...' she gabbled.

His shook his head, his eyes hard as flint. 'Do you know how it made me feel to see his hands on you, to see him kissing you?'

Anger boiled through her. 'What's it to you anyway? If we were in a relationship, you'd have every right to be pissed but we're not, you don't want me enough for that. So you have no right to be jealous.'

'I have every right and you know that. And if we were in a relationship, you can consider yourself dumped, so please, go back to Zach, enjoy yourself.'

With that he moved through the crowd and was gone a moment later.

*

Joy sat on a wooden bench and stared up at the gradually darkening sky. The sun was just setting but the moon was already out prematurely.

What a mess. She had hurt Finn spectacularly just as he had been venturing out of the fortress he had built around his heart. Now he had rushed back inside, probably never to come back out again.

She had given Zach a piece of her mind in front of everyone and he had wandered off like a puppy that had been kicked. And evidently during the chocolate fountain fracas, she had inadvertently knocked the fountain over Arielle and her five-thousand-pound dress.

Although Joy was now clean and had dried in the heat, she hadn't dared show her face back in the hotel again. She had sat out on this bench ever since, in the quiet seclusion of the beautifully manicured gardens. She wanted to go home, but her money to pay for a cab and house keys were inside somewhere and she didn't think enough time had elapsed for her to go safely back in to retrieve them.

She heard someone approaching and she willed for them to walk past, for them not to notice her in the gloom.

Casey rounded the bush and grinned at her. 'Thought you might be out here somewhere. Hungry?' He offered her a heaped plate of nibbles from the buffet and she took it greedily. He sat next to her, slinging his arm round her shoulders.

'Casey, I'm so sorry, I've ruined your whole wedding.'

He shrugged. 'What's a wedding without a bit of drama? Besides I needed something to lift me out of my bad mood, I thought the whole thing was hilarious myself. Arielle was not so keen.'

203

She bit into a sausage roll. 'I need to apologise to her.'

'No, it was that nut job Chloe's fault and Arielle knows that. They had a fight you know, a proper punch up, I think Arielle broke Chloe's nose. She left not long after that. Arielle got changed and the last I saw she was drunk at the bar, happily chatting up one of the barmen. It's fine, you should come back in, it's all but been forgotten.'

'I've hurt Finn…'

'I know, but he knows he's being unreasonable. It was clear to anyone who was watching that you didn't know who you were kissing. He'll come round.'

'How are you doing?' She squeezed his hand.

'I'm OK, I guess. Still wondering how I can possibly get out of it, even though that ship has already sailed. The worst thing is, Zach was right. When I was having my little panic attack just before the wedding, he said that Mum would be even more hurt if she knew I was only getting married for her. I only did it for her, and if she finds out she would be heartbroken.'

Suddenly, there was a giggle and Casey frowned with recognition. Arielle ran past them dressed in a stunning floor length purple dress, pulling along the tall man in the grey suit behind her.

'Hurry Steve,' she laughed, as she ran through some nearby trees.

Casey was very still and quiet next to Joy. Then he stood up and taking her hand he pulled her silently in the direction that Arielle had gone. He took his phone out of his pocket as he walked, flicking on the video camera. The sounds of moans were getting louder as they rounded the bushes.

And there they were, against a statue of a large dragon. Arielle's dress around her waist, her legs wrapped round Steve's hips, his spotty bum pale in the moonlight as he thrust against her. Her head was thrown back in ecstasy, gripping his shoulders.

'Harder Steve, for God's sake harder.'

Joy squeezed Casey's hand next to her as he calmly recorded the whole thing on his phone.

'Fuck me like that little prick can't.'

Joy stepped forward, furious, but Casey, still holding her hand, pulled her back.

Simmering with rage, she found her hands clenched into fists. How could Casey just stand there and let her carry on? Why was he not shouting at her? It was his wedding day and his wife was shagging someone else. If he didn't say anything in a minute then she would.

The sex was over very quickly – poor Steve, with probably a few too many drinks inside him, didn't perform as Arielle would have liked. After what seemed like less than a minute he groaned, shuddered and stopped, leaving her with an enraged and wholly frustrated look on her face.

'Was that it? I didn't risk my marriage for that.'

'Oh, but you did.' Casey stepped forward. 'And "that" is what you call grounds for divorce.'

Arielle's head snapped round in their direction, the colour draining from her face. But Casey was already tugging Joy away, walking purposefully back towards the hotel.

'Casey I'm so sorry,' Joy whispered as she struggled to keep up with him.

'Why? I'm delighted, I've never been happier. I never wanted to be married to her, you know that.'

'Yes, I know, but still the betrayal must hurt?'

'No, I knew she was seeing other men behind my back, I just didn't have any proof. God, I feel so relieved.' He laughed, a bubble of happiness erupted from him. He quickly scrolled through his phone again and dialled a number as the bright lights of the hotel drew nearer.

'Hi, it's me. It's over… I'll tell you all about it when I see you. Yes, I'm coming round now. Be about half an hour… OK.'

Casey shoved his phone in his pocket and she looked at him in confusion. Who had he been talking to?

He pulled her through the bar area where the guests were in

varying stages of drunkenness. She saw Zach flirting with a blonde who he seemed very keen on. Some things never changed. And then there was Finn, and that same desire that she had every time she saw him ripped through her. He was alone – emanating a dark cloud so thick you could practically see it. He stood when he saw her, but she didn't have a chance to stop as Casey was pulling her towards the band.

Finally he released her hand and climbed up on the stage, he mumbled something to the lead singer and the song stopped immediately.

Casey took the microphone and with a big grin on his face he addressed the room.

'I'm afraid the party is over, as is my marriage. I've just caught my wife shagging another man in the grounds of this hotel. Thank you for coming, but you can go home now. Feel free to take your wedding gifts with you and get your money back. Goodnight.'

Casey hopped down from the stage next to Joy and chaos ensued.

Everyone was shouting, some people were cheering.

Arielle's dad lunged drunkenly for Casey. 'How dare you speak about my daughter like that, you little prick.'

He took a swing for him but he missed and ended up falling straight into Joy, knocking her to the ground, landing with his face in her cleavage. She struggled against him, but he was big, drunk and immobile.

Finn was suddenly standing above them, he looked furious. He bent and yanked Arielle's dad off her and to his feet. Arielle's brothers came running – one of them, either the bravest or the stupidest, punched Finn in the stomach, obviously thinking that Finn was hurting his dad. Finn stared at him unmoved and clearly unhurt as the man leapt back, clutching his hand in shock,

Then Arielle was there, her face puce with fury. There was screams, shouts, more punches thrown. Joy scrabbled to her feet, and through the chaos she saw Casey hugging his mum who looked stunned. He kissed her on the cheek and ran outside. She watched him jump into a waiting taxi, and with a wheel spin of gravel it sped away into the night.

*

Joy walked up the drive with her heels in her hand. There was no light apart from that of the moon. The fight had dissipated very quickly after one of the bar staff threw a bucket of ice over everyone. Then the guests had started to leave.

She had expected Casey's mum to be horrified but she seemed somewhat relieved by the whole thing.

Joy had decided to walk home as she had been unable to find her purse with her money for a cab. Zach had disappeared completely and Finn was still not speaking to her, so it seemed the only logical solution. It would probably take an hour, maybe more, her feet were aching already and she still hadn't made it out of the hotel grounds yet.

A cab was winding its way up the drive, another one of the guests leaving. She stepped onto the grassy verge, waiting for it to pass. But as it did, it slowed and stopped. The door opened and Finn got out. She could barely see his eyes, but she knew he was staring at her in his way. She felt her skin prickle, as it always did when he looked at her.

She walked towards him, sighing inwardly.

'Get in.'

Doing as she was told she slid into the back of the taxi. The car shifted under his weight, the same weight that had pinned her to the bed temporarily that morning. She closed her eyes, trying not to remember what it felt like to have his hands on her, to have him touch her.

'Here, I found this.' He passed her purse to her. 'It was under a table.'

'Thanks.'

He looked away, out the window, closing any further conversation.

'I really did think I was kissing you,' she said, quietly.

He didn't say anything. She wouldn't apologise again. He knew he was being very unfair about the whole thing. It was just unfortunate that she had been inadvertently kissing Zach of all people. It must have brought back unpleasant memories of Pippa all over again.

The taxi pulled up outside Finn's house. He leaned forward and paid, before Joy had a chance to even open her purse. He was out and striding up his path a second later.

She climbed out after him, determined to talk to him.

'Finn, wait…'

But he had already disappeared into his house and closed the door.

She stood staring at his door for a moment. It seemed their tentative friendship was well and truly over. He was wrong for her in every way; moody, unpredictable, unable to commit and trust… but her heart ached now so much more than at the ending of any previous relationship, and this one hadn't even started yet.

*

Joy sat on the swing chair, sipping some orange juice and watching a squirrel eating a cracker as it sat on the dividing fence between her and Finn's gardens.

She looked towards the shed, where her chainsaws lay unused and lonely. It had been days since she had carved and her fingers were getting itchy because of it. She still had one more local job to do, courtesy of National Heritage who had hired her to do the three strikes in the woods that stretched alongside all the local villages.

Although the press had not been interested in the new sign that had adorned the entrance to the village, the villagers themselves had apparently been full of excitement at the prospect of The Dark Shadow living amongst them. Mark Dempsey, the supposed Dark Shadow, had reportedly had cakes, pies and casseroles made for him. Casey had said that Mark had been invited to barbeques, dinner, to go hunting, he hadn't paid for a drink in The Pride in the last week. He was thrilled because before he was unveiled as The Dark Shadow, the villagers had ignored him completely, treating him with the same contempt as all newcomers. Well, not all newcomers – Joy was sure Mark hadn't had eggs thrown at him and dog shit posted through his letterbox on a daily basis. He had even been asked to do a carving at the Friendliest Village fete at the end of the month. He of course denied any knowledge of chainsaws and carving, but the villagers had all just smiled knowingly at him.

Whilst the attention was on him, it might be easy to slip out and do the last strike, but the threat of getting found out was not a pleasant one. She had other jobs to do, further away. She could do those and do the final local job in a few weeks' time.

She diverted her attention back to Finn's garden. She really needed to talk to him. Maybe they didn't have a future together, if he couldn't trust her then they definitely didn't, but she didn't want to go back to how they were before – bitching and sniping at each other over misplaced feelings.

Right on cue he stepped outside. He froze when he saw her, then he turned away and walked towards his shed.

'Finn, wait.' She ran through the connecting gate. 'This is silly, you know I thought I was kissing you. I lay in bed with you yesterday morning kissing you, we had been dancing together mere moments before…'

He turned so quickly that she nearly ran into him. 'I would have thought you would have been able to tell the difference between his kiss and mine.'

'I did, that's why I stopped, I realised it wasn't you.' She reached for him but he stepped away.

'It took you long enough to come to that conclusion.' He sighed. 'Look, me and you being friends, or friends with benefits or whatever the fuck it was, it's a really bad idea. Someone would get hurt. I clearly can't do relationships, I'm rubbish at them. So let's just say we gave it our best shot and leave it at that.'

'Gave it our best shot? Are you kidding? You didn't even give me a chance. If that's your best shot then you have a hell of a lot to learn about relationships.'

He stormed away and slammed the shed door behind him.

That man. Why did he infuriate her so much and why did it hurt her so much too?

*

Finn was on his hands and knees weeding in the back garden, when he heard Joy's back door open. Despite his best intentions, he peered through a tiny hole in the fence to look at her. She came out with Alex to stand on the decking. She passed Alex a beer and sighed. She looked so small and vulnerable then and Finn found, despite the betrayal, that the overwhelming need to hold her, to protect her was still there.

Alex, obviously very good at the big brother job, picked up on her mood immediately. Without even stopping to ask what was wrong, he immediately pulled her into a big bear hug, holding her tight. She stood limp in his arms for just a second, obviously trying to pretend nothing was wrong, before she wrapped her arms around him and clung to him.

Finn swallowed uncomfortably as he watched, angry that she could still have this effect on him. Alex held her for a while, then pulled her to sit in the swing chair next to him.

'Come on Joy, tell me?'

'I've missed you.'

'Is that what this is about? Because that's silly, you know you are welcome to come and stay any time you want. Hell, you can come back and live with me if it's not working out for you here, you know that.'

'It's just been a long week.'

'Casey told me a bit about the wedding, sounds eventful. He also said that you and Finn were…'

'There is no me and Finn, I guess that's part of the problem.'

'Casey said that Finn looked after you when you were sick, that you spent the night together before the wedding. That sounds like something to me.'

Finn watched her pick at a small scar on her knee – she looked so small, so forlorn.

'He doesn't want anything to do with me.'

'Why not? You're brilliant, funny, beautiful – the man must be stupid if he can't see that.'

'After I lay in bed with Finn and kissed him, I went to the wedding and kissed another man.' Her voice was hollow as she spoke, though her eyes were filled with real pain.

Alex gasped whilst Finn blushed at the raw honesty that Joy and Alex had in their relationship.

'Joy, that's not like you.'

'I thought I was kissing Finn. Long story short, I got pushed into a chocolate fountain, got covered in chocolate and when my neighbour kissed me, the same neighbour that slept with Finn's ex-wife two years ago, I thought it was Finn and kissed him back.'

Alex to his credit only blinked once at the chocolate fountain part, clearly this sort of thing happened to Joy all the time.

'And now he's angry? Idiot.'

'God Al, he's behaving like a child that's been bitten by a dog. After what happened with his ex-wife, he's too scared to go near women again, afraid that he'll get hurt all over again.'

Alex picked at the label around his bottle. 'You need to give him time. You don't know what it's like to have your heart broken. You've never been in love, not with Ed or Jake. But that moment

211

when you realise the person you're completely in love with doesn't love you back, that feeling is unbearable.'

Finn watched as Joy sighed heavily. He tried to ignore the huge lump in his throat, the feeling of guilt, of needing to protect her, crashing through him like a tidal wave.

'I'm falling for him,' she said, quietly.

Alex leaned forward to study her face, his mouth dropped slightly. 'Oh shit Joy, you're not?'

'I can't help it, there's something between us and it won't go away. I've never felt this way before, with anyone. He's all I can think about, his kiss, his touch, his unbelievable kindness. It's driving me mad.'

Finn felt his heart crash into his stomach because he felt exactly the same

Alex stared at her for a moment. 'Then he's worth fighting for.'

Joy shook her head. 'I'm not what he wants. He won't fight for us and I can't win this battle on my own.'

'Then the man really is a bloody idiot.'

They sat in silence for a while as Finn stared at the woman he knew he was in love with. She was going to ruin him, she was going to break his heart into a million pieces but he couldn't keep away from her either. Joy was right, there was something between them and sooner or later it was going to come to a head.

'Look, change of subject before I'm forced to go round there and teach the man some manners.'

Finn saw Joy smile at this.

'I got some legal advice about the shit that the villagers are putting you through. My solicitor said you'd have a very strong case for harassment. He gave me this, it's basically a letter saying that you're going to take them to court if they do not cease and desist all actions against you.'

'I don't know who to give this to, we still don't know who it is that's targeting me.'

'Then you post it through every damn door in the village, with a big pile of dog shit too.'

Joy laughed and Finn hated that he wanted to do everything in his power to keep that smile on her face.

*

The sun was just beginning its descent into the hills, leaving behind trails of candy floss pink and tangerine in the pale blue sky. Joy had already loaded her car with her chainsaws and other power tools and was just wandering back to collect the little power generator when she noticed Darcy lying at the back of the garden.

She had to get her in; the job wasn't a local one tonight and she would be gone for several hours. Fishing out one of the dog treats she habitually carried round in her pocket, she walked over to her.

'Darcy!' She changed her tone to one of excitement, expecting to get an enthusiastic tail wag, as was her usual response. Nothing. The great lump was probably very deeply asleep. She stroked her gently, waiting for her to stir, she didn't want to scare Darcy out of her dreams. Still no response. Feeling cold prickle her skin, she scooted nearer to Darcy's head and felt the bottom fall out of her world. Darcy's eyes were open, but were misty, glazed over, unseeing, unknowing.

Chapter Fifteen

'Shit, no, no, no, no. Darcy, please, wake up, look at me baby, I have your favourite treat here look.' Joy waggled the treat under her nose, shaking her hard but there was still no response.

With her heart racing, she pressed her ear to Darcy's mouth. The dog was still breathing, but it was erratic, faint, laboured.

Stumbling to her feet, Joy knew she had to get her to a vet. Finn would know the nearest one… God no, he wasn't speaking to her. She didn't have time for grovelled apologies and angry looks now. Zach would help.

She ran through the house, out the front and hammered on Zach's door. But there was no answer. She looked round at the other nearby houses, but there was no one here that would help her.

Finn. He was her only answer now and if she had to get down on bended knee she would do it.

Wiping the tears from her eyes she banged on Finn's door, as new tears coursed down her cheeks.

He opened the door and immediately stepped forward towards her. Was he still angry?

'Finn, it's Darcy…'

'Where is she?'

214

'In the garden… please…'

He turned away from her and she was horrified that he wasn't going to help her.

He glanced back as he strode purposefully away, in two quick strides he was back in front of her, he grabbed her hand and pulled her through the house towards the garden. Relief coursed through her as he dragged her through the connecting gate and looked around.

'At the end,' Joy managed weakly and Finn let go of her hand and hurried to Darcy's side. Joy quickly followed him.

He peered in her eyes, listened to her breathing just as Joy had done, then prised her mouth open and reached inside to see if anything was stuck in her throat. Of course, she could be choking. But Finn shook his head.

'Get my keys; they're in the bowl by the front door, open the truck.'

He stood and with a bit of effort he picked Darcy up, her great head lolling in his arms as he carried her. Joy sprinted back through Finn's house, grabbed the keys and opened the back door of the truck for Finn as he struggled out with the huge dog in his arms. He laid Darcy down carefully, with such tenderness, then ran round to the driver's side. Joy quickly closed the front doors to her and Finn's houses as Finn fired the engine behind her.

A moment later, she leapt into the passenger seat and Finn took off up the road.

*

Joy shielded her eyes against the glare of the sun as it rose above the hills. Her eyes were raw from all the crying and she was beyond tired. Finn was silent next to her, as he drove her back towards the village, though he hadn't said much for the last ten hours, since she had knocked on his door.

Rat poison? How on earth had Darcy eaten or come into contact with rat poison?

She turned around in her seat and watched Darcy lying in the back. Darcy eyed her sleepily, her expression almost sheepish, almost as if she was apologising for all the worry she'd put her through.

Finn had driven her to the emergency vet in the next town of Ashton Woods. The vet had examined Darcy and declared it was almost definitely rat poison and had kindly said she was unlikely to make it through the night. Joy hadn't heard what he had said after that, about the medical procedures he would try to save her or how much it would cost, she had just nodded numbly.

Time had moved slowly in the waiting room and it seemed to Joy like she was in a bubble, unaware of anything that had been going on around her as she sat in the hard plastic chairs waiting for news. At one point, through the numbness, she had realised she was sitting on Finn's lap, his arms round her as she sobbed against him. She had no recollection of how she had got there or how long she had spent on his lap, but she made no attempt to move and he did nothing to move her either.

A little after midnight the vet came out to say that Darcy was responding well to treatment, that she was conscious but not out of the woods yet. She remembered telling Finn to go home, that he didn't need to wait with her, but he hadn't moved.

It had been one of the longest nights of her life. Though at around four in the morning it was clear that Darcy was alive and kicking and Joy had been allowed to sit with her for a while as Darcy revelled in the attention that Joy lavished on her.

The vet had kept her in for another few hours before she had finally been discharged. The vet had been stunned by Darcy's miraculous and quick recovery and said that it helped that Darcy was so big, that a smaller dog would probably have died instantly, and she probably had not ingested as much poison as originally thought.

216

Finn pulled up outside her house and Joy hopped down and opened the door for Darcy. She seemed a bit sleepy still but managed to get out OK and ambled slowly up the path towards the front door. Joy let her in and followed Darcy down to the kitchen where she put down fresh water and food for her. Darcy drank greedily and had a few mouthfuls of food and then climbed onto the sofa and was snoring loudly a few moments later.

Joy watched her, smiling to herself.

'You should try to get some sleep yourself,' Finn said from behind her and she jolted slightly, not realising that he had followed her in.

'I will. You too. You didn't have to stay.'

'I wanted to.'

She swallowed and moved towards him quickly before her brain woke up and stopped her. Reaching up she kissed him on the lips, his mouth instantly responding against hers, his hands round her waist pulling her close. She pulled away, staring into his eyes.

'Thank you.'

He stared at her, then kissed her briefly on the forehead. 'I'll check in on her later.'

With that, he was gone, letting himself out through the back door.

Wrapping herself in Finn's blanket, she lay down on the other sofa to watch Darcy sleep.

*

It was late afternoon when Joy woke, stiff from lying on the sofa – it really was uncomfortable. She immediately sat up; startled that Darcy was gone from the opposite sofa. She got up and saw Darcy sleeping in the sun out on the decking. Her food bowl was empty so obviously she was feeling better if she was eating.

She stepped out onto the decking, wrapping the blanket round her.

'Darcy!'

Darcy looked up at her, wagging her tail, still with that sheepish look on her face.

Joy giggled and knelt down next to her, intending to spend the whole day stroking Darcy.

Though as a slight breeze stirred around them and she caught a whiff of her skin, she thought maybe a shower would be more timely before the stroking marathon started.

*

Joy had just finished unloading her car as the sun was setting over the tiny village. She didn't like to leave her tools in the car overnight. The sum total of the tools' worth was more than the value of the car itself, and if someone broke into her car and stole them it would take her weeks to amass such a varied collection again.

The job could wait a few days; that was the great thing about being The Dark Shadow, she could set her own timetable.

She noticed that people were leaving their houses and heading for the pub. As she looked around and her eyes cast up the hill, it seemed that every single person that lived in the village was heading that way.

Finn's front door opened and he came out too.

'What's going on?' Joy said.

'I've called a village meeting,' Finn said, closing his front door behind him.

'Well, I'm coming too.'

'No, I don't want you there.'

Joy stepped back as if he'd physically hit her.

He walked straight up to her and put his hands on her shoulders. 'We're fighting back baby. They're not going to get away with this shit anymore.'

He kissed her head and strode off into the sunset. Her knight in shining armour. All he needed was the white horse.

Finn stood outside the pub as he waited for everyone to arrive. There was a frisson of excitement amongst the villagers. They loved him, he could do no wrong in their eyes. They smiled at him indulgently as they walked into the pub. He was their hero and he was about to hit them where it hurt.

As the last straggler walked into The Pride, he followed them in, moving his way through the crowd of people who had filled the pub. He didn't even care about his strict rule to not get involved anymore. He was beyond angry. As he reached the front of the pub the villagers fell quiet. Some were smiling, some were excited, some were just curious. He had never done anything like this before so no one quite knew what to expect.

'I'm leaving Bramble Hill,' Finn announced.

There were murmurs of disbelief and shock.

'Why? You're happy here,' cried Mrs Yates.

'What you guys are doing to Joy Cartier is making me sick and I cannot be a member of this village anymore.'

'No, she's not one of us,' someone else shouted from the back of the pub.

'She needs to leave.'

'We want her out.'

There were other shouts and people started talking between themselves, nodding, plotting, creating new plans to fight against the witch. He had riled them up and in a minute they were going to march from here, gather their pitchforks and burn the witch at the stake.

He slammed his fist down on the table and they all grew quiet.

'She has nothing to do with Mrs Kemblewick being ousted from the village – and I know none of you believe that but it's true. Her only crime is having a similar name to her landlord Joe Carter but you sick fuckers poisoned her and then tried to kill her dog. What the hell is wrong with you? If I catch who is responsible for that I will tear you apart with my bare hands. As it is, I will be leaving in the next month unless I see that this hate campaign against her has stopped. But in the meantime, if any of you go anywhere near her house you will have me to answer to – and if you think I'm angry now, this is nothing if she gets hurt.'

There were more murmurs and then a voice rang out from the back of the room.

'Thanks Finn.'

The crowd parted like the Red Sea and Joy was standing there, looking wild and insanely beautiful. The villagers shifted angrily around her. Good god, they were going to kill her and she had no idea. He hurried towards her, casting evil glances at anyone who was close to her. They backed off, slightly.

'I have sought legal and criminal advice and every single one of you is going to be contacted by the police over the next few days. Fingerprints will be taken and you're going to have to account for your whereabouts over the last few days.' She passed out copies of the letter that Finn knew Alex had given her. 'The faeces that has been posted through my letterbox is being analysed and it's only a matter of time before they find which dog it belongs to. If it's your dog, you're looking at a criminal record and a hefty fine at the very least. I have already given the police the names of the people that threw eggs at me and spat at me—'

Jesus, she was spat at, this was getting worse and worse. Finn moved to her side, wanting to protect her from everything.

'—and the police are very interested in speaking to those people especially. Fingerprints have already been lifted off the pie dish that the poisoned quiche was in and the brick that was thrown through my window. It won't take them long to trace where they came from. Attempted murder has a very hefty prison sentence. Some of you are going to jail for a very long time and quite honestly I hope you rot there. And the rest of you that have not been involved in the poisoning of myself and my dog, my solicitor is very confident they can take you all to court for harassment. If you want to kick me down, I'm going to bring every single one of you fuckers down with me.'

With that, Joy turned and walked out the pub and Finn hurried after her.

She didn't stop walking as he fell in at her side. She was breathing deeply through her nose as she strode back to her house, with her head held high. Eventually, he caught her hand and pulled her round to face him.

'That was incredible.'

'Well, I couldn't let you have all the fun. You were prepared to fight my corner and I wasn't prepared to fight it myself. Enough is enough. Someone is going to pay for what they did to Darcy.'

'I love this fiery side to you.'

'I love this side to you that fights back. If you fought as hard for us, we could be lying in your bed round about now, having hot passionate sex. Instead, you were willing to throw it all away over one stupid kiss.'

She turned away. Wow, she was going all out to fight everyone tonight. He caught her hand again and before she could say another thing he kissed her, hard.

She didn't even protest, she kissed him back with equal vigour, her hands immediately in his hair as he yanked her against him. He could feel her heart thundering against her chest as he slid his tongue into her mouth, tasting her, devouring her every breath.

He pulled away slightly. 'Let's go back to mine, we can talk about this some more.'

She shook her head. 'No talking, we've talked about it enough. This thing between us isn't going to go away, so let's have one night, no rules, no promises, no labels – and let's see if we have something worth fighting for.'

'Agreed.'

He grabbed her hand and marched the last hundred yards back to his house. He pulled her inside and pinned her against the door, kissing her again.

Chapter Sixteen

God, his kiss, it was insane the feelings it sparked in her. He pulled away slightly to look at her, his eyes dark with lust and need, he looked like he wanted to devour her. It sent a rush of longing straight to her groin.

'You call the shots, you're in control. I'm not going to do anything here that might intimidate you.'

She wrapped her arms round his neck and kissed him again. This man. How could he be so ferocious, so sexy and still so caring at the same time? Right then and there she was willing to surrender every single bit of control to him. 'I'm not scared of you.'

His hands travelled all over her body, barely touching, just skimming her ribs, her arms, stroking through her hair. She seemed to have forgotten how to breathe. Her body was shaking with suppressed need,

His taste – salty, earthy, sweet – she couldn't get enough. He moved his mouth to her throat and she felt him smile as he no doubt felt her pulse hammering against his lips. His kisses were relentless as his mouth travelled slowly over her collar bone and back up her throat. She felt her breathing accelerate as he slipped a hand inside her dress, running his fingers over her nipple.

'Tell me to stop and I'll stop.' His voice was no more than a whisper now.

There was no way that word would pass her lips.

He grabbed the material at her hips and yanked the dress over her head. She was shocked by this sudden need, but not nearly as shocked as when he filled his hands with her breasts, running his fingers over her nipples through the material of her bra. As he kissed her, urgently, her bra came off and his hands were back on her breasts again. His skin was rough, but his hands were gentle.

With a noise that sounded like a growl escaping his throat, he lifted her. She wrapped her legs round his waist as he pressed her into the wall with his enormous frame. That feeling, that need, travelled quickly down her stomach and straight to her groin. She arched against him, desperate to feel him between her legs. His mouth was on her breast, his tongue rough as it travelled across her nipple. Sensation ripped through her and she grabbed his hair as her body shuddered against his.

His mouth was back on hers as he carried her to the top of some drawers, where he sat her whilst his hands explored her body again.

Realising that he was still fully clothed, she quickly rid him of his shirt and let her hands travel across his chest. She found his pierced nipple and tore her mouth from Finn's as he was shifting her legs further apart.

'Wait.' She was thrown for a second by the guttural moan of frustration from Finn. 'No, just a second, I promise.'

She lowered her head and licked his nipple. She remembered doing this when she had been high on poisonous mushrooms, but with her addled brain it didn't feel half as good as it did now. The feel of the metal under her tongue, the feel of the nipple – hard through the metal – made her gut clench. He groaned loudly as she quickly undid his jeans and pushed them and his pants off his hips. She sucked on the nipple, twirling her tongue around the metal as he took the brief interlude to rid her of her pants.

The sound of material tearing snapped her out of her reverie. She stared at the scraps of material in his hands, he had pulled them apart as if they were made of paper. He didn't even look guilty.

Taking her face in one hand, he kissed her again, whilst she heard him fumbling in the top drawer.

He tore his mouth away from hers for a second as he ripped open the condom wrapper and her attention was finally drawn down as he rolled the condom on. She felt her eyes widen and a frisson of nerves sliced through the desire.

'Don't look at it like that, I know what I'm doing.'

'I'm sure you do.' She wrapped her legs around his hips again, pulling him closer.

His hands moved to her hips, tilting her back slightly.

'Is this OK?'

She nodded.

He kissed her again, his tongue writhing against hers as he shuffled closer. She could feel him, tantalizingly close but still the kiss continued.

'Finn, please.'

He tilted her back even more, leaning over her as he kissed her and with his large hands gripping her hips, he gently pushed inside.

She let out an embarrassing noise that was half between a moan and a gurgle and he smirked. She tightened her grip around him with her legs, pulling him close with her arms, and with no gap left between them, with his eyes staring into hers, he started to move against her.

*

Joy lay on the sofa staring out the window, with Finn curled around her back, holding her against him. What had just happened? Sex wasn't supposed to be like that. If it was, no one would ever get any work done, no one would leave their homes. She thought back to her previous sexual partners; none of them had come anywhere close to what had just happened with Finn.

It had started off gentle as Finn, determined not to hurt her, had held himself back – but suddenly all at once, by some unspoken mutual agreement, everything had changed. It was urgent, a desperate need – lips clashed, hands grabbed, she couldn't take enough, she wanted more and he gave her everything he had. Where before her orgasms had been slow to build and then culminated in a ripple of pleasure, with Finn her orgasm had ripped through her so fast she wasn't even prepared for it. And it wasn't a ripple of pleasure but a tidal wave that seemed to roar through her body and went on and on as Finn poured himself into her again and again.

It had been over half an hour since they had moved to the sofa, and although her body had finally stopped shaking, her heart was still pounding against her chest.

'Did I hurt you?' Finn asked, as he kissed the top of her spine.

'Not for one second.'

'You haven't said a word.'

She turned around in his arms and as she stroked his face, she saw the concern fade from his eyes. 'I'm still in shock. Is that what sex is normally like for you? Was that just a normal regular shag for you because I can honestly say I've never had sex like that?'

'No, that was incredible.'

She smiled. 'For me too.'

She leaned up and kissed him softly, and he pulled her gently against him but as it seemed it was going to turn into something else he pulled away.

'Let's go to bed.'

He climbed off the sofa and offered her his hand. She took it willingly as he led her up the stairs. She only hoped there was going to be more hot sex to come.

*

She woke in the muted greys of the early morning as Finn ran soft kisses across her collar bone and gentle caresses up and down her hip.

'Hello,' he whispered.

'Hi.'

He resumed his kisses, trailing his hot mouth across her throat and slowly leaning over her so he could carry on his kisses on the shoulder that was the furthest away from him. His hands caressed as he peppered her body with gentle kisses, but slowly, inch by inch he moved so he was on top of her. There was no weight on her at all and he watched her carefully as he carried on kissing her. There wasn't a single part of her that could find any fear in what he was doing. He was big and strong but the only thing she wanted was to feel that strength against her. As he slowly moved his way back up her body, nudging her legs apart, she could see he was waiting for permission. She wrapped her arms round his broad shoulders and pulled him close to her, kissing him hard. He slipped ever so slowly inside her, and as he started to move she waited for that same passion as before to take over, for that mindless, animalistic, raw sex. But this time was very different – every move was slow and considered, every touch was tender and loving, it was sweet and incredible and wonderful all at once. He didn't take his eyes off her for one second as he made love to her. This was infinitely worse than the time before because with every gentle thrust, with every kiss and every caress she could feel herself falling deeper and deeper in love with him.

*

Joy woke the next day, lying on Finn's chest. He wasn't awake yet, his breathing was heavy, his hand was in her hair.

Making love had not been part of the plan. The kisses, the touches, the looks had been soft and languid. The tenderness he had shown her had made her feel so cherished. It was hard to believe that he only wanted sex from her after that. The worst thing was, that thing she had been looking for, that feeling of home she had spent years searching for, she hadn't found it in the brick walls of a house, but in his arms. With his mouth against hers, when he was buried inside her, when their arms and legs had been tangled together, she had felt more at home there than any house she had ever lived in before.

If the night before was meant to eradicate that need for him from her system, it'd had the opposite effect. Now she'd had a taste of him, she needed more. But that wasn't what it had been about for Finn, she knew that and she didn't think she could bear to be there for the 'let's just be friends' speech later that morning. It was time to go.

She slipped quietly from the bed and as he slept on undisturbed, she ran from the room and down the stairs. She found her dress, pulled it on and ran out the back door and into the safety of her own home.

It was half an hour later before Finn came to find her as she tried to distract herself with some atrocious sketches.

He was wearing shorts and nothing else, and by the sleepy, dishevelled expression, he'd only just woken up.

'Are you OK?'

'Yes. No. I'm not really sure.' She shaded the fur of a black panther so ferociously that she tore the page. She threw her pencil across the room and it bounced off the wall by Finn's head.

'Do you want to talk about it, did I do something wrong?'

'Yes.' She stood up. 'You made love to me. It was supposed to be a night of hot, hard sex and you made love to me, that wasn't part of the plan.'

'You left this morning because I made love to you?' Finn was clearly confused.

'I really didn't want to be there for the "that was a great, meaningless shag" speech. I don't do one night stands Finn, I never have, I'm not sure what possessed me to start now.'

'It doesn't have to be a one night stand, we could do it again if you like, we can do it every night if you wish.'

She shook her head. How could it mean so much to her and so little to him?

'And how would that work? Would we shag monogamously?'

She saw his eyes darken, what right did he have to be angry? 'Yes, of course.'

'That's starting to sound a bit like a relationship to me and you don't want one of those.' She sighed, all the fight going out of her. 'Someone would get hurt Finn and most likely it would be me. Despite your moods, and your silly, grumpy, gorgeous face, despite the fact that you stomp around like a child half the time and like a bear with a sore head the other half, you're kind and sweet and protective and funny and amazing in bed – and I've stupidly gone and fallen for you.'

She watched the fear in his eyes but he didn't run away.

He moved closer. 'What is it you want?'

She laughed hollowly. 'I don't know. The whole caboodle. Picnics in the woods, walking our dogs together over the fields, meals out in little country pubs, dancing in the moonlight, lying in front of the fire and making love on a cold winter's night. I want the cliché, I want my happy ever after.'

She flushed. Really, she should run through what she wanted to say in her brain at least twice before she allowed her mouth to articulate it. Where was the rulebook when it came to playing the game? Surely she shouldn't be so honest with him. Indifferent, blasé maybe, but not honest to the point of blunt. They hadn't even been out on a date yet and already she was telling him she wanted to marry him. No guy wanted to hear that. How humiliating.

She moved to walk away from him but Finn caught her hand.

'I'm sorry that I can't give you what you want. I'm trying really hard to be ready for a relationship. I'm just not there yet.'

'You know the best way to find out if you can trust somebody is to trust them.'

He ran a finger down her cheek. 'It's not like lending you some money and waiting for you to pay it back, or leaving my wallet in your house to see if you return it. This is my heart. It's already been stamped on once and the pain was unbearable. I'm not willing to get hurt like that again.'

Touched by his vulnerability and candour, she held his hand against her lips and kissed him. 'And I'm not willing for us to have a purely physical relationship either, so I guess we have ourselves a stalemate.'

He stared at her for a moment, kissed her on the forehead and walked away.

It seemed she wasn't worth fighting for after all.

*

Joy took a long swig from her beer as Casey settled himself into the chair opposite, his eyes hidden by the sunglasses he was wearing. Grateful that her own sunglasses would hide her red puffy eyes, she watched him carefully. He looked happy and relaxed sitting barefoot in her garden, but his smile was hiding something. His happiness rubbed off on her and she leaned forward smiling. God, it was good to see him.

'Come on, Fallowfield, out with it.'

He laughed. 'Jesus Joy, want a job with CID? We could do with someone like you.'

Giving him a few minutes' grace as he shifted awkwardly under her gaze, she leaned back in her seat and watched a huge group of people trudging from the village and up into the hills.

'Where are they going?'

He swivelled round to look and turned back. 'Deer hunting.'

'You're kidding?'

He shook his head.

The villagers really were a sick bunch if they could kill something so pure and innocent as a deer.

She changed the subject. 'Aren't you supposed to be on honeymoon round about now, lying on a beach in St Lucia being served mojitos by some hot barman?'

He smiled. 'Damn it, why didn't I think of that? Actually, I didn't really want to go on my own. There would have been something very depressing about lying in my honeymoon suite all alone for two weeks.'

'Hell, I would have gone with you, we could have pretended to be husband and wife for two weeks. I would have rubbed suntan lotion into your back and turned a blind eye whilst you fooled around with the pool boy.'

'Very sweet of you, but I've spent the last fifteen years pretending to be someone I'm not, I couldn't do it anymore. Besides, going on holiday kind of felt like running away; it's time to face the music.'

She grabbed a handful of cashew nuts and shoved the bowl across the table towards him. 'So your mum now knows the reason your marriage broke up.'

'Joy the reason my marriage broke up was because my wife was caught shagging another man, you know that. If that hadn't happened I'd be sitting on a beach in St Lucia wondering about faking my own death round about now, just so I could finally start to live the life I want to live. However, now the deed is done, I spent a very long time yesterday talking to my mum about my sexuality. She cried buckets.'

'Oh god Casey, of disappointment?'

'No, because I never felt I could tell her that I was living a lie and that I was only marrying Arielle to keep her happy. She was distraught. But finally, after the tears had stopped, she told me how happy she was for me, that I had finally come out. I told her that if she wanted to keep it quiet I would understand and I would ensure I was very discreet. But she was adamant that she wasn't ashamed of me, that she loved me and was very proud of me and if I was to bring a man along to any of the many functions… she would be happy as long as I was happy.'

'That's great. Oh, I'm so pleased for you.'

He swept his hair from his face. 'I know, all these years of hiding and it was for nothing. I feel an idiot. You don't know how light I feel, like a weight has been lifted from my shoulders. I'm gay and now I can finally shout about it.'

She laughed, then moved in for the strike. 'But that's not what has you smiling like the cat that's got the cream.'

He blushed as he examined a stray thread on his shorts. 'I've met someone.'

'Good god, that was quick. When did this happen?'

He smiled again and she wished he would take his glasses off so she could see his eyes. 'Yesterday, Alex took me to a gay bar, my first one, I was so excited.'

'And this man was there? What's he like, what's his name, did anything happen?'

Casey smiled that sweet, happy smile again. 'We're taking it really slow, seeing how things go. We kissed, that was it. But I'm seeing him again. I'd like you to meet him, at some point. Not yet, but if it turns into something more then I definitely want you two to meet.'

Stunned by this huge gesture of friendship, she took a huge swig of beer. 'I would love to, anyone that makes you this happy must be pretty special.'

'I think he is, but as I said, we're taking it slow.'

'Was there Zing?'

He laughed. 'There was definitely Zing.'

'Ooh, what about Alex? Did he pull? Was there anyone that took his fancy?'

He frowned slightly. 'Shouldn't you be asking him those questions?'

'Oh, he rarely tells me anything about his love life. He was involved with someone, quite seriously about two and half, three years ago but that ended sourly and Al ended up with a broken heart. As far as I know there hasn't been anyone serious since. I'd love for him to find someone special, for him to be happy too.'

Casey took his sunglasses off and rubbed his head. 'I don't want to speak for him but there was one man who he seemed to spend more time with than anyone else. When we left, he was grinning hugely.'

Joy clapped her hands together excitedly.

Just then her phone rang on the table between them. She leaned forward and saw that it was Alex ringing. 'Oh, talk of the devil.'

Casey leapt up and grabbed the phone from her hand before she could answer it.

'Don't you dare say I told you that! If he wants to tell you about his mystery man then that's down to him. But you didn't hear it from me.'

Burning with curiosity, she nodded reluctantly and he passed her back the phone.

'Hey!' She answered it whilst Casey watched her intently.

'Hey, my lovely little sister, how are you?'

'All the better for speaking to you.' And that was the truth.

He laughed.

'You sound happy.' She ignored Casey's scowl. 'Casey said you went to a gay bar yesterday.' Casey reached across and pinched her. 'Ow!'

'What's up?'

'Nothing, just stubbed my toe.' She returned Casey's glare.

'You're so clumsy. Yes, we went to Dazzles; you know I can't resist that place.'

She laughed. She'd been there a few times with Alex herself – it was a cheesy place, but the drinks flowed cheaply and the clientele were a happy, laidback bunch.

'You sure know how to show a man a good time.'

'Hey, he had a good time,' Alex said defensively. 'Did he say he had a good time?'

'Yes, he did. He said he met someone nice.'

She could almost hear Alex smile on the other end. 'Yeah, he did, well, the other guy seems nice. Not bad for Casey's first night out. I'm quite proud of him.'

Still ignoring the scowl, she pressed on. 'Take care of him though Al. I don't want to see him get hurt.'

The scowl fell from Casey's face immediately, his mouth hanging open slightly in shock.

'I will, I promise.'

Joy smiled. 'And you? Was there anyone that grabbed your eye?'

The scowl came back on Casey's face again.

'Well… yes. Someone I've known for a while actually, but he was involved with someone else and I've never really looked at him like that before. But my god, does he kiss well. I like him, a lot, but we'll just see how it goes. It's early days.'

And that was as much as she was going to get out of him for now, she knew that.

'How's your love life?' Alex asked pointedly, deftly turning the tables on her.

She sighed heavily. 'Non-existent.' Eyeing Casey across the table, she glanced down. 'I slept with him.'

'And?'

There was no judgement from Alex, just unwavering continued love and support.

'And it was bloody amazing, but we're still no further along than we were when I saw you. He still doesn't want me.'

'Did you sleep with him hoping you could change his mind?'

'No, I knew he didn't want me in that way, but I just couldn't stay away from him any longer.'

Alex was quiet for a moment, clearly sensing her discomfort and unwillingness to talk. 'Would you like me to change the subject?'

'Yes please.'

'I have the results back from the CCTV footage.'

Her heart leapt and she sat up in her chair, ignoring Casey gaping like a goldfish.

'And?'

'There is absolutely nothing on there that can link you to Menton Hall. There are no reg plates, no redeemable features on the car and there is absolutely no way you can tell who is driving. It could be a yeti behind the wheel or a smurf and you wouldn't be able to tell.'

'Are you sure?'

'Yes, I swear, I'd be prepared to stand up in a court of law and say the same thing, the tape is clean.'

'Could it be enhanced further to give a different result?'

Casey realised what she was talking about and in a huge sign of solidarity he leaned across the table and took her hand, his face etched with concern.

'No, my friend enhanced it as far as humanly, mechanically and electronically possible. There is nothing on there.'

She smiled with relief. 'That's brilliant news. CID won't be happy that that particular lead was a dead end, but I'm over the moon about it.'

Casey broke into a huge grin and squeezed her hand in celebration.

'But Joy, maybe you should invest in some tinted windows, just to avoid anything like this happening again.'

'Not a bad idea.'

'I'd better go; we're blowing up London Bridge today.'

'Something CID would be very interested to hear about I'm sure.'

'Nah, this one's only three foot high. Love you kid.'

She hung up, still smiling.

'OK, good news aside, which I am very, very happy about by the way, let's cut to the most interesting piece of that conversation. You slept with Finn?'

She took her glasses off and rubbed her eyes. 'Yes.'

Casey studied her face for a moment. 'This doesn't end up with a happy ever after, does it?'

She shook her head.

'Oh crap, am I going to have to go round there and rough him up for treating my friend so badly?'

She laughed, she couldn't help it. 'Oh, my hero, would you?'

Casey let his head fall into his hands. 'Oh crap, I'm going to die.'

'But my honour would be restored.'

'In that case I'm going to need another beer.'

*

Joy was just getting up to see Casey out when Finn came out into his garden. He stopped when he saw them.

'Hi.' Finn's eyes burned into her.

'Hi.' So reserved, polite acknowledgements it was then. It was better than going back to the evil glares and bitchiness at the start of their friendship, better than him telling her to get lost.

'Finn.' Casey acknowledged his friend coolly and Joy smirked at his loyalty.

Finn glanced at Casey in confusion and then returned the greeting. 'Casey.'

'Do you still want me to beat him up?' Casey asked, theatrically in a stage whisper.

Finding it hard to suppress her grin, she shook her head.

'Thank god for that. So I'll see you on Friday for your birthday then.' He leaned down and kissed her, hugging her briefly. 'I'll leave you two to... glare at each other. I'll see myself out.'

235

With that he left, leaving her and Finn to, as he put it, glare at each other.

Finn moved closer to the fence. 'I don't want this to be awkward between us. I really am very sorry.'

'Stop apologising. You didn't force me, I wasn't drunk. I went willingly and if given the choice I'd do it again. Yes, I'm hurt that after the way you touched me, made love to me so lovingly last night, you still don't want me for anything else but sex, but you made it very clear what you were offering and I didn't expect anything else.'

He ran his hand round the back of his neck. 'So we can be friends again?'

She nodded grudgingly.

He paused, clearly trying to find some safe ground. 'So, I thought your birthday was tomorrow?'

'It is but Alex is blowing up the Houses of Parliament tomorrow and Thursday, it's a huge job and he can't get out of it, so we're going out Friday instead.'

It seemed obvious to extend the invite to him too but did she really want him there at her birthday celebrations, staring at her, making her stomach clench with desire? The tension would be unbearable. She had already invited Casey along to her favourite restaurant but he and Alex were friends now, so they would be fine. Alex would be decidedly frosty towards Finn for making her so miserable. It would probably be best if she didn't invite him. So not friends at all then, if they couldn't enjoy a simple meal out without that agonising friction bubbling between them.

'Are we still OK for tomorrow, we had plans to go out?' he asked.

He was so awkward. Men and women really couldn't be friends, especially not after they'd slept together. Joy had forgotten that they were supposed to be going out for the day. At this moment she would much rather spend the day alone doing her ironing rather than deal with this atmosphere hanging over them.

'Please. Besides it's already booked and paid for.'

She nodded reluctantly. And the silence stretched between them.

'Right, well, I've got things to do,' he said, and casting her another guilty look, he walked towards his shed. Sighing inwardly, she went back inside.

*

It was late afternoon when Finn knocked on Joy's back door. She was surprised when she answered it to see him dressed in a black tuxedo. He looked stunning.

'Hi, erm, could I borrow Darcy for ten minutes or so?'

What a weird question, especially dressed as he was.

'What for?'

'Lily wants Darcy and Billy to get married. After going to Casey's wedding at the weekend, she's become obsessed with weddings. All her toys have been married off and now she thinks Billy needs a good wife.'

This at least explained the tuxedo. 'And you've dressed up for the occasion?' There was something so endearing about this.

'What can I say, the girl has me wrapped around her little finger. I did make the fateful mistake of promising she could do whatever she wanted when she came round today. I didn't quite envisage this.'

'Do you always give her what she wants?'

'Pretty much, I'd be a lousy dad.'

Joy ignored the lump in the throat that wanted to contest this statement and whistled for Darcy. She came running over, wagging her tail furiously.

'Thanks.' Finn made to grab Darcy's collar.

'Oh no, I'm not missing out on this. Someone needs to make sure Billy's intentions to Darcy are pure and that he can financially support her. Shall I get changed?'

Finn looked her up and down. 'You look beautiful Joy, you always do.'

Joy stood still for a moment as she watched Finn and Darcy go back into his house. It was such a genuine comment.

Lily shrieked with delight when she saw Darcy and after giving the big dog a hug, she ran straight into Joy's arms.

'Hello ragamuffin! So Darcy is getting married?'

'Yes, Billy is lonely, he needs a good wife.' Lily disentangled herself from Joy's arms.

'Perhaps he's happy being miserable and alone,' Joy said and saw Finn wince.

'No, he can't be, he'd be happier with Darcy to play with every day.'

'You would think that, wouldn't you Lily, but sometimes it doesn't work like that.'

As Darcy sat down next to Billy, he snuffled in her ear and she licked his nose. Joy smirked and Lily clapped her hands with obvious excitement.

Lily tied a piece of net curtain over Darcy's head and attached a flower to her collar.

'It's probably a good thing that Billy's going to make an honest woman out of Darcy,' Finn whispered. 'I meant to tell you – when I took Darcy out for a walk the other day, I got distracted for a moment and when I turned around Billy was...'

'Bumping ugly bits?' Joy said.

'Yes. I presume she's been done?'

'No. When I got her a year ago, the vet said she hadn't but was probably too old now to breed anyway. He said I should think about it but there were risks about putting a dog that was her age under anaesthetic. I decided against it. Has Billy?'

Finn shook his head. 'He's less than a year old. It was on my to-do list for this summer.'

'Oh.' She smiled slightly at the thought of Newfoundland puppies. They would grow quickly and eat a lot. But before she could get carried away with knitting patterns for woolly booties, the wedding was under way.

'We are gathered here today…' Lily started in a near-perfect imitation of the same speech Joy had heard many times in weddings up and down the country.

'Still, I don't see why Billy should have to marry Darcy because he had a quick… thing with her.' Joy said sarcastically, so only Finn could hear as the ceremony continued. 'Heaven forbid that that should be the social convention in this country. You bump ugly bits with someone you care about and then you have to marry them.'

'I am not marrying you just because we… played hide the sausage,' Finn hissed.

Joy nearly laughed at this but Lily shushed them.

'This is the important bit. Does anyone here present have any reason why these two should not be married?'

'Is Billy gay?' Joy asked.

'I don't think so, he seems quite keen on Darcy.'

'Again, not a good enough reason to marry it seems.'

'So I now pronounce you man and wife, you may kiss the bride,' Lily said.

Billy lay down and closed his eyes.

'Oh look, he's bored of her already,' said Joy.

Finn rolled his eyes, though she could see he was fighting a smirk.

'Now you two can get married,' Lily said, her eyes shining happily as she looked at Finn and Joy.

'No,' Finn said.

'No.' Joy folded her arms across her chest.

Lily's bottom lip wobbled. 'Why not? We're just playing. You said we could play anything I wanted Uncle Finn.'

'Fine, fine, we'll get married.'

Joy felt her eyebrows shoot up. 'We will?'

'Just say "I do" and it will all be over in five minutes.'

'So just like last night then?'

Finn gave her a dark look and quite rightly so, he had tremendous stamina.

Lily was already tying the net curtain round Joy's head. 'You should learn to say no to her, it will prepare her for when she's let down by men in the future.'

'You must hold hands,' Lily declared.

Joy saw Finn's jaw clench as he took her hand, sending a jolt of lust spiralling through her.

'Do you take Joy to be your awfully wedded wife?'

Joy snorted

'Yes. I do,' said Finn.

'Do you take Finn to be your awfully wedded husband?'

'I do.'

'I now pronounce you man and wife, you may now kiss the bride.'

Finn bent down and gave her a short, sharp kiss on the cheek. 'Now, how about we let Joy get back to her busy life, and me and you could take Billy for a walk before your dad picks you up?'

'No, you need to kiss her properly. On the mouth.' Lily giggled. 'With tongues.'

Joy felt her eyebrows shooting further into her hair.

'No honey, that's not appropriate. You shouldn't really kiss someone like that unless you love them.' Finn knelt down to Lily's level.

'Like that stopped you last night,' Joy murmured.

The wobbling bottom lip was back. 'But you do love Joy, I've seen the way you look at her, the same way Daddy looks at Mummy – like she is a big piece of chocolate.'

Finn brushed his hair off his face and tears smarted in Lily's eyes. 'You do love her, I know you do.'

'Just kiss me Finn, for God's sake.'

He stood back up. 'You're caving now as well?'

'Yes, we'd both make terrible parents, just kiss me.'

Lily's tears vanished. 'Joy, you have to stand on one leg, I've seen it in the movies and then you have to smush your faces together like this.' She moved her hands against each other like she was squashing a bug in between them. 'And Uncle Finn you have to hold her face.'

Finn took Joy's face in his hands and she leaned into him, lifting one leg obligingly. He kissed her and as with the night before the chemistry between them was almost tangible. A desperate need crashed through her and as he trailed his hands to her waist and pulled her against him, she could taste the urgency in his kiss as well. The kiss lasted mere seconds before Finn snatched himself away, his eyes dark with lust.

'Yay!' Lily clapped enthusiastically.

Joy put a hand to her lips, which were tingling with his taste. Why did every kiss from him have to feel like the prelude to sex? Could the man not just kiss her normally without firing her up? Good lord, her hands were shaking. He stared at her for a moment and thankfully the unbelievable tension was broken when someone knocked on the front door.

'Yay! Daddy's here.' Lily ran to answer the door and Finn tore his attention from Joy to go and greet his brother-in-law.

Joy tried to straighten her thoughts as Lily's dad came in. He laughed when he saw the net curtain tied round Joy's head. 'She got to you two as well, did she? She's marrying everyone at the moment.'

Finn came to stand next to her and slung a casual arm round her shoulders. 'Yep, we're now man and wife.' Finn laughed, though his hand traced over her bare skin at her neck – sending shudders down her spine. 'Darcy and Billy are married too.'

Lily's dad laughed. 'Well, we'd better get off Loodles, we've got to pick your mum up and then we're going to Pizza Hut tonight.'

'Yay!' Lily ran straight out to the car and her dad gave a little wave of thanks and followed her out.

The tension between Joy and Finn returned as soon as the

door was closed. His hand at the top of her neck was now playing with the zip at the back of her dress. Through the frosted glass of the front door, Joy saw Lily's car drive off up the road. She turned to Finn and he immediately kissed her again. There were no protests this time as she pushed Finn's tuxedo jacket from his arms. He lifted her onto the nearby dining table as the kiss continued, frantically undoing his trousers. He slid her backwards and climbed up onto the table too. There was no time for any more clothes to be removed and Joy didn't care. Without taking his mouth off hers, he pinned her with his delicious weight and was inside her a second later.

Had she known that when Finn said he'd take her as his wife that he would take her as spectacularly as this, she perhaps wouldn't have given him so much grief to start off with.

*

Joy knew she had to get to work. The job list for The Dark Shadow was getting longer. It would give her something to do rather than lying in bed, just feet away from where Finn lay, thinking about his hands on her, his mouth against her own. She wasn't sure where she stood with him now. After they had finished on the table, he had kissed her for a very long time and of course she had kissed him back. He hadn't apologised again but it had been very apparent that she'd wanted him as much as he'd wanted her, so he'd had nothing to apologise for. Eventually, he'd climbed off the table and helped her down too. She'd kissed him briefly on the cheek and left.

So she would go to work and let her mind be filled with something other than Finn. It would be good to get back to it again, she'd left it too long since her last carving.

It was almost a two-hour drive though to her next job. It would be a long night. Ignoring Finn, who was steadfastly watching her as she loaded her car, she packed up all her tools and left.

Finn knocked on her door the next morning and before Joy had even opened it she felt that rush of desire for him again. Would that ever go away? She just hoped that the awkwardness of the day before would be gone... or the day would feel painfully long.

He was dressed casually, just overly washed jeans and a black T-shirt so she didn't feel out of place in her similar attire, though he still looked stunning, he always did.

'Ready?'

She nodded and noticed he hadn't kissed her or greeted her in any way that might offer a gleam of hope that they had a future together. But he'd made that very clear, and these plans were made before they'd slept together. They were silent as he drove slowly out of the village and up the hill, past the sign that outed them both as residents of Bramble Hill.

'I hope you like your birthday present,' Finn said, quietly.

'You've bought me a present?'

'Well, not something you can unwrap, today is your present.'

She felt impatient. 'You're so fickle. You tell me you don't want me, which was obviously a lie after the amazing sex we've had. You tell me it was just sex but you clearly care about me or you wouldn't be feeling so guilty about it. You tell me you don't want more but then you do things like this. You're so confusing.'

He concentrated on the road as he drove through Ashton Woods. 'You know I like you Joy...'

'Yes, but not enough.'

'No, I like you too much.'

'What?'

He sighed. 'We're here now. We need to talk Joy, but now is not the time. Go and have fun.'

She looked around in confusion. They were sitting outside his mum's pub, but there was no other sign to indicate what she was doing that day. She turned back to him. 'Let's talk now.'

'No. For one I have no idea what I'm trying to say, every time I'm near you my brain turns to mush and I need to clarify what it is I want – secondly, people are waiting for you.'

'Who?' This was getting more and more bizarre.

'Go inside and see.'

'You're not coming in?'

'No, I'm not part of the present.'

Feeling even more confused, especially over Finn's attempts to tell her how he felt, and disappointed that she wouldn't be spending the day with him, she unbuckled her seatbelt and opened the door.

He caught her arm and pressed his lips to her temple. 'Happy birthday Joy.'

She stumbled out of the car in shock and he drove off without a backward glance.

Feeling slightly hurt and beyond confused, she pushed the door of the pub open. She froze in shock and then burst into tears.

*

By the time the taxi dropped her off outside her house it was gone three in the morning, but the adrenaline and excitement of the day was still buzzing through her veins – plus a few cocktails were making her feel very warm and happy.

Finn had somehow arranged for all her university friends to be there. Eve hadn't been able to make it from Texas but she was there on Skype for some of it. But Libby, Annie and Suzie had been there all courtesy of Finn, who had seemingly paid for plane tickets and accommodation for them all. A car had been laid on for them which whisked them off to some posh spa hotel so they could be massaged, manicured, pedicured and thoroughly spoiled whilst they sipped champagne and ate the finest foods. They had stayed in the hotel all night and it was like all those years apart

244

had never happened – they just picked up where they had left off, chatting, giggling, exchanging stories. She had been touched that her friends had gone to all the trouble just to be with her on her birthday. But the most touching thing was that Finn had organised and paid for the whole thing.

That had been beyond doing something nice for a friend, it was in fact the kindest, nicest thing that anyone had ever done for her. It gave her hope. And now, thanks to long, convoluted, champagne-induced talks with her best friends, she had a plan. She would sneak it up on him slowly so he was in a relationship before he noticed. A dinner here, a walk over the hills with their dogs there, maybe an odd picnic thrown into the mix, add a liberal amount of amazing sex and they'd be halfway there. At the back of her mind a little voice was telling her it wouldn't be that easy in the cold light of day, but regardless of what the future held for her and Finn, she knew that tonight, now, she had to see him.

*

Finn woke with soft kisses being peppered across his cheeks. Sleepily, he reached up and ran his hands through her hair, knowing from the sweet smell that it was Joy.

'Finn, wake up,' she whispered.

'I'm awake,' he muttered grumpily. He eyed the clock and realised it was after three in the morning.

He sat up, pulling the sheet around him to hide his nudity. She was wearing that beautiful green dress that he had squirrelled away and left to Libby to hand over for their posh meal that evening. The moonlight gleamed off it, making her look ethereal in her beauty.

'I came to say thank you.'

'You're welcome…' He trailed off as she kissed him on the mouth briefly – but then she stepped back just as he was reaching for more. He frowned, at the feelings that crashed through him.

She giggled. It was such a beautiful sound. 'Why are you scowling?'

'Joy it's 3.15 in the morning, there are rules about waking up men at such a stupid time. Don't do it.'

'No exceptions?'

He smirked. 'Sex, that's the only exception. So unless you want to thank me with a night of unbridled passion, could we save the thanks for tomorrow?' He rubbed his eyes, embarrassed by his own candour.

'Then I'm glad I came.'

He looked up in time to see her undo the bow at the back of her neck and let the dress pool to her feet, leaving her naked standing before him.

'Jesus!' He yanked the sheet back and pulled her towards him. She handed him a condom as she straddled him. A quick frustrating second later, he was buried deep inside her, his mouth pressed to her throat as she kissed his head. 'I love naked gratitude, it's the best kind.'

He ran kisses across her throat, filling his hands with her breasts. He was never going to get enough of her.

His brain cleared slightly. 'Wait, I don't want to hurt you again. I didn't do all that so you'd sleep with me.'

She moved, taking him with her, arching back against him and sending all clarity from his brain.

'Why did you do it?' She wrapped her arms round his neck, kissing him lightly.

He buried his face in her throat, revelling in her scent, her touch, her skin against his. 'Because…'

She moved again, so slowly, but the movement sent need crashing through his stomach straight to his groin. He fought to gain control, at this rate he wasn't going to last five minutes.

'Finn…' She tipped his head back so she could look at him. 'Do you want to know why I came here tonight? It's because I love you.'

He stilled; his heart in his mouth.

'I know you don't want to hear that, I know you don't feel the same way, but I love you.'

There was so much he wanted to say, but he couldn't find the words. His brain was clouded with sleep, desire, her smell, her taste... words eluded him.

'Just make love to me Finn. I know you need time to think, but you don't have to do that tonight. Tomorrow you can be angry or withdrawn or scared or whichever mood you choose, but tonight it's still technically my birthday, sort of, so just make love to me.'

There was no escape now. He knew it and it scared the crap out of him. But tonight he could just be with her, enjoy the moment, and deal with his demons tomorrow. She was already kissing him, her tongue in his mouth, running her hands down his shoulders, urging him to respond. He rolled her over so she was under him and kissed her slowly, gently as he moved against her.

*

Joy woke the next day with soft caresses going up and down her bare back. She kissed Finn's throat and looked up at him. His eyes were guarded and wary as he watched her. There was a silence that hung between them like a thick velvet curtain.

She smiled and sat up. 'Don't worry, you don't have to say anything.' She kissed him briefly on the mouth. 'I meant what I said last night – I love you. I know you feel something for me, what you did for me yesterday was... wonderful. No one goes to that amount of trouble for someone they just like. But you're scared and I get that too. We don't have to have a relationship Finn, we don't have to put a label on it, but I love you and I want to spend time with you, no matter what form that takes. Can I come round again tonight?'

'Yes.' He didn't hesitate.

'Good, because the sex part is pretty damn amazing.'

He smiled. 'For me too.'

'And maybe I could come for dinner before. You could teach me how to make something and I'll make pudding, I'm good at that.'

'I'd like that. And maybe we could take the dogs for a walk together later.'

She felt the breath catch in her throat and he frowned slightly.

'As friends,' she quickly clarified. She wouldn't push it, she didn't want to scare him off.

'Of course.' He nodded thoughtfully. 'Though maybe we could be friends that could hold hands when we walk.'

She couldn't help the grin that split her face and she kissed him, deeply. 'Who says men and women can't be friends?'

*

Finn was standing in his kitchen, thinking about Joy. Of course he was thinking about her, she was all he could think of ever since she had stepped from that car on that fateful morning. He smiled at the thought of what that night would hold. The smile grew as he thought about walking the dogs together later that day, of dinner and cooking together. It seemed he was embarking on a relationship whether he wanted one or not. It terrified him. The wall he had carefully constructed around his heart was tumbling down and he had no control over it. He was still poised to flee, he could sense that. There was still a big part of him that wanted to push her away. But for now at least, the part that wanted to spend every single waking second with her was greater than the part that wanted to run.

He suddenly heard raised voices coming from the back garden and hurried out to see what was going on. Zach and Casey were standing in Zach's garden, clearly angry. Finn had never seen Casey so angry, in fact Casey didn't do angry at all.

Letting himself through the connecting gate he moved quickly across Joy's garden and let himself into Zach's, ignoring the pointed glare from him.

'What's up?'

Casey looked up at him, real hurt in his eyes. 'The diamond thief, she struck Mum's place, two nights ago. Thankfully she was away Tuesday night when it happened, got back yesterday and found out.'

Finn felt himself go cold. The night that Joy had disappeared dressed in black again and didn't come back till the early hours of the morning.

'She cleared out the safe, took everything. The worst thing was she was in my parents' room, stole all my mum's jewellery including a starfish necklace from Dad. Mum's absolutely gutted. The attack is personal, I'm sure of it. She's deliberately hitting houses that are in my patch, and some of them, the most recent are friends of the family, people I know – and now my parents' place. It feels like this is aimed at me.' Casey sighed, throwing himself down on one of the garden chairs.

Guilt ripped through Finn. Why had he covered for Joy? All this time she was moving in for the kill on Casey and he could have stopped it. Forcing his voice to sound as normal as possible, he focused on the one thing Casey had said that had made his heart stop.

'She?'

Casey gave a small, cold smile. 'We caught her on CCTV. All the big houses in the area are being targeted, it was only a matter of time before she struck Ashton Manor. I persuaded Mum to get some cameras inside and we caught her. She's clever though, kept her face hidden or averted from the cameras. I've got a friend that might be able to enhance the footage, maybe get a clear ID. But it's definitely a woman, we think she might be a redhead.'

Finn hissed and he couldn't help but glare at Joy's house.

Chapter Seventeen

Casey clearly saw his gaze. 'Don't be so ridiculous. It's not Joy.'

'She's been out dressed in black every night there's been a diamond robbery in the local area. She was out Tuesday night too.' It was a cathartic relief to be finally saying it, he should have said it ages ago. Casey was his best friend, and he'd known Joy for two seconds – he should have been more loyal, told Casey what he'd seen instead of trying to protect her. 'I've seen her covering her number plates, wearing a bandana over her face...'

Zach gasped

'Stop!' Casey was really furious this time. 'You can't just go around accusing somebody like that, that's her reputation you're tarnishing there...'

'I don't give a shit about her reputation, not now she's messed with your family.'

'Oh, don't get all 'Godfather' on me, seeking revenge for the wrong exacted on my family. This has nothing to do with Joy. She's got enough shit from the villagers to deal with without you adding your misplaced anger to the pot too.'

'That's a bit too much of a coincidence for my liking, Caz,' Zach said and Casey glared at Finn for putting the idea in Zach's head in the first place.

'You see, you start spreading that kind of shit around and people start to take notice.'

'She's rich and her parents certainly didn't have any money. She doesn't work.' It was like a floodgate, now he'd started Finn couldn't stop.

'Stop it.' Casey pushed his hair off his face, his hands shaking with suppressed anger.

'Look, I'll prove it to you.'

He moved quickly, letting himself through Joy's back door, which he knew she always left unlocked now. To his annoyance, Casey didn't follow. Joy wasn't there – by the sounds of it she was upstairs, singing badly.

Opening the kitchen drawer, Finn took out the three plasticine animals he had hidden in there when Joy was sick. He moved back outside and thrust them out for Casey to see. 'I found these in her kitchen the other day, when she was sick. I hid them, I didn't want anyone to know...'

Casey stared at them for a second and groaned.

'You said that the diamond thief always left behind plasticine animals, linking herself to each robbery.'

'This isn't what it looks like.' Casey grabbed the plasticine animals from Finn and squashed them in his hands so they were no longer recognisable.

'Casey! That's evidence,' Zach scolded. 'I think we should call the police.'

'I am the goddamn police. This has nothing to do with her and if we involve the police it could ruin her.'

Just then Joy appeared in the back garden, looking across at them in confusion. Her face lit up when she saw Finn, but quickly fell at their stony expressions.

'I need a word,' Finn growled, stalking towards her, but Casey snagged his arm.

'Leave this – I'm asking you to leave this. You'll hurt her, you'll feel like scum after and if you take this any further it will ruin everything she has worked so hard to build. Please drop this.'

But anger boiled through Finn – Casey was loyal to the bitter end and Joy had betrayed that. If Casey was too stubborn or too loyal to do anything about it then he sure as hell would. Removing his arm from Casey's grasp, he grabbed Joy's arm and marched her back inside.

*

'Ow, what the hell are you doing?' Joy fought against him and he let her go as he closed the door behind them. She could hear Zach and Casey arguing still out in the garden, though she couldn't hear the specifics. 'What's going on?'

'You need to give it back,' Finn's voice was low, sinister, his eyes dark.

'Give what back, what are you talking about?' She had spent the morning drifting round in a glorious bubble of bliss. After Finn's suggestion that they could be friends who hold hands and cook dinner together, and knowing that the amazing sex was now going to be a regular feature, she didn't think anything could break her mood. Now Finn was shouting, looking at her as if she was something unpleasant he had stepped in. Her bubble had just burst spectacularly.

'Don't play coy with me – the diamonds, everything you took from Ashton Manor Tuesday night. Give it all back or I'll go to the police and I'll tell them everything.'

'What?' Her brain raced whilst she tried to piece together the limited information that Finn had given her. 'There was another diamond robbery at Ashton Manor. Oh God, that's Casey's parents' place, isn't it?'

He let out a low snarl. 'Give it back. I don't care how you do it, whether you break back in there or post it through their letterbox, but you'll give it back.'

'What?' Hurt sliced through her like a knife. 'You think I'm the thief, that I would steal from Casey? How dare you suggest that?'

He stepped towards her so menacingly that she took a step back. 'I covered for you, I never told the police when you concealed your plates, when you went out dressed in black every night there was a robbery. I hid those bloody plasticine animals so Casey wouldn't see them – and then you betrayed him and me. Now you've made it personal, you've attacked someone I love and I'm not going to let you get away with it. You'll take it back and then you'll pack up and leave this village and never come back.'

Joy felt hot angry tears prick her eyes but when she spoke her voice was low. 'I know you don't trust me, you've made that very clear with your refusal to give me your heart…'

'That has nothing to do with this…'

'It has everything to do with this, because if you trusted me enough with your heart you wouldn't be standing in front of me now accusing me of something so appalling. I don't have many friends as you are well aware and I'm not in the business of stabbing in the back those that I do have. I would never do this to Casey and he at least knows that.' God, she hoped he did.

'So where were you Tuesday night, you were out for hours?'

'I can't tell you that. I'm hoping that if we have any kind of future together, you can find it in you to trust me in this. Trust me when I say I didn't have anything to do with the theft at Casey's parents' house or any of the other robberies.'

Finn opened his mouth to speak but then Casey burst through the back door. He took in the situation in seconds – Finn's angry stance, the tears in her eyes – and quickly moved between them.

'Get out,' he said to Finn. 'You have no right to come in here accusing her like this. This is my business, my case and it's mine to deal with how I see fit – and accusing one of my friends is not how I wish to play it. If you wish to pursue this, if you go to the police behind my back, then our friendship is over, do you understand me.'

Joy was stunned, riddled with guilt that Casey would choose her over Finn, the man he had loved for fifteen years. She couldn't allow it. 'Casey, no, you don't have to do that.'

Finn stepped back, shocked. 'Casey, I'm doing this for you...'

'Just get out.'

Finn glared at her for a moment, then left, slamming the door behind him.

Casey watched him go and turned back to face her. He was livid.

'Casey, I swear, I didn't...'

'I know.'

She stared up at him, furiously wiping the tears from her eyes. Suddenly, an idea came to her. 'I can prove it.' She moved quickly to her rucksack and rummaged inside for her camera. 'I have photos of my latest strike, from the other night. They're time stamped, I haven't loaded them onto the website yet, look let me show you...' She trailed off as Casey stopped her with his hand.

'I don't need to see any proof, Joy. I know you didn't have anything to do with this. I pride myself on being an excellent judge of character; it's one of the most important parts of my job. Finn, sadly, has never been a good judge of character. As far back as I can remember, he's made bad decisions. The women he slept with who sold their stories to the papers, Pippa who I hated from the first moment I met her, and now this. He can't see the good from the bad and the ugly.'

Joy laughed despite her tears. 'Am I the good or the ugly?'

'Oh, hideous, grotesque, some might say.' He wiped her tears from her cheek and pulled her into a big bear hug. 'Finn is fiercely loyal to me and if he knew you a little better he would do the same for you.'

She released her face a little from his chest so she could breathe and speak. 'He sort of did. He said he hid my maquettes so you wouldn't see them. It just hurts that he would think me capable of doing this.'

'He doesn't know you, he's tried to push you away because he's afraid of getting hurt. If he knew you like I do, he wouldn't think it. But we've known each other for over thirty years, when it comes to loyalty he's bound to choose me over you.'

'He doesn't have to choose at all.'

'I know, he'll come round, don't judge him too harshly.'

'I'm not sure if I want him to come round at all now.'

Casey sighed into the top of her head.

*

Joy had waited for it to get completely dark before she loaded her gear back into the car. National Heritage had emailed The Dark Shadow that morning, saying how impressed they were with the two strikes she'd done in the local woods so far but how they were hoping to have all three done before the forthcoming bank holiday as they wanted to have a nature trail including the three strikes en route.

She was out tomorrow night for her birthday so she knew she had to do it tonight. It was just an inconvenience that her last local strike was so close to Ashton Manor, there might be some kind of police presence.

Finn's house was in darkness so she guessed he was already in bed. Safe in the knowledge that he hadn't seen her, she got in her car and drove off.

*

Finn sat up in his car as he watched her drive off. So she was taking the stuff back. That was something, he supposed. But he wasn't going to lose Casey's friendship over this; he had to prove to him he was right. Or maybe he just had to prove it to himself that she wasn't to be trusted, then he wouldn't feel such a fool for pushing her away so spectacularly when he loved her so much.

He had seen her loading her car up and as she went back to her shed for more boxes he had hidden himself in the front seat of his car.

He watched Joy round the bend and disappear from sight. He turned the car on and pulled out onto the road. He kept his headlights off as he picked his way round the quiet country lanes, following her tail lights as she made her way towards Ashton Manor.

*

Joy had spent the day stewing about Finn and how hurt she had been by it. But he'd got one thing right. It was time to leave the village, time to move on and put the whole nasty episode behind her. After being let down by the villagers, the only thing that had been keeping her in the village was Finn, but now he'd let her down too. The threats from the villagers had stopped for now, but they would always hate her and there was seemingly nothing she could do about that. There was nothing keeping her in Bramble Hill anymore.

But she still couldn't get Finn out of her head. Every time she closed her eyes, he was there, touching her, kissing her, caressing her – and now it hurt even more after his betrayal. She had to exorcise her demons somehow and it wasn't until she had been carving unseeing for about ten minutes that she realised what she was creating. For the first time in her life, her art had become personal. Even though she knew it was a mistake, that she would regret it after, just like her night of passion with Finn, now she'd started she couldn't stop.

*

Finn stood, touched at the magnificence of it. He was stunned at the fine lines, the detail, the muscles, the contours of the flesh,

256

all captured intricately. Every line, every groove erotically captured in full – the night before with Joy. Carved into the fallen oak was a life-sized Finn and Joy, limbs tangled, eyes closed with desire, her head thrown back in ecstasy as he kissed her throat. It was beautiful.

He had seen her car disappear into the trees and he'd got out of his own car and followed her on foot. Knowing she was heading for Ashton Manor, he had pulled his camera out of his pocket and primed it ready for filming as he stealthily made his way through the trees.

He had watched unseen as she unpacked her trunk with chainsaws and other power tools and then to his utmost confusion, he'd watched in horror as she had started to carve.

The camera lay forgotten in his hand as he stood there over the three hours it took for her to finish her masterpiece. He felt sick at the accusations he had foisted on her earlier that day. Now it all made sense – the secrecy, the black clothes, even the plasticine models. Joy was The Dark Shadow.

She finally turned off her chainsaw and ran her fingers over the shoulders, the arms and the back of the wooden Finn, carefully brushing off all the sawdust. She sighed sadly and he found himself stepping forward to hold her.

Suddenly, she turned around and she froze when she saw him. Then her face crumpled and she launched herself at him, hitting and slapping every part of him she could reach.

'You bastard. You couldn't just trust me, could you? This is all I have, this is all I am. My parents are dead, I haven't had a home in eleven years. I've moved around so much I don't have any friends. I gave you my heart and you threw that back at me. This is the only thing I have – but now you've ripped this from me as well.'

Keen to avoid the bruises, he pinned her quickly to the nearest tree with his weight and caught her hands to stop her hitting him.

'I'm sorry.' She struggled against him, but he was stronger. He brought her hands to his mouth and impulsively kissed her knuckles. 'I'm so sorry.' He felt the fight go out of her and she slumped against him. He kissed her forehead. 'I swear, I'll never tell anyone who you are or what you do. You have my word on that.'

She pushed him away from her and he let her.

'Until the next time you fall out with me or decide you hate me again. Then you'll decide that will be an opportune moment to out me.'

'And don't you think your talent will be enough to carry you? Joy, you're amazing…'

'It's the mystery that is the success of The Dark Shadow – the creations that appear overnight, no one knows who did them or even when as sometimes my sculptures take days to be discovered. Without the mystery, the intrigue, there is no Dark Shadow.'

He watched her as she walked back towards the carving, shaking her head sadly.

'Casey knows?' he asked quietly.

'Yes.'

Crap. Casey had warned him not to accuse Joy and he hadn't listened. He had been determined to prove he was right – and hurt her spectacularly in the process, more so than when he had slept with her.

He approached her and she stiffened when he touched her.

'Joy I'm sorry, I truly am, I should have trusted you, I'm really sorry. Can I make it up to you, somehow, please?'

She turned back to face him. 'I don't want anything to do with you now.' Her voice was empty, devoid of emotion and this scared him more than the violent outburst moments before. 'I'm leaving at the end of the month. You won't see me again.'

Panic ripped through him. 'What? No. Where are you going?'

She shrugged, indifferently.

'Why, because of me?'

Her eyes flared and he took a step back.

'You arrogant sod. Since I've been here I've been attacked in the toilet of a pub, thrown in a pond, had dog shit posted through my letterbox on an almost daily basis, had eggs thrown at me, been spat at, had bricks thrown through my window, my dog has been poisoned and so have I. There is nothing for me in Bramble Hill. After today… well, that just really brought it home to me that there was absolutely nothing here worth sticking around for. Now I need to get rid of this, so I suggest you stand back.' She picked up the chainsaw and moved back towards the carving again.

He quickly grabbed her arm. 'No! Why are you getting rid of it, it's stunning.'

She smiled, thinly. 'Because it's pornographic and not exactly what the National Heritage were thinking of for their nice family friendly nature trail. Don't worry, I'll keep you, I'll just get rid of me.'

'Wait, hang on, let me just take a photo of it before you do.'

She stood back, her eyes cold, impassive as he quickly fired off a few shots with his camera.

Once he was done, she put her ear defenders back on and within a few minutes the wooden Joy had been eradicated, leaving behind a bed of leaves and flowers instead, other leaves and flowers covered his bare bum and with a quick flick of the chainsaw, the wooden Finn soon had pointy elf ears.

Without another word, Joy packed up her car, extinguished the lights and left, leaving Finn alone in the moonlight staring at the sculpture. In a short few minutes, Joy had been erased figuratively and literally – not leaving behind a trace of her presence – and by Tuesday she would be gone from his life too.

*

Joy sat and stared at the photo of her latest carving on The Dark Shadow website. Now titled 'The Fairy Prince', she had managed to capture Finn's magnificence perfectly. She wondered, idly, what she would have called it if it had been left as it was. 'Village Porn' perhaps, 'The Orgasm', or more personally, 'The moment I felt my heart breaking.'

She looked around the room; she had quite a bit of packing to do. She had phoned Joe and given her notice, though as she had paid until the end of the month he wasn't expecting her out until then. He had been very apologetic about the whole Mrs Kemblewick fiasco that had forced her out and as such had not enforced the two months' notice she should have given as part of her contract.

She just had to keep her head down over the next few days, try to avoid Finn as much as possible. It was already early after-noon and she hadn't seen him all day, just another few more days and she could escape for good.

There was a soft knock on the back door and Finn stepped in. She automatically snapped her laptop closed so Finn didn't see The Dark Shadow website, though clearly, on hindsight, it was too late for that now.

'Hi.' He stepped towards her much like he was approaching a wild animal.

She rubbed her head and sighed. 'What do you want?'

'I… can't take back what I said, what I did yesterday. I wish I could, so we could be friends again…'

'We were never friends Finn. You hated me, you shagged me, then you betrayed me. Definitely not friends.' She ignored the look of hurt that crossed his face.

His jaw clenched determinedly. 'You don't accept apologies easily, do you? Forgiveness not one of your strong points, is it?'

He stepped closer and she had to ignore his glorious earthy smell, the way his eyes burned into her, the charge of desire that crashed through her at his proximity.

She looked away. 'Saying sorry isn't enough. This is never going to work between us, you don't trust me.'

'What about you, you didn't trust me enough to tell me about The Dark Shadow. Trust works both ways.'

'I would have, eventually. I would have shared that part of my life with you. But I can't just tell every man I'm involved with what I do – The Dark Shadow's success depends on my identity being kept a secret. That kind of trust takes time.'

'For me too, I just need more time.'

'I thought that too, that you just needed time to heal, time to think… but I was wrong. If you loved me, if you felt for me a tenth of what you felt for Pippa, you wouldn't have to think. You'd just dive headfirst into it and to hell with the consequences, because being with me would be the only thing that mattered. But let's face it, there's no point in risking your heart unless it's for the stupid, mindless head over heels type of love. You can't risk it on someone you just quite like to shag.'

She heard him step closer, she could feel the heat from him now.

'I'll be gone by Tuesday and then you can go back to your nice uncomplicated life without me.'

'So that's it. One little disagreement and you're running for the hills?'

She glared at him. How did he have the right to be angry? 'I'd say that making me feel that I'm not good enough for you, not trusting me with your heart and accusing me of being a thief is a bit more than a little disagreement.'

'You told me you love me.'

'Yes, and what did I get in return?'

He shifted awkwardly. Exactly, she'd got nothing other than his accusations and betrayal, hardly a fair exchange.

She stood up, grabbed Darcy's lead and whistled for her. Without another word, she let herself out the front door and closed it behind her.

*

The Glasshouse at The Grove Hotel near Watford was one of her most favourite places in the world – the food was amazing and there was so much choice she wanted to eat it all. Tonight there was an all-you-can-eat buffet and she had gone there with that exact intention, to eat it all. Sadly, it was not to be. She stared at the strawberry mousse topped with chocolate cream despondently. It looked delicious, but there was no way she could fit it in. After the amazing red pepper bread, the huge king prawns, the smoked salmon, the chicken, beef, pork, turkey Sunday roast, the Chinese ribs, the cheeses, the crème brûlée and the passionfruit sorbet, there was simply no room for the strawberry mousse.

She sat and patted her rather full belly, taking a sip of her champagne cocktail in the hope to dispel some of the fullness. It didn't work.

She eyed Casey who had admitted defeat about ten minutes before, though Alex was still picking at the few slices of cheese that were on his plate.

It had been a lovely way to celebrate her birthday – Casey and Alex got on so well and the three of them hadn't stopped talking all night. It had been an excellent way to help her forget about Finn too, albeit temporarily.

She sat back in her chair, shifting uncomfortably. 'I've eaten too much.'

Alex sat back, finally admitting defeat too.

She picked up her champagne flute and peered at the strawberries sitting at the bottom, wondering if it would be completely uncouth to stick her tongue in the glass and lick them out. Deciding The Glasshouse was slightly too upper class for that kind of behaviour, she put the glass back down again. 'And these cocktails are making me very fuzzy, think I need to go home and sleep it all off.'

'Lightweight,' Casey said. 'I was going to suggest making it an all-nighter.'

She moaned, resting her head on the table. 'No, definitely need to sleep.'

'That's a shame, I have some very nice rosé champagne and strawberries back at my house, I was going to suggest we go back there to celebrate. Alex, you up for a few more glasses?'

Joy lifted her head. 'Rosé champagne, you say, I could be tempted by that.'

Casey smiled and out the corner of her eye she caught Alex suppressing a smirk. 'You just said you were going to bed.'

'Yes, but it is my birthday and rosé champagne sounds like a nice way to finish it off.'

Alex coughed, still smirking to himself. What was he up to? She watched him fish in his wallet. 'I have to be up early tomorrow so I'll have to decline – you kids enjoy yourselves though.'

Casey rolled his eyes, also suppressing a smile. What had she missed? 'Just me and you then, kid.'

'I'll get this.' She fished in her handbag to find her purse.

'You will not, it's your birthday, I'll pay,' insisted Alex.

'You two can argue this out between yourselves but I've already paid,' Casey said, standing up. He offered her his arm. 'Shall we?'

She leaned over and kissed Alex goodbye and then took Casey's arm. 'I hope you're not going to get me drunk and take advantage of me.'

Casey looked back at Alex. 'That wasn't my intention for tonight, no.'

Leaning her head against his shoulder, she smiled sleepily.

*

'So what makes you think these robberies are personal and not just coincidence?' Joy asked as Casey pulled into his driveway.

'I'm a detective, we don't work with coincidences.' He was silent for a moment. 'Have I told you she leaves behind plasticine animals at every robbery?'

'No… oh, that's why Finn hid my maquettes, the plasticine models I make before I do my strikes.'

Casey nodded as he turned off the engine. 'The first one she left was of my old dog Max. He died about two years ago. He was a border collie. It wasn't just a border collie model though, it was Max, down to the very distinctive three little black spots above his right eye. I knew then it was someone that knew me. But since then, the animals have had no connection whatsoever and I've kind of shrugged it off, I thought maybe I had been too paranoid.

The one before my parents' house, she left a lion, but I didn't see it. I was still dealing with wedding stuff so I was just told about it. That's what was so annoying; if I'd seen it I would have known she was going to break into my parents' house next. It was an exact replica of the lion that sits outside their front door, a copy of one of the lions on the Marco Polo Bridge in Beijing where my dad proposed to my mum.

When she broke into my parents' house, she left a note – it's the first time she's done that.'

Joy swallowed uneasily. 'A note addressed to you?'

'No, it just said, "*You think the net is closing in, you have no idea.*"'

He moved to get out the car but she took his hand, suddenly feeling very sober. 'Are you scared?'

'No. We'll catch her, you can be sure of that. She's making mistakes and despite what she thinks, the net is getting tighter. We know she's a redhead, that's something.' He smiled as he eyed her hair. 'Redheads, they're all trouble.'

He got out and as he moved towards the house, he switched his mobile on. She followed him as he went round the side and unlocked the back door. His phone burst into life from his pocket and he answered it as he switched the lights on, illuminating a huge kitchen with bright red units, a white marble effect top and a little black log burner in the chimney place.

He frowned as he listened, then he spoke, his voice serious and authoritative. 'Casey Fallowfield. Alpha, Foxtrot, Romeo, India, Charlie, Alpha…'

Ooh, he was speaking in code, how exciting. He eyed her watching him and turned away. Oh, maybe it was private. She decided that using the bathroom might be a good idea, so she set out from the kitchen to find it. She was met with a large house, a wide staircase and a lot of doors to choose from. She caught sight of the sink through one of the doors and was just about to go inside when she heard what sounded like a faint cough coming from upstairs.

Frowning slightly, she took the stairs quietly. At the top there were more doors, but one, open a crack, immediately drew her attention. She was sure that as she reached the top stair a faint light went out, leaving behind only darkness. Someone was here.

She stole across the landing as quietly as she could and stopped just outside the door. What was she doing, was she really going to confront the thief? She could have a weapon or be a black belt in martial arts. Really, she should go downstairs, tell Casey and let him handle it – he was CID after all, he was trained to deal with this kind of thing.

There was a cool draught coming from inside the room, the window was clearly open. If Joy didn't act now, the thief would be gone. This was her only chance to stop her once and for all.

Without thinking she barged into the room, slamming on the light and was immediately thrown face down to the floor. As she struggled she felt something cold and metallic thrust against the base of her skull and she stilled, her heart pounding furiously.

Chapter Eighteen

'Well, well, well, what do we have here?' A quiet, cold female voice came from behind her, poking her hard with what felt like a gun. 'Casey Fallowfield with a girl. Now that is a turn up for the books. I'd always assumed he was gay. Yet you're here, he has candles in his bedroom ready for a night of romance, champagne chilling in the fridge... he plans to seduce you. Well, you being dead might put a dampener on his plans slightly. Still, he took away the man I love, it's only fair to return the favour. Stand up.'

Joy did, slowly, her blood roaring in her ears. Who the hell was this crazy bitch? The safe in the wall next to her was already open, but inside diamonds glittered in the light. There was a diamond dragon, several diamond rings, a diamond owl brooch, and the diamond starfish Rose had worn to Casey's wedding. Crazy Bitch was trying to plant them on Casey, make him out to be the diamond thief all along. That's why she had targeted people he knew, to make the connection to him even stronger. The window was open a crack. Joy had been right, another few seconds and she would have been gone, though in hindsight that probably would have been the safer option. Casey had said the attacks were personal, well Crazy Bitch breaking into his home with a gun didn't get any more personal than that.

'Turn around,' said Crazy Bitch.

Joy did and had her first glance of her attacker. She was tall, at least a foot taller than she was, with long red hair right down to her bum – she was thinner too, pretty with those large brown doe eyes.

Crazy Bitch was clearly assessing her as well, as she held the gun pointed at Joy's face. Joy couldn't help feeling that Crazy Bitch's gaze was less than complimentary.

'This is what's going to happen.' Crazy Bitch licked her lips nervously. She was clearly out of her league here; getting caught had not been part of the plan. Joy had cocked it up for her and she looked pissed. 'You're going to help me escape by creating a diversion. I want you to go to the safe, take some stuff out. Casey will come running in here, see you stealing from him and whilst he's dealing with your betrayal, arresting you, doing what he does best, I'll slip out unnoticed. If you say one word, if you somehow signal that I'm here, if he suspects in the slightest, I'll shoot you both.'

'Wait, wait.' Joy found her voice. 'He won't believe for one minute that I'm involved in this, he'll know you're here. I'm not going to let you shoot him, just because you're stupid enough to get caught.' She ignored the furious look on Crazy Bitch's face. 'Just go out the window now and I'll give you a five-minute head start before I raise the alarm.'

'The window has locks on it you idiot, I can only open it an inch, something I'd just found out when I heard you coming up the stairs.' Crazy Bitch looked around, panic-stricken, and quickly turned off the light. 'When he comes, you'll attack him – wait for him to get into the room and then launch yourself at him. As he tries to fight you off, I'll slip out. But one word from you and you're both dead.'

'No, listen…' Joy trailed off as they both heard footsteps come quietly and quickly up the stairs.

Crazy Bitch moved behind the door, priming her gun with a sickening click. 'Not one word,' she whispered.

Joy stood in the moonlit gloom, feeling sweat prickling across her neck. Her heart was roaring, her mouth was dry. Casey's shadow stole across the landing as he moved slowly towards the room and she saw to her horror that he had a gun too. Nice, sweet, laidback Casey, holding a gun at arm's length, his eyes cold as he listened and approached the doorway.

That's when she struck. Joy charged forward and at the movement from the shadows, Casey swung the gun to the right in her direction. Wincing she leapt through the air and threw her whole body weight against the door. It slammed backwards, a gun went off, Casey threw her to the ground, landing hard on top of her and everything went black.

*

Joy was aware of pain before she could open her eyes. Aware of voices too; she tried to tune into them as she became more conscious.

'I knew she was trouble as soon as I met her, it was only a matter of time before she did something stupid like this,' Casey said.

Another voice answered from further away and she couldn't make out the words.

'Yeah, you can take her now. I'll come down and interview her at the station tomorrow when she's less groggy. She's going to have a hell of a sore head.'

That was the understatement of the year, her head was pounding.

Suddenly, she was aware she was moving. The police were taking her away? That meant that Casey thought she was involved. Did that mean that Crazy Bitch was still in the house waiting for her chance to attack?

She struggled. 'No, wait.' Her words sounded so muffled and slurred.

The movement stopped.

'That's OK, you guys go. I've got this. Cheers boys,' Casey said.

The movement started again and as she struggled against the strong arms that were around her, the movement stopped and it felt like she was being laid on a bed.

She forced her eyes open, the light was so bright, she immediately closed them again, struggling to sit up. She had to tell Casey.

'Hey, keep still for a moment,' Casey's voice came from close by and she felt herself being pushed back down.

She forced her eyes back open again and blinked against the bright lights a few times. Slowly the room came into focus. She was lying in what appeared to be Casey's bedroom, with Casey sitting next to her watching her carefully, his eyes filled with concern.

'Where is she?' Joy tried to sit back up and again was pushed back down.

'Do I need to tie you up? Stay still. She's gone, you're safe.'

She groaned. It was actually Casey's safety she feared for most but regardless, they were both safe now.

She felt her heart rate slow, the panic ebbing away.

'Are you in pain?'

She nodded. 'My head is killing me.'

'Stay here a moment, I'll get you some ice.'

He quickly scooted out the room and she took the opportunity to raise herself on her elbows and look around. Crazy Bitch had been right; Casey had placed candles over every surface. They weren't lit but the intention was clear.

Casey came running back in and helped her to sit up, then pressed the ice to the back of her head. 'I'm so angry with you right now, what the hell were you thinking?'

'I didn't want her to get away with it. You'd said the robberies were personal, that they were aimed at you. I wanted to stop her.'

'And you honestly think that a few hundred pounds, some

silver cufflinks and a few letters regarding stocks and shares were more important than the life of my friend. She could have taken every single penny I have and I'd still want you over all that crap.'

'I wasn't thinking.'

She eyed him, his eyes were angry now.

'Evidently. I could have shot you when you leapt out at me from the darkness.'

This all seemed a bit unfair – she had been acting in Casey's best interests, trying to keep him safe. 'I wasn't leaping out at you. I was trying to stop her from hurting you. She said if you knew she was there, she'd kill you.'

He sighed, as he shifted the ice slightly. 'I already knew she was there, why do you think I came upstairs with a gun? You should have let me handle it.'

She took the ice off him, but kept it pressed against her head as she shuffled back so she could lean against the headboard.

'How did you know? What happened?'

'The phone call, it was my security team. I have sensors on all the windows and doors – if one of those gets tripped, my security team get notified and they contact the police immediately. She arrived about ten minutes before we got home. Reinforcements were already on their way.'

'That seems a bit over the top for a few hundred pounds and a pair of cufflinks,' she muttered.

'As I said before, I knew the robberies were aimed at me. So I had these special measures installed so we could catch her if she tried anything. My security team tried to contact me straight away, but as I was out, my phone was off. When they phoned, they said the sensors had been tripped on the downstairs bathroom window and on my safe. I thought you were in the bathroom, so I grabbed my gun and went to face her. Next thing, a screaming banshee leaps out of the darkness, a whirlwind of red hair and flailing arms and legs. I aimed my gun. You threw yourself into the door, broke her nose, knocked her out cold, her gun went off and I threw you to the floor where I knocked you out. Sorry about that.'

She arched an eyebrow. 'Banshee?'

'Good god yes, you sure can scream.'

'I didn't even know I had screamed.' She giggled with embarrassment. 'Did you throw me to the floor because you thought I was attacking you?'

'No, it took me about a split second to realise the banshee wasn't aiming for me. When I realised it was you and the gun went off I threw you to the floor so you wouldn't get shot.'

Joy smiled. 'So you really are my hero?'

He laughed. 'Looks like you were more mine actually.' He leaned forward and kissed her forehead. 'Thank you.'

'She was trying to plant the diamonds on you, they were all in your safe. Did you know her?' Her head was feeling better now, so she placed the bag of ice on a small set of drawers, amongst all the candles. She smiled to herself as she realised what Casey's intentions had really been for that night.

'Yes. Do you remember me telling you about Bonnie and Clyde?'

'The husband and wife crime duo?'

'Yes, it was her, Bonnie. She was pissed off at me for putting poor Derek in prison and wanted to get back at me. She wanted me to go to prison too. The great thing is, we now have all the diamonds she stole so they can be returned to their owners. I honestly thought she would have sold them.'

'Do you think she would have killed you?'

'I doubt she was the murdering kind. But then you never know what some people are capable of.'

'Well, at least you can tell Finn now that it definitely wasn't me.'

Casey rolled his eyes. 'I take it you still haven't forgiven him for that yet. You have to let that go. You've got to remember that he was prepared to cover for you, to lie to me and to the police for you. The only reason he got upset was when it affected me.'

'Some things are hard to forgive.'

'Yes, being unfaithful and physical violence are two things that I would find very hard to forgive. This is a mistake. To be fair, if I hadn't seen the chainsaws and I saw you going out dressed in black on the night of the robberies, I would be quite suspicious as well. If you love him then you have to move past this now.'

'Loving him isn't enough. He has to give me something here. It can't just be about the amazing sex.'

Casey smirked. 'I don't see why not.'

She scowled at him.

'He loves you Joy.'

Her heart leapt. 'Has he told you that?'

He hesitated. 'Yes.'

The pause was just enough to make her think he was lying.

'Did he actually say those words?'

'Yes, after he saw you in the woods, he called me the next day to say what an idiot he'd been and then he told me you were leaving and that he loved you and couldn't bear for you to go.'

She stared at him, somehow finding that impossible to believe.

'I need to hear it. It's not like I want a big proposal or to see it written across the sky in one-hundred-foot letters, I just need to hear him say it. I need some glimmer of hope that we have some future together.'

'You can see it – think about all the lovely things he's done for you over the last few weeks, how many times he's been there for you. Surely it's better for him to prove he loves you, than say those three little words.'

Joy picked at a stray thread on the duvet. Casey was right. What Finn had done for her birthday had been wonderful. How he had been there for her with Craig Peters and the nonsense from the villagers. But were those three little words too much to ask for?

Casey stood up. 'I think it's time to call it a night. I'll just go and check everything is locked up downstairs and then I'm taking you to bed.'

She quirked an eyebrow up and Casey laughed, breaking the tension. 'To sleep. You're really not my type.'

She smiled as he walked out the room and then waited patiently for him to come back before she tackled the most important subject.

'Casey.' She stopped him as he walked back in the room and she gestured to the candles. 'So what was your intention for tonight?'

He flushed. 'You know?'

'I do now.'

He fiddled with the cuff of his shirt. 'Are you OK with it?'

She felt her mouth fall open. 'Oh my god, Casey, of course I am. I couldn't be happier. But I thought you were taking things slow?'

He visibly relaxed at her blessing. 'I don't know Joy, we were both wary of getting involved in a serious relationship. But when we're together... that wariness, the fear of getting hurt or rejected... it just goes away. We both decided that being together was more important than taking things slow. Carpe Diem, seize the day, and we'll deal with the consequences later if we have to.'

She smiled. 'That's a good philosophy. My dad always used to say that we should worry about tomorrow, tomorrow.'

'Alex said that too.'

'So I really ruined your plans tonight then?'

'Not one bit, I love spending time with you. Besides, nothing kills a night of romance quicker than a crazy lady wielding a gun. It will keep.'

She smiled as Casey disappeared off to the bathroom. So it seemed that Casey at least might get his happy ever after. She just had to work on her own.

*

Joy woke late the next day. Casey had already gone, leaving her a note saying he had to go down the station to sort out the Bonnie debacle, but that he had left out towels and a new toothbrush for her and there were croissants downstairs, if she wanted them for breakfast. She smiled. He was the perfect host.

She quickly got washed and grabbed a taxi home. She hadn't slept well the night before. The natural noises of the house, the pipes creaking and floorboards settling kept making her jump. In her half-asleep state she kept thinking it was Bonnie coming back. But the main thing that kept her awake was what Casey had said. That Finn loved her. Would she stay in Bramble Hill if he told her he loved her? Was that all it would take? There were an awful lot of coincidences that made Finn think she was the thief and as Casey said there was no such thing as a coincidence. She couldn't really blame Finn for thinking that. Everyone makes mistakes. But Finn had to give her a reason to stay now, he had to give her something.

Darcy greeted her joyously when she walked in, and Joy grabbed her lead and headed out.

*

It was early evening as Joy stood staring out of her bedroom window, watching the sun sink behind the hills. She hadn't seen Finn at all, though she knew he was in. Sad, haunting music drifted out from the open windows and she'd heard him clanging around in the kitchen earlier. She had wanted to tell him about Bonnie, to maybe start back on friendly ground, but she hadn't quite forgiven him enough to face him. She had tried to keep herself busy all day, planning some strikes, correspondence with future customers, taking Darcy for a long walk – but the more time alone, the more she had a chance to think. If he loved her, wouldn't he tell her? He knew she was leaving, that she was only going to be there for a few more days. Wouldn't he do something to stop her from going?

She sighed sadly and moved to go downstairs to start dinner. At the top of the stairs she stopped in confusion as something was being posted through her letterbox. It looked like a bundle of rags tied together, with one end of the rag still sticking out through the letterbox. Something else horrible from the villagers, no doubt. Furious at their continued hatred, she stormed downstairs to finally give at least one of them a piece of her mind. But halfway down the stairs, the sharp smell of petrol hit her nose and she froze. The rags were soaked in it. And as she watched, a flame quickly travelled through the letterbox, down the rags towards the bundle. She stood paralyzed with shock and fear. Then her brain finally caught up with what was about to happen.

She tore down the stairs and everything happened in slow motion. As the flame hit the rags, a great ball of fire engulfed the front door.

Chapter Nineteen

She threw herself back, hitting the floor hard as the fire licked hungrily up the door. The heat was immense.

She scrabbled up quickly, staring at the fire in shock. Reacting on instinct alone she ran into the kitchen, grabbed the emergency fire blanket and ran back to the front door. She yanked the blanket from its case, kicked the rag free from the letterbox and as it hit the floor, she smothered the fireball with the blanket, patting and rolling it to put it out.

Slowly the smoke disappeared, and she was vaguely aware that the ear-piercing sound of the fire alarm had finally stopped, but she couldn't stop clinging to the blanket.

Eventually she sat up, uncurling her fingers from the blanket, and leaned against the wall. She curled her knees up to her chest, put her head into her hands and let the tears that the adrenaline had been keeping at bay finally come.

*

Finn found her like that a few minutes later, sobbing into her hands. He had heard the fire alarm go off again, and assumed it was her dodgy cooking that had set it off. He'd wandered out into the garden just to surreptitiously check she was OK. The fire alarm stopped but there was no sign of her in the kitchen at all. After a few minutes anxiously waiting, and with still no sign of Joy, he'd let himself in to her house and his blood had turned to ice at the sound of her sobbing.

He quickly ran through the house and stood aghast at her curled up and crying. He checked her over, but she wasn't injured at all. Without thinking, he knelt next to her, taking her hand.

'Joy, love, what's happened?'

There was a smell, an acrid, burnt stench in the air.

She let him take her hand from her face, but she looked at him without seeing him, which made him go cold. She didn't even know he was there.

'Joy.' He stroked her hair and slowly her eyes focused on him. Her tears dried, her face taking on a determined resolve.

Without a word, she scrabbled up and flew upstairs.

He looked around and spotted the fire blanket on the floor. Kicking it open, he was confused to see what looked like a burnt roll of clothes. But the smell of petrol was unmistakable. The area around the letterbox was burnt too.

He felt his fists clench at his side at the sickening reality of what had happened and quickly ran up the stairs after her.

She was in her bedroom, throwing clothes into a suitcase, she wasn't even bothering to take them off the hangers, they were going into the suitcase as well.

'What are you doing?'

She didn't answer as she ran past him into the bathroom and came back a few seconds later shoving her toothbrush, toothpaste and shampoo into a small bag. She threw that into the suitcase too, then slammed it closed, wrapping the strap around it and doing the buckle up tightly.

She looked around the room, her eyes wide, but not looking at him at all.

'You're leaving? You said you'd be here till Tuesday, you can't leave.'

Finally, she looked at him, her eyes cold. 'Finn, they want me dead. I'm just some prey for them to hunt like those poor deer. I'm not sticking around for the next attempt on my life.'

She lifted the suitcase and struggled downstairs with it.

A slick feeling of panic ripped through him. He was going to lose her.

He tore downstairs after her but she was already outside, loading her car.

'Wait, wait… what about fighting back, not letting them win?'

'You said it yourself Finn, "Don't put yourself in harm's way unnecessarily, don't tempt fate. If you're there when some nut job is trying to kill you, run as fast as you can in the opposite direction." This is me running. Staying here any longer when they want me dead would be phenomenally stupid.'

She moved quickly back towards the house.

'What… what about us?'

She turned to look at him. 'There is no us, Finn. Is there?'

She stood waiting for an answer but when none was clearly forthcoming she disappeared back inside. A moment later, she reappeared with Darcy hot on her heels, and closed the front door behind her.

'Car!' she ordered and Darcy duly obliged, leaping in, her tongue lolling out of her face excitedly.

She closed the back door and opened the driver's door, stepping up to the footplate so she was closer to him.

She took his face in her hand and kissed him, sending his heart into overdrive.

'I would have given you everything,' she whispered.

Then she sat down, closed the door and drove off.

He stared after her, and was still standing there long after she had disappeared from sight. His heart clenched painfully. What had he done? How could it hurt so badly? When Pippa had betrayed him, that had hurt – but this was real, acute pain, so much so he found himself rubbing his chest to try to alleviate it. His throat was raw, his hands were shaking.

He turned away from the road and saw Zach watching him from his doorway. He stormed back towards his house.

'Finn, wait.' Zach grabbed his arm.

Angry and hurt and wanting to lash out at someone, he turned and slammed Zach into the wall.

'If you want to punch me, then go ahead, but you'll listen to what I have to say first. You know in your heart that I would never have betrayed you had I been sober and properly awake – and you know if it wasn't with me, Pippa would have cheated on you with someone else. I can't go back and change what happened between me and Pippa, I wish I could. But I won't stand by and let you lose the woman you love for the second time in your life. Don't be an idiot. Don't throw away a chance of real happiness just because Pippa couldn't see how fantastic you are, and because your best friend was a complete and utter dickhead. You need to go after her, tell her how you feel. There are no guarantees in life, least of all in love, but when you find someone you love like that, someone who clearly loves you back, then don't let her slip through your fingers.'

Finn relinquished his hold on Zach and stormed back to his house. It would be a cold day in hell before he took relationship advice from Zach Fallowfield.

*

Joy pulled up outside Alex's house an hour later. It was just starting to get dark. She parked on the street and walked up the short narrow drive which curled round tall conifers blocking the house from the road.

As the trees ended and the front door came into view, she stopped because waiting on the doorstep was Casey. He seemed nervous somehow, and suddenly not wanting to be seen, she ducked back a bit so she could peer through the leaves.

Alex opened the door and as soon as he saw Casey, he broke into a huge grin. He took Casey's face in his hands and leaned forward and kissed him. The kiss was so sweet, so tender, so loving that despite what had happened just an hour before, Joy couldn't help but match Alex's huge grin.

Alex drew back, smiling and Casey followed him into the house, and the door closed behind them.

Still with the smile plastered on her face, she walked back down the drive and got back into her car.

Now where? She leaned her head on the steering wheel for a moment, feeling incredibly lonely all of a sudden.

There was only one place she could go now. She started the car again and drove off.

*

Joy was woken in the early hours of the morning by the noise of the door to the barn opening. Lights were snapped on and she quickly covered her eyes, sitting up, blearily.

She knew who it was, without even seeing him, somehow, blindly her body was already reacting, her gut clenching, her heart racing.

'You're trespassing,' Finn said softly as he walked towards her. Treacherously Darcy scrabbled up and ran to greet him. As she peered through her fingers, willing her eyes to become accustomed to the bright lights, she saw Finn rubbing her great dog's head affectionately.

'So call the police,' she snapped.

'Not a morning person then, I'll have to remember that.'

Her heart leapt a fraction. Why would he need to remember that?

'You should never wake a woman up in the middle of the night, there are rules about that kind of thing,' she muttered.

'No exceptions?' Finn knelt in front of her.

'No.'

'Pity.' He took her hand and pulled her gently to her feet. 'Come on, we need to talk.'

He started pulling her towards the door but she yanked her hand free of his grasp.

'No, we don't. You had plenty of opportunity to talk. It's too late now.' She realised inwardly she might as well be stamping her feet and folding her arms petulantly across her chest.

'Stay there then. I've just cooked a full English breakfast. Billy will be delighted if you don't want it.'

Finn left and she walked to the door, blinking at the early morning light. The sky was tinged with the palest pink, the sun just peeping over the edge of the fields that sloped down to the river. Large black blobs peppered the fields, where the cows were still sleeping. Her stomach rumbled loudly in protest and reluctantly she walked up to the farmhouse and round to the kitchen door where the delicious smell of bacon was drifting through. Darcy followed and Billy greeted her in the yard, nuzzling her gently in the ear. It made her smile to see.

Finn gestured for her to sit down at the breakfast bar opposite him, where a plate was already heaped with appetizing foods and, still scowling at him, Joy did as she was told.

She took a big bite of crusty toast and Finn opened his mouth to speak, clearly waiting for her to eat so she couldn't answer him back.

'Joy, I love you. I...'

She swallowed the toast quickly and it lodged in her throat. She spluttered, coughed, heaved, tears spurting to her eyes as she tried desperately to breathe. Her chest convulsed, her lungs screaming at the lack of air.

'Jesus.' Finn was at her side instantly, slapping her hard on the back – it did nothing to retrieve the piece of bread. She coughed, clutching at her throat. He yanked her off the stool to stand in front of him. With his hands round her chest he slammed her against him in what she presumed was a perfect Heimlich manoeuvre as the piece of bread shot out of her throat and sailed across the room where Billy leapt in the air to catch it neatly in his mouth.

She gasped in good, clean air, finding it hard to get enough as she leaned against Finn weakly. His hands were on her shoulders, holding her steady whilst she caught her breath.

'Well, I pictured this conversation many times in my head, played out every scenario, how might be best to tell you how I felt, but nowhere in my wildest imaginings did I foresee it panning out like this.'

She grabbed a glass of orange juice and drank it down quickly, cleansing and soothing her throat. Finally, she straightened herself and turned to face Finn, frowning. 'You love me?'

He nodded.

She stared at him for a moment, the silence lasting seemingly an eternity. Then anger took over. She pushed him away from her and stormed out.

'Oh no you don't.' Finn reached the door before she did and slammed it shut. 'You've been running your whole life, you're not going to run from this. You'll damn well listen to what I have to say.'

'You don't love me Finn. You like me, at best you care for me – and the sex has been fantastic – but you don't love me. Love is stupid and crazy and hedonistic. If you were in love you'd jump in without looking, you wouldn't be standing on the side afraid to get your feet wet. Look how you were with Pippa, you were married just six months after you'd met. That's how it should be – impetuous, reckless…'

'You don't get it do you? I jumped before I looked with her and I got hurt spectacularly. So yes, I was cautious about falling in love again.' He looked around trying to find inspiration. 'Look, you were attacked walking the streets alone after dark. Although logic says lightning isn't going to strike twice in the same place, and you are obviously more than capable of looking after yourself if the way you attacked me in your bedroom is anything to go by, you're not going to be stupid enough to tempt fate and walk the streets alone again, are you?'

She reluctantly conceded this. 'You learn from your mistakes.'

'Exactly. So when another beautiful redhead moves next door – someone with a zest for life, someone who wanted to see the world, someone with vulnerabilities, someone I wanted to protect and hold – I was scared that it was happening all over again.'

'I'm not Pippa.'

'I know.' He swept a stray hair out of her face. 'I know. There are so many things that stand you apart from her. Casey adores you, and he's always been such a good judge of character. You risked your life for him, which I owe you a debt of gratitude for. Your friends, I know circumstance means you don't see each other that often, but they dropped everything to be with you on your birthday. That says a lot. Your love for Darcy makes me smile… and Lily, a little girl who has nothing to do with you, and you treat her like she's your own. That fills my heart. I love your honesty. You just say what you feel. With Pippa it was lies and games. I love that you love the fresh air as opposed to air conditioning. I love how you dance. I love your optimism, that you see the good in everything, that nothing seems to keep you down. Your talent, you don't get how extraordinarily talented you are, that you have a real gift. Look…'

He dragged her towards the end of the kitchen. He tore some brown paper off a huge canvas that she hadn't noticed before, revealing a huge photo of the original Fairy Prince – her and Finn, in the throes of passion, captured in wood. The light of the lanterns cast over the pale wood of the oak set against a backdrop of black trees and the inky blue sky was breath taking. She had never seen her art in such a way before. Finn was looking at it in awe. To have it so appreciated moved her deeply, in a way she didn't expect.

He ran his finger lightly over the picture, almost as if he could feel the curves. 'You know I love you Joy. I might be able to lie to you with my words, but I couldn't lie to you with my body.'

She looked away. The way he had held her, touched her with such love, such reverence, that had been the thing that made her think that they had a future together. That's why it had left her so hurt and confused the next day when he hadn't wanted more, that seemingly it had just been about sex.

'I was trying to protect myself,' he said, almost as if he was reading her mind. 'I know you're not like Pippa because what I feel for you is so much more than I ever felt for her, so much more than I could ever imagine. And that terrified me – if I loved you more, then I could get hurt more and I knew the pain of losing you would be more than I could bear.'

Though her heart was racing, her blood pounding through her veins, she knew she had to let him finish. She'd said everything she could, it was down to him to take that step now. Though him being here certainly spoke for something.

'I think it took you leaving to make me finally realise what I was losing. When you left, I cried.'

She swallowed. 'What?'

'I don't cry, Joy. I can count on one hand the times I've cried in the last twenty years. When a bone burst through my skin when a stunt went wrong on the *Darkness* set, when Pippa had an abortion and when you left. I didn't even know I was crying until I felt my cheeks were wet. I was trying to protect myself against being hurt and by pushing you away I got hurt anyway. That's when I knew what I wanted.'

'What do you want?' Her voice was barely a whisper.

He turned to her. 'I want the caboodle.'

Her heart soared.

'I want to build a life with you Joy, I want to wake with you in my arms every morning, I want to grow old and grey with you. I want to be your constant, I want marriage and kids, the whole caboodle.'

'A happy ever after?'

'Yes, I want that more than anything. We could live here, raise our kids here, make new memories together. Or if you want a fresh start for us both, we can sell this place and find somewhere else.'

She looked round at the kitchen, the early morning sunlight drifting through the windows, spilling over the large granite topped breakfast bar and across the warm terracotta floor. Could she build a future for herself here when it held so many memories of the past? Would it be taking a step back, to live here again? Beyond the window lay what used to be the back yard, it was now much more than a scrap of land – it was a garden, with paths and benches and places to sit in the sun and the shade. Finn had created a home here.

'Say something.' He stepped closer to her.

She turned back to him. He was her future now, regardless of where they lived.

'Yes.'

'Yes, to living here?'

'Yes to the happy ever after, wherever that is. I love you, that hasn't changed.'

He smiled hugely and took her in his arms and kissed her, deeply, sweetly. Finally he pulled away, leaning his forehead against hers.

Holding his face, she stepped back. 'Oh, I have something to tell you. How do you feel about the pitter patter of tiny feet?' She pulled out the pregnancy test she had taken the day before. 'It's not conclusive but…'

His face was a picture – his smile slid off as he looked down at her belly. He rested his hand on her stomach gently. 'God, I will carry you everywhere, I will massage your back every day and night, I will rub cocoa butter into your bump so you don't get stretch marks. I…' He trailed off as she giggled.

She circled her arms round his neck and she kissed him briefly. 'That's very sweet, and I'll remember that when I am pregnant, but you might want to direct that lavish attention about two feet to your right.'

He stood confused for a moment, then his eyes cast down to look at Darcy fast asleep in the sunlight. His smile grew again.

'Oh, thank god. I want kids, loads of them, but I was kind of hoping to have you to myself for a little while.'

She pulled herself against him. 'And what will you do, now that you have me to yourself?'

He scooped her up and she giggled as he walked towards the stairs. 'I'm sure I can think of something.'

She wrapped her arms round his neck. She had spent years looking for home, but in his arms she had finally found it.

'Finn, I'm thinking of getting my nipple pierced.'

He groaned with desire against her throat and she laughed.

Epilogue

Joy bent to slip on her silver heels then stood to admire herself in the mirror. The silvery dress showed every curve of her body, she ran her hands over her hips and stomach, loving how it clung to her.

She looked down at the local paper again and smiled. The Dark Shadow, into her third year, was still making the news. Though more recently, her more astute followers had deduced that The Dark Shadow had fallen in love. Several of her latest carvings had shown a couple entwined, arms and legs wrapped round each other, so you couldn't tell where one body ended and the other began. She had been careful not to reveal her or Finn's identities in the carvings, but the amorous creations had actually gained more coverage than her previous attempts of unicorns and dragons. Many people who were getting married or cele- brating anniversaries had contacted her asking for miniature versions to be carved as gifts. It was a new road she had not gone down before and she loved the freedom of being able to carve in one of the barns at the farm as well as travelling the country. It also meant she could properly finish the pieces, sand them, polish them and stain them before she posted them out. That was something she could never do with her strikes because the finishing process took days.

Her latest strike had made the front page of the local paper, not only because it had been a local one, but also because there was now speculation that The Dark Shadow was expecting a child. She looked at the picture and smiled hugely, the entwined couple, kissing, with the very obvious bump between them.

She stroked her belly fondly as another smaller article caught her eye.

'Bramble Hill wins Most Miserable Village award for the second year running.'

She smirked at this. The day after she had fled Bramble Hill the year before, she had decided she wanted to fight back somehow, hitting them where it hurt the most. She had phoned Casey to say she wanted to take him up on his offer for revenge. It had been childish, she knew, to tell Casey's mum all about the vendetta that the villagers had exacted against her, when Rose Fallowfield had called to gather details. Rose could practically be heard rubbing her hands together with glee on the other end of the phone.

When she put the phone down she felt a huge sense of satisfaction, but doubted that anything would be done.

Joy had clearly underestimated Rose. On the day Bramble Hill was supposed to be crowned Britain's Friendliest Village for the tenth year in a row, Rose turned up with a thirty strong-committee and the local press and loudly awarded Bramble Hill, Britain's Most Miserable Village.

Things turned ugly, with many of the villagers throwing cakes and throwing some of the committee into the pond. Their wrath was captured for all to see the next day in the local paper, showing the village in their true colours.

Unfortunately, things didn't stop there as the national press also got hold of the story. Bramble Hill was even listed in several national newspapers and magazines as the worst place to live.

The national press turned up to take more pictures and interview people – and the grumpier they appeared in the papers, the more press turned up to capture it.

Bramble Hill took the huge, bizarre and expensive decision to make their village private. Rather than waiting for the furore to die down, they erected an eight-foot fence around the entire village and put a gate across the entrance so only the villagers could enter.

This of course did nothing to dispel the rumours and stories of rude, grouchy villagers – and one humorous documentary showing the villagers at their worst went viral, with over two million hits on YouTube within the first week. That was probably in part the reason for the Most Miserable Village award being awarded again this year.

Joy felt no guilt at all.

She put the paper down and turned to face Alex who was struggling with his cravat, trying to arrange it artfully. She smiled and stepped forward to help him.

'You look lovely.'

'So do you.'

'Thank you for giving me away, you don't know what it means to me to have you standing next to me today.'

'I wouldn't have it any other way. Are you nervous?'

'Excited.'

She finished the cravat just as a knock came on the door. Leaving Alex to fiddle with his cufflinks, she went to answer it. Finn and Casey were standing there, she quickly scooted outside, closing the door behind her.

'You're not supposed to be here,' she said.

Casey, grinning hugely, rolled his eyes as he walked through the door that led to the barn where the wedding was to take place. She caught a glimpse of flowers entwined with fairy lights, before the door closed behind him.

'How you doing?' Finn asked, running his hand over her ample belly.

She smiled. 'Reminds me of my own wedding day.'

'Happiest day of my life, followed almost immediately by the announcement that we're expecting a baby girl. I do so love you Mrs Mackenzie.'

'I love you, I always will. You make me so happy.' She leaned up to kiss him and knew she would never tire of doing so. 'Go and look after Casey and make sure Rose is OK, though she hasn't stopped grinning all day. We'll be through in just a second.'

He kissed her, his eyes meeting hers intently and then he disappeared through the door.

She went back in to see Alex and, seeing he was no longer faffing, she offered him her arm.

'Are you ready?'

He grinned and took it.

'I've been waiting all my life for him Joy, I'm more than ready.'

She smiled and to the beautiful strains of Pachelbel's Canon she escorted her brother down the aisle.

Acknowledgements

Thank you to everyone at HQ Digital who has supported me in making my dreams come true, and to my friends and family who have stood by me as I've slowly gone insane with self-doubt and hysterical with joy, you are all amazing and I love you all.

Dear Reader,

Thank you so much for taking the time to read this book – we hope you enjoyed it! If you did, we'd be so appreciative if you left a review.

Here at HQ Digital we are dedicated to publishing fiction that will keep you turning the pages into the early hours. We publish a variety of genres, from heartwarming romance, to thrilling crime and sweeping historical fiction.

To find out more about our books, enter competitions and discover exclusive content, please join our community of readers by following us at:

🐦 *@HQDigitalUK*

f *facebook.com/HQDigitalUK*

Are you a budding writer? We're also looking for authors to join the HQ Digital family! Please submit your manuscript to:

HQDigital@harpercollins.co.uk.

Hope to hear from you soon!

**Turn the page for an exclusive extract from
Holly Martin's *One Hundred Proposals*…**

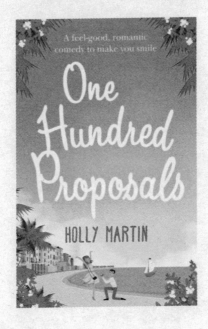

PROLOGUE

'Ok, you can open your eyes now,' Harry said.

I blinked in the gloom of the cave. Moonlight tumbled through the opening above us, reflecting off the waterfall as it cascaded into the pool below. We had been in Australia for just a few days but I knew it would never cease to amaze me. Dancing in the pockets of the cave walls were hundreds of fireflies, sparkling like fairy lights.

Nothing could have prepared me for what happened next.

The fireflies started to gather together and slowly a shape was formed. I frowned in confusion and then within seconds the words, 'Suzie, Marry Me,' stood proud against the cave walls, written by the fireflies.

I whirled round to face Harry in shock. 'How did you do that?' I looked back at the fireflies, not wanting to miss anything. Would they perhaps move to form the lyrics of my favourite song? Were they super trained fireflies and in a minute they'd all whip out their mini cheerleader pompoms and start some kind of dance where they would balance precariously on each other's backs?

'It's some kind of fruit juice, they love it.'

I fumbled in my bag for my camera. 'We have to get a picture for the website.'

I fired off a couple of shots and I could see a few other tourists had entered the cave and were clearly waiting for my answer. They'd be waiting for a long time.

'So what do you think?' Harry said. 'Is this the perfect proposal?'

'It's definitely one of your best, very romantic.' I focused my attention on the photos I was taking. They were going to look fantastic with the waterfall in soft focus in the background and the fireflies in sharp detail set against the inky blue light of the moon.

'But still not the perfect proposal?'

'Not for me, but someone else would love it.' I watched the faces of the other tourists fall at my callous response. 'We're not together, we just work with each other.' One couple looked at me dubiously, so I pressed on. 'Our company creates the perfect proposal, this kind of thing is our bread and butter.'

I resisted the sudden urge to rush over to them and start handing out business cards. As if reading my mind, Harry slung an arm round my shoulder, restraining me with his hand.

I looked up at him innocently but he didn't seem convinced.

The tourists moved further down the cave, leaving us alone.

'You always do that,' Harry said.

'What, promote our business? I know, I can't help it. I'm just so proud of what we've achieved that I want to tell anyone that listens and anyone that doesn't.'

'No, not that. You always say *our* company, *our* business. It's yours, you started it. I'm just the tech guy.'

It was just me to start with. I created the.PerfectProposal. com over two years ago when my boyfriend at the time proposed drunkenly to me over a greasy kebab. It struck me that maybe the menfolk of this world might need a little helping hand to create a proposal their girlfriends would remember forever. Although the greasy kebab is not one I'm likely to forget.

Harry was my web designer. When the business first started he would come by my office, the back bedroom in my home, every day to help update the website with my new ideas, photos and special offers. In the end it made sense to make him a permanent feature. Our website looked fantastic and as an online company this was integral to our success.

But Harry wasn't just the geeky IT guy, far from it. He was the biggest man I had ever seen in my life, with large thighs and big feet. He had stubbly, dark hair and chocolate eyes. But he also had a vivid imagination – where I was organising the logistics for a champagne helicopter trip, he would be the one that would come up with something completely unique like using fireflies.

'And you always put yourself down. We're equal partners now, you helped to make the company a success too,' I said.

He shrugged, never keen to accept that he played such an important part in it. He gestured to the fireflies that were starting to break formation now. 'Is it too sickly?'

I let my camera hang round my neck and leaned into him, I loved the way I fitted against him. 'I love it, I really do, it's… magical. But there's still something missing.'

Was there really such a thing as a perfect proposal? Three months ago, just before Valentine's Day, Harry had made it his mission to provide me with one. But deep down I knew what I wanted and I doubted Harry would be able to deliver it. I should have told him that when he first started this wild goose chase. It would have saved me a lot of heartache.

CHAPTER ONE

Three Months Before

I put the phone down on another excited client and sighed. It was February 11th and we'd had a surge of customers all desperately wanting to propose on top of the Eiffel Tower on Valentine's Day. I felt like screaming. It was only by careful planning that I'd arranged that my customers weren't going to be there at the same time. That's just what a girl wants to feel special, to see other girls being proposed to at the same place and time that she was. Was there no originality anymore? Harry was brilliant at coming up with unique proposals, but no matter how many times I had tried to sell Harry's ideas to them, they wanted the traditional and that was that.

'Another Eiffel Tower?' asked Harry as he absentmindedly uploaded photos to our rolling gallery.

'He wants a dozen red roses delivered to the observation deck at eight.' I rubbed my head in defeat. 'What about something different, going to the ballet or proposing over a bag of chips at the end of Brighton Pier?'

He swivelled in his chair. 'What would be your perfect proposal?'

I looked at him and had a sudden flash of him holding me in his arms and asking me to marry him.

'I don't know, the perfect guy would definitely be a bonus.'

'Ok so you have your perfect guy and it's not greasy kebab boy –'

'Let's be clear, it was the kebab that was greasy not the man.'

He waved away the details. 'So Orlando Bloom or some other non-greasy hunk is asking you to marry him, how would he do it?'

I took a sip of tea whilst I pondered this. If one of my customers phoned up at a loss for inspiration I had a hundred ideas. But for me, my mind was blank.

'I have an idea.' Harry's eyes were suddenly bright with excitement. He whirled round on his chair and started tapping away furiously on his computer. I peered over his shoulder at our website.

Proposer's Blog

How Do You Propose to a Proposer?

Over the next hundred days I intend to find out. I will find one hundred ways to propose to our Chief Proposer Suzie McKenzie, and post the results here for your enjoyment. One thing's for sure, not one of my proposals will be on top of the Eiffel Tower with a dozen red roses.

'You can't put that, we've had fifteen customers who want to propose like that over the last week,' I said, ignoring the sudden thundering of my heart that Harry was going to propose to me.

'Then maybe they'll have a rethink.' Harry was already uploading a picture of a diamond ring onto the blog.

'Or ask for their money back.'

But Harry was still writing.

Day 1: The Traditional Proposal. Location: Our office.

He stood up and got down on one knee – yanking the snake ring off his thumb, he held it aloft to my shocked face.

'Suzie McKenzie, you are my best friend and I cannot imagine finding anyone I would rather spend the rest of my life with. Marry me.'

The world stopped. My mouth was dry. How unfair was it that the one thing I wanted most in the world was happening right in front of me and it was as real as a pair of breasts on Sunset Boulevard.

I wanted to snatch the ring off him, stuff it on my finger and march him down to the nearest registry office. But I didn't.

I cleared my throat of the huge lump. 'Too clichéd, wrong location, wrong ring.'

He grinned as he appraised his ring and stood up, clearly not fussed by this rejection. He started typing.

Crashed and Burned. Apparently a snake ring with evil red eyes and the beige walls of our cramped office isn't good enough for her. I'll try again tomorrow.

Surely not. A hundred days of this torment? I didn't think I could bear it.

He looked at his watch. 'Oh, I've got to go, hot date with Sexy Samantha again tonight.'

Samantha was his first girlfriend in nearly a year. When I first met him he seemed to go through a different girl each week, so I wasn't sure why he'd gone through the sudden dry patch. But Samantha was definitely the type to tempt him out of it.

I'd had the pleasure of meeting Sexy Samantha the night before. Suspicious of Harry's relationship with his best friend, she'd barrelled into my home and demanded that Harry introduce me. I came downstairs in leggings and an oversized black hoodie – I knew I was hardly dressed to impress. And impress her I didn't. The look of relief when Samantha saw me was palpable. She, on the other hand, was a vision of heavenly loveliness. She was almost as tall as Harry, with long blonde hair and curves everywhere. My eyes were immediately drawn to a big pair of breasts, squeezed into an overly tight top. Harry was definitely a breast man. All of his girlfriends were very well-endowed in the breast department. Some of the breasts, I suspected, weren't even real – though Harry didn't seem to mind. I was more in the straight up, straight down department, definitely no curves and not really any breasts to speak of.

I watched Harry log off his computer with haste and obvious excitement about what Sexy Samantha had in store for him that night.

'I have a hot date too,' I blurted out, watching for any flicker of jealousy. Of course there was none.

'That's great Suze.' He looked genuinely pleased. 'You haven't seen anyone since Jack…' He trailed off. My life was defined into two segments. Before Jack and After Jack. I wondered if Jules felt the same. Harry grabbed his jacket, averting his eyes from me, perhaps knowing that he had said something he shouldn't. 'It's about time you got back on the horse again. We can swap notes tomorrow.'

'Or not.' I couldn't bear thinking about that conversation. The literal ins and outs of Harry's date would be something I really didn't want to hear. I'd changed the subject twice that morning already when he started giving me explicit details that would be right at home on the pages of an erotic fiction novel. Sexy Samantha was far kinkier than those baby blue eyes might suggest. Besides, what did I have to contribute to that conversation? My hot date consisted of a tub of Ben and Jerry's and a night in with the beautiful Brad Pitt. I logged off my own computer, keen to show him I also had something exciting to run off to.

'Where did you meet him?'

I racked my brain as I fluffed out my hair in the reflection of a photo showing me and Harry covered in snow and grinning ear to ear after sledging at the indoor Snow Zone. Before Jack.

'Skiing,' I said, then wished I hadn't.

He stopped in his hasty exit. 'Skiing? When have you been skiing?'

'I go every Sunday, skiing lessons, he's my ski instructor.' I was making it worse.

'You hate skiing.'

I had said that, hadn't I. Because this photo was taken when we had our first and last skiing lesson a year before. I had spent forty minutes falling on my bum – as kids as young as five glided effortlessly past me – and the last twenty minutes of the lesson, after Harry had been upgraded to the adult slopes, trying to get up and rolling around on the floor with my skis in the air, looking like an oversized beetle stranded on its back. Harry had felt sorry for me because I had failed so spectacularly and had taken me sledging instead. Much more up my street. There was no skill at all involved in sliding down a slope in a red plastic sledge.

'I like it now. I'm very proficient. Obviously just needed the right instructor.'

'Well that's great, maybe we can go together sometime.'

I fixed a smile onto my face. 'Maybe.'

'What's his name?'

I cast around for a suitable name and a suitable adjective to describe him, something comparable to Sexy Samantha. I had nothing, no names in my head at all. The only name in my head was Harry and that would be too weird. He was staring at me, waiting for me to come up with a name, the silence stretched on. I had to say something.

'Tim.' I almost shouted out with relief. 'Tiny Tim.'

Great. Just great.

Harry's face fell. 'Tiny Tim?'

'Yes.'

'As in…' he waggled his little finger at me.

'No, no, of course not, he's very big in that department. Big all over in fact. Huge. It's kind of an ironic name.'

'Big like me?'

'Well I have no idea how big you are in that department.' My eyes cast down to the sizeable bulge in his jeans and I felt my cheeks burn as he clearly saw me checking him out.

'I meant in height,' Harry said. I'm sure I saw his mouth twitch as he supressed a smile.

'Oh yes, he's very tall.'

'Good. That's good. I have a friend who's a ski instructor at the Snow Zone, he might know your Tim. What's his surname?'

'Timmings.'

I was a terrible liar.

'Tim Timmings?'

'That's right.'

A horn tooted outside and Harry peeled back the net curtain to wave at Sexy Samantha as she leaned on the bonnet of her sexy red convertible. I didn't think I'd ever be so relieved to see her again.

'Well have fun.' Harry threw me a cursory wave as he thundered down the stairs. A second later I heard the front door slam.

I peered out the window, hoping not to be noticed as Harry swept Sexy Samantha into his arms and swung her round as if he hadn't seen her in months. As he deposited her on the floor she waved up at me and I was forced to wave politely back.

With a wheel spin and the stereo blaring out something young and hip, the red convertible roared up the road, taking my heart with it.

I'd been in love with Harry for two long, painful years and we were further away today from getting together than we had been when we first met. We were now firmly in the friend zone and there was never any coming back from that.

Two years was way too long for unrequited love. It was time I moved on with someone else. I would just fall out of love with him, simple as that.

I sighed as I walked into my bedroom and got changed into my cow print onesie. I flicked through some songs on my iPod until I found something suitably rousing and as Gloria Gaynor started belting out '*I am what I am*', I turned up the volume, leapt up onto the bed and danced and wiggled my bum in time with the lyrics. I was highly skilled in the playing of air drums and as Gloria reached a crescendo so did my frenetic drum playing. As the instrumental kicked in I leapt off the bed, doing the splits mid-air. I pulled a muscle in my groin and as I flicked my hair theatrically out of my face I saw Harry's eyes widen in horror as I landed on top of him, one leg somehow hooked over his shoulder as my other foot kicked him square in his crotch.

He screamed in pain. I screamed with embarrassment as he staggered back and landed hard on his bum, my leg still wrapped round his neck.

Gloria was still singing loudly in the background as we stared at each other. Finally I managed to speak.

'What are you doing here?'

'Currently, wondering if I'll ever be able to have sex again. Can you please get off my lap?'

I quickly climbed off him, kneeing him in the face as I tried to stand up. He slowly staggered to his feet, doubled over in obvious pain.

'I forgot my wallet,' he said, by way of explanation.

I swallowed. 'You saw me dance?'

He lifted his head and this time there was no mistaking the grin. 'From the very beginning to the dramatic finale.'

I groaned.

'I better go, Samantha will be wondering where I am. Nice onesie by the way. Does Tiny Tim have one too? A horse or a pig perhaps?'

I stared down at myself, at the pink udders hanging limply from my stomach, and wanted the ground to swallow me up. 'He's not coming round till later.'

'Of course not. And I imagine he thinks you look quite cute in it.'

Cute? Puppies were cute. Is that how he thought of me, as a cute little puppy?

He moved to the top of the stairs and I followed him.

'Do you think I look cute in it?'

He turned and walked back up a few stairs, kneeling on the stair below me so we were eye to eye. 'Yes.'

My heart dropped. I was so far in the friend zone I was now categorised as cute. He'd be patting me on the back next and telling me he saw me like a sister.

'Sexy cute?'

'No.'

My heart sank into my feet.

'I bet Samantha would look sexy in it?'

'I doubt it. I don't think it's possible for anyone to look sexy in it.'

I felt slightly better at this.

'And don't underestimate the value of cute, it's a great quality to have.' He leaned forward and kissed me on the nose. 'And don't stay up too late, I have a big day planned for you tomorrow.'

He ran down the stairs and was gone a second later.

I touched my nose, still feeling the softness of his lips. He thought I was cute. I smiled as I fell in love with him all over again.

If you enjoyed *A Home on Bramble Hill*, then why not try another delightfully uplifting romance from HQ Digital?